Nationwide praise for Ronald Ruiz
and for his best-selling first novel,
Happy Birthday Jesús

"A talented, painstaking, and intelligent writer."

—*The Houston Post*

"The sparse, simple prose lets the story tell itself . . . The supporting characters are briefly but fully drawn . . . Few readers will be able to forget the chilling experiences of a forlorn hero who's destined to take his place next to Bigger Thomas [of Richard Wright's *Native Son*] in the honor roll of seminal characters in American literature."

—*Publishers Weekly* (featured review)

"Undeniable raw power and genuine feeling for the downtrodden . . . Riveting . . . Frighteningly real."

—*New York Newsday*

"Savage and searing . . . A rare degree of intensity . . . His narrator's voice is convincingly authentic . . . What might otherwise be merely shocking is written with such burning conviction, and with such obvious dead-on accuracy, that it casts a dazzling light . . . [Ruiz] knows his characters intimately, and he renders them on the page so vividly that only a reader with a heart of stone could ever forget them."

—Alan Ryan, *San Jose Mercury-News*

"Powerful . . . important and illuminating."

—*Houston Chronicle*

"Gripping . . . Thrusts us vividly into the consciousness of those members of our society who may become the ruin of all of us . . . Ruiz's novel has earned an important place in our literature for the courage to shock us from our complacency."

—Gerald Nicosia, *Los Angeles Times*

"There's no redemption here for anybody . . . You can agree or not, but you won't be the same after reading this book."

—Carolyn See, *The Washington Post*

❧ Giuseppe Rocco ❧

Ronald L. Ruiz

Arte Público Press
Houston, Texas
1998

...gh grants from the National
...agency), Andrew W. Mellon
...Digest Fund and the City of
...Council of Houston, Harris
County.

Recovering the past, creating the future

Arte Público Press
University of Houston
Houston, Texas 77204-2090

Cover design by James F. Brisson

Ruiz, Ronald L.
        Giuseppe Rocco / Ronald L. Ruiz.
                p.   cm.

        ISBN 1-55885-228-X (pbk. : alk. paper)
        I. Title.
        PS3568.U397G5 1998
        813'.54—dc21   98-12848
                                                            CIP

8 9 0 1 2 3 4 5 6 7   10 9 8 7 6 5 4 3 2 1

"¿Y quién eres tú?"
"Yo soy tu mujer."

And who are you?
I am your woman.

❧ Book One ❧

Chapter I

Giuseppe Rocco left Naples for America at the age of fourteen. An orphan since he was three, he had lived with an uncle on the outskirts of a small village outside Naples. By the age of twelve, he was the size of most men in the village. People said he was going to be a giant. But he didn't grow any after twelve, although he continued doing the work of a full-sized man. Many before him had gone to America and he had heard stories of money and land and riches to be had everywhere there. But when he heard that Mario Lopopolo, a neighbor, a man with whom he had tilled the land, had become rich in America, he left for America. If Mario Lopopolo could be rich in America, so could Giuseppe Rocco. It was as simple as that.

He stowed away on a ship bound for the United States and, once at sea, befriended and became part of a family that was on its way to the coal mines of Pennsylvania. Once at work in Pennsylvania, it took Giuseppe Rocco but a few weeks to decide that he would never get rich in the coal mines. All the while he thought of Mario Lopopolo, a man he could out-till, out-prune, out-harvest and out-think, even at the age of twelve. He had heard that Mario Lopopolo had gone to a place called California and he knew that if Mario Lopopolo could become rich in California, so too could Giuseppe Rocco. As soon as he had saved the train fare, he went to California. He arrived in San Francisco on the last day of his fifteenth year.

For two years, he worked twelve and fourteen hours a day, seven days a week in the slaughterhouses of San Francisco, among the blood and stench and cries of terrified animals. He lived but a block from the slaughterhouses, and at night he could still smell and hear the animals. He lived with an Italian family in a tiny shed that had once been part of their outhouse. Week by week he stuffed first coins and then small folded bills behind loose boards in his shed, saving toward that day when he would buy himself a plot of ground in San Jose, some forty miles south of San Francisco. That's where they said that Mario Lopopolo had gone. That's how he had made his fortune: with land and orchards and a climate like they had at home. So each week, after he had paid his room and board and set aside a few pennies for the three

Toscano cigars that he allowed himself (one to smoke after he had stuffed his weekly sum away, a second to smoke at mid-week, the third to smoke on the night of the sixth day to remind himself that he had but one more day to go), he would carefully loosen his chosen board with his thick fingers, just enough so it wouldn't show, and then, savoring the excitement of that week, he would feel and then listen to the rasping of the bills and coins as he pushed them slowly and carefully toward his fortune.

He went to San Jose on his first day off from the slaughterhouse, on his first Christmas in America, to look for Mario Lopopolo. He did not find Mario, but instead found the orchards, leafless and bare on a warm Christmas day. He scooped up a handful of the rich, moist, almost black earth and rubbed it between his fingers and smiled: yes, riches could be had here.

He returned on the fourth of July. Now the trees were green and heavy with fruit. Still no Mario Lopopolo. But the climate was warm and mild, perhaps a little hot in the early afternoon, but then there rose a wonderfully cool breeze in mid-afternoon. And the sky was blue, blue, and the air fresh—he could taste the freshness. That day he realized for the first time that San Jose lay in a small valley, bounded on the west by a low range of green mountains and on the east by dry brown hills that rose and rose until they too seemed to be mountains. And each range was close, so close that Giuseppe Rocco was certain that he could hike from one to the other in less than a day. He liked that.

On his second Christmas in America, Giuseppe Rocco went to San Jose again, despite an invitation from the Signora Sabbatini to have Christmas dinner in the front house. "But what will you do in San Jose on Christmas day all by yourself?"

"I have much to do there, much to prepare."

"Prepare what? You have nothing there," she said to the serious manchild for whom her heart ached. "Stay, eat with us. We are like your family. Christmas can be lonely without family."

"But I have family there. I have a cousin there. His name is Mario Lopopolo."

So he went again. This time it was raining in San Jose. But even the rain was not uncomfortable in San Jose. It was a warm rain, one in which he thought he could walk forever. When he reached downtown, he began to feel chilled. He went into a small Italian restaurant to dry himself and wait for the rain to stop so that he could walk out into the countryside and continue his search for Mario Lopopolo. He ordered soup. Two men at the table next to him stared at him. They laughed and one of them said, "Hey, Sicilian boy, this is America. When you come into town on Christmas day, you change your boots." He brushed aside their insult as best he could.

It was true: he was dark enough to be a Sicilian, but so what. Then he saw that his rain-drenched boots, his only shoes, were shedding blood on the clean wooden floor. He panicked, wanting to clean it up, yet not wanting to acknowledge it, not wanting them to see him acknowledge it. He tried erasing the blood by rubbing it with the sole of his boot. But that just spread it, making it worse, as the two men howled with laughter.

He returned again on the fourth of July. The year was 1925. This time he walked directly into the countryside. There was much to do and only a day in which to do it. Now there was no pretense of looking for Mario Lopopolo. Now he went from house to house, from small ranch to small ranch, asking if anyone would sell him land. There were questions, many questions, many mixed with surprise and amusement. Who are you? Where are you from? How can you have money to buy land? How did you get that money? How old are you? By that afternoon he found an old Italian who would sell him an acre of bare land for two hundred dollars, a hundred dollars down and five dollars a month for twenty months. He told the old man that he would return with the hundred dollars within four weeks, and he gave the old man the dollar he had brought with him as a sign of good faith. As the old man took the dollar, he asked Giuseppe if he was sure that he wanted to buy the land. Giuseppe replied that in two weeks he would be seventeen and already he had spent too much time at a job in San Francisco that would give him only bondage.

He returned four weeks to the day later with a small knapsack in his hand. In the knapsack he had a change of clothes and a jacket and a wadded handkerchief filled with coins and bills. Slowly he counted out his down payment: one hundred dollars to the penny, reminding the old man that he was not counting the dollar that he had given him four weeks before. Then they walked off the acre, with Giuseppe Rocco driving stakes at the four corners. It was flat, unimproved land, overgrown with dead grass and weeds, situated behind the old man's furthest orchard. There was nothing signed, nothing measured, just the nod of the old man before each of the four stakes was driven into the hard earth and a handshake after the fourth stake had been driven. Then the old man asked Giuseppe Rocco, "And what will you do with the land?"

"I will plant it and live on it."

"When will you live on it?"

"Now."

"But where?"

"There," he said, pointing to the center of the acre. That night he slept exactly where he had pointed, using his knapsack for a pillow. The next morning he arose, telling himself that he had never slept so well.

That day Giuseppe Rocco looked for a job. But there were no slaughterhouses in San Jose, and the small ranches would give him little more than room and board when he needed capital. He searched for work in town, but his blood-stained clothes and his smell offended anyone in close quarters. By his calculations, he had barely enough money left to eat for two weeks and he didn't dare buy clothes. That night, as he looked up at the stars, he thought and thought of places that might hire him despite his appearance and smell. The next morning he sought out Salvatorre Garofoli, the man who owned the San Jose Garbage Company. Like Giuseppe, Salvatorre was a short, dark, squat, husky man who said bluntly, "I don't need nobody right now."

"You need me."

"What? Something wrong with your hearing? I said I don't need nobody right now. So beat it! Go! Go on, go!"

"But you need me because I'll work twice as hard as anybody you got for half the price, just so long as I can save seven dollars a month. And to prove it, I'll work the first week for free."

So Giuseppe Rocco began his career as a scavenger, not needing to worry about his appearance or his smell, needing to worry only about saving seven dollars a month and feeding himself. He soon realized that he could feed himself by sorting through the refuse at the markets and the butcher shops. Doing that, he was able to save almost nine dollars a month. In mid-September, he bought a small tent to keep the increasing night crispness and moisture off him. Then, when he discovered that Salvatorre Garofoli would not accept rags with the other garbage, he began collecting the rags himself and piling them on his acre until he could find a market for them—surely there had to be a market for useable cloth. He eventually found a market for his rags among the Chinese in San Francisco. Thereafter, once a month, he took his mountain of rags to San Francisco on an overnight trip, for which he soon made almost as much money as Salvatorre Garofoli paid him in a month.

He woke to the first rain, cold and soaked, and then, startled, thought of his rags. He crawled out of the tent as quickly as he could, running into the pouring rain in his underwear. He ran to his rags. No one would buy wet rags, not even the Chinese. But his attempts to cover them were futile. That afternoon he built platforms a foot off the ground for his rags, and the next afternoon he erected roofs of tin scraps and discarded wood over his rags.

The old man said, "You take better care of those rags than you do of yourself."

Giuseppe Rocco answered, "Right now they're worth more."

The following week, he put his tent on a platform and erected a lean-to roof over it. Then he bought a lantern. Those were the only amenities he allowed himself that winter, and despite the winter darknesss, he continued working fourteen hours a day, using his lantern to sort and stack and bundle his rags each night. The following year he bought another acre of land from the old Italian, paying for it in cash. He also bought an old battered truck, which he used only to haul his rags and for which he promptly built the most elaborate structure yet on his land.

Again the old man said, "You take better care of that machine than you do of yourself." And once again he seemed to react to the old man's words. He bought a bigger, thicker tent, one designed for a stove. To his platform he added three-foot sides of wooden planks. When he bought and installed a stove, he felt as satisfied and happy with his new home as any man could hope to be.

Word began spreading among the Italians of San Jose's east side about the serious young man who worked day and night and lived alone in a tent, surrounded by piles of rags on two acres of bare land. Giuseppe Rocco began seeing signs that people had come onto his land while he was gone. Usually they looked through only his rags and truck, but occasionally they entered his tent in which there was nothing but the rags he slept on, his stove, and two lanterns—he had bought a second lantern for a better night sort. Now and then curiosity would get the best of someone and he would go out to Giuseppe Rocco's land in the darkness to find the young man sorting his rags.

"Good evening. I was just passing through and I saw the lights and I thought I'd stop and say hello." They said this even though there was no public road to Giuseppe Rocco's land and they would have had to walk through three acres of the old man's darkened orchards to see the lanterns.

"Oh, hello!" he would answer with a big, toothy, clumsy smile, already knowing that he could get farther with that warm, open awkwardness than he could with any other demeanor.

"I don't mean to bother you, but isn't it a little late to be working?" or, "My God, you work so hard."

"I never got much education," he'd say, flashing that clumsy smile again. "All I know how to do is work. I don't make very much money and a man's got to eat. I don't mind. I sleep good at night."

But within days after he bought another acre of land, he found holes dug up all over his three acres. "They're looking for my money," he thought. "Better they should look for my soul."

⟶

It was Angela Garofoli who got Sundays off for him. "Salvatorre, it's not right, it's not fair. He's worked for you two years now, and he still has no day of rest. Everybody else gets Sunday off, and you pay them more."

"What are you, his mother? He likes it. You don't hear him complaining."

"Because you'd run him off if he did. He knows that."

"He never had it so good. He's a *Napolitano.* There they barely eat. Ask him."

"But he's hardly more than a boy. That's no life. All he does is work. And he's getting to the point where he should have a wife. How can he meet anyone if he's working every day? I tell you, it's no life, Salvatorre."

"You love him so much, you marry him. The two of you deserve each other. Besides, he's got way more than any nineteen-year-old I ever knew. He owns land, he's got a truck, he's got his home. I should have been so lucky."

"Come on, Salvatorre, you've told me about that land. No water, no lights, no outhouse, no nothing. You've told me about his tent and rags. Just let him be like the others. Let him rest on Sunday."

"And if I did that, he'd probably play with his rags all goddamn day. He doesn't know how to rest."

Salvatorre Garofoli was almost right. Thereafter, Giuseppe Rocco did spend each Sunday with his rags, working them, sorting them (because the Chinese knew cloth and now he too knew cloth), and loading them onto his truck for what now became a weekly trip to San Francisco to dispose of the growing number of rags he collected. It didn't take long for the Italians of east San Jose to note that regular, unfailing trip each Sunday. It puzzled them because Giuseppe Rocco showed absolutely no signs of increased income. The rumor was that he still ate from the garbage cans, that if he changed clothes, it was into others that had been discarded. He still lived in his tent and no one ever saw him go to the bank. And yet, he had to be paying for gasoline. He wasn't taking those piles of rags to the Chinese for free, or because he was a missionary or something. Rumor also had it that once his beat-up old truck had broken down in Redwood City and that he had to pay a lot of money, cash money, to have it fixed. So what were those Sunday trips about?

And as Sunday after Sunday passed, Salvatorre Garofoli became more and more uncomfortable. He had given this idiot Sundays off, against his better judgment, and now this idiot was hauling rags, his— Salvatorre's—rightful rags, rags that he had long since decided were not worth picking up, to San Francisco where he had to be selling them. Finally he confronted Giuseppe Rocco.

"What do you do with those rags?"

"Nothing."

"Nothing! You mean you collect them, stack them, sort them, and haul them in your truck every Sunday, and you do nothing with them? You want me to believe that?

"I just take them and get rid of them. The people like your service better that way, Salvatorre Garofoli. That way you're taking all their garbage."

"Please, don't bullshit me, Giuseppe. You mean you take the rags, they say to San Francisco, every Sunday, and you do nothing with them. And you do it for me?"

"That's right."

"Oh, shit, get out of here."

Salvatorre Garofoli was not a man to be lied to. The following Sunday, he borrowed a cousin's car, one that Giuseppe Rocco would not know, and left early that morning for San Francisco. When he reached the city, he parked the car on a hill from where he could see the approaching northbound traffic. Then he waited. Near noon he saw the old truck loaded with rags waddling towards the city. Then he followed the truck to an old wooden warehouse. There the truck stopped and Giuseppe Rocco tooted the tired horn three times. Two Chinese men came out of the warehouse and Giuseppe Rocco got out of his truck and met them. They greeted each other with smiles and nods of their heads. Giuseppe Rocco motioned to the truck and one of the men climbed on the rag pile and began looking through its many stacks as the other two men quietly waited. Then the three men had a discussion, not so much with words as with their hands and heads. There was much disagreement, much shaking of their heads, no, no. Twice Giuseppe Rocco turned and began walking away only to stop and return with more hand motions than before. Then there was agreement, slight noddings at first and then full, complete nods from all three. One of the Chinese men took out his wallet, withdrew some bills and then began counting them. At this point Salvatorre Garofoli leaped from his car and ran across the street shouting, "I caught you, you son of a bitch, I caught you!" startling the other men and causing the man with the money to stuff it back into his pocket.

"That's my money!" Salvatorre Garofoli shouted at the stunned man. "Those are my rags and that's my money." And when that got him only wide-eyed stares, he turned to Giuseppe Rocco and said, a bit more calmly, but even more firmly, "Tell him to give me my money!"

Giuseppe Rocco stared at Salvatorre Garofoli, saying nothing, explaining nothing, asking nothing. Salvatorre's demands were only met with stares. Some other Chinese men came out of the warehouse to see what the commotion was. Soon he was badly outnumbered, and rather than lose face completely, he pointed his finger at Giuseppe and said, "I'll see you in my office tomorrow morning before you go out on the route!" He turned and left.

"I don't have any money," Giuseppe Rocco said the next morning.

"You're lying! I saw them paying you!"

"I said I don't have any of your money."

"It's *all* my money! Those are *my* rags! You got them while you were working one of *my* routes with one of *my* trucks! They're *my* rags, and any money you get for them is *my* money. It's as simple as that!"

"I said I don't have any money!"

"Then you don't have a job! Because I want *all* the money you got from *my* rags, not just yesterday, but since you started doing this two years ago!"

"Then I don't have a job."

It didn't end there. Later that week, Salvatorre Garofoli heard that Giuseppe Rocco was now using his old battered truck to canvas and collect rags from his customers. This time he promised himself that Giuseppe Rocco would be stopped. So he hid in the front yard of a friend, and, when Giuseppe Rocco tooted and then came bounding into that front yard with that awkward smile thanking his friend's wife ever so much even before he reached the porch, Salvatorre Garofoli was ready.

What happened next neither man would ever say, and the friend's wife saw only part of it before she fainted: the beginning of what had to have been a vicious beating, one in which the younger, smaller man attacked Salvatorre Garofoli with such force that she thought he would surely kill him. Aside from what she saw and the fact that Salvatorre Garofoli stayed at home for a week, nothing else was ever known about the altercation. From then on, Giuseppe Rocco went about his business collecting rags unmolested, not only in San Jose, but soon throughout all of Santa Clara County, still with his smiling, awkward manner, but now with a new-found respect.

Again Giuseppe Rocco approached the old man with the idea of purchasing more land from him, this time two acres. The old man was reluctant at first. "No, better you should build yourself a house. You work like a dog and live like an animal. How long are you going to live in that tent with no water and no light and no outhouse and barely enough room to stand?"

"If you want I should have a house, then you should build me a house. Me, I don't want a house. I go in my tent only to sleep. I don't need a house."

"But that's no life."

"No, it's my life."

In the weeks that followed, Giuseppe Rocco all but convinced the old man that he didn't need a house. But before they could agree on the particular acres, the old man died.

Giuseppe Rocco went to the old man's funeral. It did not once occur to him not to go, nor did it occur to him that, aside from Christmas and the Fourth of July, this was the only day he hadn't worked since coming to San Jose. He was surprised to see that, besides himself, only the neighbors on each side of the old man attended his funeral. The old man had always said that all of his people were in the old country and he had never married, but still, thought Giuseppe Rocco, a man would make some friends after thirty years. He was shocked when he learned that the old man had left him his ranch. The will said simply, "I leave all of my real property to Giuseppe Rocco." That was sixty-eight acres.

Suddenly Giuseppe Rocco was a very eligible bachelor. (Despite what the daughters in the Italian community said, their mothers knew better.) But it was difficult, if not impossible, to arrange anything. For one thing, the dirty little man continued to live in his tent. He rented the old man's house out to a family who, besides paying rent, agreed to tend the orchards. This meant not only that he never took a bath, but also that any mother interested enough would have to trek across three acres, usually in the darkness, with a protesting daughter in tow. On his rag route, he was so dirty and awkward that no self-respecting girl dared or wanted to be seen talking to him. Soon it was said that the reason he didn't make himself available was that he used Chinese women in San Francisco or Mexican whores in the labor camps. Some even said that he didn't like women, that he was "queer." Eventually, the mothers gave up on him.

Once Giuseppe Rocco established his county-wide route, he began collecting scrap metal too. Salvatorre Garofoli did not take metal and the Chinese said they would buy it. Now there were new mounds of refuse on the land surrounding his tent, and now his old truck carried both metal and rags to San Francisco each Sunday. But the old truck wasn't big enough, and each week the mounds grew. It was plain that he was losing money. So he bought another truck—paying "cash money" for it, all the Italians said. The truck was bigger and better than any truck on the east side. Now the Italians wondered anew how much money he did have and where he kept it, because no one ever saw him go to the bank.

For the next ten years, Giuseppe Rocco continued to baffle the Italian community, working day in and day out, twelve to fourteen hours a day, living in his tent, even though by then he owned at least a dozen houses and hundreds of acres of land. As ever, he was friendly to everyone, but was without a friend. Quietly, he continued to buy more ranches and untold acres of unimproved land. On each of the ranches he brought in poor families who, in exchange for rent and half the share of the harvest, tended the orchards and crops for him. Soon it was common knowledge that "the rag man," as they called him, owned more real estate than any other Italian in the county. Still he wore discarded clothes and shoes, and no one knew when or where, if ever, he bathed. He did make one change. Now one of his tenants' wives cooked for him, bringing his supper and the next day's lunch to his tent every night at seven, although he was seldom there to receive it, and retrieving the empty plate the next day.

Suddenly, after almost two years, the tenant's wife began finding the previous day's plate untouched. The number of untouched plates increased until they were left almost every night. It had to be a woman, they said. And it was.

Her name was Angelina Mendoza. She was a Mexican woman of forty-five who was widowed and lived alone on five acres of land at the end of a dirt road, two miles from any neighbor in the southern tip of the county. He had heard about the woman in Gilroy. Rather, he had heard about the abandoned automobiles that the widow's husband had hauled onto his land. And everyone was certain that those automobiles were still there. That was all that mattered to Giuseppe Rocco. It mattered not that everyone also said that the widow was strange, if not crazy—harmless enough, but strange or crazy—and that she had five big, black, ferocious dogs that guarded every inch of her property. Giuseppe Rocco had already decided: sooner or later those automobiles would be his.

It was a burning, late-August afternoon when he started down that dirt road for the first time. Fifty yards down the road he was very much aware of the thick cloud of dust that his truck was creating as he went. He had hoped to take her by surprise or at least be on her land before the dogs started barking. Now he was sure that he could be seen from miles away and that she was watching the dust cloud moving toward her and that she had already signaled the dogs. Slowly he crept along the rutted road. No one remembered seeing her in town after her husband's death. The more time she had to think about his coming, he thought, the more suspicious she would become. He had planned to be at his clumsiest: to relax her, to put her off guard. He had hoped that the dogs wouldn't throw him too much off stride. Slowly, too slowly, the big truck churned over the pitted road. The two miles seemed like two hundred. If it weren't for the dogs, he probably would have done better going in on foot the first time. But the dogs would have never let him get on the property on foot, let alone close enough to the widow to talk to her.

Yet when he reached the bare fence posts of the widow's property, he neither saw nor heard any dogs. Carefully he squeezed the big truck past two posts that defined the road as much as the fence. Two hundred yards away was a small, unpainted, wooden house. Nowhere did he see any sign of life, and worse, no vehicles. He inched the truck toward the house, looking in every direction. No cars. All of this effort and worry, and no cars. No, something was wrong. Too many people had said there were cars there. He stopped the truck. The small parcel seemed deserted. Everything was either broken or run down: there was nothing worth salvaging. He had decided to leave, when he noticed what had to be the front end of a rusty old car protruding from behind a shed. He went on to the house.

The front door was open, but the light was such on the screen door that it was all he could see. He revved his engine before turning it off, hoping to draw the dogs while he was still in the truck. Nothing. Even the air was still. He got down from the truck, bracing himself for the dogs as he walked toward the porch. *"¿Quién eres tú?"* a thin voice said from behind the screen.

He couldn't see her, but he knew it had to be her and he knew enough Spanish to answer, smiling his awkward smile, *"Yo soy*

Giuseppe Rocco, para servirle, señora." He stumbled deliberately on the porch steps and recovered, smiling.

"¿Quién eres tú?" the voice asked again.

Now he was in the porch shade and he could make out a silhouette. *"Yo soy . . . "* he said again, except that this time he clumsily remembered, and just as clumsily took off his cap and finished with exaggerated respect, all the while smiling his shy, awkward smile.

"¿Quién eres tú?"

Now he was next to the screen and he could see her staring at him. It was a woman shorter than he, a woman neither stout nor slim, hidden by the plain cotton dress that she wore. He said it again, taking care to be just as deferential, just as awkward and pleasant as he had been the other times.

"¿Quién eres tú?"

Now he looked at her, stared back at her, and he saw that she was staring at him without seeing him. He answered again, smiled again. Now she simply stared. She had a fine face. She must have been beautiful, he thought. No, she was beautiful. The nose was sharp yet delicate, and her skin, though creased, was smooth and light brown. Her eyes were not the brown or black of Mexicans, but rather a kind of hazel, almost green. He looked at her as he had looked at no woman, mainly because she was not seeing him. The white of her hair enriched the brown of her face. He felt stirrings that he seldom permitted himself. He shook his head and reminded himself about the rusty old car behind the shed and all the other cars that had to be somewhere on the property. Somehow he had to get her to focus on those cars.

"¿Quién eres tú?" she asked again without so much as blinking.

He started to answer again, as he already had, but instead he stopped and said, *"Yo soy el Niño Dios."*

Now her eyes sparkled and she smiled a big wonderful smile and said, *"Ah, sí, sí, tú eres el Niño Dios,"* and she unlatched and opened the screen door for him.

"Ah, yes, my dogs told me that you would come. They've been telling me that for a long time now. They said they would hide under the house when you came and that by that sign I would know. And this morning when we saw that great cloud of dust and then saw your giant truck, they ran and hid under the house, and I knew you had come, my *Niño Dios*. I just asked you to be sure. Come, come into my house, my

Niño Dios. Come into me, my *Niño Dios.*" And she took him by the hand and led him into the small front room.

"For a long time my dogs have told me that I was a chosen one, that God Almighty had chosen me to challenge the Virgin Mary who had become lazy and much too satisfied with herself, that I was to bear a man-God. Come, my *Niño Dios,* fill me with your son."

And she took him to her bedroom, where she let the cotton dress fall and waited for him to do what he had never done before. And he did, with her help the first time, and then again and again and again and again, until it seemed that his penis would burst.

And when it was dusk and he lay still on the small, sweat-soaked bed next to the woman who said only, "My *Niño Dios.* Oh, my *Niño Dios,*" he examined her body. It was the first female nakedness he had been next to. Her body was so different from his, so soft and big where his wasn't. He studied it boldly in the oncoming darkness, knowing that there would not be another time. And when darkness came, he lay back exhausted, enjoying that exhaustion, wanting to enjoy it that one time. Then, suddenly, the strong chirps of crickets jerked him from a sleep.

"I've got to go!" he said, sitting up, his movement waking her. He wished that it hadn't, that he could have slipped out unnoticed, never to return.

"What's wrong, my *Niño Dios?* Where are you going?"

"Home."

"But why? We are so happy here."

He didn't answer. There was no answer. You didn't talk to a crazy woman. He dressed in the dark as quickly as he could. But not quick enough, because then she was up too, naked still, embracing him, clinging.

"Don't go, my *Niño Dios.* Stay. When your Son comes, all of mankind will rejoice."

No, it was he who was crazy. What had possessed him to make love to a crazy woman, to do to a lunatic what he had steadfastly avoided doing with normal women? Then he couldn't find his belt.

Panicking, he said, "Turn on the light."

"I have no light, my *Niño Dios.* I have only a kerosene lamp, but no kerosene. All of which is a sign that your Father wants you to remain here with me until His Grandson is born and the world rejoices."

"Stay, my ass."

15

"What?"

"I said I'm going. I'll get the belt another time."

"Don't go, my *Niño Dios!*" she said, following him onto the porch, naked still, clutching at his arm. "You'll come again?"

He nodded, thinking it was a small price to pay for his freedom. He hurried to his truck, worrying that it wouldn't start. As he drove, he chastized himself. He had worked so hard, had deprived himself of so much . . . to come to this? They had laughed at him when he had first come: an ugly, awkward stump of a teenager with blood on his shoes and but one change of clothes, and those blood-stained and worn too. He lived like a smelly old billy goat, he had heard some of them say, staked to the middle of his bare acre with no water or light or even a hole for his waste. The young Italian girls laughed and snickered as he walked through their yards with huge sacks of their garbage on his back. In those first days, he had taught himself to expect it, to ignore and accept it. But gradually, as he accumulated land, as he showed signs of money, there were changes. Middle-aged women began stopping him on the street, trying to engage him in conversation, all to the end of introducing their daughters to him. He avoided those introductions. Then he was invited into the kitchens and front rooms of the homes from which he took rags and scrap metal. He declined. Nothing gave him more pleasure than his awkward excuses: "Oh, no, thank you so much. But I'm so dirty . . ." There was still the disdain on their faces, no matter how they tried to hide it. It was still hard for them to look at him, to smell him, harder still, he thought, to be seeking him out for their daughters—but he had money. And he knew that the stories about his money continued to grow. The men were envious: it was in their eyes. On the one hand, they loathed him; on the other, they sought him out, inviting him to their clubs and their hunts and their festivals. Those too he declined, knowing that he had long since surpassed them in wealth and that they now needed him, and not he they.

All of this he had accomplished without a woman; better, he had accomplished it because he had not had a woman. Women meant children and fancy houses and fancy clothes and fancy meals. Women meant obligations and limitations, in exchange for which they gave you their bodies. That had never been a fair exchange as far as Giuseppe Rocco was concerned. And he had proven himself right. He was now the richest Italian in San Jose. (Oh, how he loved the buzz that followed

him about the streets of east San Jose once or twice a year after the purchase of another piece of real estate, a "cash money" purchase.) In a
few years, he would be the richest Italian in the entire county. Then he
planned to show the Italians of San Jose who he really was.

Long ago in the slaughterhouse, there had been an old Italian who
had been laughed at by most everyone. The old man was a miser who
lived like a pauper, spending only what was absolutely necessary. But
the reason they laughed at the old man was that he openly said that he
was saving his money toward that day when he could return to Italy and
marry a countess. Giuseppe Rocco had never laughed; he understood
that dream. Outside his boyhood village, at the top of the hill, a count
had maintained a magnificent summer home. For a few months each
year he had seen the countess. She was as beautiful and elegant and
desirable a creature as he had ever seen. Whenever she was near, he
would hide so that he could freely watch her. He had known then what
love was. Now he had a similar dream; no, he had always had that
dream. Now he was nearing a position where he could realize that
dream. In a few years he would return to Italy and not only marry a
countess, but also bring her back to live in as magnificent a house as
the Italians of San Jose (peasants all) had ever seen. Once and for all he
had planned to show them who Giuseppe Rocco really was.

But not now, and perhaps never, if he continued fucking a lunatic,
and a Mexican lunatic to boot. Not only would he be a laughingstock
if anyone found out, but what if she became pregnant and then sued
him. He had heard stories of rich men in America being sued by pregnant whores and losing fortunes. He could not understand what had
possessed him. As he neared San Jose, he felt another fear, a fear that
his rags and metals and tent would be gone, gone because he had been
out fucking a lunatic. He pushed the big truck as hard and as fast as it
would go. The closer he got, the more certain he was that it would all
be gone. He banged the truck over that last stretch of dirt road and, as
he reached the site, he searched and waited and sighed as the truck
lights showed first the rags, then the metals, then the tent. He ran to the
tent and lit his lantern. He was there. He was home. He wasn't out fucking a lunatic now. Thank God, he thought, blessing himself. Never,
never would he do that again.

The next morning, he watched for a sign that someone knew. By
mid-morning he was certain that no one knew, that to everyone he was

still the same old Giuseppe Rocco, the Rag Man, as even the children called him. As far as anyone was concerned, save himself, there had been no change. He had begun the morning prepared to give up his weekly route to Gilroy if that was what it took to keep anyone from knowing. By noon, by the end of the day, throughout the next two days, and on Sunday too, he was still ready to give up Gilroy. By Monday, he seemed far removed from that lunatic lady, and there seemed little need to do anything so drastic. He could easily stay away from her, and besides, he hadn't given any of his Gilroy customers notice. And then, too, there was the matter of money: Gilroy had become far more profitable than he had expected. By Tuesday he had made his decision: there was no reason to give up Gilroy's sizable profits because of a danger that he had completely under control.

He went to Gilroy on Wednesday, feeling no apprehension whatever. The only change he made was his pace: he worked as fast as he could, there being no need to tempt the fates. He was ready to leave by one o'clock. He tied down the tarp quickly, tightly, now and again a little too quickly, fumbling, as if someone were, if not chasing him, then about to chase him. There was a clumsiness in his fingers. He stopped, breathed deeply, and then tied the knot and walked deliberately to the cab. There was no need to be alarmed: he was leaving.

Someone waved to him. He saw the wave and returned it instinctively. The key skirted the ignition. It angered him. He forced the key, but missed the ignition again. He looked at the ignition, held the key firmly, inserted it, pushed firmly until it stopped. Then he turned it hard, thinking, the son of a bitch better start. But it didn't start. Instead, it ground and ground until people began looking. He stopped, feeling the sweat on his forehead and thinking, I haven't sweat this much all goddamn day. He waited. I don't need these bastards looking at me. He tried it again. Again it ground on and on. He stopped. All I need is to burn out the battery and get stuck in this fucking place. Sweat stuck to the front of his shirt.

On the next try it started. He gunned the engine, wanting to recharge the battery, in case it died, and he had to start it again. He needed to be on his way to San Jose, out of Gilroy. People turned. He took his foot off the accelerator. The engine didn't die, as he had expected. Still, slowly, carefully, he put the truck in gear. It moved forward; the first step, he thought, toward getting out of Gilroy. He drove toward Main Street, which was also the highway. He would stop there, turn left, go two blocks, stop again, and then in another two blocks, he would be out of Gilroy. It was the second stop he was anticipating, even though he was blocks away from the first stop. At the second stop, if he turned right, he would be on the road to her house, not that he was going to her house. But if he turned right, it would be the road that led to her house. He gripped the steering wheel hard; there would be no going to her house.

A small, rickety old truck pulled out of a driveway, stopped, and then died directly in his path. He honked, but the bony driver just shrugged his shoulders and opened his hands. "Move the goddamn thing!" he yelled, before it could occur to him that that was not the way a rag man could or should behave. He honked again, leaning on his horn. When people began coming out onto their porches, he got out of his truck—he was certain to leave the engine running—and helped push the small truck to the side of the road. Maybe there was something making it difficult for him to get out of town, he thought, as he began to pass the bony old man and his truck, cursing him as he drove by it. All he needed now was for someone to bring a flock of goats onto the street. He'd run over every one of those bastards if they did. Nothing was going to stop him from getting out of Gilroy.

At the first stop sign, he looked in both directions and then fixed his eyes on the second stop sign two blocks down the street. That was the street. If he turned there . . . there would be no turning there. Now the sweat ran down the sides of his neck, and his body itched, and his breathing quickened. He shifted in his seat, moved his legs back and forth as he looked down at the stop sign. If need be, he wouldn't even stop there; if need be, he'd drive straight through it. He moistened his lips, tasting the sweat above them. Then someone honked a long shrill honk, startling and angering him. He turned and saw the bony man in his rickety truck motioning for him to go on.

He went on, flipping the bony man a finger, turning left slowly, moving forward again, slowly, wanting to think things through before he got to that second stop, though he couldn't have told anyone, including himself, what those things were that he had to think through. Now there was another honk behind him, and he saw the bony man motioning him on. "Fuck you!" he yelled, shaking his fist at the bony man, but pulling over, letting him pass. He didn't want to be rushed into anything: he needed time to think, though he had not yet dared to think about what there was to think about. He focused on the stop sign, on its redness, and then the sign became a blur. No, no, he had worked too hard, had sacrificed too much to lose it all now. No, he put the truck in gear and drove on to the stop sign, stopping only long enough to shift gears, looking neither to his left nor to his right, and proceeding on across the intersection, on to safety, on to San Jose.

His body ached and his arms twitched, and he felt as if bugs were trying to eat their way out of him. Once again he pulled over, but now only to make a U-turn. Still he didn't admit what he was doing or where he was going. Even after he turned left, he thought, "Hell, there are a lot of houses out this way. I could probably make this a good part of my route." But he didn't stop at any of the houses, and in moments he was out in the country. She had a lot of stuff just laying around out there, he thought. "I'll just stop and say hello and see if I can help her get rid of some of that junk." Now he knew he was lying, but he denied the lie. Once he turned onto the dirt road, it didn't matter. Then all that mattered was whether or not he would have to fight off the dogs to get into the house and, yes, to get to her. "My dogs said that when you came they would hide under the house, and by that sign I would know it was you, my *Niño Dios*." He shifted into a lower, louder gear, and sped up, pushing the truck, making as much noise and raising as much dust as he could. He was determined to scare those bastard dogs as they had never been scared before. Yes, yes, *Niño Dios* was coming.

Then he saw the small faded house deserted in the sun, and he raced the motor louder, pulled into the yard with a cloud of dust, slid to a stop inches from the porch, and jumped out of the truck onto the porch in one motion. For a moment he didn't see her and he panicked. Then he heard her behind the screen. "Ah, it is you, my *Niño Dios*. You have come to make me big with God."

He mounted her again and again, without care or concern, and then lay next to her, exhausted, as night came. This time he didn't worry or bolt as he had before. There was something peaceful, soothing in the way she pressed herself against him gently, softly touching and kissing his back and his arms. It was a sensation he had not known, but one that he did not question. Yes, he was truly her *Niño Dios*.

He left at daybreak, letting her kiss him as he left, knowing that he would return, but not knowing why. What was it? What had happened?

What if people were to find out? What of his dreams and his countess? He had no answers. All he knew is that he would return. And return he did, two days later, at night, after he had begun sorting rags and had fought off that gnawing ache for as long as he could, for as long as he could chase away the thought of her under him, holding him with her arms and her legs as she kissed him. Then there was no chasing it; then all was lost. And he ran and climbed up onto his truck as the quiet light was fading through the trees and drove it as hard and as fast as he could to that tiny deserted house and those soft hands and thighs. And once his passion was spent, he lay there again, enjoying her kisses and caresses and listening to, or at least hearing her crazy mumblings about her *Niño Dios*.

And then it was more than caresses and kisses. Then it was also the humble offerings of beans and tortillas and water in the still of the night. Then it was her precise and careful and loving straightening and smoothing of his side of their tiny bed before he returned to it. And it was the way she picked up and folded and smoothed his pants and shirt and dusted his shoes before she got back into bed. The next morning as she clung to him at the door, he turned and kissed her and said, "I'll be back."

And return he did, night after night, always to that fury and then to that peace and wonder. Now it was he who asked, "Who are you?"

And she who answered, "I am your humble servant, my *Niño Dios*, someone who was put here to love you and serve you and to bear you another God-man."

"Are you crazy or am I crazy?"

"Neither, my *Niño Dios*."

And he would ask again, "Who are you?" though never once questioning the passion and the kisses and the caresses, and yes, finally, the love.

Now he thought of her constantly. He saw her and heard her *"¿Quién eres tú?"* everywhere: in the trees, in his rags, on his routes, in his truck, in the frames of the Italian mothers who still sought him for their daughters. "Angelina," he would mumble, so often that others would notice and wonder. *"¿Quién eres tú?"* He resisted being with her every night because that would ultimately mean that he would have to bring her to his tent, to his land, to keep her and care for her there, regardless of what anyone might think or say. But she overcame his resistance with her love as much as her body, and he had decided to take her to his tent no matter what when she told him, "My *Niño Dios*, you have finally made me big with your son."

"What?"

"Yes, now I am certain. But I must be careful because I am old. I must not disappoint you or your Father or mankind."

"What?"

So he didn't tell her, he didn't take her, because it was different now. He let her stay in that deserted house a few days more until he could decide, decide once and for all, what it was he would do with her and, now, with his child. But before he decided, it was decided for him. He learned of that decision six days after she had told him of her pregnancy. He had gone to her house that day, distracted, still undecided. He had entered the tiny house. "It's me, Angelina, your *Niño Dios*." He found her next to their bed, bloodied from the hemorrhaging that must have come first, and then bloodied from the self-inflicted slit in her throat.

For eight days Giuseppe Rocco remained in his tent. *"¿Quién eres tú?"* On the third day people came to see what was wrong. "I'm all right. I'll be okay," he said through the tent's closed flaps.

He returned to his route on the ninth day. People said that it was the first time in almost twenty years that the man had missed a day of work. "It was just the flu," he said to anyone that asked, because his face still sagged and everywhere he went he saw her still and heard her *"¿Quién eres tú?"* And to them it seemed no more than that.

It was after his brief absence that the stories increased, that people began believing, as they had suspected all along, that there was another side of Giuseppe Rocco. It was said everywhere that at night Giuseppe Rocco visited the Mexican labor camps, not just to drink with those dirty little brown men, but to share their whores. It was said that he visited only those camps on those nights that they were to have whores. The stories were that at those camps he became a brute of a man, taking or buying whatever he wanted. And the stories were that this miserly man spent money like water around the Mexicans.

If these stories were true, Giuseppe Rocco never once acknowledged it. Occasionally there would be remarks or hints of the camps, but Giuseppe Rocco simply ignored them, never giving anyone the satisfaction of a reaction. Every now and then someone would become bold enough to confront him: "We've heard what you do in the camps, Giuseppe Rocco. What's the matter, aren't our women good enough?" But not often. And when it did occur, his cold silent stare was enough to silence anyone.

Some five years later, when Giuseppe Rocco saw Rita Verducci for the first time, he was certain she was a countess.

"Who is she?" he asked as he watched her walk from Maria Luca's house to a fancy car, where a driver waited.

"I don't know," said Sophia Bagigalupi. "It's some rich friend of Maria's."

"But who is she?" he asked again, standing in Sophia's front yard with his big burlap sack humped over his back.

"All I know is that Maria used to work for her family in the old country. I think maybe even Maria took care of her as a baby. Something like that. Anyway, the woman likes her and she comes to visit her every now and then from San Francisco."

"She must be a countess."

"That I don't know. All I know is that her family is very rich."

"She is a countess. You can just tell."

Over the next weeks he thought of the countess each time that he passed Maria Luca's house. Once he almost brought himself to ask Maria about her, but was finally too embarrassed to ask. Men like him didn't ask about countesses. So he forgot her.

Until he saw her again. It was months later when he saw her again, or thought he saw her again, because he wasn't sure. He had seen no fancy car, no driver. He thought he had seen her standing in Maria Luca's screened porch, staring out into the street as he had seen so many women do. In fact, he had paid little attention to her as he had gone into Sophia Bagigalupi's yard. Had his sack been full, he probably wouldn't have noticed her on his return. But his neck was free, and for a moment he saw that fine profile and knew it was her even as he was turning away. And he became nervous, so nervous that he couldn't look back, couldn't confirm that it was her.

He returned the next day, though he was not due to return until the next week, and explained to Sophia Bagigalupi that he had lost one of his sacks along that part of his route. Then he asked, as he was leaving, as an afterthought, "The countess was here yesterday?"

"Yes, and she's still here."

"Really."

"Yes. And she might be here for a long time, according to Maria. Something happened to her father, and now the man she was to marry won't marry her because she has no dowry. Somehow her family lost everything. I don't understand it at all, but Maria knows everything. And the poor thing doesn't have enough money to go back home, although, according to Maria, there's nothing for her there either. And the poor thing is so used to the finer things. And now there are no finer things. She may be here a long time and she hardly knows the language. Who knows, she could end up working like the rest of us."

"How long?"

"How long what?"

"How long is she going to stay here in San Jose?"

"I don't know. Ask Maria. All I know is that she's got no money and nowhere to go."

That night he drove his truck past Maria Luca's house as many times as he dared—everyone knew the truck and it was so big and made so much noise; it wouldn't take long for people to wonder. The next day he moved out of his tent, as simply as that, telling no one and taking nothing, so that the tenant's wife continued to leave and pick up the untouched plates of food for more than a week. When it was learned that he had moved into one of the houses on one of his ranches, they found him painting every room and wall inside and out with that same fierce energy with which he did everything. Still he gave no reason, no explanation. When he stopped in the middle of his route the following Saturday and went into town and bought the first new suit of clothes and shoes and shirt and underwear that anyone could ever remember him buying, the women knew.

It was just a question of whom. Most of them guessed that it was one of the daughters of the new Italian families in south county, because there wasn't the slightest hint that it was anyone in San Jose. Some of them giggled and said it was probably one of his Mexican whores. Giuseppe Rocco didn't keep them guessing for long. The next day he left much earlier than usual for San Francisco and returned much earlier than usual. Upon his return, he quickly bathed (the house had a tub) and shaved and dressed himself in his new clothes. Then he climbed back into his truck and drove directly to Maria Luca's house.

"*Signora,*" he told the startled widow, "my intentions are honorable . . ." It took Maria Luca a while to understand that the object of Giuseppe Rocco's intentions, the countess, as he called her, was Rita Verducci, who, fortunately, had gone to San Francisco that morning. It was fortunate because Rita Verducci laughed when she heard of Giuseppe Rocco's honorable intentions. And then, as she thought more about it, became outraged. "Filthy swine! The man I was to marry was a nobleman. Does this depraved garbage man really think that I . . ."

"I wouldn't be so quick to dismiss him if I were you, my dear," said Maria Luca. "If you were in a different situation, then maybe . . ."

The next day Rita Verducci looked at Giuseppe Rocco for the first time from behind a window curtain as he went into Sophia Bagigalupi's back yard for the third consecutive day. "Oh, he's so ugly, Maria. What woman could ever bear having his hands on her?"

"But he's rich."

"It doesn't matter."

"It does matter. It matters whether you live and work here like a peasant for the rest of your life or whether you live in the manner in which you're accustomed to. The plain truth is that unless something happens soon, you'll have to work soon, get a job soon, a miserable job like the rest of us from the old country. But we were used to it. You aren't. You won't want that."

He came again the following Sunday in his stiff new shoes and suit and shirt, the collar a little stained now. This time he held a hat in his hand.

"Is the countess here?"

No, the countess was not there. She had gone to San Francisco, lied Maria Luca. Rita Verducci had spent the afternoon in church because she could not have faced the garbage man. She needed time to think and she had no place else to go.

"He thinks you're a countess."

"Does it matter?"

"Oh yes it does. Titles have a way of making people worth more than they are. And besides, people expect counts and countesses to have big houses and fine cars and good food and drink. They expect them to be used to those things, to need those things. And once it's expected, it shouldn't take much for a smart woman to get an able husband to provide those things for her. And remember, countesses are not expected to work."

That week Maria Luca watched for him, and when she saw him come, she crept out of the house and waved frantically but silently to him, and then went quickly up to him and in a low voice, barely more than a whisper, so that he would think that the countess did not know, said, "She'll be here this Sunday."

He was there that Sunday at two, his new shoes showing creases, the shirt collar a little more stained, his trousers gathered and wrinkled at the crotch. In one hand he carried his hat, and in the other a bouquet of flowers.

"Is the countess here?" he asked innocently.

Yes, Maria nodded, opening the door and pointing to the front room, where the countess sat reading. He saw her sitting erectly and quietly with the dignity, grace, and beauty that only countesses had. He looked back at Maria Luca, back at the door which she had already closed. There was no turning back, nowhere to go but to the countess. He tried walking as softly as he could, but his new shoes were like iron on the floor. Still the countess read, not once distracted. She was beautiful, but more than that, stately and intelligent. (What would she say if she knew he couldn't read?) He looked back. Maria Luca was still at the entry as if blocking the doorway. There was nothing to do but what he had come to do. He took two more steps; he was close enough to be heard at a whisper.

He cleared his throat and said, hardly above a whisper, "Excuse me, my countess, my name is . . . is . . . Giuseppe Rocco and I . . . I . . . I have come to declare my intentions."

She continued reading. She must not have heard.

He cleared his throat again, louder, and said again, louder, "Excuse me, my countess, my name is . . ."

"Yes, what is it?" she said, faintly turning her head, moving her eyes more than her head. "What is it?"

"My name is . . . is . . ."

"Your name is?"

"Giu . . . Giu . . . Giuseppe Rocco."

"And what is it you want?"

Only to leave. But he couldn't say or do that, and he didn't say or do that. He simply began nodding his head as if he were trying to shake loose words.

So she said, "You said something about your intentions?"

He nodded all the more, all the faster.

"What did you say about your intentions?"

"To . . . to . . . declare . . ."

"To declare your intentions?"

"Yes, yes," he nodded.

"Very well. I will consider that. You may go now," and she returned to her book.

He turned quickly and walked quickly, as happy to be excused as he was to have declared his intentions. At the door he smiled and waved and nodded at Maria Luca, who was standing next to him, but said nothing to her, too excited and elated to say anything, taking with him the flowers he had brought, but too happy to notice or care. The countess was going to consider his intentions! He had declared them and she had not laughed at him, had not spat at him, or thrown him out. She was thinking about his intentions, "considering" them. Were it out of the question, she would have said no then. But she hadn't said no. And there were few happier than he as he drove around in his truck aimlessly. The countess was considering his intentions.

And she was. "A baser, uglier man I have never laid eyes on in my entire life, Maria. I could smell his foul odor from the moment you opened the door. No, I can't, Maria, I really can't. I don't care if he's the richest man in America. I can't."

"Well, if you can't, you can't. But the man is crazy about you. He adores you. It would take so little on your part. He would do anything for you, anything you wanted, anything you asked, even bathe."

"No, I can't. It's totally out of the question."

"He could be taught to dress properly, to groom properly, simple cleanliness. Then he would not look all that bad. And he works all the time, day and night. You would never have to deal with him . . . think of your alternatives."

Again Maria Luca watched for him at mid-week. Again she appeared to sneak out of her house and surreptitiously wave to him and speak in hardly more than a whisper, apparently planning what had already been decided.

"You should come again on Sunday. But take a bath and change your suit and bring money for a nice restaurant for the three of us. And is there any way you could bring a car? Anything other than that truck. A countess can't be seen riding around in a garbage truck."

He came the following Sunday, just as she had told him to come. He came in a shiny red convertible roadster that reeked of perfume and belonged to a Mexican pimp. He came in a shiny new black suit, or almost new, one that the Chinese told him was practically new and traded him for pennies, one that they said fit like a glove and which in fact ripped somewhere when he got into the roadster. Maria had said nothing of the shoes and shirt. So he wore the same brown shoes, dustier and with cracks instead of creases, and the same shirt with its collar now evenly soiled. Still he did not forget the money; it bulged out of both front pants pockets. And he brought two bouquets of flowers.

Now Rita Verducci also watched from behind the curtain as he crossed the street. "That car! Oh, my God! That car! I'll never ride in that car. And that suit! It's so tight, it makes him look like a gorilla. I thought you said you gave him instructions!"

"But I did, *signorina*, I did!"

When the door opened, Giuseppe Rocco looked past Maria Luca to the cool of the living room where the countess sat reading just as she had the previous Sunday, just as she probably did every Sunday. Elegant, stately, beautiful, he thought briefly until he heard Maria Luca hissing at him.

"That car! That car! The countess will never ride in that car! The countess can never ride in that car!"

"But you told me not to bring my truck. So I got a car. What's wrong with that car?"

"If you don't know, I can't tell you! Whores would ride in that car but not a countess. And that suit . . ."

"But it's almost new."

"I don't care if it *is* new! It's too tight. It's too small. Look where the sleeves are. It makes you look like a gorilla!"

"You said not to wear the other one."

"I know what I said! You don't have to tell me what I said. That shirt! It's filthy. Why didn't you change?"

"You didn't tell me about the shirt. And I just took a bath. And I brought plenty of money. See?"

He held out two huge wads of bills, and that stopped her. She had never seen so much money.

"Wait here," she said, "I'll have to talk to the countess."

She went into the living room, closing the doors behind her. And he waited, wondering what was taking so long. At times he could hear Maria Luca's voice, and at times he thought he could hear the countess's voice, but he couldn't hear what they were saying. At times, it sounded as if Maria Luca was arguing; no, countesses didn't argue.

When Maria Luca returned she was calm, matter of fact. "I have told the countess of your desire to take us to an early dinner. She has agreed. We will go to Dante's and we will walk. No one, not even you, Giuseppe Rocco, can expect a countess to ride in that car. And of course, I will act as the chaperone."

They left the house together, walking together, Giuseppe Rocco on the outside, Maria Luca between him and the countess. He was elated. He was with the countess! It didn't matter that once they were on the sidewalk he found himself walking on plants and rocks and grass and the gutter because there wasn't enough room for the three of them.

It bothered the countess, who nudged Maria who quickly snapped, "It really would make more sense if you walked behind us, *Signore* Rocco. You're stepping on people's plants, on people's lawns. You're walking in the gutter. Nobody walks in the gutter. What will people think?"

He stepped behind them. But close behind. He was still elated because now he was closer to the countess than he had ever been, so close that the countess jerked to one side and Maria Luca immediately hissed, "Stop it, *Signore* Rocco, stop it! You're much too close! You don't treat decent people like that."

When they had walked less than a block, people began noticing them and openly came out on their porches to watch Giuseppe Rocco, who in more than twenty years had never been seen with a woman. Now he was openly courting, or at least attempting to court, the stranded woman from the old country who was living with the widow Luca. Giuseppe Rocco beamed. He was delighted, beside himself, that people should see him with the countess. He waved. He grinned. He bellowed. "Hello, *Signora* Capriola! Good day, *Signore* Telesco! It's a good day! A wonderful day!" And they returned his greetings. Until the countess told Maria Luca, "Tell him to stop. It's embarrassing."

"Stop it!"

"Stop what?"

"Stop making a fool of yourself."

"I'm not making a fool of myself."

"Then stop making fools of us."

"What am I doing?"

Maria Luca could not answer, not immediately, and so she turned to Rita Verducci and asked, "What is he doing?"

And they both heard her say, "He's too loud."

And then Maria Luca turned to him and said, "You're too loud."

It dashed him. But only for a moment, because it didn't take more than a moment for him to realize that perhaps he was too loud. For a woman of the countess's sensibilities, yes, he was definitely too loud. So from then on he just waved, beaming, trying to answer any comment or question from the porches with a nod or a grin or a shake of the head.

Then they were at Dante's. Everyone said it was the best Italian restaurant in town. Giuseppe Rocco had never been there, having long ago decided that it was much too expensive for him. It was filled with Italian families, and a hush fell over the room when they entered: Giuseppe Rocco with a woman, Giuseppe Rocco in a suit, Giuseppe Rocco about to spend money. Giuseppe Rocco broke the hush, waving, smiling, nodding to all, looking from them to the countess and back at them, beaming. Then he began to speak again, being careful not to be loud, acknowledging everyone, with a good word for everyone.

Rita Verducci reached the table first and quickly seated herself against the wall, signaling to Maria Luca to sit next to her. Once the beaming Giuseppe Rocco had acknowledged everyone, he sat directly across from her.

When he saw that she had the menu in hand, he said loudly, "Order whatever you want, countess. I mean it. Anything you want. Money is no object," causing her to raise the menu and nudge Maria Luca under the table.

"*Signore* Rocco," Maria Luca muttered under her breath.

"What?"

It went no further: the waiter was there. "Will you be having anything to drink, sir?"

"Yes, the best!"

"The best of what, sir?"

"The best."

"Champagne. Wine. Whiskey. The best of which, sir?"

"The best of whatever the countess wants to drink."

But the countess was not to be seen or heard from. The menu was completely covering her face.

"May I suggest a red wine, sir," the waiter said, turning again to him. "We have . . ."

"Yes, the best. Bring us the best red wine."

The waiter left. The countess continued holding the menu up high. The silence at their table quickly became awkward. Theirs was the only table at which there was no conversation. So he asked Maria Luca, "Does the countess like this restaurant?"

"Yes, I think she does."

"Does the countess like San Jose?"

"Yes, I think she does."

"Is the countess still considering my intentions?"

"Yes, I believe she is."

"Have you told her about my ranches?"

"Yes, I think I have."

"Have you told her about all the houses on those ranches. Some of those ranches have very nice houses. Good houses for a family."

His voice was rising and Maria Luca felt another nudge.

"*Signore* Rocco . . ." but the waiter had returned with the wine.

He poured a portion into Giuseppe's glass. "No, no, serve the ladies first."

"Very well, sir."

The countess continued studying the menu. When the waiter finished pouring the wine, he asked, "Have you decided, sir?"

"Decided what?"

"On what you will have for dinner, sir?"

"Ask the ladies. They're first."

"*Signorina*."

Then the countess ordered. Only then did she lower the menu. Maria Luca ordered.

"And you, sir."

Now Giuseppe Rocco stumbled. He hadn't picked up the menu and he wouldn't pick up the menu because he couldn't read.

"Give me the same."

"The same as whom, sir?"

"As the countess," he said, pointing to her and seeing her redden.

Again they sat in silence, except that now the waiter had taken the menus and the countess was sitting close to him, face to face with him. He could not look at her, not even in her direction. He felt so unworthy. His discomfort grew. He shouldn't have sat so close to her. He shifted in his seat and asked again, "Have you told the countess about my properties?"

Rita Verducci nudged Maria under the table just as the waiter arrived with the first entree. As he served, Giuseppe Rocco asked, "How much does this cost?" The waiter stopped and looked up in disbelief. The countess asked to be excused and Maria Luca followed.

Giuseppe Rocco sat stunned as the food arrived, not knowing where the countess had gone or why, sensing that he was responsible but not knowing how and, worse, not knowing if she would return, ever. He ate unaware that he was eating, eating from each plate as much with his hands as with his fork, unaware also of the noises he made as he ate and the complaints others made, which prompted the waiter to approach him and ask, "Sir, will the ladies be returning?"

He looked up at the waiter, still stunned, and answered, "I don't know."

The next day, he went to Sophia Bagigalupi's, though he knew there would be no scraps or metal there. He went, hoping against hope, that he would get a glimpse of the countess, but arrived willing to settle for a glimpse of Maria Luca instead. He saw neither of them, despite having gone in and out of Sophia Bagigalupi's yard three times, staring all the while at Maria Luca's house and sitting in between trips in his truck for long intervals. He returned on each of the succeeding days, but there was no sign of the women.

On Friday, Maria Luca snuck out of her house and in her most secretive manner said, "I think the countess would like for you to come for a few minutes tonight." He was there that night and every night thereafter for the next three months, arriving exactly at seven and leaving exactly at eight.

The neighbors gossiped. There was nothing more they could do than gossip, because no one ever saw them come out of the house during those three months. They did notice changes in him. He was clean and freshly shaven, and his hair now seemed regularly cut by a barber, and each day he wore a change of what appeared to be new clothes. Then, towards the end of the three months, he drove up one evening in a new car.

What the neighbors did not know, could not see, were the lessons that went on every night in Maria Luca's kitchen. They were lessons that covered everything from how to bathe and wash and comb to how to dress and eat and how to greet and introduce and order for a lady. Maria Luca demonstrated and he copied, over and over until she was satisfied. But not once during those three months did the countess show herself. Some nights he thought he heard her moving about in other parts of the house, but not once did he see her. But that didn't matter, because she had agreed, through Maria Luca, to hold the declaration of his intentions in abeyance for ninety days so that he might train and improve himself before she decided. It was enough to know that by not refusing outright, she was, in fact, considering; and it was enough to know that she was under the same roof as he was.

He applied himself. ("If you want to court a countess, and because of the work you do, Giuseppe Rocco, you will have to master the use of a fingernail file.") More than anything, he wanted to court this countess; he would learn to use anything; he would do anything to court this countess. Even spend money. ("If you want to court a countess, Giuseppe Rocco, you must be prepared to spend money. Countesses are accustomed to spending money, you know.") He spent money as he had never spent it before. He spent money on clothes which Maria Luca bought for him ("This is the kind of suit that countesses like to see their men dressed in, Giuseppe Rocco."), on food which Maria Luca prepared for him ("This is the kind of food that countesses will expect you to know and know how to order and eat."), on toiletries ("Countesses not only expect their men to look fresh and clean, but to *smell* fresh and clean as well."). Finally, he bought a new car. ("Really, Giuseppe Rocco, if you are serious about courting a countess, you will have to buy a car. We can't walk, and I can tell you right now that the countess will never ride in a truck.") It was a new and very expensive car. ("You really can't expect the countess to ride in anything less than the best, can you, Giuseppe Rocco?")

Four days after Giuseppe Rocco arrived with his new car, the courtship began again. It was on a Sunday afternoon, and he came to

33

the door dressed in a well-fitted suit, with money in his pocket, prepared to take the countess and Maria Luca for a drive and then to dinner. He was delighted when she chose the front seat without any hesitation and left the back seat to Maria Luca. Slowly, he drove through the east side, waving to people, but in a subdued manner, as a gentleman would. Soon he was in the country.

"This is the beginning of one of my ranches, countess," he said, pointing and then chancing a glance and catching a bit of a nod of approval.

"These are my orchards. They bore good fruit last year."

Again he saw the slight nod. But that was enough. He drove on.

"This, too, is a ranch of mine, countess."

Again the quiet, firm approval. He drove the entire length of the ranch and then down a dirt road to a house and barking dogs.

"The house is mine, too. It's nice, huh? Sometimes I think of living in it, but I'm alone and it's too big for one person. But if I ever got married, well . . . then . . . Do you like it, countess?"

He thought he saw the nod. Then he drove by four more ranches and up to three of their houses.

As they started back toward town, Rita Verducci said, "Maria, ask *Signore* Rocco if those are the only ranches he has."

And he answered before he was asked. "Oh, no, countess. I have many other properties all over this county."

They returned to Dante's resaurant. Inside, the reaction was much the same as it had been three months before, except that now Giuseppe Rocco merely nodded to the people and helped the countess into her chair. He ordered wine before dinner and dinner for three. He was careful to use his napkin and knife and fork, as Maria Luca had taught him. He spoke softly when he spoke and waited for those moments when the countess looked at the waiter or about the room to sneak glimpses of her.

For several succeeding days, there were evening drives. The scenario was the same. No sooner would he knock than Maria Luca would open the door and usher the countess out and then follow. Only the routes and properties were different. But each night he had less to say about his properties and each night became a bit more awkward until, toward the end of the second week, Giuseppe Rocco said little, answering the countess's silence with silence.

That night, after the drive, Maria Luca said, "You're going to have to speak to him, my dear."

"I can't, Maria. I can't. He's such a thick, ugly man."

"If you don't speak to him soon, he might stop coming. The car felt like it was going to explode tonight, and I was in the back seat. You've got to say something, my dear, and not just to me. To him."

"I can't, Maria. He's so repulsive to me."

"Look at it this way, my dear. Is he more repulsive than a job as a maid?"

She spoke to him the next night. Once they were in the country, she said, "This is a very nice car you have, *Signore* Rocco."

He beamed. "You like it, countess?"

"Yes, I do."

And on Sunday, she spoke directly to him at Dante's, not much, not often, but directly, and often enough so that the others could see.

But Maria Luca thought there should be more. "Why do you keep calling him *Signore* Rocco, my dear? You've known the man almost four months now. It won't hurt you to say Giuseppe or at least Giuseppe Rocco. After all, that is the man's name, you know."

The next night Rita Verducci asked, "Are you going to buy more ranches, Giuseppe Rocco?"

The following week, he did what all three of them knew he had to do, what all three of them expected him to do: he touched her. And she screamed. And he insisted that it was an accident, as he tried to calm her and Maria Luca too, who couldn't understand what had happened, because now the countess was shaking uncontrollably and crying.

"I thought she was going to fall. I meant no harm. I was trying to help her. I only took her by the arm."

That night, Maria Luca was firm. "There is nothing wrong with his touching your arm. There is absolutely nothing wrong with it."

"But he lied. I wasn't falling. I had one foot firmly on the ground."

"It doesn't matter if you had both feet on the ground. It's natural that he should want to touch you and, yes, that he should touch you."

"But if I let him touch me now, what will it be tomorrow and the day after that and the day after that?"

"You know, my dear, there were times when women were just given away to neighboring tribes, to merchants passing through, to conquering armies. One day they were in their father's home, the next day they were in their husband's home, a husband and master that they had never seen before."

"What's that got to do with me? That was years and years ago."

"Well, it wasn't so long ago as you might think, my dear, and I'm sure that in the old country, in other parts of the world, even today, even today, arrangements are made and girls, young women are given over to husbands that they must loathe."

"What's that got to do with me?"

"Nothing, my dear, except that soon, and I don't know just how to put this, because I do love you and you are welcome here . . . but soon you will have to get a job. I know I don't live very well, and it's far beneath what you're accustomed to, but I am a widow, the widow of a working man, a plain and simple hard-working man, and my funds are limited. I don't know how to tell you except that soon you will have to get a job here or go back to the old country. And from what you tell me, there is nothing in the old country for you now except poverty. And if you do get a job here, my dear, with all due respect to your background and breeding, because of the language problem, you will probably have to work in the lowest of jobs, as a maid or a washerwoman even. I think you would die in that kind of work."

Two nights later as they drove up to Maria Luca's house, Rita Verducci said, "Giuseppe Rocco, would you please help me out of the car."

And the startled, overjoyed Giuseppe Rocco stumbled in his haste to help her. The next night she asked him to help her into the car, later up the front steps. It was a custom he quickly established, helping the countess in and out, up and down everything, eager for the opportunity to touch either of those soft, wonderful arms, touching, on each occasion, as much as he could of each arm, if only through the cloth that always covered them.

None of this passed unnoticed. "He grabs my arm at the slightest excuse. Sometimes I don't think he's going to let go."

"He's harmless, my dear. He's so much in love with you and you're in complete control. I don't find him *that* offensive."

"Yes, but he's not touching you."

"True, but how offensive can a man's hand be on the fully clothed arm of any woman?"

"It depends on who the man is."

"Has he hurt you in any way?"

"Oh, I can feel the lust in those thick fingers of his. He'd like to touch much more. Much more."

"My dear, I'm sure you've also noticed that, except when Giuseppe Rocco takes us to dinner, we are eating only pasta and vegetables. It's not that I don't like a steady diet of pasta and vegetables; there's only so many ways you can fix pasta and vegetables. But it's all I can afford. I'm afraid you're going to have to decide soon, very soon, whether you want a job or Giuseppe Rocco."

It was the Blackwell house that made her decide. The Blackwell house, as the home of a widow named Blackwell was called, was a resplendent Victorian house with windows and gables everywhere. It stood on a beautifully shaded half block lot across from the city park. It was considered by many to be the finest house in San Jose. About that time, Mrs. Blackwell died and the house was put up for sale. Rita Verducci had long admired the house. It was on one of their evening drives that she saw for the first time that it was for sale.

"Oh, my God!" she exclaimed. "The only house in all this barrenness that would be fit for anyone of breeding to live in, and it's for sale. If Papa were alive, I would make him buy it for me."

Maria Luca seized the moment. "With all your ranches, Giuseppe Rocco, could you buy that house?"

"I could buy that house and keep my ranches."

"No!"

"Yes."

That night Maria Luca was as direct as she had ever been. "You have no excuse now, my dear. The man has declared himself. He now says he can provide for you in the best of fashion, give you what no other woman around here has. I don't understand your hesitation. Frankly, my dear, I don't see how I can continue to feed both of us, even if it's only on pasta and vegetables, much past next week. You have to decide, my dear. You have to act."

The next night when Giuseppe Rocco knocked, Maria Luca surprised him by inviting him in. "The countess would like to speak to you privately in the living room. Don't look at me. I haven't the faintest idea what's on her mind. All she told me is that she wants to talk to you privately. So I will leave the two of you."

The countess sat reading beside a dim lamp, looking up only after Giuseppe Rocco's heavy shoes had clumped several times on the hardwood floor. "Oh, it's you, Giuseppe Rocco! Come in. Come in, please." Slowly she marked her place in the book. "Won't you sit down, please," she said with an elegant extension of her arm. He sat down and for a few moments she studied the book cover, smoothed it over with her hand, and then set the book on the sofa alongside her. She looked up at him.

"Giuseppe Rocco, quite some time ago you declared yourself. I have come to the conclusion that it is not fair to you to keep you in suspense any longer."

He felt his heart thumping. This he had not expected, not tonight at least, perhaps never.

"I have studied your proposal carefully. I have watched you steadily improve yourself and I now find myself in the position of having to decide once and for all whether I should return to my country or remain here. Undoubtedly you have heard that my family has suffered reversals. Life for me in Italy will not be what it used to be, at least not at first. But a woman of breeding and education should not have too difficult a time making a comfortable life for herself. On the other hand, you have offered things, have implied that you are prepared to offer a woman of my standing the kind of life she is accustomed to. Am I correct?"

"Yes, my countess," said his voice and his eyes and his head and his entire body. "Yes."

"Good. But you know that providing a woman of breeding with the kinds of things that she is accustomed to will be expensive. You are aware of that, are you not?"

"Yes, my countess."

"I must tell you that I am very seriously considering your declaration of your intentions. But there are some very specific matters that we should discuss and reach some agreement on. In some countries, I'm told that these matters are reduced to writing so that the parties can be sure. That is not the custom in my country, but then, had there been a little more care on my family's part, I would not be in the predicament I'm in now. Can you understand that?"

"Yes, my countess."

"Need we reduce the terms of our agreement to writing?"

"I am a man of my word, countess. And even if I were not, I would never deceive you."

"Good. Very well then, shall we proceed to specifics? First, there is the matter of a suitable residence. I want the Blackwell house. Without the Blackwell house I doubt that I could or would stay in this country. True, you see me in these humble surroundings, but it was a completely unforeseen catastrophe that put me here. Believe me, it has not been easy. Not that the *Signora* Luca hasn't tried to make me comfortable. God knows she has. But the poor woman simply hasn't the means. I can't stay here much longer. I can't bear it much longer. I've given myself until the end of the week to decide. I don't mean to rush you, but I will have to know your position on each matter of importance by tomorrow evening. Is that clear?"

"Yes, my countess."

"First then is the Blackwell house. I want it. Yesterday you said you could buy it. Was that just inflated talk or can you buy it?"

"I can buy it, my countess, I can buy it."

"But *will* you buy it?"

"Yes, my . . ."

"No, no, don't answer now. Think about it. Think about all the things I'm about to propose. All of them. Think about them carefully tonight. I want you to be firm in your answer. Then there is the matter of help. You should know that I am totally unaccustomed to physical labor. And, of course, we must talk of family."

Giuseppe Rocco returned the following evening. Yes. Yes to everything. And when Rita Verducci had Giuseppe Rocco sign a document written in her hand, she learned that he was illiterate.

Then all of east San Jose was abuzz. The man had to belong to the Mafia, or at least have some connection with one of the Chinese tongs. Didn't he see the Chinese in San Francisco every Sunday? Not only was he buying the Blackwell house, but he was also buying furniture and furnishings, clothes for Rita Verducci and himself, and another car. Never had east San Jose seen such an outpouring of money. And though neither he nor Rita Verducci had a single friend in the entire town except for Maria Luca, theirs was to be the biggest wedding ever in east San Jose.

A week before the wedding, Rita Verducci and Maria Luca moved into the Blackwell house. Had they not, thought Maria Luca, there

might never be a wedding. For now, Maria Luca had a stake in the wedding: it had been agreed that she would serve as Rita Verducci's maid, drawing a monthly salary as well as her room and board. All week long Maria Luca encouraged Rita Verducci's joy. "Isn't this a wonderful house, my dear!" she said as Rita Verducci walked about basking in the airy light of the high-ceilinged rooms. "You'll be so happy here!" she added, playing to the gleam in her face. "Finally you'll have a home that suits you!" She was ever fearful that Rita Verducci might still waver before Sunday. And then what would either of them do?

By Sunday, Rita Verducci had reconciled herself to the fact that what would take place in the church later that morning was nothing more than a fair and simple exchange. So she calmly prepared on Sunday morning, far more calmly than Maria Luca, who was helping her dress and who was babbling the whole time about how happy she would be and how, in time, she might even grow to like Giuseppe Rocco because, when all was said and done, he wasn't a bad man, and he loved her so much that he would never abuse her, and . . . It was an exchange, as simple as that, nothing more, nothing less. In exchange for that lovely house and all the fine things that went with it, in exchange for the security he would give her, she was prepared to be his wife. But in name only.

Once the vows had been exchanged and the first dance had been danced and the cake had been cut, Rita Verducci immediately retired to her room to pack for their honeymoon, she said, but really to weep.

"I can't, Maria. I can't."

"But he's your husband now, my dear. He has every right to it."

"I can't let him touch me."

"It is his . . . it is his right."

"I think I would rather die than have his thick hairy body on top of me."

"Look at it this way, my dear. For those few nights, and they are few when you compare them to the rest of your lifetime . . . for those few nights until the children come, you are guaranteeing yourself a very fine, comfortable life, one that any woman would want. Think of all the scullery maids who slave day in and day out and still must go home to those beasts they have for husbands and let them do it. If I could only tell you of all the loathing I have heard, of all the nights of misery that I have heard about in my lifetime, and all of that from women who had so much less to gain than you. It is endured countless times every night in every little town and in every big city across the face of the earth."

And she too could endure it, thought Rita Verducci.

"Look at it this way, my dear. It is something they want and need desperately. They will do anything for it when they are needy, and they seem to be needy all of the time. It is for us women to make the most of it. Thank God that we are by nature more interested in love than in base pleasure. Where would this world be if we had the same wild, uncontrollable lust that they have? Can you imagine everyone walking around at all hours of the day and night mounting each other any time and any place the urge arises, as it does with them? It is us women who keep some semblance of order in this world. No, you must use his awful hunger to build what you want, to have and raise your blessed family in the manner God chose."

If there was some comfort for Rita Verducci in being reassured that she did not suffer alone, that hers was a common suffering, it lasted only until they had left the house, because she cried all the way to San Francisco, the first stop on what was to be a two-week honeymoon.

"Why are you crying, my countess?"

"Because I don't feel well."

"What's the matter, my countess?"

"I must have drunk too much champagne."

"But I didn't see you drink any champagne."

"Are you trying to tell me what I drank?"

"No, my countess."

"I'm not your countess."

She continued weeping as they drove into the city, so much so that Giuseppe Rocco was afraid that the hotel people would think that he had kidnapped her or beaten her. When they reached the hotel, he said, "Countess, we're here. Do you feel well enough to go in?"

She nodded.

"Or maybe we should go back home. Would you rather go back home?"

She shook her head. There everybody would know. Here only she would know.

A bellhop took them and their luggage to their room and then stood at the door.

"Tip the man! Tip the man! Can't you see he's waiting!"

Giuseppe Rocco rummaged through his pockets, retrieving a few coins.

"Why must you be so cheap! Don't embarrass both of us, give him more!"

Then, as Giuseppe Rocco fumbled through his pockets again, she went into the bathroom, locked the door and began crying again. She had all night to cry.

Giuseppe Rocco stood bewildered. Never had he been in such an opulent room. Everywhere was the excitement of what was to come. They were alone in this magnificent room with but one bed in which they would both sleep before the night was over. Carefully he touched the bed, the dresser, the chair, the curtains, his fingers rasping on each. His bride had cried all the way to the city. But that didn't matter—women cried for anything—and before the night was over, she would be his. That was all that mattered; that reverberated everywhere. Then he was aware that she was in the bathroom. Somehow he had never thought of countesses going to the bathroom. At one and the same time he strained to hear and not to hear, not wanting to embarrass her, or was it him. What to do . . . what to do? He was unable to decide or even think because of his anticipation.

Then he heard her move and his confusion and excitement grew, not knowing where he should be or what he should be doing when she came out. What would cause her the least embarrassment, make it easiest for her? She had to be a virgin. She *would* be embarrassed. He turned off the lights and got into bed before he realized that he was still dressed. He jumped out of bed and quickly undressed, except for his shorts, because he was swollen now, and if she saw his size, it would probably frighten her. He got into bed shivering. Light shone from under the bathroom door. He turned himself on his side to face the door. The instant the light went out, he would be ready. He was ready now, as ready as he would ever be, as ready as he had ever been. Still he fought off vulgar thoughts about the countess. She was not one of his whores. She had to be a virgin. He would be gentle with her, go easy with her, be careful with her—after all, the whores did say that his was one of the biggest. He would proceed slowly. But once she got a taste of him, she would never want another. He could guarantee that: they all liked big ones and his was one of the biggest. Once he showed her what

a real man was like, then things would be more like they should have
been, then she would forever want to be pleasing him. The light in the
bathroom continued to burn. There was no movement, no sound. What
could she be doing?

She was crying. And recalling her happy life as a child, recalling
her family and friends. How could she have come to this? Her friends
had married well. Every one of them. Few, if any, had the intelligence
or poise or character that she had. But for a quirk in her father's business, she would have married as well as any of them. Now she sat in
the bathroom of her wedding night suite, locked in that bathroom
because she was terrified of the ape who waited for her on the other
side of that locked door: the ape, her husband, one and the same. Why?
What had she done to deserve this? All she had ever wanted, dreamed
of, was a husband that she truly loved. She wept all the more. But
silently, for fear that he might hear and begin making inquiries, for fear
that he would never fall asleep.

For his part, the longer she took, the more determined he became.
If it took all night for her to come out of that bathroom, he would be
ready. Before the night was over, he would have his countess; there was
no mistaking that. But he was beginning to hurt. He took off his shorts
to give himself room. His skin was so stretched, he was afraid it would
tear. Still she didn't come out. What was she doing in there? He got out
of bed to walk, to calm himself. But when he saw his size, he got back
into bed. If she saw that, it would be too much for her. He stared at the
light for what seemed like an hour. Not once was it broken by movement, by anything. There was no sound. Had she fallen asleep? He
listened. Maybe she had fallen asleep. He strained to listen. Nothing.
He got out of bed, covering himself with his hand, tiptoeing to the door.
He knocked lightly. Nothing. Again. Harder.

"Are you all right, countess?"

She stiffened with both fear and rage. Oh my God, she thought, and
yet how dare he, too. But it was best to be still, to be silent. Each time
he knocked, she stiffened all the more. When he spoke, she shook her
head. And then he tried the door, softly, stealthily at first, then a bit
harder, then more openly, harder still. And then the door burst open,
and she saw him, hairy and big, and she screamed, screamed as loud
and as hard as she could, until people began pounding on the walls and
the door, until four men had wrestled the naked Giuseppe Rocco into

submission, while two others led her to the manager's office, where she spent the rest of the night.

They returned to San Jose the next day. She cried all the way home, just as she had cried all the way to the city. She was weeping still when Maria Luca talked to her later that night.

"You know, my dear, without it, no matter how disgusting it might seem, the marriage is not consummated. He can walk away tonight or tomorrow, and you will be no better off than you were two weeks ago. All of this will have been for nothing. In fact, we would be worse off, much worse off. We couldn't show our faces in this town. Can you imagine the laughingstocks we would be? This big house, the big wedding, two cars, I gave up my home. All of that gone because you couldn't let him. Oh, they will laugh. We will seem like schemers, connivers, old maids. And once this is known, who would ever seriously consider you for a wife again? Not here. Perhaps in Italy. Perhaps some penniless peasant in Italy, because your father has closed all the doors. And you're not getting any younger. In a few months you'll be twenty-eight. I've seen the wrinkles just as you have. You'll be giving all of this up. Just look at this room, at this house, at the grounds. All of it gone because you can't let him.

"Now, now, my dear, we're reaching the point where I don't think tears are going to be enough. Excuse me, but I do think you're being a bit too refined . . . You say it will hurt. Use oils, salves. The pain can't be unbearable. Most women have endured it since the beginning of time. And it lasts but a few seconds. They're usually so anxious, so hungry, that they pop in seconds. You say he stinks and you can't stand the smell of him. Tell him he has to bathe beforehand. You'll see how quickly he bathes. You say you won't be able to bear his hairy body on top of you. Drink a little wine. Start sipping it early. You'll hardly feel him. No, no, my dear, it's entirely up to you. Continue to deny him and we'll be out of here in a week. And where will we go? My house is gone.

"But I don't know why I'm wasting my time. It's not going to be enough to let him once. You're going to have to make up your mind that you're going to let him as much as he wants. Until you conceive. Not just once, or even twice, but three times at least. Because each child secures your hold that much more. And then his fortune will become the family fortune, your fortune."

❧ Giuseppe Rocco ❧

And so Joey and Johnny and Matthew were born, each no more than fifteen months apart. Joey was named for his father. Johnny was named for Giuseppe Rocco's father. Finally, Matthew Rocco was named for Rita Rocco's father.

Chapter II

Each time she made him wait just a little longer. First it had been thirty-five days, then forty-five days and now fifty. And he was beside himself. It was not that he had been without sex during her pregnancy, because there had been the Mexican whores. Nor was it that sex with her had been particularly good, because it wasn't. In fact, it was among the worst. She would lie motionless and speechless, under covers and in a long thick nightgown, no matter how warm the evening. He would feel his way in the darkness of her room, to the far side of her bed and raise her nightgown under the covers, never past her navel and never near her brassiered breasts. He smelled the salves and the lubricants as his body raised the dormant blankets and he took his pleasure, knowing but not caring that she was watching silently and motionless until he finished. Then he would leave her room as carefully, quietly, and silently as he had come. But she was his countess, a countess, something he was never meant to have.

Still, it was the fiftieth day and there had been no sign, no hint from her at any time, as if they had never known sex, as if the boys had been immaculately conceived. And he had kept himself clean, away from the whores since Mateo's birth, hoping perhaps that somehow his cleanliness, his abstinence would change their wooden ritual. He waited all day, that fiftieth day, for some sign, but in vain. On the fiftieth night he could wait no longer. So silently and carefully he opened her bedroom door and just as silently crept into that dark room, naked and extended. But even before he could close the door behind him, she said, "No, Giuseppe, do what you want, but you will never touch me again." The words were firm and final, so much so that he turned, like the intruder that he was, and left without a word, as if he had never entered.

He left that night, within minutes of those words, just as long as it took him to dress and slip down the back stairs to his pick-up truck. He went to his second house, as he often thought of it, to the small, worn, faded, wood-framed house east of Gilroy. And he wept. And later, much later, he slept in that small metal bed that had been theirs so long ago. "*¿Quién eres tú?*"

❧ Giuseppe Rocco ❧

The first October sun of 1955, hot on his face, woke him. He shifted in the bed, shading his eyes to look up at the parched golden hills behind the house that were now his too. He had come to the tiny house at least twice a week since Angelina's death. To feed the dogs, he had told himself in the beginning. But the practice had continued for years, and he would stay long after he had fed and watered the dogs, often hiking along those golden hills, occasionally spending the night there when others said that he was with his Mexican whores. He often sat, sometimes for hours, in her old wooden rocker on the porch, looking acoss the valley to the green of the coastal range to the west.

He had not only fed the dogs, but he had bred them as well, to perpetuate and increase their numbers, so that they could better guard the vacant house. That was the only change he had made. He had bought all the surrounding parcels to insure that the house and the hills and the road and the views would remain as they were when he had known Angelina.

He stayed for four days, beginning each of those October mornings behind the small house, sitting on a bench that her husband had made long ago from the branches of an unknown tree. He munched on tacos of beans and tortillas as he had when she was there, looking up at the bare golden hills and the pristine blue sky above them until the sun drove him to the shade of the porch before noon. There he spent those four afternoons, looking across the valley to the west as the sun continued its never ending journey. He sipped dago red wine from a flowered kitchen glass that was once hers. And for those four days he thought and remembered and imagined. By the fourth day some of those thoughts, some of those images were constant.

The strongest was his earliest and most vivid memory. His father was on his death bed, smiling, his face drawn and tired, holding his hand in that huge rough paw and repeating, "You be a good boy, Giuseppe, you be a good boy." And then there was a series of neighbors and uncles and aunts and strangers for whom he became an inconvenience. So, by the age of twelve he was living alone in the shed of a man who worked him as he would have a man while giving him only his room and board. And there were the images of his sons, of Giuseppe and Giovanni, the light of his life, and now Mateo, of their delicate limbs and their wide and trusting eyes. They were his family, his bloodline, the only family he would ever have. They would never experience the harshness and loneliness of his childhood. He was a wealthy man now.

On the morning of the fifth day, he returned to San Jose, stopping first to see his lawyer, Carlo Rossi, a man also of humble origins.

"I come today to speak to you, Don Carlo, about more than money. I come to speak to you about matters of the heart."

It was the first time that the forty-seven-year-old Giuseppe Rocco had spoken of such things to another man, and he was both embarrassed and at a loss for words. There was some shame too, shame that Don Carlo would surely know that it was the countess who had rejected him and not he the countess. He had always expressed himself directly and forcefully, if simply. But now as he sat across the polished desk from one of the few men that he respected, fingering his grey khaki J.C. Penney hat, nothing came from him except stammering starts.

Finally he said, "Don Carlo, I want to know if it is better or worse if I stay with or leave my family. And if I stay, which is the best way to do it?" He had already decided the first question; it was only the second that troubled him.

That evening he returned to the house at precisely six o'clock, startling the countess and Maria Luca as they were beginning dinner and surprising little Giuseppe and Giovanni, who cried happily, "Papa! Papa!"

"Maria, will you excuse us please," he said without looking at her, but in a tone of voice that made it clear that she was to be excused. "And take the boys." Then he sat next to the countess, removing his hat, but not touching the napkin or the utensils.

"Rita, I will never touch you again. That I promise you. But as long as my sons remain in this house, I will remain in this house. If you cannot live with me in this house, then you are free to leave. It is my house. The lawyer tells me you have no claim to it. You can go wherever you like, but my sons stay. You can return to the old country if you like. I will support you. You will never want for money or the things that are important to you. But my sons stay. If you decide to fight me for my sons, then you will have to leave. And a fight it will be."

It was not a threat. He did not need a threat. Rita Rocco was in shock. His voice was scarcely more than a whisper. His grey eyes were fastened on her as they had never been fastened before. She had reacted to his first words by sitting back in her chair. Now the palms of her hands were taut against the edge of the table, tilting her back. He, in turn, was almost crouched at the table, and the more she tilted backward, the further he bent forward.

"And if the courts give you my sons, believe me, it will not end there. You will regret the day that you laid eyes on this peasant. But I have touched you for the last time. Of that you can be sure, Rita Verducci."

That night Giuseppe Rocco slept as well as he had ever slept in that house. The next morning he was back to his daily routine. Up at 5:30, in his pick-up truck by 6:00 to begin a day that would eventually return him home for dinner at 6:00 that evening, except that today, even before he left the house, he had decided that he would return at 4:00.

He drove to Nick's Cafe, which was four blocks from his home at the edge of downtown San Jose. He drove there for breakfast as he had almost every morning at six o'clock for the past four years, Monday through Saturday. It was still dark and he zipped up his leather jacket as he got out of his pick-up. The nights were getting longer and the mornings cooler: winter was on its way. As he stepped up onto the sidewalk, he could see Nick Petrakis, the old Greek, twisting from his work space to the stove with a pan in hand. The old son of a bitch is probably dying to know where I've been, but he won't ask, he thought. He pushed on the door as he always did, and the old Greek turned as he always did, and their eyes met as they always did, his from under the brim of his grey khaki hat and the other's from under thick, bushy tufts of eyebrows. They nodded almost imperceptibly. That was all, that was all that was ever said. Then the old Greek picked up a bright red slab of meat as he always did when Giuseppe Rocco entered and placed it on the grill as Giuseppe Rocco walked by.

He walked along the forty foot counter, shunning the booths and tables on his left, as he had done from the beginning, to the last two chairs, which were separated from the rest of the counter chairs by an entryway. He took off his jacket and laid it across the swivel chair nearest the entryway and then sat, as he always did, on the chair next to the wall.

"We missed you, Giuseppe," Annie said quietly as she gently, caringly slid his coffee cup near his right hand. Giuseppe nodded and examined her widening hips as she turned for his sweet roll, examined them as he hadn't in some time. She was still very much the female.

"Is everything all right, Giuseppe?" she said softly as she gently slid the plate with the sweet roll across the counter top toward his left hand. He looked at her as he stirred his coffee and saw the tired but caring blue eyes of a fifty-year-old Norwegian waitress. She did care for him, and he for her, but never as she would have wanted. Giuseppe stirred his creamless, sugarless cup and nodded yes, yes, yes.

"You know I put aprons on these two chairs every one of those mornings from six to nine, until I was sure you weren't coming. I told everyone that those two seats were reserved, even when it got busy. Nick didn't care; he was wondering where you were too. Even Debra, you know, the new girl who comes in at seven, asked where you were. We missed you, Giuseppe."

She wouldn't go much further. "I had to take care of some personal business, Annie." He owed her that much.

"But everything's okay now, Giuseppe?" Her thin pursed mouth authenticated her concern.

Yes, he nodded.

"That's good," she said with a trace of a smile and turned and started for a booth where two men had just seated themselves. If only he could care for her as she cared for him. Would it be enough if he could want her?

Another man, thin and bony with age, entered the restaurant. He too wore a khaki hat. He too moved along the counter without hesitation, greeting no one until he reached Giuseppe Rocco. Annie watched from the cash register. If Giuseppe removed his leather jacket from the vacant seat, she would take the man a menu; if he didn't, the man would just as likely leave the restaurant without ordering anything. Everyone that wanted, or needed, to know, knew that Giuseppe Rocco ate breakfast at Nick's Cafe every morning at six and that he conducted business there at the counter in those two red Naugahyde swivel chairs, sometimes until nine. Annie waited.

"Good morning, Giuseppe."

"Good morning, Dino."

"I came three mornings and you weren't here. I kept coming back and looked through the window, but you never came. Nobody knew where you were."

"What's the matter, Dino?"

"My wife's mother's worse. They only give her six months to live. My wife wants to go right away and I don't want to stay. So we need to know real soon from you, Giuseppe, are you going to buy the ranch?"

Giuseppe Rocco removed his leather jacket from the vacant seat and said, "Sit down, Dino."

Annie removed a menu from the metal menu holder.

"There's no telling about these things, Giuseppe. Sometimes they say six months and it's six years or six weeks. But I'm ready to go back to the old country. I always said I wanted to die there. Now with my sons dead and the trees bearing less and less fruit—they're getting old too, Giuseppe—there's no reason to stay."

Annie placed a menu before Dino Restelli along with a glass of water.

———

Giuseppe Rocco left Nick's Cafe and drove south and east into the foothills to the Haney Ranch, which like many of his ranches, still bore the name of his predecessor. Once there, he left the paved road and drove on a dirt road alongside an irrigation ditch for almost a mile. Then he turned onto another dirt road toward the heart of the orchard, drove for a few hundred yards, and stopped. He stood outside his truck for several moments, enjoying the stillness. Except for the occasional chirping of a bird, the orchard was silent and the air was fresh and clean. He walked down a long row of apricot trees, examining the newly exposed branches for the December pruning. Under his boots he could feel and hear the crackling of the fallen leaves. Then he passed on to the plum trees. At the end of those rows he could see San Jose below. As he reached the clearing, he stopped and knelt down over the mound of a fresh gopher hole. There had been little rain the past two years and some of the growers were thinking of irrigating their trees before the pruning. Giuseppe Rocco thought this ridiculous. Now he sifted the freshly excavated earth in his fingers, hoping to get some sense of its dryness. It was dry, how dry he could not tell. But after all those years, he was still impressed by the richness of the dark soil: soil like this was rare indeed. As he knelt with the earth in his hands, he looked down at the bulging, encroaching city. The day would come when those trees would be uprooted for the city's asphalt and cement. But they would pay dearly for it.

Next he drove south and west to the vineyards in the small fertile valleys behind Morgan Hill. This was the last cutting. There were about twenty Mexicans, mostly men, picking wine grapes and dumping them into gondolas. He knew none of these people, and Miguel, the labor contractor, was nowhere to be found. Yet they were deferential as he walked among them, examining their work. He was white and had parked his pick-up as if he owned the land and walked among them with authority.

Once he had walked several rows, he went to the gondolas to examine the fruit's color and taste its sweetness. While he was there, he asked one of the men, *"¿Y Miguel?"*

"No tarda, señor."

He smiled to himself. *No tarda.* With Mexicans, that could mean tomorrow or next week. Crazy Mexicans. But he loved them, loved those little brown people from villages far away. *Indios*, Ramiro called them. And Indians they were, with that dark chocolate skin and their thick coarse black hair. He drank with them, got drunk with them, ate with them, slept with them, slept with their women. As a group, he was more comfortable with them than with any other. Now he watched them hurry lopsided down the rows with their buckets full and in one motion dump their loads into the gondolas and hurry back to the vines. It was piece work and they pushed themselves. One concern was that they pick the vines clean. Today, from what he had seen, that was not a concern.

Two women approached, walking side by side, talking, their upper bodies tilted towards each other with the weight of the buckets. They were dressed in men's clothes, layers of over-sized men's clothes. Their hair had been braided and wrapped in kerchiefs that were only partially visible under baseball caps. Except for their eyes, their faces were covered with kerchiefs too. The kerchiefs said they were women. They were speaking Spanish, quick, rapid exchanges, until they came within earshot of Giuseppe Rocco, the white man, a *patrón* of some sort. Then they became silent: short round figures bearing their loads. The first woman grunted a bit as she hoisted her bucket up over her shoulder onto the lip of the gondola, not once looking at Giuseppe or even in his direction. The second woman waited, and, just as the first woman started to move from the gondola, she looked at Giuseppe and their eyes met. They were clear, young, beautiful, dark eyes that for a moment taunted him, teased him, sought to bring him down from the *patrón* that he was. And his eyes rose to the challenge, and he raised his head to show his interest. She turned from him and lifted and emptied her bucket and turned again to the waiting first woman. He watched her as she walked back down the dirt road to the vines, imagining what had to be under those layers of loose fitting clothes. Tonight he would go to Watsonville.

He drove back to San Jose, back to Garofoli Scavenger Company, the business he had bought out of receivership some two years earlier. On the way there, he stopped to call Ramiro. *"Esta noche llego,"* he said in his halting Spanish. *"Sí, como a las ocho. Quiero música, comida, y viejas."*

Sal and Tony Garofoli were only shadows of their father, timid souls who had lost the company until Giuseppe Rocco had purchased the company and left them in charge. But he didn't trust them. It was just that no one else in San Jose knew the scavenging business, except himself, and he was too busy to return to it. So he made a practice of stopping in every day to question, listen, watch, and decide. Business had never been better.

As he started up the office steps, Sal leaned out of the doorway and said, "Giuseppe, Mr. Rossi's been trying to get hold of you all morning. He says it's important."

He called Carlo Rossi.

"Giuseppe, where you been? I've been calling everywhere. Federated has accepted our counteroffer."

"Federated?"

"The sixty-four acres, Giuseppe. They've accepted. They'll pay thirty-two million."

"Oh."

"You don't sound very excited, Giuseppe."

"I should have asked for more."

"More! There's a limit, Giuseppe. Thirty-two million dollars is a lot of money, Giuseppe, especially when you consider that you paid nothing for most of the land."

"Yes, but they want what *I* have more than I want what *they* have."

"They've sent someone out with the papers. They want to sign them today. John Lucas from the planning department wants to be there. I was hoping you could meet us for lunch at Alfredo's."

As he drove to Alfredo's, he thought of the land. Most of it was the ranch that the old Italian had left him years ago when he was still a boy. The city had all but encircled the ranch. Federated had plans for a huge shopping mall there. He had been careful to exclude his original two acres. He would never sell those. He wondered what the old Italian was thinking wherever he was. They had originally offered twenty-two million and he had countered with thirty-two million, never dreaming that they would accept. Sooner or later, he told himself, they could probably force a sale, have the city condemn the land. The impending sale did little to raise his spirits. He was a multi-millionaire already. He didn't need this money. He couldn't spend it in his lifetime. It would have to be reinvested to avoid taxes.

He drove on. At this point, money was power, but little else: there was little else it could buy him. He probably spent more waking hours in his pick-up than in any other confine. It had been with him six years now and was a companion; at times he spoke to it. He didn't want or need another vehicle. He wore his grey khaki hat and grey khaki shirts and pants and work boots and worn leather jacket everywhere he went. And everywhere, people still made fools of themselves trying to win his favor. He had twenty-one ranches, twenty-three houses, and fourteen apartment complexes by his last count. If his sons could not make their way in the world with what he now had, they would be a sorry lot indeed.

"This sale will make you one of the richest men in the county, Giuseppe," Carlo Rossi had said. And Giuseppe Rocco was revisiting those words when he reached Alfredo's. Power. Nothing more, nothing less.

The parking attendant simply nodded to Giuseppe Rocco as he drove past him. He had made it clear long ago that he would park his own truck. Men in business suits converged at the entrance. Most greeted the squat, thick man who to a stranger might have been a custodian or a repairman. "Hello, Mr. Rocco." Today Giuseppe Rocco looked and nodded. More often than not he would have simply looked, a blank hostile look, that more often than not would have made the greeter uncomfortable. No one wore a hat except Giuseppe, and inside no one asked if they could take his hat, not anymore. He walked past the hostess with her cradled menus towards the table where he saw Carlo Rossi and two other men. "Hello, Mr. Rocco," she said after he had passed her.

Carlo Rossi stood when he saw Giuseppe Rocco, and the two other men followed suit, stiff grey men in starched white shirts. Giuseppe Rocco knew one of the two men: he was a big shot in the planning department. It was the stranger, the man from Federated, who was uncomfortable, uncomfortable with his work boots and worn leather jacket and shapeless khaki hat in that carpeted room of white tablecloths and fine dinnerware. So Giuseppe Rocco cocked his head to one side and looked at him before Carlo Rossi could introduce them. It was a look that became a stare, making the man nervous. Carlo Rossi introduced the man, but Giuseppe Rocco didn't listen for the man's name because the man was of no interest to him. He met the nervous man's extended hand with his own belated, firm hand. Then he sat down, before the others, and tipped his hat back, exposing the sun's brown red line across the top of his forehead and a strip of white flesh as well as his greying, sweat-matted hairline. Once again he looked at the man from Federated until the man from Federated looked away. Then Giuseppe Rocco reached for a piece of bread and slowly, calmly, evenly buttered it.

A waiter came. "Are you gentlemen ready to order?"

Giuseppe Rocco said, "I'll take my usual."

"Your usual?" the young waiter answered.

And Carlo Rossi said, "He'll have spaghetti with meat sauce and a garden salad with three diced filets of anchovy added. He'll add his own oil and vinegar. And bring him a glass of house Chianti."

As Carlo Rossi spoke, Giuseppe Rocco felt the Federated man's displeasure, and so he looked directly at him again and scared away that displeasure.

Then he listened as Carlo Rossi outlined the terms of the sale, and then as the man from Federated said that they drove a hard bargain, that Federated had never paid that kind of money for unimproved land, which made him look at the man again, to stop him in mid-sentence with that look. Bullshit! They wouldn't spend a dime if it wasn't worth their while. But he had seen the huge losses that the Caparellis and the Piazzas had suffered, families that had refused to sell, only to have the city take their land for pennies. So he lowered his eyes and listened again, saying nothing, having nothing to say, occasionally thinking back to those first days when he walked over that land through those orchards to get to his tiny parcel.

They signed the papers over coffee and dessert, a stack of papers with hundreds of words on each page, words that he could see but not read. Slowly, laboriously, he scrawled his name next to the X's Carlo Rossi had placed before blank lines, scrawled it with big uncertain letters that he had slowly and laboriously taught himself to make long ago. Before each signing, Carlo Rossi gave him an explanation, sometimes long, sometimes short. But he wasn't listening. It was a loss. They wanted what he had more than he wanted what they had.

After the signing, the man from the planning department spoke excitedly about the mall and San Jose's growth. Outside of Los Angeles, it was the fastest growing city in California. They expected the city's population to top a million, and the county's, three million. When prodded by the man from Federated, the man from the planning department said that the city was anticipating huge developments in South San Jose around Greenlee Road. Then Giuseppe said, "Greenlee? Greenlee and what?"

"Greenlee, from Wilson Avenue to Lowell."

Those were the only words Giuseppe Rocco said to the man from the planning department. They were the only words he wanted to say.

He drove to the land that he had just sold, to walk through it unimpeded one last time, to remember and appreciate what it was and still was. He touched the bark of several trees, strong, healthy trees, some that had preceded him and some that he had planted himself. He looked up at the yellowed, rapidly vanishing leaves, a never-ending cycle, death and resurrection, unlike man's, but soon to be ended by man's machines. They called San Jose "The Garden City." It was the land, the soil, as rich and wonderful as any he had ever seen. And this parcel was particularly blessed. He knelt down near the center of what had been the old man's orchard and brushed back the fallen leaves with his hand. Then he took out his pocket knife and a small jar that he had brought from the truck and he broke the soil, crushing the resulting small clods with his fingers until their powder filled the jar. Then he left.

He drove to South San Jose, to Dino Restelli's ranch, whose northern boundaries bordered on Greenlee Road for at least half a mile. It was just past two and he wanted to be home by four. There wasn't much time.

A short, round, grey woman answered the door, wiping her hands on a stained apron, which was as much a part of the dress as the dress itself.

"Mrs. Restelli, my name is . . ."

"No, no. I know you, Mr. Rocco. Everybody knows Giuseppe Rocco. Come in. Come in, please, my husband has been expecting you."

She showed him into a room just off the entry way. It was a room for special occasions. The clear plastic on the sofa and chairs said so, as did the cellophane paper on all the lamp shades and the carpet remnants that covered the carpet, covered every conceivable area of the room's carpet that could be walked on.

It wasn't my idea, he thought, as he waited for the old man. He came to me. I didn't go to him. Who knows how long it would take him to sell, and he needs to sell now, he needs to take the cash money with him, now.

He went to the window and looked out at the orchard. They were old trees, and he doubted if Dino Restelli was making much more than a living, if that. His machinery was worn and some of it was in disrepair. It wasn't a big ranch, fifty-three acres all told, but it was too much for a man Dino's age, even now in the fall, and Dino hadn't mentioned, nor was there any hint of, hired help. He moved closer to the window and from there could see a patch of Greenlee Road.

When Dino Restelli entered the room, he was followed by his wife, who was still wiping her hands on her apron.

"Sit down, Giuseppe, sit down. Make yourself comfortable. Make yourself at home," Dino said.

And Giuseppe sat down on the thick, clear plastic, making it crinkle as he did.

"You've come to see the ranch?"

Before Giuseppe could answer, the small, round woman came and knelt before him with her hands clasped as if in prayer and said, "Please, Giuseppe, help us. You are the only one that can help us." There were tears in her eyes. "My mother is dying. I have to go back to the old country. I can't leave Dino alone here. He'll die here and she'll die there. The real estate men are thieves. They want twelve percent of our land. Why should we give them twelve percent of our money? And they won't guarantee that they'll sell or how we'll get our money. Maybe they'll never send our money. And then, what will we do from Italy? By then we might be too poor to come back for our money. You're the only one that can help us. Dino says you can give us our money tomorrow and we can be gone tomorrow." She squeezed her eyes shut, releasing tears. "Please, Giuseppe, please help us!"

"Lucretia. Lucretia," Dino Restelli said, getting her to her feet. "Come, come."

"Maybe we should look at the land, Dino," Giuseppe Rocco said.

They left the small, round woman crying in her special room and went outside.

"The trees are old."

"I know."

"What kind of a yield did you have this year?"

"Not very good, Giuseppe."

"They don't have too many more years left."

"I know."

"Did you plant them?"

"Only some."

"So some were here when you came?"

"Yes."

"If I buy your ranch, I will probably have to pull them out right away."

"But you can do it, Giuseppe, you have the money."

"If I plant trees again, it will be years before I see a penny. And who knows, the ground may need a change. I might have to go to row crops, and that will mean a lot more costs in the beginning."

He could feel Dino Restelli's doubt, his confusion, his desperation. He had bought many parcels of land in that valley, some from people in need. He could feel Dino Restelli's need.

"I saw your tractor as I came in. How long has it not been working?"

"Just a few weeks."

"What's wrong with it? You know what a new tractor costs these days."

"Giuseppe, I'm not trying to steal from you. All I'm asking is a fair and honest price."

On Greenlee Road, Giuseppe Rocco heard the sounds of passing cars, and he stopped himself. "How much is it you're asking for, Dino?" And when Dino Restelli told him, he said only, "Go to Carlo Rossi's office tomorrow afternoon. He'll have the papers and the money ready."

———————

Giuseppe Rocco arrived home at 3:55. He surprised Maria. "What are you doing home at this hour, Giuseppe? You're never home before six."

"Get the boys ready."

"What boys?"

"Giuseppe and Giovanni."

"Ready for what?"

"Ready to go with me."

"Go with you? Where? You never take them any place."

"I said get them ready to go with me."

"Does the countess know about this?"

"I don't give a damn what Rita Verducci knows or doesn't know. Get the boys ready."

"Rita Verducci!"

"Did you hear me?!"

"Yes, I heard you," Maria said shaking her head as she took off her apron before leaving the kitchen.

It was Rita Verducci who returned. "What is this about getting the boys ready to go with you?"

"And what is wrong with taking my sons out with me?"

"Where are you taking them?"

"Downtown."

"Downtown?"

"Yes, downtown. And we will be back for dinner by six."

"What are Giuseppe and Giovanni going to do downtown?"

"I want my sons to know my friends and for my friends to know my sons."

"Your friends?"

"I'm not going to argue with you, Rita. I want my sons dressed and ready so that I can take them downtown to meet my friends."

At that moment little Giuseppe burst in, "Papa! Papa!" The three-year-old ran to his father and wrapped his arms around his leg. "Papa! Papa!" Jumping up and down.

But Giuseppe Rocco was locked in a battle of stares with Rita Verducci, and he paid no attention to the boy other than to try to hold him still with one hand. They stared at each other, the peasant and the noblewoman, hating each other, each determined to outstare the other as the little boy jumped up and down and tugged and shouted, "Papa! Papa!" Finally, Giuseppe Rocco bent down and hissed, "Silence!" and with one motion yanked the boy away from him without breaking his stare. Rita Verducci had stared him down for the last time.

So they stared and stared some more. And then Giuseppe Rocco was aware of a clump at the kitchen door and then the toddling footsteps of his two-year-old son, Giovanni. "Papa," he slurred. "Papa." Approaching. "Papa." Clutching. This time Giuseppe Rocco bent and picked up his son, staring, and brought him up to him, staring, even though the child picked and poked at his face.

"This is ridiculous," Rita Verducci said, turning, giving up the stare. "If my sons are not home, seated at their places at the table by six o'clock, I will call the police." Then she left, left him staring, and he smiled and kissed his smiling son.

As they started out the back door, Giovanni in his arm and Giuseppe at his hand, Maria Luca appeared with a stroller. "Wait, Giuseppe, you'll need this."

"Ah!" he grunted. "We don't need your stinking strollers. We are not women."

Slowly, carefully, he took his sons down the back stairs. Just as carefully, he seated them in the pick-up, sliding Giuseppe in first, two-thirds of the way across the seat and then placing Giovanni next to him. "Hold on to your brother," he said as he climbed in and saw the awe and excitement on their tiny faces. They watched and grinned as the ignition sounded and the motor turned, and their eyes widened even more.

"Who in the hell said me and my sons can't go anywhere we want to," he said to them and himself as he drove slowly out of the yard with his thick right arm clasped around their little bodies.

He started at State Street and walked down Montgomery with Giuseppe on his left and Giovanni on his right. Slowly they made their way past the Italian stores and shops, each boy anchored by the stump of a man in the middle whose arms reached down to his knees. The thin, slight boy on the left was light on his feet, almost skipping as he walked, chattering constantly; the other boy, the toddler, was thick like his father and plodded heavily, silently along. They left a trail of people as they passed. Shoppers and shopkeepers came to the windows and doors and some even onto the sidewalk to watch the spectacle. The man they all knew, or at least knew of, but who seldom mingled, the man who was always the subject of their gossip and speculation, but to whom they seldom spoke, the wealthiest Italian, and some now said man, in the county was now walking down the street, alone and unattended, with his two infant sons. Women began coming up to the little boys, especially to the wide-eyed toddler: *"Que bello. Que bello."*

Some of the men shook their heads, others shrugged, others looked at each other and smirked: men didn't do this, at least not at mid-week, and not without their wives.

Slowly the trio made its way onto the second block. A few women followed, curious but at a distance. At almost every store Giuseppe and his sons drew more attention. Twice on the second block the older of the two boys left his father's side, bolted in front of him, turned and then on tiptoe, with his arms raised, asked to be picked up. Each time the stump of a man merely shook his head, and the boy retreated to his side again. That was the only breaking of the rank, because the younger boy was intent on looking at all that he had never seen before and Giuseppe was intent on feeling what he had not felt before. And if Giuseppe saw the gawking, as he surely must have, or the spectators behind him, he gave no indication, acknowledging no one, not even the people who passed them or the women who came up to say, *"Que bello."*

At the beginning of the third block, Giuseppe bent over and said something to the boys, which made the older one jump with joy and the younger one smile. Behind them the curious had grown. A few doors down, they turned into Giordano's Market, causing most everyone in the store to stop when they recognized Giuseppe Rocco, who never went into the store, let alone with his young sons.

The two checkers and some of the customers were still sneaking glances at the squat man and the two boys standing in the doorway when Ralph Giordano came out from one of the aisles. "Giuseppe

Rocco!" he said, approaching quickly and warmly. Giuseppe had purchased property from Ralph Giordano's father on two occasions, and each time Ralph Giordano had meddled in those purchases. Giuseppe knew him, knew him well.

"What's the matter, Giuseppe, is anything wrong? I know we sent a delivery up to your house this afternoon. Was something wrong with it, something missing or broken?"

Giuseppe shook his head and extended his hand to the outstretched hand before him. "No, my boys just want some ice cream."

"Ice cream! My God, you boys came to the right place. We got lots of ice cream. Come on, let me show you."

When the boys returned with their ice cream, they sat with their father on a large rice sack that was stacked with other rice and flour sacks along the store's front plate glass window. A few people still watched from outside the store as did a few women inside the store. Ralph Giordano tried to make small talk with Giuseppe Rocco, but Giuseppe Rocco was busy giving small dabs of ice cream and soft words to the younger of the two boys on his lap.

After a while, the older boy slid off the sack and stepped inside his father's open legs to his free leg and said, "Up, Papa," and when his father ignored him, he tried climbing up onto that leg, spilling ice cream on his father instead.

"Stop that, Giuseppe, you're too old to be on my lap."

Then as he cleaned himself and put the boy back on the sack, the younger boy crawled up onto the flour sacks, coating himself with white powder as he struggled upward. Women laughed, and Giuseppe turned and saw him and smiled and reached for him saying, "You little rascal, I can't turn my back on you for a minute, can I?" He scooped him up and kissed him and brought him back to the rice sack and his lap.

When the older boy saw this, he too started for the flour sacks, but Giuseppe stopped him. "No, Giuseppe, we don't need two messes."

Leaving Giordano's Market, he drove the boys to the land he had just sold. This time he carried them, one in each arm, through the orchard telling them time and again, "This is how I used to come when I first came here, when I was not much more than a boy too." And when he reached the first two acres, he carried them to the middle of those two acres, where the tent had been so long ago and upon which there had never since been anything planted or erected, and he said, "This is where your Papa first slept when he came here. It was just like this. There was no house, no tent, and I slept on the ground right here, and I looked up at the stars at night before I fell asleep, because they were my only friends then." Then he put them down to run and crawl and play among the leaves and the trees that he had first planted.

They were home at two minutes to six and were seated at the dinner table at two minutes past six. They ate in silence, she not asking, not wanting to give him the satisfaction of asking, even though she wanted to know where he had taken them; he, knowing that, and therefore determined not to speak, chewing his food deliberately, intensely, hating her as much as she hated him.

And then as they started on the pasta, little Giuseppe said, "Papa got us ice cream."

And the silence became more silent, and she put down her fork and turned to the boy and said, "What, what did you say, Joseph?" even though she had heard every one of the boy's words.

"Papa got us ice cream."

She absorbed it, thought about it for a few moments before she said, "Only peasants give their children ice cream before dinner."

He bolted from his chair, throwing the glass that he held as he did, and ran around the table to where she was seated and grabbed her by the top of her blouse and pulled her to him, to within inches of his face. Maria Luca was on her knees as close to them as she dared be, praying. Little Giuseppe was wailing.

"You sit here at this table because of this peasant! The clothes you wear, everything you own comes from this peasant! Were it not for this peasant, you would be in the street! And let me tell you something else, my fine, educated noblewoman. I have accomplished more in my life than all of your refined, educated friends put together. You and they can only talk. Talk is as close as all of you will get to what I have done! Don't you ever use that word in this house without my permission!"

And with that he threw her back into her chair and left.

He drove south, his body still twitching with anger, through Gilroy and then west, up into the coastal range toward Hecker Pass. For years he had visited the labor camps outside of Gilroy, but with the birth of Giuseppe, feeling he was too well known in Santa Clara County, he had moved his nocturnal visits to labor camps outside of Watsonville and

Salinas. Crossing the pass, he stopped after a few hundred yards along the roadside on the western slope of Mount Madonna. It was his favorite time of year. The summer fog was gone and for several weeks the coastal nights would be clear, mild, and windless. The moon was rising before him, defining the glistening bay and the agricultural parcels that would otherwise be just a black mass. Below him too were the lights of Watsonville, to his right the lights of Santa Cruz some twenty miles north. He leaned his head out the window and smelled the freshness of the ocean air and the redwood trees. His anger was gone. It was a wonderful night for a fiesta. Slowly he wound his way down the narrow serpentine road. About a mile from the bottom he could make out the lights of Ramiro's labor camp; a half mile farther and he could see the colored lights that Ramiro had strung out for him behind the ramshackle cabins that made up the camp. And then, at the end of the colored lights, he saw the orange flames of an open fire licking the night air. In a few minutes, two freshly slaughtered goats would be laid across the fire's coals. He loved barbecued goat, and the thought of it watered his mouth and brought a smile to his face. The things Ramiro wouldn't do for him.

As he drove onto the camp's pitted dirt road, children sprang up on each side of the truck. *"¡Aquí viene el patrón! ¡Aquí viene el patrón!"* they screamed, leading and chasing the truck into the camp, announcing his arrival. In his headlights he could see their thin, dark limbs and their smiling, excited faces. *"¡Aquí viene el patrón!"* He smiled. It was good to be back.

He parked in front of the tiny cabins, and the children circled him, happy and excited, now screaming, *"¡Patrón! ¡Patrón!"* many with their arms and hands stretched up to him. He rubbed the tops of heads, nodding and smiling, savoring their joy, and bent down to kiss some. Then he started toward the cabins with the children milling around him. A small, wiry, moustached man came out from between the cabins, moving quickly, *"¡Quítense! ¡Quítense!"* he said as he waved at the children. But the children paid little attention, knowing that the *patrón* would answer as he did, *"Déjenlos. Déjenlos."*

The wiry man went up to Giuseppe Rocco and hugged him.

"¿Cómo estás, patrón?"

"Bien. Bien. ¿Y tú, Ramiro?"

Ramiro smiled and said, *"Pues bien, también."*

And the two men laughed, full guttural laughs, the laughs of two old friends, or at least the laughs of two men who had shared many fiestas.

"Todo está listo, patrón." And with that, Ramiro turned and led the way.

At each passageway one or more small dark men or women paid their respects. *"Buenas tardes, patrón."* And Giuseppe Rocco greeted them too, nodding and smiling and adding the names of those he knew to his *"Buenas tardes."* At the end of the cabins a small crowd waited for him. He stopped to greet them, talking and laughing with them before walking on toward the strands of red and blue and green and orange lights in the open area behind the cabins.

As he moved toward the lights he could see four men tying the split bodies of two extended goats to makeshift grates. And then, just as he walked under the first lights, Ramiro gave the signal, and from the darkness came the first blast of mariachi music. Throughout the camp high-pitched cries rose into the night sky. Then Giuseppe saw the band of musicians in their vaquero dress emerging from the darkness, playing quickly and loudly "Guadalajara." And he laughed and pushed his head back and raised two fists and cried out too, "Aiyee! Aiyee! Aiyee!" setting off another round of cries throughout the camp. Ramiro nudged him and handed him a glass of tequila. The band reached him and, there before him, sang and played the rest of the song. When they finished and the applause died down, Giuseppe Rocco toasted them and in one swoop downed the tequila. There were more cheers. The fiesta had begun. It was good to be alive.

Children ran in every direction. Men and women left the shadows of the cabins dressed in their best and followed Giuseppe Rocco and Ramiro as they made their way to three pits at the other end of the colored lights, where tables and chairs had been set up. In one pit was an open fire; the goats were now stretched over the coals of the other two pits. On each side of the pits were food and drink of every kind. Two women knelt near the open fire, rolling out corn tortillas and cooking them on a metal sheet that was suspended over the edge of that pit. The mariachis waited until Giuseppe Rocco was seated at the head table before they began again. Giuseppe's favorite appetizers were brought to him: *ceviche, ostiones, guacamole, salsa,* and fresh wrapped tortillas along with a bottle of tequila. People danced. Giuseppe sipped and listened and munched and watched. People approached him, usually over Ramiro's objections, to ask for *consejos*, which more often than not became requests. Others thanked him for past favors. A thin shrunken Indian woman came up to him and knelt before him and began kissing his feet. He rose, wanting none of that, and lifted her so that they were face to face.

"No, *señora*," he said gently.

"But you saved my son, *patrón*. You saved my son," she said crying.

He answered in Italian because he wanted to know about her son. But all he could make out was, "You saved my son, *patrón*. You are a good man, a saint. May God always be with you and bless you and protect you."

The goats hissed behind him and occasionally he went to the pits to smell the cooking meat and watch their dripping fat ignite the smoking coals. "*¿Qué tal, muchachos?*" he'd say to the young men that were tending the goats, and each time they would smile up at him with smiles as warm as the tequila itself. He asked for a *salsa* of *tomatillo* because he wanted to compare the tart, wild taste of the green fruit to that of the tequila.

About that time Ramiro leaned over to him and said, "I have a good one for you tonight, *patrón*."

"Where is she? Show me. Point her out to me."

"Oh, *patrón*, I couldn't do that. That would take half the pleasure away. Believe me, she is good. You will like her. Has Ramiro ever lied to you, *patrón*?"

"Better said, has Ramiro ever told me the truth?"

And they laughed as only old drinking friends could.

Later as he stood watching the goats, he noticed one of the two women who knelt making the tortillas. She was a woman who was at least in her fifties. Her white and black hair was pulled straight back into one large thick braid. Her skin was copper brown, her eyes, almond shaped and her nose, though thick, was sharp. She was beautiful. Beautiful still. The lines in her face strengthened rather than weakened, and the loose skin on each side of her chin did nothing to detract from her full, proud mouth. He stared at her, busy with her *masa*, and wondered of her loves. And soon he saw not her but Angelina, as beautiful as her, as beautiful as any. "*¿Quién eres tú?*"

When the goats were ready, the music stopped and the people went to their tables. Ramiro clanked two pans together, and when he had their attention, began his toast. "I would like to take this opportunity to thank *el patrón*, this great man, for all he has done for us, the one who never forgets us, who not only makes these fiestas possible, but does countless things for us in our everyday lives, never asking for anything in return except our simple thanks. *¡Qué viva el patrón!*"

"*¡Viva! ¡Viva!*" came the shouts from the people now standing at their places. "*¡Viva!*"

Giuseppe Rocco in turn rose, glass in hand, and raising it, toasted them, nodding his thanks.

Then they began eating and the mariachis, as was the custom, came to his table to play the first song of the meal. They played his favorite song, knowing for some time now what that song was. "Tú, Sólo Tú." It was a song he had first heard in the cantinas and camps just after Angelina's death, a song that made grown men cry, men who would have fought and perhaps killed at the slightest challenge to their manhood. It was a song best heard when a man was drinking.

> *Mira como ando mujer*
> *por tu querer*
> *Borracho y apasionado*
> *Nomás por tu amor*

At the first words, shrieks rose all around. The words cut deeply. *See how I am, woman, because of your love.* Giuseppe thought back to that face in the darkness long ago . . . "My *Niño Dios*" . . . He reached for his glass in anticipation of the drunkenness and perdition that were to come.

> *Mira como ando mi bien*
> *Muy dado a la borrachera*
> *y a la perdición*
> *Tú, sólo tú*

You only you. As it had always been, as it would always be. Would she ever leave him? "*¿Quién eres tú?*" Not in all these years.

Tú, sólo tú
Eres causa de todo mi llanto
de me desencanto
y desperación
Tú, sólo tú

You, only you. And now he wept, openly and without shame. And when the song ended, he asked them to play it again and again. And again he wept. And he asked himself for the thousandth time, no, the millionth time, what his life would have been like had he not been so weak, had he taken her to his tent, as he had decided, before she told him.

Later, before he was ready, the ever watchful Ramiro said, "Your bed is ready, *patrón*."

He poured himself more tequila and more after that, until he felt the chill of the night air and he said to Ramiro, "I'm ready."

Then Ramiro led him to the cabin, the best cabin. "You will like her, *patrón*. When I first saw her, I knew she was for you, just what you'd like. She's pretty and clean and she has such a good body. And she belongs to no one. As far as I can tell, she hasn't been touched by anyone in years."

The room was dark and warm and quiet. He listened for breathing, but could hear none.

Then she said, "I have been waiting for you. Don Ramiro said not to turn on the light unless you did."

He went to her in the darkness, to the open, giving warmth of her body, of a woman's body, a warmth and a pleasure that he had not known for many months. His moan was long and loud. And she held him through that moan. When he collapsed on her, she welcomed him again, but now with kisses and caresses.

When he recovered, when he turned from her to sleep, she said, "My name is Yolanda."

Chapter III

Yolanda Parra lived in a small house in the row of small houses at the edge of Salinas. She lived there with her two sons and her two daughters. She was thirty, and her children ranged in age from five to eleven. She had been married once, but her husband had gone to the store one winter afternoon some four years before and had never returned. He left no note, no message, but she knew. He had not worked in six weeks. The rains had been unusually heavy, and even if it had stopped raining on that day, it would have been weeks before the fields would be dry enough to work. All day long the baby had been howling for milk, and Yolanda herself had been crying for days. They had sold everything and were sleeping on the floor. Her children's stomachs were bloated, and their meals had become the soup of boiled bones, bones that she told the butcher were for her dogs. That afternoon when the small, dark, bewildered Indian from Michoacán, Jesús Parra, went to the store for a can of evaporated milk without a penny in his pocket, it didn't surprise her when he never returned.

Yolanda Parra not only endured, but survived, first with the help of a church group and then with welfare, but always with her own bone-grinding work. Unwilling and unable to leave her children, she worked out of her home, beginning by preparing breakfasts and lunches for a few *campesinos* and then by washing and ironing their clothes, gradually increasing her clientele until she had not only her children helping her but also another woman. Yolanda was a pretty, light-skinned woman; *La Güera*, they called her, whom many a man was taken with. But she was not interested. She had her children, her independence, and a financial stability that she had never had with a man. And she was more of a man than most men she saw.

Even Ramiro showed an interest in her. Having heard of *La Güera* from some of his men, he had gone out of his way on several occasions to have breakfast at Yolanda Parra's home. He had offered her money. But the thought of the greedy, grinning, little man on top of her repulsed her, and she just as firmly said no to him as she had to the others. In fact, she had enjoyed rejecting him, because in many ways he was less of a man than many of his uncertain crew.

Ramiro never quite gave up. He continued occasionally to have breakfast at Yolanda Parra's home and then began having her cater special gatherings. It was at one of those gatherings that she first saw Giuseppe Rocco.

"Who is he?" she asked as she saw the excited children gathering at the gate and the lights being strung and the camp being cleaned.

"He's probably the richest man in all of San Jose."

"If he's so rich and white, what is he doing eating and drinking with Mexicans?"

"You'd better ask him that."

She watched him through three fiestas. He was not a handsome man, but a strong man and, despite his gruffness, a warm man, whom the Mexicans clearly loved just as he loved them. He drove an old pickup truck and always wore the clothes of a ranch foreman. But he paid for all the fiestas, and Ramiro, who worshipped money, idolized him. And there were stories of enormous hospital bills that he had paid and monies and food that he had given to families in need, but always on the condition, poorly kept, that no one be told that he was the donor.

Then there was the matter of his cabin and the women. When Yolanda Parra first learned of it, it angered her. He was no better than the rest; in fact, he was worse. He posed as a Good Samaritan when all he wanted was what the lowest of the low wanted. But in time, in between fiestas, she had to concede that he was paying much too much for a whore, that he could have had the best of whores for twenty-five dollars, whereas each fiesta was costing him hundreds and there were families on whom he had spent thousands. So she asked Ramiro, at the next fiesta, "Who is the woman tonight? Show me. Point her out to me."

"Why?"

"I want to see what kind of a woman would stoop to that." And then, "She's not worth twenty-five dollars. Two at most."

She asked again at the next fiesta. And when Ramiro pointed the woman out, she said, "How much does he pay?"

"You'd better ask him."

"No, Ramiro, I'm asking you."

"Why, are you interested?"

And when she answered, "Perhaps," Ramiro felt a twinge, but only momentarily, because it didn't take him long to recognize the chance to make more money.

"How much would you charge, Yolanda?"

"Fifty dollars. Not a penny less."

———————

The morning after, Giuseppe Rocco was up at 5:30. He turned on the cabin light, which, according to Ramiro, was a good sign. When he saw her pale skin he said, *"Ay, Güera."*

She smiled, responding to what his eyes, rather than his mouth, said.

He went to her again. And when he was finished, he said, "I want to see you again."

"When?"

"Soon."

"When?"

"Sooner than the next fiesta."

"When?"

"Next week."

"Yes. But you know, this is not for love."

"Please don't cheapen it. I understand. You will be paid."

———————

The next morning Ramiro drove to Salinas for breakfast and to pay her.

"Is he married?"

"Yes."

"Does he have children?"

"Three small boys."

"Does he love her?"

"You'd have to ask him that."

"If he's with all these other women, do they still have sex?"

"My understanding is that she is sick and they don't."

"Sick? Physically or mentally?"

"You'd have to ask him that."

———————

For months Giuseppe Rocco made a weekly trip to Salinas, arriving at Yolanda Parra's home no earlier than ten in the evening and leaving the next morning no later than five. As he left, he would place fifty dollars on the bureau beside her bedroom door, in part because she would often remind him that, "This is not for love."

They continued with those hours until Sonia Parra turned twelve and asked her mother, "Why does your friend come only late at night and leave early in the morning, *Mamá?* Are you ashamed of him? Or of us? Or of yourself?"

Yolanda Parra said only, "That is none of your business." But the following Sunday Giuseppe Rocco was having his breakfast when the four Parra children came into the kitchen.

Little else changed outside the bedroom. Within the bedroom, their passion grew. They said without words things that could only be said through sex. Now she rarely said, "This is not for love," because after a while, it had no place, no meaning in that room. More and more it became a frail, helpless phrase. One day, she said it no more, even though he continued to leave the fifty dollars.

Then one night, as he was about to enter her, in the throes of their excitement, she asked, "Do you love me?" He paused, hesitated just long enough for her to turn from him and say, "If you have to think about it, Giuseppe, there is no need to answer."

There was no need to think about it. He had already thought about it long and often and had always ended with the same uncertainty, knowing only that to love her meant leaving his sons, and he would never leave his sons. Still, they went on, week after week, even after she threw his fifty dollars at him and screamed that she didn't want or need any of his filthy money. He returned the following week with arms full of food and presents for all. They went on, each careful to skirt that edge. Week after week after week, he was content to continue with things as they were, and she hoped for the change that had to come.

He had been with her at least once a week for some three years when she said one night as he had begun touching her, "Giuseppe, I can't go on like this anymore. I love you and I want you, but not just like this anymore. You're going to have to . . ."

He left within the hour. She had given him until the following Friday night to decide.

That Friday morning, when Giuseppe Rocco walked into Nick's Cafe at 6:03, a young Italian was sitting in the chair reserved for Giuseppe's business clientele. He introduced himself as Pete Antonino, a new neighbor in Hollister, who owned the forty acres adjoining the hundred that Giuseppe Rocco had recently purchased.

"They tell me that if a person wants to talk serious business with you, Mr. Rocco, this is the time and place to do it."

Giuseppe Rocco had yet to look at the chirping, red-headed young man when he said, as Annie gently slid his coffee toward him, "You must have gotten up at four to get here this early," thinking as he watched her long, thin, fine fingers that Annie would never have given him that ultimatum, that for Annie it would have been enough for him to be with her whenever he wanted. "You know what they say, Mr. Rocco, the early bird catches the worm." And then he launched into his business proposal as Giuseppe Rocco quietly ate, first his sweet roll, and then his steak and eggs and potatoes. The young Italian spoke rapidly and with animation: everything was possible. He was prepared to lease up to forty acres of Giuseppe Rocco's land that was now laying fallow for as long as Giuseppe chose. Payment would be half of whatever the profits were for the crops he raised on the land. And there would be profits, good profits, because the land was rich. He would have purchased the hundred acres himself, but he had no money. He had just taken over the family ranch, which had been sorely in need of the improvements that he had just made.

Giuseppe Rocco said little, quietly eating and listening, liking what he heard, but aware of Yolanda too, as he had been all week long, knowing that tonight was the night. Second-generation Italians had all but left the family farms and ranches. Few had any sense of or love for the land. His sons would probably be no exceptions. He had already decided before the young Italian was finished, well before he said, "What do you think, Mr. Rocco?"—even as he heard Yolanda say, "I love you, Giuseppe." And behind that, the frail voice was repeating, *"¿Quién eres tú?"*

"How old are you?"

"Twenty-eight, sir."

"I think we should go look at the land and see what you're talking about."

Not that he needed to look at the land. What he needed was a distraction, something to pass the time, somebody to be with until the time for the decision came and went, a decision that he had long since made without ever acknowledging to himself that he had made it. Because he loved her, had ached for her for a week now.

At the ranch outside Hollister, the young Italian showed Giuseppe Rocco his improvements: the new irrigation pumps and tanks, the new fencing, the rebuilt tractor, and the repairs to the barn.

"It took every penny I had and then some. And then the land you bought came up for sale. It's such a beautiful piece of land. I remember how much I liked it as a boy. Let me show you . . ."

And Giuseppe Rocco allowed himself to be shown what he did not need to be shown, what he had no interest in being shown. Because the time, the hour for decision was upon him.

"My father died two years ago and my mother didn't want to leave here," he said, taking a shovel from the barn and starting towards Giuseppe's land. "All of us kids had moved to San Jose and nobody wanted to come back except me. I was there six years and I had a good job. But I missed the ranch. I missed the sky. It had no meaning in town. I missed the rain. Rain just makes it harder to drive in town. Here you can see it wash and feed, watch it help the seasons along. And I missed the smells. In town all you can smell are the fumes."

Somewhere, probably in that small house across from the lettuce fields, she too was waiting, as she had to have been waiting all week long, for the appointed hour.

They squeezed through Giuseppe Rocco's barbed wire fence.

"And of course I missed the land. I missed feeling it in my hands." With that he sliced into the ground and scooped up a shovelful, turned it and broke it, and then stooped and picked up a handful. "Just look at this, Mr. Rocco, look," he said, as he rubbed the dark rich soil in his fingers. "I could grow anything here. Lots of it. And make us some good money, too."

Giuseppe sighed. "How old are you again?"

"Twenty-eight."

He thought back to his twenty-eighth year, thought of Angelina. Everything had been possible then. But he was fifty now and that was no longer the case. Yolanda might be the last woman he could or would ever love.

They walked the land for the better part of an hour, stopping when the young man chose to dig up samples, examining the slope of the land and Giuseppe's fences. Giuseppe envied the young man's exuberance and his ignorance, too. Without that ignorance, little could be accomplished. She was only fifteen miles from him then. But he couldn't go to her, not then. There was time still.

When they were finished, the young Italian said, "Stay for lunch, Mr. Rocco, my mother makes the best pasta anywhere. It takes her two days to make the sauce. It's none of this stuff out of a bottle . . ."

He thought of staying, wanted to stay, wanted to taste the old woman's pasta, but there was Giovanni and Giuseppe to pick up at school. No, there was Yolanda. And he wanted to stop, needed to stop, in Gilroy before he picked up the boys, if only for a little while.

———

He had been to Angelina's house east of Gilroy on Wednesday to feed and water the dogs, and they had enough food and water until Sunday. Carlo Rossi had said later on Wednesday, "If you move out of the house, Giuseppe, you become a weekend father, a good time uncle, who is forever creating good times on Saturdays and Sundays to make up for what he hasn't given his kids the rest of the time, which is of course himself. If your sons mean to you what you say they do, and I believe they do, then I think you must stay. You cannot be the father you want to be and not live under the same roof with them. Of course, you could always try to take them with you, but few courts would be sympathetic, given their ages and their surroundings."

Yolanda was a good woman. And she had said before he left, "I can make you happy, Giuseppe," with all the certainty of a woman in love. At fifty he might not ever have another chance. And dinner that Wednesday night had been especially difficult: forty-five minutes of swallowing every one of Rita Verducci's many faults and wondering how many more thousands of such dinners his thirteen-year sentence—until Johnny was eighteen—carried.

When he arrived, the dogs yelped and leaped and whined and pranced. As he petted and stroked them and mumbled to them, he thought, Everyone needs love. Slowly he lead them up to the porch, stroking them and soothing them as he went. The old porch creaked. It was tired. Maybe as tired as he. He unlocked the door and closed the rickety screen door behind him. It was noon, but the house was dark. He stood in the doorway absorbing the darkness and then said, without speaking, I have not come to blaspheme, Angelina. You know all too well that I can never replace you.

He stood as the tiny house took shape. The bare front room with an old wood rocker and a small oval table next to it and two chairs and no more. The doorway to his left through which he could see a corner of their iron bed. Through the doorway before him, he could see part of the stove against the back wall some fifteen feet away, and two more doors, one that opened onto the bathroom and the other that opened onto a smaller bedroom that she had used for storage, storage which like everything else in the house was still there, still as it was. And everywhere were the planks, dark unpainted planks, darkening still with the years. They were twelve inches wide and an inch thick, rough ripped planks that made up not only the floor but the walls too, planks that had never been smoothed or softened save by the shoes and later the bare feet that wore them down, leaving shiny paths of habit just as the deer did up on the hillside. He had lost a woman that he had never forgotten. Would Yolanda be the second?

He went to the kitchen and warmed the beans and tortillas that he had brought from Gilroy and then sat and ate, as he had sat and eaten so many years before, watching her warm each tortilla and stir and re-stir the beans for her *Niño Dios*. As he ate he looked out at the hillside, dressed in its new green life, just as it always had been, just as it always would be, long after he was gone. He had looked at the hillside a thousand times, and still it fascinated him. Now as he looked, his mind repeated the obvious: It was a matter of his sons, of Giovanni and Giuseppe.

"If you take them with you, the courts will force you to return them to Rita. Even though they are boys, and even though you want only the two older boys, they would still be considered children of tender years in the eyes of the court, and in that instance the courts favor the mother. If you move out of state, those courts will take the same position. And if you were to take them to Italy, Giuseppe, you will be uprooting those boys in a very harsh manner. I can't believe that you would want to cause that kind of hurt or shock to your sons, Giuseppe. And you would become a criminal; you would never be allowed to return to this country without first being subjected to criminal prosecution for child stealing."

He walked the hillside following the narrow path that the deer's hooves had cut for generations in the search for food and water. He walked through the tall, lush grass that would begin to die in but a few weeks, walked past the lone scrub oak to the top of the hill and then looked down at the tiny, faded house which seemed smaller still, an intrusion even. If he left, he might never see that house again, that house in which it now seemed that much of what had really mattered in his life had been lived.

He left a half hour early because today he would pick up Giovanni first. As he drove, it seemed all but decided. Yet he wavered. At fifty . . . He needed to be with his sons. Still he wondered: had he not vacillated years ago, had he decided sooner, had he not abandoned her, had he followed his instinct, his heart, what would his life be now.

<hr />

As he drove alongside the play yard, Giuseppe Rocco saw the children in the yard and honked his horn three times. A ruddy-faced boy with a shock of light brown hair stood up from a group of bent children, looked for the truck, saw it, burst into a smile and shouted, then bolted from the yard toward the house. Giuseppe laughed. The sight warmed him as no other sight on earth could, even though he saw Loretta Logoluso start for the house too, shouting, "Johnny come back here! Johneee!"

He parked and hurried to the foot of the walkway where he squatted some fifty feet from the front door, arms opened wide, grinning, waiting. And then the door flung open and the boy shot out, his face stretched with glee, his eyes wild, as he leaped over the two front steps and bounded down the walkway towards Giuseppe. "Papa! Papa! Papa!" Giuseppe Rocco moved not an inch, watching the streaking boy. And then the boy hurtled into his father's arms and Giuseppe Rocco hugged that taut, small, wiry body and kissed him and said, "Giovanni. Giovanni." Yolanda seemed distant indeed.

Then Loretta Logoluso was there. "Mr. Rocco, you promised me just last week, just seven days ago to be exact, that you would stop honking. And that wasn't your first promise. When you do that I lose all control, not only of Johnny, and he's not an easy boy to control, but of all the children, because then I have to leave them and chase him for fear that he'll run into the street or something and . . ."

He had heard it many times before, too many times. But he had made the promise. So he let her talk, as he stroked Giovanni, running his hand through the boy's tousled hair as if to calm it, brushing the sand and dust from his otherwise soiled T-shirt, tugging at and hoisting his sagging pants, which on Giovanni seemed like an afterthought. Talk, after all, was all she could do, because Giuseppe Rocco owned the day care center's house as well.

Then they drove off, with Loretta Logoluso wanting to set a time for discussing "the latest of Johnny's behavioral problems" and Giuseppe answering only, "I'm late. We'll have to talk about it next week."

Within two blocks of Saint Albert's grammar school, children were already walking home from school. At the truck's window, Giovanni began taunting older boys, shouting threats and dares at them as they passed.

"Sit down and roll up that window, Giovanni, before you fall out of this truck."

But Giovanni continued his taunts and Giuseppe repeated himself and then finally shouted, "Giovanni!"

Now the boy did turn to his father protesting, "My name's Johnny. My name's Johnny."

Giuseppe didn't answer, and the boy turned back to the open window and leaned out again, waiting for the next group of boys.

Turning a corner, Giuseppe saw his other son waiting patiently, just as he had been told, in front of the school gate. He was as neat and clean in his school uniform as he had been when he left home that morning. He carried a small blue lunch box, and he waved and grinned when he saw the truck. Giovanni leaned out of the truck even further and began shouting, "Hi, Joey! Hi, Joey!"

Little Giuseppe opened the truck door and said, "Hi, Papa," as he climbed in.

"Hello, Giuseppe," said his father which prompted Giovanni to say, "His name's Joey and my name's Johnny."

Giuseppe Rocco ignored the boy and started driving again. Within the block, Giovanni shouted, "His name's Joey and my name's

Johnny!" When Giuseppe Rocco ignored him again, the boy screamed, "His name's Joey and my name's Johnny!"

Giuseppe Rocco stopped the truck. Nobody spoke to him like that. He glared down at the boy and, as he did, he saw the other boy watching, saying nothing but watching intently. He remembered the time not long ago when that boy had said quietly, "Papa, they call me Joey in school," and he had said, "I don't give a damn what they call you in school! Your name is Giuseppe! I gave it to you and that's it!" But Giovanni's face was cracking now, tears were rimming his eyes. Giuseppe Rocco's heart ached, and he said, "I know we're in a different country now, and I know all your friends call you Johnny and Joey," and pausing, sighing, he finished, "and that's okay with me."

It had been a long day. His sons were growing up. They needed him. There could be no leaving them now.

⎯⎯⎯➤

They started at Columbia Street as they always did.

"Why can't we just park in front of the store, Papa?" Johnny asked, as he always did. "Because I like to walk. Exercise is good for you."

A group of boys had already gathered there, waiting to join the procession which would end at Giordano's Market with free sodas and ice cream.

Johnny immediately paired off with five older boys as wild as himself and ran off ahead of Giuseppe. Joey walked a step or two behind his father. No one came out of the stores to stare at or acknowledge Giuseppe Rocco and his sons, but he knew that they were aware of them and that was enough. The five older boys were soon chasing Johnny half a block ahead. Quick and well coordinated, Johnny easily outdistanced them at first. Then, as they neared him, he stopped dead in his tracks, ducked under them and started back, in and out of doorways, around a fire hydrant, then back in their original direction, onto the bumper and hood of a parked car and off again before Giuseppe could shout. Time and again he squirted out of their reach, laughing and screeching as he did so. Giuseppe walked and watched, shaking his head and smiling. When the biggest of the boys finally caught Johnny, Johnny collapsed on the sidewalk, giggling and exhausted, and the bigger boy fell too. And as soon as he did, Johnny rolled out of his grip and jumped to his feet, winded but laughing, and the chase began anew.

Giuseppe smiled and said to Joey, "Go play with your brother."
The boy shook his head no.

"It's good for you to run and play." The boy looked straight ahead. Giuseppe sighed and let it be.

They walked on with one son dodging and ducking and climbing and running and screaming before him and the other walking a step or two behind him. When they crossed over to the next block, there was another group of boys waiting, and Joey caught up to his father and reached for his hand.

"Don't hold my hand!" Giuseppe said, yanking his hand away from the boy, "Go! Go play with your brother! You're no baby!" But the boy only tucked his chin in his chest and walked as closely as he could to his father without touching him until they had passed the new group of boys.

At the first sign of Giuseppe and the boys, one of the checkers at Giordano's Market retrieved sodas and ice creams and placed them on a counter. Each boy took one of each and then went to the far front corner of the store, where sacks of beans and rice and flour were stacked. Giuseppe Rocco joined them, sitting on a sack of rice, propping his back against another sack while the boys sat on the dark, oil-stained wood floor, eating and drinking and trading bottle caps. Today was no different from any of their weekly walks, except that Giuseppe was irritable. In a few hours she'd know; in a few hours it would be over.

Ralph Giordano joined them. Other men joined them, older Italians who came into the store on those afternoons for no other reason than to speak to Giuseppe Rocco, who was usually approachable then. But today, when one of the men questioned his opinion on real estate values in San Jose, Giuseppe Rocco responded brusquely, "Please don't argue with me. I've spent my life in real estate. I know what I'm talking about. Just like I wouldn't argue with you about how to fix a pair of shoes, since all you've done all your life is fix shoes."

Then, when Joey began mingling with the other boys, he seemed to lose some of his testiness. After a while, the boy rose and, leaving his soda and ice cream behind, walked dejectedly back to his father and pressed against him.

"Go on, go play," Giuseppe said, nudging the boy. "Can't you see I'm talking."

The boy only pressed closer against his father. Giuseppe pushed the boy away from him with a firm hand. When the boy came back, he shoved him. The boy stumbled and fell and began to cry and returned to his father, rubbing his teary eyes and pressing against his knee. This time Giuseppe swung, hitting the boy across the face with his open hand, sending the boy reeling down past the other boys. The room fell silent until the boy saw the blood and let out a terrified scream that went on and on as blood spilled from his nose.

Everyone froze. Giuseppe went to the boy and picked him up and called back to his other son, "Come on, Giovanni, let's go!" Giuseppe carried the screaming boy out of the store and down the street without regard for the freely falling blood and tears. When they reached the truck, he finally heard Johnny's screams: "Papa! Papa! Joey's gonna die! He's gonna die, Papa!"

He laid the boy on his back on the truck's seat and propped up his head with his jacket. Gradually the bleeding slowed. Then Giuseppe Rocco began to cry and he started cleaning the boy's face with his handkerchief, even as his own tears smeared some of the blood. It occurred to him that everywhere along that empty street others had to have been watching, were watching still. But their meddlesome eyes meant little now. And he said to the boy, "I'm sorry, Giuseppe, I'm sorry. You are my son and I do love you. Believe me, I do. I have never hit you before and I will never hit you again." And it was all true.

He could never leave his sons.

———————

Dinner was eaten in silence as it always was, except for the requests for more meat or pasta or the clink of utensils or glasses. But tonight he expected more. Because she had seen the blood. She said nothing. She was as stubborn and hate-filled as he, so she said nothing. Rather, she left it for Mateo, her son, to say, not with his mouth but with his eyes.

By then Giuseppe Rocco was convinced that Mateo had hated him even before birth, that Rita Verducci had taught him to hate him even as she carried him. When he had first held the infant, Mateo had cried and writhed. The more Giuseppe held him, the more he cried until his mother, and only his mother, took him and soothed him with her arms and words. Even when he approached the crib, the infant screamed.

And that was before she had moved the crib into her room, where it remained and where he had slept even to that day. Although she had not done it with his brothers, Rita Verducci breast-fed him.

Mateo was almost two before Giuseppe began to see the boy regularly at the dinner table, but nowhere else. He sat immediately next to his mother in that huge, hand-carved, wooden high chair. From the first day, he stared down at his father. Giuseppe Rocco immediately realized that it was too late, that the boy was irrevocably filled with her hate, that he thought his father to be the beast that his mother thought him to be. Never a word, it seemed, but a hate-filled stare consumed more of his time in that high chair than the food ever did. With him she will destroy me, he often thought, it's just a matter of time.

That night was no different. That night the boy sat, as always, at the opposite end of the long table, next to his mother, eating little, staring at him with her hate. From time to time, Rita Verducci leaned over to him and in hardly more than a whisper pretended to remind him of his dinner. Pretended, because she had to have been ecstatic with the hate that her son had fixed on his father.

That night was worse. That night an alternative was slipping away. And he vacillated once again, however briefly, thinking that perhaps he should leave after all. As he sat fifteen feet from that hate, he thought, when he is twenty-three, I will be seventy; when he is thirty, I will be seventy-seven; when he is in his prime, I will be a stumbling, bumbling, old man and he will devour me as she watches. If I stay, I let him. I need only stay until Giovanni is eighteen, only thirteen years more, because Giovanni will leave by then, and Mateo will be just sixteen, and although I will be sixty-three then, he will still be too young to do what she will have been waiting for him to do all these years. And I will leave then.

He looked at little Giuseppe, who was quietly, politely, eating his vegetables. If it were only him, I might go now. It's not. He looked at Giovanni, the uncombed, unkempt boy of five who was still sporting the stains of the day on his shirt and who at that moment was attempting to tear a piece of meat from the huge slab that he had stabbed with his fork. Giovanni. There was no decision to make. He could never leave his sons.

After dinner, he kissed Giovanni and Giuseppe good night and went up to his room and lay on his bed and began his wait. Within three hours she would know. Because he never arrived after ten. Ten came and went in the darkness and he stared up into that darkness for hours afterward; there was nothing else he could do, nothing else to do.

The following days were hard. He saw her everywhere. By Sunday he decided that there had to be some compromise, some meeting of the minds, a promise, a guarantee, a written contract even, that in time, in a few years . . . On Tuesday when he could stand it no longer, he loaded his truck with gifts and groceries and flowers and drove to Salinas, drove down those familiar streets to that familiar neighborhood, to that familiar house across from the lettuce fields only to find it empty, deserted, void of all persons and things, even the window shades.

A neighbor said, "I don't know what to tell you, Mr. Rocco. All I know is that yesterday I went to work, and she and the kids were there. When I came home, everything was gone. She didn't tell nobody nothing."

Chapter IV

Annie carefully, gently slid the saucer towards him, averting her eyes as a young girl might. He took her hand in his and said, "How are you, Annie?" forcing her to look at him.

"I'm fine, Giuseppe."

He held onto her hand. It was the first time he had deliberately touched her in more than thirteen years.

She reddened and blushed and her eyes fell more than before. She said, "There's a man at the register waiting to talk to you, Giuseppe."

"But you don't look fine . . . Forgive me, Annie, but should you be working so soon?"

"It's been three months, Giuseppe."

"I know. But it was cancer."

She nodded and looked back up at him. For a moment their eyes locked as intimately as any embrace, spoke more candidly and meaningfully than words. They were the eyes of a man and a woman, each in their fifties, who knew life now perhaps as well as they would ever know it, and their eyes spoke of the affection that each had for the other, of what might have been, and of mortality too.

"Annie, if it's the money that's making you come back to work, you know that I'll pay for anything you need. I don't want to see you down here killing yourself."

"Thank you, Giuseppe. It's not the money. I needed to get out of the apartment. I needed to be around people again. I need the job more than I need the money."

"Are you sure?"

"Giuseppe, I'm going to cry." With that she withdrew her hand, picked up a menu and started for a booth where two men had seated themselves.

It was to be a busy week. Today, he and Carlo Rossi would sign the papers for the mall. Johnny was twelve, and tomorrow would be his championship game. On Saturday, Johnny and Joey would be confirmed. Added to that, Refugio and Ramiro had promised that the work on the house in Gilroy would be completed that morning. He spoke to

Joe Biggio about an apartment complex in Santa Clara. Then he slowly finished his breakfast. When he was ready to leave, he looked for Annie. She was at a back booth with a coffee pot in each hand, bending, smiling, pouring as she had for more than thirteen years now, the hips wider with time, the smile tired, but still the same pleasant, affable Annie. He stood at his red vinyl chair to draw her attention. She saw him, nodded, and came.

"You're all right?"

"Yes, Giuseppe, thank you."

He drove to Gilroy, wanting to see the house before Refugio left, before he paid Ramiro. He had known Refugio Apodaca for many years. He had seen the old man in the fields and in several of Ramiro's labor camps. He had seen Refugio work with wood when he wasn't in the fields, making furniture and cabinets. He had seen the love and respect that the old man had for wood. When the toilet fell through the rotted floor of the colorless house and then the porch collapsed, he went to the old man.

"But I am not a carpenter, *señor.*"

"I don't want a carpenter. I want you."

The old man had little choice, because after speaking to him, Giuseppe Rocco went directly to Ramiro, his boss. "I don't care what it costs. I'll pay his wages and I'll pay for his replacement in your crew. And if he does a good job, there'll be a bonus in it for you and him."

"But, Don Giuseppe, I can get you a young carpenter who can make those repairs in half the time for half the money."

"If I wanted a young carpenter, I wouldn't be coming to you, Ramiro."

And so it was that in early September, while the great black dogs sniffed and jostled around the apprehensive old man, Giuseppe Rocco stood just inside the gate of the colorless house and in his best Spanish-Italian-English said, "I don't care how long it takes you, or what kind of tools you need or use, but all the wood must come from what's already here, probably from the barn, because I don't want anything else taken from the house, probably from the two sides of the barn that can't be seen from here or from the house."

The old man nodded, as much to convince himself as to pacify Giuseppe Rocco.

His work was good but slow. It took him three weeks to replace the small floor surrounding the toilet. Whenever Giuseppe Rocco seemed to be prodding him, he would simply say, "You want it done right, don't you, *señor?*" And it was right. Once completed, it was the floor he had known twenty-five years before.

One morning when Giuseppe arrived, the old man was sweeping the newly completed porch. The old man went on sweeping until he was finished before looking up. Then he said, "Do you like it, *señor?*"

"Oh, yes, Refugio, I like it very much. There's no way you can tell it's a new porch. Maybe the edges give it away a little, but a few winters and summers will take care of that."

Once the old man was gone, he brought the old rocker out onto the new porch. Then he sat and thought, looking past the golden brown hills to the evergreen coastal range to the west. Once again his life was changing. Today he would become wealthier than he could have ever imagined. And he thought of his voyage across the Atlantic, years before, when he was young and penniless and unable to speak the language of the vast new country to which he was going. He thought of the deep, dark shafts and the cool, compacted air of the Pennsylvania coal mines. He thought of his move to San Francisco and of his work at the slaughterhouses and of his first nights on his open acre in San Jose. And he thought of Angelina too, and of Johnny and Joey and Yolanda. The past enriched the present and he wanted to savor both.

He had insisted on this date for the signing of the papers, nine years exactly from the day that he had purchased the fifty-three acres from Dino Restelli. It was to be at the same hour and at the same restaurant, at which he and Carlo Rossi had signed similar papers nine years earlier. It would mark the beginning of the construction of the second largest shopping mall west of the Mississippi. It was a major step forward for San Jose. So many people had mentioned the event to him that, just a few days before, he thought of buying and wearing a business suit for the occasion.

He had gone to J.C. Penney, where he had bought all of his clothes for the past thirty-five years. He had gone to the men's department and had purchased a pair of work socks, even though he needed none. He had lingered long enough to study a brown business suit on a mannequin. Later that day, he had spoken to Carlo Rossi, had awkwardly asked him where he bought his suits. Carlo Rossi had casually answered that he had his suits tailored at Professional Tailoring on San Fernando Street. And he had timidly asked how long it took to have a suit tailored. Carlo Rossi had laughed and slapped his thigh and said, "You! In a suit! Giuseppe Rocco in a suit!" Still he had driven past Professional Tailoring six or seven times anyway, getting as close to it as the windows of his pick-up would allow. Ultimately he didn't stop. Because he couldn't.

As he neared Alfredo's, he saw a crowd gathered at the entrance. Then he saw television cameras and the crowd as he pulled into the parking lot. Slowly, deliberately, heavily, he got out of his truck like a man who had already put in a full day's work but still had several hours before him. Slowly, he moved toward the crowd. Cameras flashed and whirred and people called out his name, "Giuseppe Rocco! Giuseppe Rocco!" Someone shouted, "Giuseppe Rocco, you've put San Jose on the map!" He looked for that voice, but saw only a host of smiling faces and nodded.

Inside there was more of the same. People stopped eating and talking when he entered. Several men approached him with hands extended, but he moved past them without so much as a nod and entered a private dining room where some twenty men sat at three tables. Again, conversation stopped and cameras clicked and whirred. Slowly, he made his way to the head table, acknowledging no one until he reached the head table.

Carlo Rossi hugged him, and as he did, quietly complained, "Jesus, Giuseppe, where you been? These are important people. You don't keep them waiting."

Giuseppe mumbled back, "I had something important to do."

"As important as this?"

"Yes."

They ate and drank as speaker after speaker rose and toasted and extolled the mall and Giuseppe Rocco. Several speakers asked for a few words from Giuseppe Rocco, the man who had helped make this possible. Giuseppe simply shook his head, enjoying each refusal. There was no need to speak. The moment was his.

Finally the principal speaker, a man from New York, asked for a few words from Giuseppe Rocco. Carlo Rossi leaned over to him and whispered, "Please, Giuseppe, for my sake if nothing else."

For a long moment, Giuseppe Rocco looked down at his glass. Then he rose slowly and went to the podium. The crowd, which had grown, broke into applause. He stood at the podium, hunched and with eyes downcast, until the applause died down. Then he raised his head and pushed the brim of his hat back and said in an accent that he had long since abandoned, "Thank you. But I'm just a hard-working Italian. I didn't have too much school, so I don't talk too good. So I just want to say that I'm happy to help San Jose."

Later, much later, when all had gone and Carlo Rossi and Giuseppe Rocco sat alone in the private dining room sipping Chianti, Carlo Rossi said, "Giuseppe, there's still two things we have to talk about."

"So let's talk."

"The governor's re-election committee called again this morning, and when I couldn't give them an answer, the governor's office called."

"So?"

"They really want you to be at the big fund-raising dinner at the St. Claire."

"Carlo, they don't want me, they want my money. I don't need those fancy dinners and those fancy people, and I don't want nothing from the governor. Tell them if he wants my money bad enough, he can come to my house and ask for it . . . And besides, what's he gonna do if I don't go, cut off my Social Security?"

"Okay, Giuseppe, I'll tell them. But I think it's a mistake."

"So it's a mistake. What else do we have to talk about?"

"Don't be offended, Giuseppe, but I noticed again today that you examined some of the papers before you signed them. Do you read now?"

"I can read."

"You can read! How did you learn? Who taught you?"

"My son taught me."

"Your son? Johnny?"

"No, Joey."

❧ Giuseppe Rocco ❧

The lessons had their beginning some four years earlier. It was at the dinner table. Johnny and Joey still sat across from each other along the sides of that great table, and Rita Verducci and Giuseppe Rocco still sat at their accustomed places at the head and foot of the table some fifteen feet apart. The only change was that Matthew's high chair was gone. In its place, exactly where the high chair had been, was a fine high-back chair. In it sat Matthew, the right arm of his chair touching the left arm of his mother's. Although he was just six, Matthew had already been enrolled in three schools across town, the latest of which required that he wear a sport coat and tie. Rita Verducci drove him to those schools just as she drove him to his music lessons and Italian classes after school, and to San Francisco to buy his clothes and books and special foods for his lunches. Each evening after dinner, she spent at least an hour with him doing his homework. On the other hand, Johnny and Joey walked to school, Maria Luca bought their clothes and made their lunches, and they did their own homework.

Giuseppe had only to look at the boy to know that he was his mother's son. Not only did he carry his mother's delicate features and thin body, but he still carried hate for him as well. They seldom spoke. When they did, the boy's tone and look always said, "I hate you."

Dinner was almost over on that evening and Johnny, as was now his custom, was speaking through the silence. "That new kid says we get way too much homework."

"What new kid?" Joey asked.

"You know, the one with the funny eyes."

"Johnny, I can read! I can read, Johnny!" Matthew piped in.

"So, big deal."

"I've already read two books at school."

"So, everybody can read when they're six."

"Uh, uh. Papa can't read and he's way past six." And he laughed.

No one else laughed with him, and when his smile died, a much heavier silence fell on the room. Johnny and Joey sat motionless, looking wide-eyed at their father. And then Giuseppe Rocco, angry and ashen, rose, and for a long while stared at the two downturned heads at the other end of the table, saying nothing, moving nothing, oblivious to the two small, upturned faces on each side of him. Then he turned and left.

Later, when he heard the faint knock on the door, he knew it was
Maria Luca coming to plead for peace. He rolled off his bed, ready with
a response that neither she nor Rita Verducci would soon forget. But
when he yanked the door open, he startled only Joey, who was standing in the hall's darkness. He caught himself as best he could, held back
as much as he could before saying gruffly, "What the hell do you
want!"

Joey said, "Papa, I can teach you how to read."

That was how it began. Thereafter, every Monday through Friday
evening, the fifty-three-year-old father met with his nine-year-old son
for an hour and a half in the boy's room and learned, just as the boy had,
how to read and write. Joey had saved everything: every worksheet,
every workbook, every textbook, every assignment. They started with
the alphabet, slowly sounding out each letter. Then came the words:
can, man, ran. Then came the stop, top, spot, pot books—slowly, just as
the boy had read them—with no one the wiser, except for Johnny, who
was sworn to secrecy.

They struggled through the fall and into the winter with the hulk of
a man seated on one of the two tiny chairs beside the small desk, cast-
ing an enormous shadow against the back of the room and ceiling.
Night after night they plodded through the worksheets and workbooks.
Giuseppe Rocco was learning. Every day he saw proof of that in the
words he recognized on street signs and buildings and windows and in
the newspaper. And that brought him back with renewed determination
to that tiny chair in the room upstairs next to his at the far end of the
hall. It brought him closer, too, to the lesser of his sons, the plodder, the
son whom he had always considered the slowest, the most cautious, the
most frightened, and therefore the one most likely destined for medi-
ocrity or worse. It also gave him a different view of that son, the son
who that year had been made to repeat the third grade.

"You're not dumb, Joey, you're not stupid. You're teaching me.
Why did they keep you back in the third grade?"

"Because I wanted them to, Papa."

"You wanted them to?"

"Yeah, Papa, I didn't want to be Johnny's older brother any more."

"What!"

"I didn't want anybody telling me anymore about all the things my
little brother could do that I couldn't do. So I never turned in my home-

work. I did it. See, I did it. I just never turned it in. And when the teacher used to call on me, I'd say I didn't know when I did know. I just didn't want to be his big brother anymore."

He had, in fact, done all of his homework the year before and had saved it, which meant that he now had no homework and each day he could turn in work that had sat in his desk for a year. Each night he could teach his father to read and write.

They worked through the Christmas vacation. At the end of the vacation, the man asked the boy the question he had longed to ask. "Can I read as good as your brother?"

"No, Papa, Johnny can read almost as good as me."

"Not Johnny."

And the boy paused and looked and said, "Matthew?"

The man nodded.

But Joey didn't know. "I never hear him read. Him and Mama work in the study, just like we work here."

Giuseppe could not rest. And the following week he asked, "Can you bring me one of his books?"

"Matthew's?"

The man nodded. The next afternoon while Matthew was at his music lesson, Joey brought him a first grade reader. Giuseppe read, "Tom went to the . . ." slowly, struggling, knowing he was struggling. When Joey said, "That was good, Papa," it meant nothing because he knew he wasn't ready, that they would have to work through the summer too, while Matthew wasn't studying, so that he would be ready.

When spring came and suddenly the days were longer and the evenings mild, they could hear Johnny outside through the open window playing baseball with the neighborhood kids. And the man knew that even if Joey didn't play, he at least went outside and watched.

"You want to go play?" Giuseppe Rocco asked.

The boy shook his head and said, "No, Papa."

They continued on into the summer in that same room that was now cooled by the wind that chased the afternoon fog down the peninsula, while Johnny played baseball below loudly, constantly, incessantly. Rita Verducci became suspicious and asked Johnny first and then Joey, what they were doing.

"We just talk," Joey said.

When she asked about what, he said, "About when he was a boy in Italy."

So they moved down among a patch of bamboo and ferns along the banks of the Guadalupe River, just a few blocks away. There, hunched and huddled together, the man started on the boy's second-grade reader with his finger on the page moving from word to word while the boy watched and corrected, and the now dammed but not yet polluted silver stream of water ran obliviously over slabs of sandstone and granite.

At the end of the summer he was ready. Now he needed only the opportunity. And the opportunity presented itself when Rita Verducci began attending the Wednesday afternoon teas of the San Jose Auxilliary of the San Francisco Symphony, leaving Matthew behind to do his studies. As confident as the man was, he still found it necessary to say to Joey, "Bring me his book." And Joey did, and together they read and re-read the first three pages and the last three pages until the man knew them almost by heart. Then he strode into the study, a room that was now theirs, as casually as if he spent his days in it, and smiled and nodded at the startled boy who was startled for just a moment before the cold hate appeared.

His father walked up to him and said pleasantly, "Oh, you're doing your studies. That's good, Matthew. It's good that you're becoming so educated so early in your life."

The boy watched him wordlessly as he picked up the reader and then opened the book and read, "When Tom met Susan he was in the second grade . . ." He read on without pausing until he stopped abruptly midway through the third page.

"Do you know how it ends?" he asked, seeing, reveling, gloating in the boy's shock. "Have you gotten that far? Can you read to the end yet?" not needing or wanting an answer, because the boy's eyes held all the answers he needed. "Here, let me read the end for you." He read to the end, smoothly and flawlessly, smiling as he closed the book, and then nodded pleasantly to the wide-eyed boy and left.

———

Thursday of that week, Giuseppe and Joey went out the back door to the pick-up at exactly 4:15.

"I don't want to be late."

"We're not gonna be, Papa."

"Not for the game. I want to see Johnny warm up. I want to see how he's gonna throw today."

He had been aware of the game almost from the beginning. He had seen grown men wasting away their Sundays playing it. And then it was everywhere: in the schools, in the parks, in vacant lots, on the streets. It was a stupid game. You threw the ball, you hit the ball, you ran to a place. He had loathed Johnny's love of the game and had refused to watch any of his games. But all that had changed some three years earlier when the coach's car wouldn't start and he had to drive his sobbing son, resplendent in his new white and black uniform, to the Little League park.

He had stayed only to make sure Johnny had a ride home. What he saw was a revelation. There, among boys two and three years older, and in some cases almost twice his size, Johnny Rocco was outplaying them all. He dove for balls, he caught them in mid-air, he caught them as he fell, and threw them as he ran or jumped. But it was the fierceness, the sustained intensity with which his son played that captivated Giuseppe Rocco. The boy was obsessed, consumed; he was in another world, aware of nothing, responsive to nothing except what was happening on the ball field. Each time he did something more, each time the crowd marveled, Giuseppe Rocco simply shook his head, not so much for what the boy had done, but rather for the ferocity with which he had accomplished it. Every time the announcer rolled his name, "Johnnneee Rrroccooo!" the entire crowd rose and cheered. And that was often.

At the end of the game, Johnny's teammates ran to him, surrounded him, hugged him, lifting him and slapping him until the coach came and picked up Johnny and held him high for all to cheer. Only then did the boy smile, did the ferocity wilt. Later when the coach said to him, "You should be proud of him, Mr. Rocco," Giuseppe Rocco had answered, "I am." And for the next three and a half years, Giuseppe Rocco did not miss a single one of his son's games.

Today he wanted to watch Johnny warm up, because then he would know. He wanted to watch Andy, the catcher, take his hand out of his mitt and rub away the sting with his fingers after the hard throws, watch him back up a few inches after each of those throws. Then he would know. Because today was the championship game and it all depended on Johnny's right arm. He remembered what the coach had said that first year: "I'd pitch him right now if I could, Mr. Rocco. He's got the best arm and the most heart on the team. No doubt about it. But he's only nine, and the rules say I can't pitch him until he's ten, and even then I can only pitch him once a week for a max of six innings. And I have to have your written permission for him to pitch." Giuseppe remembered what the coach had said when it came time to sign: "There is nothing to worry about, Mr. Rocco, the league makes us do this because so many kids hurt their arms throwing curve balls and junk pitches. Johnny doesn't have to throw that stuff. He can blow the ball past nine-tenths of the batters right now, and he's only ten. It's his arms. They're down around his knees and his hands are huge and his wrists . . ." Then he had stopped and, looking at Giuseppe, smiled and continued, "I can see where he gets them from." Giuseppe smiled too, thinking that it was more than the arms that Johnny got from him.

They had lost the league championship on the last day of the season the first year that Johnny had pitched. They had lost in the regionals last year on a day when the league rules prohibited Johnny from pitching. This year they were undefeated, and Johnny had been both awesome and masterful. He was now an inch taller than his father, wide and wiry, with arms that still extended to his knees and carried those huge hands and wrists, and a heart, as his coach often said, bigger than any other. There had been games when he had faced eighteen batters and had struck out eighteen batters, the ball little more than a blur as it exploded from that sling of an arm, terrifying not only the batters but Andy and the umpire behind him as well. And he had hit home run after home run, batting from either side of the plate, holding the bat cocked far back and then whipping it around like some bestial weapon with those huge hands and wrists as the ball approached.

The ferocity had not only remained but had increased. Or at least it was more imposing. The boy's face at twelve now gave indications of what the man's face would be, and that look on a man's face would have brought fear to most. When he looked down at a batter before throwing a third strike, he could have been an executioner. As a batter, his eyes fastened on the pitcher as they would have on a life-or-death enemy. And with every home run, there was no smile, no clapping of the hands or jumping up and down as the other boys did when they trotted around the bases. There was only a grim, fierce, silent look of vindication and repeated stares of comtempt towards the pitcher's mound and the scum that had dared challenge him. Giuseppe knew and understood that look. It pleased him no end.

And then Johnny hit a batter. It was the most closely contested game of the regular season. In the last inning, Johnny's team was winning, one to nothing. Johnny quickly struck out the first two batters and then just as quickly got two strikes on the third batter. Johnny's next pitch was a blazing fastball for what should have been a third strike. But the umpire called it a ball. The crowd groaned and Johnny's coach and teammates protested. The call stood, and Johnny was angry. On the next pitch, in an exaggerated wind-up, Johnny kicked his left leg as high as it would go, reached far back and then lunged toward the plate, flinging his arm in one powerful motion and releasing a blur that struck the frozen batter just above the left ear and carromed twenty feet into the air off the shattered batting helmet. The batter collapsed, and there was a hush everywhere. Then coaches and parents and players ran to the boy who lay motionless on the ground. For a full two minutes the boy did not move. Then the boy began to stir while Johnny waited alone on the mound, alone on the field, not wanting to or needing to join all the others who had crowded around the fallen boy. Instead, he waited for the game to resume, pacing about the mound, pounding his fist into his mitt even as the boy got to his feet and was led off the field, looking back at Johnny more frightened than hurt.

It happened again two weeks later. The score was sixteen to zero, and it was only the fourth inning. Johnny had already homered twice, twice with the bases loaded. This time he waited taut and centered as the awkward laboring boy on the mound threw a pathetic pitch that Johnny sprung at with a savage rip of his bat, rifling the ball back at the boy at ten or twenty times the speed it had arrived. The boy hunched and tried to duck and twist, but the ball struck him with an ugly thud that had set off cries all around the park. The boy fell, writhing in pain, gripping the top of his right arm as Johnny reached first base and started for second. People poured onto the field as Johnny rounded second base and headed for third on the now empty base paths. People were shouting, "Call a doctor! Get an ambulance!" as Johnny touched third and sprinted for home. Giuseppe, who was watching Johnny, reddened when a woman planted herself before Giuseppe and said, "I think your son's sick. To keep running like that with that boy on the ground, I think he's real sick."

He spoke to Johnny that night.

"Nobody called time-out, Papa."

"Johnny, the boy was hurt."

"I didn't know that, Papa. I just hit the ball and ran."

"But he was lying on the ground when you went around first base. And the ball was right by him. You wouldn't have gone to second base if you didn't know where the ball was."

"Papa, I hit the ball and ran."

"But there was a whole bunch of people around him, Johnny. His arm is broken in many places. I know you didn't hit him on purpose. I know it was an accident. But you were leading sixteen to nothing. You didn't need that run. Why did you keep running?"

"Papa, when I play, I play to win. I didn't know he was hurt, honest. I don't even remember seeing the ball hit him, honest."

Then the boy's eyes welled with tears and Giuseppe went to him and hugged him, hugged the boy who was now an inch taller than he was. "I know, son. I'm proud of you and I love you. I understand and I wouldn't want you any other way. You remind me very much of a boy I knew a long time ago. There was no baseball then. Not for him anyway. So he did it with rags."

⬩━━━━━➤

They were almost out of the driveway when Joey said, "I forgot the scorebook, Papa."

Anger flashed. "Goddamn it! Go get it! I told you I wanted to watch Johnny warm up!"

Joey ran into the house and Giuseppe waited, fuming, knowing that now he was no different than all the parents that he had watched for years, escaping from their hum-drum lives through the lives and deeds of their Little League kids. He honked the horn. Anger rose. If there was some way to screw something up, Joey would find it. He honked again and looked up at Joey's window. He got out of the truck and started for the back door. Scorekeeper or not, they'd leave without that goddamn book. "Joey!" he yelled, before he was in the house. And at that moment the back door opened and Joey stood at the threshhold, arm extended, holding out a black spiral notebook, smiling a fragile smile, a smile that said, please don't be mad at me, Papa.

Giuseppe said only, "Shit!" and turned in disgust, leaving the boy with his outstretched arm and no sign of a smile.

It was a twenty minute drive to the Little League field. Today's silence came from Giuseppe. Usually it came from Joey, so much so that Giuseppe had several times said, "Joey, you don't have to go to these games. Johnny won't mind. I won't mind." But the boy would always answer, if weakly, "I want to, Papa." This year had been better because the coach had made Joey—out of pity, Giuseppe thought—the team's scorekeeper, which meant that he had been given a team cap, a black cap with a gold P for Pirates, a cap which he wore pulled down tight, so that its sides pressed against and marked the beginning of his ear lobes, so that the bill of the cap seemed to extend a full foot in front of his face, but low, hiding his face and his glasses, which he still refused to wear in public. He wore the cap all day, every day, even to bed. It also meant that he got to sit with Johnny and his teammates in the dugout during the games rather than in the stands next to his father. As they neared the field, the hunched boy carefully took his glasses out of their metal case and then just as carefully put them on under his cap, first over one ear and then over the other. To his father, he cut a pathetic figure.

Once they arrived, Giuseppe Rocco could see from the truck that Johnny had not yet begun warming up. He looked over at the slight, hunched boy with the huge glasses and ridiculous cap and said, "I'm sorry, Joey."

And the boy said softly but quickly, "That's okay, Papa."

As soon as they parked, Joey slid out of the truck, score book in hand, and broke into his customary run towards his seat at the end of the Pirates' dugout. It was an ungainly trot, one in which each foot flared out to the side with every other stride. He'll never be a baseball player, thought Giuseppe as he got out of the truck and started for the stands.

The warm-up began with soft tosses that gradually increased in speed until the ball was streaking past Giuseppe and the others who were watching, streaking and slamming into Andy's mitt with loud and convincing pops. And then Giuseppe saw Andy remove his reddened hand from his glove and rub it against the side of his leg, saw his fingers go to his burning palm, and saw too the inch or two that he backed up each time he squatted for one of Johnny's pitches. Those were good signs.

When Johnny stepped off the warm-up mound, he stooped for his black jacket and then inserted only his right arm and shoulder into it and started for Andy. His face was solemn and his eyes were fixed straight ahead. "Looking good, Johnny!" "Way to look, kid," "Go get 'em, Johnny," the others said. But Johnny gave no indication that he had heard them. Silently, solemnly, Johnny and Andy walked back toward the dugout, like two pallbearers.

As they walked, Johnny's jacket began slipping off his shoulder so that the limp, empty left arm of the jacket was dragging on the ground as they approached the stands.

Giuseppe shook his head and smiled. "Johnny, if you're going to wear the jacket, wear it, put it on."

"Papa, you don't understand."

"What's there to understand? You either wear the jacket or you don't wear the jacket."

"Papa, that's how the pros do it."

"What pros? You don't even need a jacket. It's too damn hot anyway."

"The professionals, Papa. The major leaguers."

"This is Little League."

"So what, Papa, it keeps my arm warm."

"How can it keep your arm warm when it's falling off your arm?" They had had that conversation many times, but it had changed nothing.

When they reached the stands, cheers rose and Giuseppe could hear his son's name punctuating everything. "Johhhnneee! Johhhnneee! Johhhnneee!" And he smiled again.

"Don't you hear them cheering for you, Johnny? How can you not hear them?"

"I hear a noise, Papa, and sometimes I don't even hear that. But I never hear them."

"What do you mean you don't hear them? How can you not hear them?"

"I guess I'm just thinking about the game, about what I have to do, about what I want to do."

"Every other boy grins at them or waves at them or tips his cap."

"I don't want to be like every other boy, Papa." Nothing could have warmed Giuseppe Rocco's heart more.

Then the two boys disappeared into the dugout and Giuseppe walked to the stands. Once there, the familiar remarks began. "Has he got it today, Giuseppe?" "Did you tell him how important this game is, Mr. Rocco?" "How's his arm?" "We're counting on him, Mr. Rocco." Twice he said, "Not to worry. My Johnny will do it."

And Johnny did do it, striking out thirteen of the first fifteen batters he faced. Only the opposing pitcher, a giant of a boy, a good head taller than Johnny, who was as tall as most, managed to hit the ball. Twice he swung mightily only to tap the ball weakly back towards Johnny, who quickly pounced on it as he ran towards the batter, not looking or even thinking of throwing the ball to first base, but rather instantly choosing to chase and catch and confront and personally tag out the giant boy hard, so hard that it brought boos and jeers from the other team's fans, but boos and jeers that Johnny didn't hear. His only concern then was staring down the giant boy with that fierce hateful look for having dared hit the ball or having challenged him, or, better, for being on the same field with him.

Johnny did do it, coming to bat in the top of the sixth and final inning with the score tied at zero. Long before Johnny stepped into the batter's box, he glared out at the boy giant on the mound, not once taking his eyes off him, even as he readied himself next to the plate, glaring, hating. Not once did the boy giant look at Johnny, even though he was facing him, looking down and past him instead for the catcher's sign, looking past him as he wound up and brought his huge left leg up and half way to the plate and threw a streak of his own. Johnny met it with one quick vicious swing and sent it high and deep and far, and watched as all the others turned to watch what there was no need to watch, what was a certainty from the moment the aluminum bat met that strip of horsehide.

And only when the ball bounced high and deep in the parking lot beyond the fence did Johnny drop his bat and begin his uncontested trot around the bases. There was bedlam in the stands and along the third base dugout, bedlam that he did not hear as he started his trot more out of instinct or memory than design. Because he was aware only of the boy giant, the stunned, crestfallen boy giant who was now fighting back tears. With each step he glared and nodded at him who would not look back. When he rounded second base, the boy giant's back was to him; still he glared. When he reached third base, he could see his face again, and he glared all the more. Coaches and players slapped at him there and ran to meet him at home plate. But he didn't see them or feel them or hear them. He saw only the beaten one. And he continued to glare even as he reached the plate, hoping beyond hope that their eyes would meet, if only for an instant, to cap what was rightfully his. Until he touched the plate and his teammates mobbed him and took his eyes, but not his consciousness, from the beaten one.

At the edge of the jumping, mobbing teammates stood Joey, unnoticed, clutching his scorekeeper's book and smiling clumsily. In the stands when the clamor died down, when he and all the others sat down, Giuseppe Rocco was not sure what he had enjoyed more: the homerun, or the trot around the bases, or Johnny's glare at the beaten one. It was the glare that returned again and again.

Giuseppe watched as Johnny strode out to the mound to pitch the final inning. All around him people were shouting, "Come on, Johnneeee!" "You can do it, Johnneee!" "Just three more!" And Johnny walked with purpose, his face grim and eager and alone. He promptly struck out the first two batters on six pitches. That brought the boy giant to the plate. Johnny threw two streaks past him for strikes. They were as hard as any pitches he had thrown, slamming into Andy's glove above the din of the crowd. Then the crowd was on its feet in anticipation of the last strike as Johnny stood on the mound looking down not at Andy but at the boy giant. And he threw another streak. But this one hit Andy's arm, and Andy spun to the ground clutching his arm, whimpering and then crying. Coaches and players ran to Andy. Johnny remained on the mound, staring instead at the boy giant who had long since looked away. Then the coach motioned for, shouted for, and then started for Johnny. Only then did Johnny move off the mound toward the plate, occasionally pounding his fist into his glove.

"Andy's hurt, Johnny." For the first time Johnny saw that Andy was crying, sitting on the ground at the center of a circle of legs, holding on to his left arm. "He's hurt, and no one else can catch you. For Christ's sake, ease up. This guy's afraid of you. He's standing six feet away from the plate. Throw him an outside strike and the game's over. But for Christ's sake, ease up. You don't have to throw so hard. You don't have to kill Andy to get this guy out." The coach had Johnny by the arm, squeezing now as the sobbing Andy looked up. "You're gonna ease up, aren't you, Johnny?" But Johnny was looking at the boy giant. He gave the slightest of nods and turned and started for the mound. And the coach said, "See, Andy, he's gonna ease up. Come on, get up, let's get this third strike. Let's get this game over with." The next pitch was harder than any Johnny had thrown. And the boy giant swung and missed, but the frightened Andy let the ball skip past him and the boy giant ran to first as the crowd groaned.

As soon as the next hitter settled himself in the batter's box, the coach went to the mound, motioning for Andy. "You don't have to throw rockets, Johnny. Did you see where this kid was standing? He's afraid of you. He's almost out of the batter's box. Anything on the outside part of the plate will get him. Ease up."

Again Johnny threw hard. The first two strikes Andy managed to catch scooting back onto the umpire behind him with both. Then Johnny threw another hard fastball and the batter timidly swung and missed. But this time Andy scooted back so far that he knocked the umpire and himself over as the ball carromed off the backstop and the runners went to second and third as Andy struggled first to get up and then to find the ball.

Again the coach went to the mound. In the stands there was concern. One more passed ball and the score would be tied; two more and the game would be over. At the mound, Andy was crying, but now for a different reason. "I'm sorry, Johnny. I'm not doing it on purpose. I'm not trying to lose the championship."

Johnny was watching the boy giant at third base, who now, for the first time, was returning his look, openly smiling, even taunting Johnny. "Just catch the ball," Johnny said coldly, abstractly, not once looking at the pleading, sobbing Andy.

"I'm trying to, Johnny."

"Just catch the ball."

"He's trying to, Johnny, but you're throwing it too damn hard."

"Put Billy in. He's not afraid," he said, still glaring at his now brazen tormentor.

"He may not be afraid to catch you, but he blinks when the batter swings. You know that. Two swings and two blinks and this game is over. We lose."

"How many guys do I have to strike out anyway. I've already struck out four this inning and I'm still pitching."

"Nobody says you're not pitching a great game, Johnny. All I'm saying is that you'd better ease up a little or we're gonna lose. Two more passed balls and we lose. How many times do I have to tell you that."

Johnny's eyes and mind were still on the boy giant who was now dancing on and off third base, returning his glare with a mocking grin.

Then he was alone on the mound again, facing a frightened batter and a frightened catcher while the boy giant yelled at him and laughed at him and bluffed a run at the plate from third base. Johnny threw another blur of a pitch that the batter swung at feebly and missed. Andy shifted again, and the ball shot past him and the umpire, untouched, and slammed off the backstop twenty feet away. The boy giant broke for home. And Johnny burst for home plate too. Then it was clear that the ball and the boy giant's paths would converge just a few feet from the plate and that Johnny was heading there too.

Giuseppe rose with the others as the ball slowly squirted toward the rushing two, the boy giant on his left and Johnny directly before him. Then he saw the boy giant lunge, leap head first, arms outstretched, diving in mid-air as if to thread past and through the driven boy and the spinning ball. Johnny dove, at both the boy giant and the ball. They collided violently: the sound of flesh slamming against flesh, the thud of bones, the fall and the dust that rose from that fall, not only from the dirt but from the base line too. There were the grunts and the gasps as the two boys lay on the ground, locked shoulder to shoulder, each with an arm outstretched, reaching, one for the plate just inches away, the other for the ball just inches away.

And for those moments, which would be forever frozen in his mind, Giuseppe Rocco saw his son's eyes, bulging and taut, wild and tormented, but determined, as if everything in life depended on his reaching the now stationary ball. Then, with one final lunge, Johnny grasped the ball and in the same motion tagged the struggling boy giant. The umpire shouted and gestured with his right arm, "You're out!"

And all around Giuseppe Rocco there was joy and rapture, screaming and shouting, laughing and embracing. Giuseppe just stood motionless, his eyes fixed on the two boys who were still spread on the ground, but seeing neither, seeing only, as he would from time to time for the rest of his days, that fierce, violent, determined look in his son's eyes, a look which could only have come from Giuseppe Rocco.

Joey had watched too, watched from the corner of the dugout as Johnny struck out batter after batter; watched his father and the people around him, watched as they stood and cheered with each strikeout, as they shouted and spoke their joy into Giuseppe's ears and even dared touch him and slap him in their excitement. He had watched his father beam, growing prouder and happier with each strikeout, watched him sitting and standing erect and proud with a look for Johnny that he would never have for him.

When Johnny had come to bat in the sixth inning, everyone in the park, except for Joey, rose to their feet. In the dugout the others moved to the dugout's edge. The cries for Johnny roared through the park. Only Johnny had hit the big pitcher; if he didn't hit him now, the game could well be lost. The cries hunched Joey closer to his scorebook, so that the bill of his cap was inches from it. So hunched, he could not see what he knew he did not want to see, what he knew they would all see. Joey knew that Johnny would not strike out. Joey knew that Johnny would hit the big pitcher. Joey knew that Johnny would win the game. And for the first time in more than three years, Joey knew, no, let himself know, that he wanted Johnny to strike out. So he busied himself with his scorebook as the crowd screamed, erasing that which did not need erasing, rewriting that which did not need rewriting. Then he heard the crack of the bat and heard and saw what he knew he would hear and see, and more: the team jumping up and down ecstatically, hugging and squeezing one another, and then running out onto the field to meet Johnny, to lift him and praise him and worship him.

And he had looked up into the stands, not to see his father's reaction, because he knew what that would be, but rather to see if his father had seen him alone in the dugout. But his father saw only Johnny. So he sat erasing and rewriting until he began to feel that the others would know, or at least suspect, what he felt for Johnny. Then it was that he ran out onto the field too, with his ungainly trot and his forced smile.

For the rest of the inning Joey had sat dreading the inevitable, as much because he would be found out as because he wouldn't be able to hide his anger and disappointment when Johnny won again. But hope flickered when Andy missed the first third strike, and he felt his heart pounding on the second missed third strike. Two more passed balls and Johnny would lose. Then there was another passed ball and he, like the rest of the team, leaped up to see, but for a different reason. Then there was Johnny's lunge, and more cheers and cheers and cheers.

Still, no one found him out, no one suspected. Because after the game, no one even noticed him.

<hr>

Giuseppe listened for them. The team and the coaches had a victory celebration at a pizza parlor, but he went to eat alone at Nick's. His two sons would go to Johnny's room and there replay the game. Just after 8:45 he heard them come up the stairs; then he heard Johnny's door close. He waited. He would give them fifteen or twenty minutes alone. They were close then, they were brothers then, Joey recollecting and recounting all that Johnny had not seen or heard. Often it seemed as if Johnny had not been there, that it was Joey who had played. Johnny would sit there mesmerized, his open, soft face absorbing and imagining and enjoying all of Joey's details.

But he could only wait five minutes. Then he moved silently, carefully, down the hall so that she and Matthew would not hear. He opened the door quietly, and only Johnny greeted him. Now there was no recounting, no celebrating. Instead they sat silently, Johnny on the bed and Joey on the floor, waiting for him. They knew he would come.

Giuseppe said, "Hey, what's the matter? You guys don't seem too happy for such a big game."

Only Johnny looked at Giuseppe, and he said, "Papa."

"Yes, son?" It was a yes, son, that said ask me anything, ask me for anything, and it's yours.

"You know on Saturday me and Joey are getting confirmed."

"I know."

"And you know Mama's throwing this big party for us afterwards."

"I know."

"Are you coming?"

"Sure I'm coming."

"Papa, can I ask you a favor?"

"Ask me anything you like."

"Papa, can you dress up for the party?"

"What?" And again the room fell silent. "Dress up! Dress up! What do you mean by that, Johnny?" he asked even though he did not want to know.

"You know, wear a suit."

"I don't have a suit."

"Buy one, Papa."

"What's the matter with you, Johnny, are you crazy?"

"He's got a girl friend," Joey said sullenly.

"Liar!"

"You have a girl friend, Johnny?"

"Yeah, Mary Ann Licalsi," Joey continued without looking up, without looking at his father.

"You better shut up, Joey."

"You have a girl friend, Johnny? Don't you think you're a little young for that?"

"I have a friend who's a girl, Papa."

"Licalsi? Licalsi? Who's her father?"

"He's the doctor," Joey finished.

"Oh, I see . . . Are they coming to the party, Johnny?"

"I didn't invite them, Papa."

"Are they coming to the party, Joey?"

"Yeah, Mama invited them."

And then for several minutes, it seemed, Giuseppe Rocco looked out at the night through the window's black glass. Then he said, "Are you ashamed of me, Johnny?"

"No, Papa."

"Are you ashamed of the way I dress?"

"No, Papa."

"My clothes are always clean, aren't they?"

"Yes, Papa."

"When you tell me that you don't want to be like all the other boys, do I ever tell you that you have to be like them?"

"No, Papa."

"Then why should you want me to be like everybody else?"

Giuseppe paused and stared at the black window. Then he said, "You know, I've never said this to either of you because I never thought there was any reason to say it. But now I want to say it. For me. Listen carefully. Saturday, your mother will probably have a hundred people here, a lot of fancy people, including Doctor Licalsi and his wife. Well, you take all those people and put them together and I can buy and sell them a hundred times over. I have a hundred times more money than all of them put together. I can buy all the fancy suits and shoes and watches and rings and cars that I want to. But I don't want to. Do you understand? I don't want to. Why? Because I don't want to be like them. Do you understand?"

Johnny stood with his head bowed.

"Do you understand, Johnny? Especially you, Johnny, who tells me you don't want to be like the other boys. I don't want to be like them."

"Yes, Papa."

"And let me tell you one thing more. Tomorrow afternoon at four o'clock, the governor of California will come here, to my house, to visit me. You'll see. How many other people in San Jose do you know that he comes to visit? The television people will be here, the newspaper will be here, the police will be here, a whole bunch of people will be here. You'll see. And you know why he's coming? To ask me for money. That's right, to ask your father, Giuseppe Rocco, for money. And I'll meet him on the porch and both of you can be there with me. And you know how I'll be dressed? Just like I always dress. Just like I'm dressed now."

———

Giuseppe arrived just after the party began, which was much earlier than he usually arrived. Usually his appearance was just that, an appearance, just enough so that everyone understood that this was his house and that he had made possible everything they were enjoying. But today he was early because Joey had burst into his room that morning with the morning paper.

"Look, Papa, you're on the front page with the governor! And everybody saw you on television last night! All of Johnny's friends called him and told him!"

He had stared with satisfaction at the photograph that took up most of the top half of the front page, a photograph that showed him, in his customary attire, shaking hands with the governor there on the front porch of the old Victorian mansion. He slowly read the caption aloud: "Local pro-min-ent business man meets with governor."

He looked at Joey and smiled. "I like that word."

"Which word, Papa?"

"Prominent."

The outdoor party was blessed with a wonderful early June afternoon. Bright awnings had been erected to shield food, and drink, and musicians, and guests. The stately old trees shaded the huge side lawn. The stark white of the outdoor furniture emphasized the lushness of the lawn, and shrubs, and flowers. Chamber music was provided by a group of eight musicians clad in black dresses and tuxedos, who sat in one corner of the lawn, sternly rasping out their music.

People were arriving when Giuseppe appeared. Rita Verducci had stationed herself and Matthew near the pathway from the front lawn and was greeting the new arrivals. She wore a long white dress that she had purchased for the party and she had her hair layered in ascending spirals. Next to her stood Matthew in a suit and tie. Giuseppe had watched them from the rose garden before entering. She looked elegant; he would give her that. She loved her role: the gracious, charming hostess, queen of all she surveyed. She had a smile and kind word for everyone, and to everyone she introduced Matthew, who in turn smiled and shook hands and held himself as if he were already the man of the house.

It didn't take long for the sight to anger Giuseppe, and abandoning his plan, he started toward them, knowing that the sight of him would wipe the smiles and graciousness from their faces and expose them, as it often did, or at least he thought it often did, for the mean, cruel, hateful people that they were. But a woman stopped him, a woman whom he recognized, but whose name he did not know.

"Mr. Rocco, Mr. Rocco. How does it feel to be a celebrity?" She was an attractive woman in her early forties. Her face was bright, and her eyes shone with admiration.

"Oh, I'm not a celebrity. I'm just Giuseppe Rocco."

"Not anymore you're not. Everybody's been talking about you. We all see how much you're doing for San Jose."

And then there was another woman, and a man too, and then several others. And the more that came, the more that were drawn, until most of the people at Rita Verducci's party had crowded around him, asking about the governor, about the mall. It was more attention than he had anticipated, and he was uncomfortable until he saw the looks on Rita Verducci's and Matthew's faces. Suddenly he relished his new role and his voice grew louder, confident, and he smiled and took a glass of wine from a server and continued.

"You know, the governor's kind of like me . . . Don't get me wrong. I'm not saying I'm like the governor. I'm just a hard-working, uneducated Italian. Look at my hands. They didn't get this way from turning pages in a book. What I mean is that the governor is a kind of an everyday fellow. I would have never believed that before. But you know, we were together for over an hour, just me and him, and he's just an ordinary guy like me and you. We talked about everyday things. About business and how San Jose is growing and the population explosion here, about our favorite food and wine. He's a nice man. He . . ." And he was growing nicer even as Giuseppe Rocco spoke, because gone, forgotten, was the tension that had built as Giuseppe Rocco had waited for the well-groomed man in the dark suit on that Friday afternoon to ask him for money in his own home, which, just before he left, he did.

The crowd grew larger. They came directly to him once they had greeted Rita and Matthew. And now he would routinely look over to them and see the hate on their faces and smile and wink. The two finally abandoned their position, angry and upset, and hurried past him and his admirers to the farthest end of the lawn.

Giuseppe Rocco was not to be denied. He excused himself saying, "I've got to see what my sons are up to, those little rascals." And then started toward the farthest end of the lawn too, and was within fifty feet of them again, when he saw Johnny under a veranda surrounded by four giggling girls. The sight stopped him. It won't be long now, he thought. Look at those little bitches. And they'll let him, too. They'd let him right now if he knew what to do. That's the last goddamn thing I need right now: a grandson. It would ruin him. Just look at him. He can get anything he wants. He can be anything he wants. Anything. If he just doesn't stray.

"Mr. Rocco," It was that first woman. She was a good-looking thing. Well preserved. And she liked him. But before he could talk to her, others surrounded them. And it irritated him, until he saw how irritated Rita and her son were again. So he relaxed and took another glass of wine from a server and talked about the governor some more, as if he were an old friend, revealing things about the governor that if they weren't true, should have been true. And now Johnny and the girls joined the crowd, and soon Joey was there too. Then almost everyone, except Rita Verducci and her son, gathered to listen to the amiable, affable celebrity.

"Like I say, the governor knows that San Jose and Santa Clara County are the fastest-growing areas in the state. He knows there are votes here. And he looked me right in the eye and said . . ." He paused long enough for a woman to interrupt, "Mr. Rocco, I see that two of your sons are here. Can we get a picture of you and your sons?" Johnny and Joey blushed, but Giuseppe Rocco said, "Sure, why not!" even as he saw that Rita Verducci and her son had had enough and were moving once again. He couldn't have been happier. As Rita and Matthew skirted the crowd, the woman said, "How about getting your wife and your other son in . . ." But Rita was shaking her head no and quickening her pace, leaving Matthew behind. The woman approached Matthew and said, "Come on, little man, let's get you in the picture with your dad and brothers too." The boy froze, and the woman tugged, and the boy's chin sank. A man who was standing nearby scooped up the boy. "Come on, big fellow, let's get you into the picture. It won't hurt you." Matthew writhed and twisted and struggled and began screaming, "Let me go! Let me go! I hate him! I hate him! He's mean to my mother! He's mean to her! He kicks her and beats her! I hate him! I hate him!"

The man released Matthew near his father and brothers. The boy slumped down on the grass and continued to writhe, face down, on the lawn, sobbing and crying hysterically, "I hate him! I hate him!"

———

Annie died that afternoon.

Nick told him on Monday morning. It was one of the few times that Nick had done anything other than nod when Giuseppe entered the restaurant. "Until she got sick we were here every morning, five days a week, at 5:30 in the morning for over twenty years, rain or shine."

Only Nick and Lorie, the other morning waitress, and himself were at the funeral chapel the next night. After the brief service, Nick said, "She lived alone. Her husband left her for another woman years ago. He brought her here from Norway and left her here. She had no children. What family she had is still in Norway. I didn't know how to reach them."

Giuseppe waited until Nick and Lorie were gone. Then he moved to the first pew and sat with Annie, watching her sleeping face in the open casket. He sat there for several hours remembering the care and gentleness with which she had slid those cups of coffee towards him for all those thousands of mornings. And he remembered too what now was so clearly the love in her eyes as she said, "Good morning, Giuseppe." And it seemed now, in the emptiness of the chapel, that it would have taken so little to have given her so much. And he cried.

"We'll be closing in fifteen minutes," said a small man in a black suit behind him. Giuseppe nodded and waited for his footsteps and then, with his hat in hand, he went up to the casket and looked down at the heavily powdered face and at the oncoming green beneath it and said, "You gave me so much, Annie. I saw it every day." And he kissed her, kissed the cold, stiff, lipstick-red lips and cried again. "You deserved better."

The next morning, the next day, had no beginning or end. It was one of those fog-soddened days that drooped from and returned to the night's grey-black. As Giuseppe got into his pick-up, he cursed the sky and thought, Today of all days, You could at least have given her a bit of sunshine.

Only Nick and he were at the funeral chapel. Just before the casket was closed for the final time, Giuseppe kissed those frozen lips. Goodbye, Annie, wherever you are. Then the casket was wheeled to the hearse and the driver said, "Well, unless somebody else shows up at the cemetery, it looks like you gentlemen are the pallbearers. I can't do it because of my back. But I'll get some of the grave diggers to help."

At the cemetery, as they circled the grave sites, Nick said, "You know, she came out here three or four years ago and started looking. She came at least a dozen times, but it could have been more. She came on the bus. She didn't have a car. And she told me that she came at different times of the day and different times of the year to see what the day and the season would be like on the plots that she liked. After that, she picked one and then made a down payment and monthly payments just like you would on a house."

When the casket was whirred halfway out of the hearse, the driver said to the two lone men, "Let me get those two boys over there," looking in the direction of two Mexicans who were standing waist-high, shovels in hand, at the opposite ends of a new grave. He motioned to the Mexicans, who immediately jumped out of the grave and walked quickly and subserviently toward the hearse. Giuseppe Rocco recognized the walk, and the shabby clothes, and shoes, and thought this was no time to be ordering anyone around.

Once the Mexicans neared the hearse, they stopped and removed their broad-brimmed palm leaf hats and blessed themselves and whispered momentary prayers for Annie. Giuseppe removed his hat, and when the Mexicans laid their hats on the lawn before touching the coffin, he left his side of the coffin and walked around to lay his hat with theirs.

There was a singular grunt when they lifted the coffin, more casket than Annie. He longed to stop and open that box and lift Annie and carry her the rest of the way to her grave.

They laid the coffin on five wooden slats over the open grave and then waited for the minister, who soon arrived with a prayer book in hand, from which he read a few prayers and then spoke of God's scheme of things. Giuseppe wondered how Annie fit into that scheme: alone, childless, and unloved. What reason could God have had for placing Annie on this earth?

Then the preacher was gone. And the driver too. Only he and Nick remained with the Mexicans, who lowered the coffin into the grave until it would lower no further. From that huge mound of dirt next to the grave they began filling what they had uncovered just hours before. Giuseppe Rocco heard the first shovelful of dirt land on top of the coffin with a heavy thud, loud, final, and resolute. Someday a shovel would release a first shovelful of dirt on him. The only consolation he had was that not a single person on the face of the earth would escape a similar fate.

As he turned to go he said, "I love you, Annie. I hope what you have now is better than what you had here."

Chapter V

Johnny was gone. He had left on an afternoon flight for Phoenix. From there he would go to Northern California and Oregon with twenty-five teammates for a summer of baseball. For twenty years, the old Victorian mansion across the street had been Giuseppe Rocco's home. But Johnny would never return, and there was no reason for Giuseppe to stay.

The scouts and the coaches had come from every part of the country, from all the major league teams and major colleges. In the end, it had been Carlo Rossi who had decided. "Giuseppe, Johnny doesn't need the money. He needs an education. He doesn't need to be trudging through the Georgia swamps for four or five years before he gets to the major leagues, if he gets to the major leagues. What the coaches said was true: many of today's big stars came off the college campuses. Even if he makes it to the major leagues, and there's no guarantee that he will, regardless of what all the scouts and coaches say, he can't play baseball forever. His career will be over by the time he's thirty-five and probably long before that. Few of them last that long. And he'll still have more than half of his life to live. What will he do then? He needs an education, Giuseppe."

Giuseppe looked over at the house, at its outline in the night lights. In fact, he was all but moved out now, having moved a bit at a time since the beginning of spring into a modest house on forty acres, tucked into a beautiful valley at the foot of the coastal range west of Gilroy and Morgan Hill. Since then, he had come and stayed at this house only on the nights when Johnny or Joey were having dinner there. Still, it was hard to leave and he didn't know why. He was sixty-three now, and he had given that house twenty years of his life, almost a third of his life. Who knew how much longer he would live?

Now it was eleven o'clock and both Rita and Matthew would be in bed. At most, it would take two or three trips into the house to load the few things that remained in his room. As he pulled around to the back porch entrance, he was surprised to see Joey's car. Joey had told him at the graduation ceremony that he was going to Lake Tahoe for three days before he started full-time at Giordano's Market for the summer. Still, he entered as quietly as he could, but once he opened the kitchen door, he heard shouting, the shouting of an unfamiliar female voice.

"I don't care whose house this is, you have no right to do this!"

From the dining room door, Giuseppe Rocco saw the back of a slender, dark-haired girl standing at the foot of the staircase with her hands on her hips. Behind her was Joey and to their right Matthew, both of whom were also looking up the staircase. Then Rita Verducci answered from above. "I've told you that this is my house and I don't want you in it. Now please leave."

"And I've told you that I'm Joey's wife, and everything in his room is his and we have a right to take it! If you don't get out of the way, I'll move you out of the way!"

"I've already called the police."

"I don't care who you've called! Call the FBI, too! I'm coming up to get his stuff and you're not gonna stop me!"

❧ Book Two ❧

Chapter I

Sally Martínez. Oldest daughter of Concepción Ramírez, who in turn was the sixth of nine children born to Ignacio and Filomena Ramírez, who left the migratory fields of central and northern California when Concepción was ten and settled in East San Jose. There Ignacio Ramírez was able to get his first steady job as a janitor and promptly lost, as he and Filomena haplessly watched, all control of their remaining offspring to the customs and values of the barrio's youth. Connie, as her peers immediately christened Concepción, gave birth, at thirteen, to Sally in the home of her fifteen-year-old lover. The scene was repeated a year later in the home of another boy after the first boy found another girl and disclaimed that first child. It was repeated again and again, until at twenty-five she had seven children by seven different fathers and her social worker threatened, and then cut off, her funds, until she finally had the operation that ended the cycles.

Sally's earliest memory was of a man. She couldn't have been more than four. He was hunched over her bed. The outline of his figure was a huge mass against the sheet-covered window. Light always filtered through that sheet, giving shape and form to the sleeping, breathing lumps in the room. For a long time, the man remained motionless. When he did move, it was only his hands that moved, and they were hidden, one by the darkness, and the other by the blanket. First came the flat object against her lips. "Candy," he whispered. And the flick of her tongue assured her, yes, it was candy. And she licked again and again. Until she felt the finger of the hand that was already between her legs move, move up to her pee-pee and begin to enter. And she screamed and screamed, and then the baby screamed, and then her brother who lay next to her in the tiny bed screamed. And the man fled out the bedroom door and then out the only other door of the cramped apartment. But Connie didn't scream, Connie didn't turn, Connie didn't wake up.

It was because Connie could not wake up. Sally would not know, understand, that for several years yet, after many men of all sizes and shapes and shades of brown had visited her mother's bed in that same small cramped bedroom that grew only by the number of children that shared it with Connie. But Sally would wake up, as would her brothers and sisters, to the creaks, and grunts, and pounding of their mother's bed against the wall, and sometimes too from the pounding and shouts that came from the other side of that sheetrock wall: "Knock it off in there! We're trying to sleep!" Too often Sally would hear, in that tumult, her mother's voice from somewhere in that darkness, from somewhere under the thrusting mass that hulked over her, from somewhere buried in that bed. "Do you love me." It was never a question; it was always a plea, a plaintive plea that sometimes became more explicit. "Tell me you love me. Please tell me." And more often than not the gasping hulk would pant, "I love you, baby. Oh, do I love you." It was always a short-lived love. Once the groans had passed, there were the flights, "I gotta go, I gotta go," or the insults, or the beatings, or simply the loud snoring.

There were times when Sally slept with a knife under her mattress. She could see in the man's eyes that Connie was just a pretext. Twice, once when she and once when Angie would have been the victims, Sally sliced a hand groping in the darkness.

And then came the jail visits. At five or six, when Sally was old enough to watch whichever brother or sister was being presented to the locked-up man as his son or daughter. Because Connie's presentation would be brief, and the man's interest even briefer, Sally would have to chase and catch and coddle and quiet the disinterested toddler of the day, while Connie visited with her caged love. And there, too, she would hear Connie's pleas for love. In that caged setting, she would hear more: vows of love, of undying eternal love, exchanged from both sides of the steel mesh, of a love that was born in heaven and was meant to be, but which too often ended once the man was released and he had taken Connie's body and whatever little money and drugs that she had. Invariably, there was talk of sex, initiated by the hungry man who brought with him every fantasy he had concocted in his cell over the past weeks.

Then, too, there were the visits, though not as often, at intervals of months and even years because of the distance, to those huge complexes in the middle of nowhere with enormous walls and fences, and above them the gun towers where capped men looked down on everything with their silhouetted rifles. The state prisons. And before, during, and after those visits came the letters in envelopes that at the very least were decorated in an elaborate fancy script or printing as if the writer had put on his best writing suit, or shirt, or jeans. Often those envelopes and the letters they contained were adorned with intricate, distinctly Mexican drawings, self-taught drawings that invariably depicted a strong, bold, defiant Mexican man and a beautiful, wistful, long-suffering Mexican woman. The drawings themselves promised love and fidelity against all odds. Many of the letters were carefully crafted. They began with, "My sweetest love," "My dearest darling," or whatever other dulcet words lurked in those dark cells. "It has been so long, much too, much too long since these arms of mine have held your warm and beautiful body . . ." They were words designed to be sweet music, words designed to hold, to clutch and hold. Connie had hundreds of such letters neatly stored in shoe boxes, shoe boxes that she somehow managed to take from place to place, despite her many moves. There were eight such shoe boxes under her bed on the day she died.

There was one visit to a California state prison that Sally always remembered. She had just turned ten, and Danny Madrid, Rachel's father, had been writing Connie for months, asking her to come and visit so that their love of three years past could be rekindled, so that he could meet his daughter for the first time, so that they could begin building a foundation, a future for that day when he would be released and they could once again be together. This time, he swore, it would be forever, this time they would marry, this time he would get a righteous job and make Connie an honest woman and become a father, not only to Rachel, but to the others as well. Connie loved the letters. She read them over and over again. She slept with them. She read parts of them to Sally, who said, "I don't believe him, Connie."

But Connie would not be discouraged. "Listen to this . . ." And she would read yet another passage.

Sally would answer, "He didn't come over that much when he was out, except when he wanted something. I wouldn't remember him, except for that time he locked us all up and then beat you up, and I had to jump out the window and go call the police because I thought he was going to kill you."

Still, they didn't visit for months, because the prison with a funny-sounding name was up in the mountains someplace far away, and they didn't have a car, and the closest Greyhound bus stopped ten miles away. One day, a letter arrived saying that Big Smiley, one of Danny's homeboys, would pick them up early one Saturday morning and drive them to and from the prison.

Then began the preparations, or better, the alterations. Connie would take the few dresses and skirts that she had and try them on endlessly in front of Sally and the only mirror they had in the one-bedroom apartment, a mirror that was fastened to the door of the medicine chest which hung over the sink in the bathroom. Connie would stand in high heels on the toilet bowl and turn and stare, and turn and stare some more, into that mirror. She would ask Sally, "How does it look?"

Sally would say, "It's too short."

And Connie would say, matter of factly, "That's how Danny likes them."

Then she would get down from the toilet bowl and take the hem up another inch, climb up on the toilet bowl again and look and say, "Not bad for a broad with six kids, huh?"

Sally would resentfully look at the still shapely, smooth, firm, brown legs and say, "Yeah, but you got no waist, and your ass is getting flatter, and you're only twenty-three."

"Yeah, but I can hide that, and with these high heels and this short skirt, he won't look anywhere past these fine brown legs."

Big Smiley arrived at the appointed day and time. He wore dark glasses, even though it was still dark out.

He said, "I'm Big Smiley. Homeboy sent me a kite saying for me to pick you up." He didn't smile.

Sally answered in a hushed tone, "My mom's not ready yet but come in. Everybody's asleep."

He came in, looked around, and sat down. Big Smiley was a short Mexican with slicked-back, black hair who wore a Pendleton shirt buttoned at the top, baggy khakis and black canvas shoes. The dark glasses hid much of his face; he could have been fifteen or thirty.

Sally said, "I'll be right back," and turned to tiptoe back to the bathroom. He still hadn't smiled.

Connie was where she had left her, as she had left her, standing on the toilet bowl looking over her shoulder into the mirror at the back of her legs.

"How do I look?"

"Like I told you all morning, Connie, you look good. Smiley's here. I got to get Rachel up and we got to go."

Connie turned one more time. This time the mini skirt flicked enough so that Sally caught a glimpse of one of Connie's cheeks.

"You got no underwear on!" she shrieked in a whisper.

"Yes, I do."

Sally didn't argue. She simply grabbed at what there was of the skirt and lifted it, exposing a clump of pubic hair above Connie's gathered legs.

"Danny doesn't want me to wear any underwear," Connie said as Sally held up her skirt.

Sally shook her head and let go of the skirt. "I'm not going. You go, but I'm not going."

"Danny doesn't want me to wear any. You want me to read you the letter. You can read it yourself. He doesn't want me wearing no underwear."

"I'm not going."

Then they stood in silence, Sally looking down at the toilet seat, and Connie looking down at Sally. Then Connie said, "All right, have it your way. I'll wear underwear. Go get Rachel ready while I finish getting ready."

"I'm not doing nothing 'til you put on underwear."

Connie sighed, got off the toilet bowl, went into the bedroom, and returned with a pair of black bikini panties, wiggled into them and said, "There! Are you satisfied now, Miss Priss?"

As they left, Sally asked, "What are you taking that for?" pointing to the overcoat that Connie was carrying.

"Because Danny wants me to."

"But it's still summer."

"Not in the mountains."

"How do you know?"

"Danny said so."

"Then why don't you put some clothes on, Connie!" she said, looking at her naked legs.

"I have clothes on," Connie answered, wriggling in her miniskirt.

They rode in silence in a primered car that had been lowered so that its floorboard was just inches above the roadway. They sat in seats that had been lowered too, so that only their heads, from the chin up, were visible in the windows. Big Smiley and Connie sat in the two front seats. Sally sat directly behind Connie with Rachel next to her, so that Sally could monitor how much of her legs or panties Connie was showing, not by looking over Connie's shoulders, but rather by watching how much, and how long, and how often Smiley turned towards Connie, even though his eyes were shielded by dark glasses. He turned and stayed turned for several moments, frequently at first, and then not at all. They drove through the great central valley as the sun came up, white and hot, in the east to continue parching the already cracked and dusty valley floor.

Not only did Big Smiley not smile, but he said nothing except for the three or four occasions when some white boys pulled up next to them and stared or grinned contemptuously down at them. "Sorry-ass motherfuckers best not be looking at us too long. They don't even know what I might be packing."

Just outside Bakersfield, Connie announced that she had to go to the toilet. Sally immediately said that she and Rachel had to go too, and when Big Smiley pulled into a gas station, Sally quickly followed Connie into the restroom. There was never any telling when Connie would resort to her syringe, and Sally did not want to arrive at the prison with a loaded mother. In the restroom, Sally watched Connie's feet under the door to see if they shifted in any way, and she watched through the crack in the door too.

"I'm taking a shit! Do you mind!" came the irritated voice from within the stall. "No, I'm not fixing!"

They left the valley floor and began climbing. The hills were hot, and barren, and dry, with nothing but an occasional giant rock to break their sameness. Big Smiley was turning again for long, longer intervals.

Sally asked, "How much longer is it?" hoping to break his stare.

"Not too much," he said while looking more at Connie's thighs than he was the road.

They were still climbing and Sally asked again, "How much longer?"

This time Big Smiley didn't answer, but he didn't stop looking either.

Sally scooted to the center of the back seat and then leaned between the two front seats, as much to interrupt Big Smiley's stare as to see how high Connie's skirt was.

"How much longer?"

"Not much," said Big Smiley, turning his head back to the road.

Connie's skirt had slid up as high as it could slide. Sally sighed and thought of the black panties: that was the most he could see. Sally stayed in her crouched position between the seats. Trees appeared, alone at first and then among rocks and then closer and closer to other trees. The constant blasts of air through the open windows became cooler and Sally turned back to see how high they had climbed. In the distance, far behind and below them lay the valley and a grey-white haze.

"Do you know how much more it is, Connie?" she said, needing to justify her crouch.

"How should I know? I never been up this way."

The blasts of air changed again, cooler, cold even.

"It's getting cool," Connie said.

"Yeah," Sally said, turning and taking Connie's overcoat from the back seat and tossing it onto Connie's lap. "You better cover yourself."

"It's not that goddamn cool," Connie said, pushing the coat down and onto the front floorboard.

The rise flattened, and Big Smiley pulled off the highway and wound the car through a row of houses, past a few stores and then more houses. In the distance were mountains, and soon a gun tower and then another and a third, and then the high cyclone fence and the concrete buildings, tall, straight, hard, shapeless, colorless, and unadorned.

"We're here," Big Smiley said.

Then Sally saw the cars and the stirring of people in the parking lot and the long line. Within minutes they were making their way to the line through the mostly worn and tired cars, without Big Smiley who had not once smiled. The line was made up mostly of women and children and an occasional man, mostly of brown and black and an occasional white. They took their places at the end of the line, which would eventually take them through a metal detector inside a shed just outside the prison gates. A cool wind blew across the open expanse from the mountains. Soon it was a cold wind.

"Aren't you glad you brought your coat, Connie?" said Sally.

"Danny told me to."

"But aren't you glad?"

"He wanted me to."

If Connie wasn't glad, Sally was. It would be bad enough when the guards made her take off the coat for the metal detector. Every male eye would be staring, devouring. And what would it be like without the coat in the visiting yard with hundreds of other men like Danny watching.

The line moved slowly, not unlike all the other lines Sally stood in with her mother and her brothers and sisters: the food stamp lines, the Medi-Cal lines, the soup lines, the welfare review lines, lines everywhere they went for everything they got. Few of the other women spoke to them. Most were fat and ugly, and Sally understood why they looked the way they did at Connie. Occasionally Rachel would stray or run after another kid. Sally would chase her and catch her and discipline her. Connie would say, "Why did you let her do that, Sally?"

Once past the metal detector, Sally held up the coat for Connie, afraid that Connie might forget it or shun it. "Button it, Connie," she said as soon as it was on. "It's going to be cold in there." Then they walked to and through the double gates and down the long walkway that led to the visiting yard. Whistling and catcalls poured out of the two buildings on each side of the walkway. The closer they got to the visiting yard, the louder and more constant the clamor became. "Oh, baby, what I could do to you!" "Looka here, baby, look what I got for you!" "Oh, sweetheart, you could sit on my face all night long!"

Inmates in the visiting yard began moving towards the gate to see what was causing the commotion. A loudspeaker blared, "Get away from the gate! Get away from the fence or all visits will be cancelled!" The surge stopped, and a slow retreat had begun when Connie and her daughters arrived at the gate. There were yelps from some of those retreating. The gate remained closed, and Connie and her daughters waited. A gust of cold wind swooped down on the gate and caught Connie's coat and skirt, lifting them. Sally saw what she thought she had seen earlier when some of the inmates had hooted and hollered from the buildings: Connie was wearing no underwear. Longer, louder cries went up. The loudspeaker blared again: "You have ten seconds to move away from the gate and the fence or all visits will be cancelled!"

The inmates retreated, and then the gate clanked and clattered and slowly cranked open. Sally froze. She looked for Danny, but could see him nowhere. Then the gate was open and Connie strode into the visiting yard confidently, head held high, as if it were her own back yard. Rachel ran after her. Sally looked up to the gun tower, hoping they would stop Connie, but to no avail. Connie was now three hundred feet into the yard and moving farther away. Sally ran after Connie. All around her she could feel the eyes of the inmates on Connie. She saw and heard the evil grins and dirty words and thoughts that came from their mouths. Connie walked on, absorbing, and yes, enjoying the looks and the words. She walked on, as if with purpose and design, to the far end of the yard, where Sally finally saw Danny sitting on the bench of the last picnic table. He faced them, grinning, just one of the many Mexican men clad in long denim jackets and rolled up denim pants. Connie quickened her pace.

When she was twenty or thirty yards from him, Connie broke into a run, high heels and all, and jumped onto the smiling, seated Danny. For a moment Sally was relieved, until she saw the gyrations and thrusts and heard the all too familiar groans and saw the two, coupled. They fell from the bench and Danny rolled over on top of her. Sally heard others running toward them, shouting. Connie was suddenly protesting and pounding on Danny's back with both fists. Shots rang out, and the oncoming men fell on their stomachs. There were more shots, and then everyone in the yard, except for Sally and Rachel, were lying flat on the ground. "Get down, kid! Get down!" Someone pushed them down. The whole yard was quiet except for Rachel's screams, and between them, Connie's whimpers.

It was almost dark when the angry guards released them. They had threatened Connie with jail and with placing Sally and Rachel in a shelter. They had called the district attorney, but he could find no statute that made it a felony, or even a misdemeanor, for a female visitor not to wear underwear into the prison. They had tried to question Connie, and in fact, questioned Sally and even Rachel about their mother's intent in coming to the prison, hoping to establish some sort of conspiracy to enter the prison to commit a lewd act. Connie only cried, and Sally only shrugged her shoulders and occasionally said no. Rachel only looked at them wide-eyed, threatening to cry.

Connie started drinking as soon as they reached the clump of stores in the tiny town outside the prison. And then she drank some more, drank all the way home. There was little Sally could do, because Connie would not stop crying, mumbling, slobbering again and again, "I got fucked but never got kissed. I got fucked but never got kissed."

It wasn't the shots, the guards, or even the coupling that would always bring Sally's mind back to that day, but rather the fact that Connie's unswerving decline began with that visit. Connie took to heroin as never before. All about the apartment, burnt spoons appeared, and with them dirty cotton balls and needles. The men increased, coming at all hours and leaving within minutes of their grunts. Connie walked or stood or sat in a dream-like state, hearing nothing, seeing nothing, feeling only the dream or trance. And when the number and frequency of the men declined, when even they found her unattractive, Connie took to stealing. Coats and jackets and sweaters and blouses and shoes and stockings and purses and shopping bags filled with cartons of cigarettes were gone within minutes of their arrival. And Sally took to stealing too. She stole from Connie, in her stupor, so that she could feed and bathe her brothers and sisters, so that she could keep them warm and dry.

Then Connie was arrested, and for Sally the horrors increased. She saw and heard the screams and pleas and tears of Billy and Danny and Rachel and Bobby as they were whisked away from the apartment, not to be seen again for more than a year. At the shelter, Elena clung to her hysterically, but to no avail. At the foster home, she and Angie were reunited. But the rejoicing was short-lived. The fourteen-year-old son of the foster parents soon discovered them and used Angie as a pawn. "If you don't, I'll do it to her and my mom will never believe anything you say."

It ended and then began again when Connie was released from jail. It was a different Connie, one who had aged ten or fifteen years in one, who sat and stared quietly out the window, or at the wall, or at her feet, without any drugs or alcohol, but doing little else. Instead of the men, there now appeared a probation officer and a social worker, randomly, at least once a week, to inspect Connie's arms and legs and feet and any other part of her body that had a useable vein, and to inspect the tiny apartment, not for cleanliness but rather for spoons and cotton balls and powdery residue. Slowly, the other children returned, one by one, until the family was completely reunited. Only then did Connie return to alcohol, but only alcohol, because it left no marks, no visible marks at least on her body.

It was about that time that Sally met Ralph Giordano, or rather that the confrontations with Ralph Giordano began. Connie had pointed him out to her from a distance. He was the owner of Giordano's Market some two miles from their apartment. It was a market at which they never shopped but one at which Connie and Sally regularly began scavenging, because Connie was convinced that, of all the markets, it threw out the best food.

They would leave their apartment early in the morning, as early as six, after Connnie had had a drink or two to steady herself, but well before she was drunk. In the beginning, they made the long walk in the winter darkness going at least every other day. It was easier in the dark. They could stand in the shadows across the street from the parking lot and watch, undetected, as Ralph Giordano and one of his workers brought out the wilting produce and souring milk and browning meat and stale bread and dumped them into two large garbage bins. Once they heard the final slam of the market's rear door and the dead bolt bang behind it, they would rush across the street with their rope bags and flashlight. At the bins, they would carefully open the lids and then Connie would boost Sally into a bin, hand her the flashlight, and then quickly take from Sally all of the food that their three bags could hold. And then they were gone.

As winter retreated, the scavenging became more difficult. If it wasn't light when they left their apartment, it was light when they reached the bins. Then they were in a neighborhood in which they were neither welcome nor wanted, in which they had no apparent reason to be. So they would keep in motion, walking up one street and down another, then over onto a different street and around and back through another, always returning to an edge of the parking lot until there appeared to be no further activity around the bins.

On the morning of Sally's twelfth birthday, Ralph Giordano confronted them. "Just what in the hell do you think you're doing!" he said in a loud, rough voice, coming out of nowhere.

Connie started to cry, and Sally stood up in the bin, wide-eyed and frightened.

"Goddamn it, Connie, it's you again! How many goddamn times do I have to tell you to stay off my property and not take my garbage! It is my garbage, you know! And now you bring your kid with you. Get the hell out of here, both of you! And if I catch you here again, Connie, kid or no kid, I'm going to call the cops and your butts are in jail!"

Connie's check came the next day, and for the next two and a half weeks there was enough money for Sally to feed everyone and keep Connie in her cheap wine. Towards the end of the third week, the money was gone. Again they returned to Giordano's Market, but now at night. It took them four nights to get there. On the first two nights Connie was too drunk to walk more than a block. On the third night, Sally made her take a nap, but she was still shaky, and they turned back after three blocks. The next morning, Sally gave Connie as much wine as she could drink. Connie was passed out by two, but by ten o'clock she was able to walk the two miles to Giordano's Market. It had been a hot day, and when Sally opened a bin, a steaming stench rushed up her nose turning her stomach. She climbed in anyway. There was nothing left to eat in the apartment. She sank into a rotting squish, waking flies and bees that had settled for the night. Taking the flashlight, she saw that she was standing in some sort of greenish brown slime. But there were several unbroken milk cartons and loaves of sealed bread and plenty of brown meat, although much of it had tiny white worms crawling about it. She took the meat anyway: the worms could be washed away and with a little trimming, the meat would almost be red. The next night, Billy and Angie were vomiting and feverish, and the following day everyone except Connie, who hadn't eaten, was sick.

They returned to Giordano's Market the next morning. Ralph Giordano saw them walking the adjacent streets, and as soon as they descended on the bins, the police were there. A tall, sandy-haired policeman with a creased face helped Sally out of the bin, where Ralph Giordano had insisted she stay until the police came. Then he took them aside, away from Ralph Giordano and the other man. Connie was crying, but that had little effect.

"Let's see your arms, Connie," he said matter-of-factly.

To Sally it seemed that everyone in the world who shouldn't know Connie knew her. Connie extended her arms and he looked closely at them.

"Just old scars. Let's see your feet and legs." He crouched down. Then he rose and said, "Well, you don't seem to be using unless you're sticking yourself in the butt. But I can smell the wine . . . Goddamn, Connie, what the hell are you doing down here going through this man's garbage? Don't you think I got better things to do than to come down here on a garbage rip-off?" Connie only cried.

Sally said, "We don't have any food at home."

For a long time, the tall policeman with the creased face looked at Sally, looked at the thin, pretty girl whose world had been, and would be, so different than his, until his eyes softened and he shook his head and said, "Goddamn it, Connie, there's a soup kitchen at St. John's Church over by where you live. They serve dinner there every other day. Take the kids there. I'm gonna let you go, but quit making my life difficult."

The soup kitchen got them to the first of the month. Connie quickly taught her kids how to hide and pilfer food from the soup kitchen for the following day. When the welfare check came, they continued going to the soup kitchen, hoping in that way to avoid returning to Giordano's Market. Two weeks later Connie disappeared.

Connie had disappeared in the past for as long as two days, but when she was still gone on the third day, Sally began looking for her. She and the older kids fanned out through the neighborhood, but there was no sign of Connie. Then Sally and Angie walked to and through the two-block skid row, peeking into the dank bars as they did: no Connie. That night Sally waited up, walking around the apartment complex and adjacent streets several times, hoping to find a fallen Connie: no Connie. Again Sally left the apartment door unlocked, but with the first sign of light there was still no Connie.

Panic set in. Without Connie, the shelter and foster homes became a reality again. If the probation officer or social worker learned of her absence, they would all be taken away. When they came the following week and searched the apartment as usual and accepted Sally's explanation that Connie had gone to Salinas for the day to visit her sister, Sally breathed easier.

There was still the matter of money. She didn't dare take the kids to the soup kitchen without Connie, because then people would know that Connie was gone. She budgeted as best she could, feeding the kids packaged soups and milk for a full week before the money was gone. There were four days until the first of the month. That night Bobby and Elena cried from hunger.

Sally left the apartment the next morning with the three rope bags while it was still dark. She dressed in pants and an old baseball jacket and with her hair tucked under Billy's baseball cap, lest anyone think she was a girl. Still, she dodged the few car lights that appeared on the deserted streets, ducking or crouching behind trees and shrubs and other parked cars. It was still dark when she reached Giordano's Market, but the sky behind her was quickly turning. She looked at the trees across the street from the garbage bins and then selected the biggest and darkest. There wasn't much time. Then she climbed the huge walnut tree, whose roots had long since uprooted the sidewalk around it and whose branches spread out across most of the darkened house behind it. She felt and climbed her way almost to the top with the rope bags hanging from her shoulder until she reached a limb that completely hid her while letting her see the garbage bins across the street.

She waited. Night became day. An hour later, Ralph Giordano drove up and walked past the bins to the store's rear door. A few minutes later, another man arrived. Still later, the rear door opened and the procession began: three boxes of produce, a box of dairy products, bread, and some dented cans, more than enough to get them through to the first. Then, after Ralph Giordano had dumped the last of the boxes, he looked around, looked, Sally thought, for any sign of Connie and herself. Satisfied, he went back into the store and slammed the lock bolt over the door.

Sally continued waiting, in case Ralph Giordano had forgotten something. Cars started using the side streets. She couldn't wait much longer. After a third car passed, she climbed down as quickly as she could, and then, looking in every direction, she ran across the street to the bins. She hoisted herself into one of the bins and had almost filled the first bag when she heard the door's bolt again. She grabbed for the bin's lid and brought it over her, letting it fall the last few inches to a bang that she had not expected. Then she crouched in the darkness, her heart racing, hoping that whoever was at the door hadn't heard the bang. If they found her, it would mean the police and then the shelter and then . . . She listened, motionless. The store's back door had to be open because she heard a man's voice. "Yeah, he's got a hair up his butt about those fricken bins. I don't see why he couldn't lock them. He was the last one there."

The words meant nothing to her except that they hadn't heard the lid's bang. If she could just stay still until they closed the door again, she would be . . . But then she heard the footsteps. She tightened, she held her breath, fear beat against every inch of her body. Then he was at the bins. He didn't raise the lid. Instead she heard some scraping at the next bin, and then the same scraping at her bin. And the man mumbled, "I'll be damned if I know why we have to lock these fricken things." Then she heard the click. And she screamed and kicked and slipped and pounded and rose and grunted against the immobile lid. "Stop! Stop! Let me out! I'm in here! I'm in here! Let me out! I'm gonna die in here if you don't let me out! Let me out!" The lid didn't budge, despite her pounding and kicking and screaming and crying for what seemed like forever. And when she heard the voices, she screamed even louder and pounded even harder. And then the lid opened, and three men looked down at her. She fell back down into the slime and covered her eyes and cried.

For a long time, Ralph Giordano simply watched. When he did speak, he said only, "Get her out of there, Fred."

Fred protested, "Hell, I'll get all that crap all over me."

Giordano pushed Fred aside and said to the sobbing girl, "Come on, let's get you out of there. Come on," he said quietly, leaning over the edge of the bin, helping her up, taking her arms and putting them around his neck and lifting the thin, slime-covered girl in one motion out of the bin and then carrying her with one arm under her knees and the other around her back to the door, saying quietly as he walked, "It's okay. There's nothing to cry about. It's okay. You're okay."

He carried her into his office and laid her on his couch and covered her with a blanket. "There's nothing to cry about, honey, there's nothing to cry about. It's gonna be all right. Just rest there for a minute and we'll get you cleaned up." He called for Jennie, and when Jennie came in, he said, "Have Fred wash out the lettuce tub and then have him put it in the women's restroom and fill it with warm water. Then I want you to give this girl a bath. Clean her up real good. And get Barbara over here."

To Barbara he said, "Find out her sizes and go over to Gottschalk's and get her some decent clothes and shoes. Get her a complete outfit. Hell, get her two oufits."

"And who's gonna watch the registers?"

"Hell, I've been checking since before you were born."

Later, when Barbara relieved him, she said, "Wait 'til you see her now."

What Ralph Giordano saw in his office this time was a beautiful, brown, almond-eyed girl with delicate features and smooth skin and fine, dark hair. Whatever remaining apprehension or reservation the girl had disappeared when he said softly, "I want you to tell me why you were in that garbage bin."

She told him of Connie's disappearance and of her brothers and sisters, of their lack of food and money, and of the shelter and the foster homes, and how much she needed to keep the family together. When she finished, he sat silent, touched, embarrassed, and bewildered.

Finally he said, "Connie will be back. She's been with you kids too long not to come back. I don't think it'll be more than a few more days. She knows her check comes on the first. Meantime, I can probably find something for you to do around here, something to get you by until she does come back."

He thought for a moment. "I know, you can do some pricing. You know, putting price labels on cans and packages. It's easy. Starting tomorrow you can come in after school for a couple of hours. I'll pay you ten dollars a day, at least until Connie's check comes in. I think she'll be back by then. I think she will . . . For now, I want you to take home whatever you need to get you through 'til tomorrow. And tomorrow you can do the same."

Sally stared at him in disbelief. "Go on. Go get your groceries. Then I'll take you home. What are your brothers and sisters going to do without you?"

In the car, she wanted to give him the name of another street, any street except Curtis Street. But she had already told him, and he seemed to know where it was because he was heading east on Santa Clara Street. She was painfully aware, but never more so than now, of how the streets and houses and neighborhoods changed once you crossed the freeway. Dirty was the only word that came to her mind: it was the only word she had. But it said it all. It described the littered, stained sidewalks, and it framed the broken-down old cars that had been driven up onto the front yards where grass had once been planted and grown, and dirt had now resurfaced, tired and marked with splotches of oil and fuel and God only knew what other substances. It captured the wide-open doors of streaked and splattered houses through which large green and black flies entered and small diapered and undiapered infants exited, as often on their knees as on their wobbly legs, to partake of the litter and the refuse on the worn dirt.

When they turned onto Curtis Street, she looked down and held her breath, not wanting to see what he was seeing, not wanting to see the shock and disgust that had to be on his face. He said only, "Where to?" confusing her.

When he said it again, she looked up and said, quietly, "Right there." She pointed to Mrs. Gómez's house, the best house in the neighborhood.

"I thought you said you lived in an apartment."

She shook her head and said, "No, I live here."

"Okay."

He stopped the car before Mrs. Gómez's house and watched as she hurriedly took the three bags out of the car and set them on the sidewalk. He wanted to help her carry the bags, but thought better of it because she couldn't look at him as she reached for and closed the door.

He said only, "I'll see you tomorrow."

The next afternoon at exactly 3:30, Sally Martínez stood in the doorway of Giordano's Market with frightened eyes and an open mouth, until Ralph Giordano, who was standing near the check-out stands, saw her and went up to her.

"Hi, Sally, come on in."

She looked from side to side, seeing no one and nothing, despite the voices and cash registers.

"Come on," he said, "I've got some work for you to do."

She looked down at her new clothes, squeezed the brown paper bag she was carrying, and followed him down a long aisle of canned goods to the back of the store and then through a set of doors that were marked EMPLOYEES ONLY, through a room stacked with cardboard boxes, and then down a flight of stairs to a huge basement, where cardboard boxes were stacked in tall rows from the floor to the ceiling.

"You can start over here," he said, leading her to a smaller stack of boxes. "Fred has marked the price on the outside of each carton. In a minute, I'll show you how to operate the labeler."

The basement was cool and quiet. Naked incandescent bulbs hung from overhead rafters every forty feet, breaking up the darkness. The more Ralph Giordano had thought of it, the more he realized that this was the only place that Sally could work in the store. She was twelve, and there were child labor laws. It would only be for three or four days. He showed her how to set the labeler and where and how to fix the labels on the cans. Then he left, walking up the stairs to the click of the labeler. He felt good.

He returned at four o'clock to find her sitting on the boxes. "What's the matter?" he said.

"Nothing. I'm finished."

"You're finished?"

"Yes."

He checked the cartons: each can had been correctly labeled. "I thought this would take you an hour, maybe even two. You want to do some more?"

She nodded.

This time, he broke down two rows of cartons, four times the amount she had had before. "This ought to keep you busy for a while." Again he left to the click of the labeler and returned to that click at five, smiling to himself, thinking: Poor thing, she's probably worn herself out.

"How you doing?"

"Fine."

"How much more you got to go?"

"This is my last box."

"Your last box?"

She nodded.

He checked the cartons. Every can sported a yellow label and none were mislabeled. He checked again. She was as fast as most and faster than some, and she had just started. He looked at her. "Are you tired?"

"No."

"Do you want a break?"

"A break?"

"Yeah, rest. Get a Coke or something. Just sit down."

"Not really."

And then he saw the huge sweat stains under her arms, almost to her waist.

"Is it hot down here?"

"No."

"Are you hot?"

"No."

He looked at her again. Except for the sweat stains, there was no other sign of fatigue.

"Maybe you've done enough for today. Maybe we ought to wait until tomorrow before you start another stack."

"What time is it?"

"It's just after five."

"You said I could work until six for ten dollars. You said—"

"Okay, okay. Go upstairs and get yourself a Coke out of the cooler, and then come on back down here and take a break while I get some more boxes ready."

He checked the cartons again, but now more carefully. Not a single omission or mistake. Incredible. When she returned he asked, "Have you ever done this before?"

"No."

"Never?"

"No."

This time he decided to watch, waiting until she had taken her break. But when she went up to the cartons, she stood motionless.

"What's the matter?"

"I don't like people to watch me."

So he left. He walked down the rows of cartons and up the stairs only to creep back down and stoop on the stairs to watch her, watch as she deftly raised the cans and clipped first the bottom can and then the top can as she let it down and picked up another. He watched her break the seal of a new carton with two tugs and then begin again, labeling as quickly as anyone in the store. She was a natural, he thought.

———————

That was all that Ralph Giordano had seen, that was all he could see. What he did not see was the worry and then the outright fear that descended on Sally the previous morning when the rejoicing and feasting from the bags of groceries had passed in the tiny apartment. It was a fear that drove her to force four of her six siblings out of the apartment and off to school even though it was near noon, to plop Rachel, who was sick with something, before the T.V., and to bloat Danny with the milk that he had been craving so that he would collapse in his crib. Somehow she had to deal with that fear. And as soon as Danny's bloated stomach had drugged him off to sleep, she closed the bedroom door on the madness of morning television and sat on her bed in the darkened bedroom and faced the fear as squarely as she had faced anything in her twelve years. What she saw was Giordano's Market. No, what she saw was white people in and around Giordano's Market, more white people than she had been around in her entire life. She not only saw them, but she heard them and felt them. White women mainly, white women in big cars and pretty clothes and hairdos, with big, gleaming smiles that said that everything was wonderful and fine, when in fact nothing was wonderful and fine in her life. White women, with whom she would be locked, sealed in that store for two and a half hours, more time than she had ever been around white people, except for a teacher maybe, and then there was always a bunch of Mexican kids in the room with her. And those white women would know with one look that she was not one of them, that she didn't belong there, that she had somehow snuck in and was blotching their clean and happy store with the stench and filth that only Mexicans carried. And they would chase her. No, they would not need to chase her, because she would not last, she would not stand it for more than a minute before she would run, run forever from their knowing and accusing eyes.

She tended to Rachel and cared for Danny for the rest of the day, and the next day too, out of memory, instinct, just as she scolded and yelled at the others. She cooked dinner from rote, just as she readied the younger ones for bed and reminded Billy and Angie that they had homework. Because she wasn't there, she was at Giordano's Market with all those white women.

She slept little that night, or rather, she rested little that night. Her body was wrenched, exhausted by her consciousness, which was still at the store, the store where they all looked and knew. She heard her brothers and sisters breathing, she heard people's night sounds fade and the wind die down once the fog left its cover and then, finally, she heard the quiet of the night in a neighborhood where, for too many, night was day. She heard all of this through the film of sleep, an exhausting sleep that would never provide rest, because she was living and reliving tomorrow afternoon.

Once again, Sally didn't go to school the next day. She needed to rest, prepare herself, and think about what she had incessantly thought about for the past twenty hours, but alone, or as much alone as she could be. So she sent all five of them, including Rachel, who was still sick with something, to school, and she bloated Danny again. Once he fell asleep, she went to the bathroom and put on the clothes that she had worn yesterday, replaying Ralph Giordano's words over and over again. "My, you look good! Doesn't she look good!" So she put them on without hesitation, leaving the other set in the rolled-up, folded brown paper bag which she had hidden under her bed from the others. Then she climbed up on the toilet seat, just as Connie had done so often. She climbed up and looked and turned and looked from every angle, as Connie had. But it was not her figure that Sally looked at, because she had no figure. No, what Sally looked for were the signs of a Mexican. The clothes hid most of them except for the arms, and the face, and the hands, and the neck. The clothes even hid the barrio, because no one in the barrio dressed in, or had, clothes like these; these were white people's clothes. Even after rolling down the sleeves and pulling up the collar, the clothes didn't, or couldn't, hide the face and the hands, or rather the skin, or more specifically, the brown of the skin which told all. It was the brown, nothing more, nothing less: the hands had fingers like any other's, the face had eyes and a nose and a mouth like any other's. No, it was only the brown. And for the brown, after almost an hour of turning and adjusting and readjusting her new clothes, of grimacing and bending, of combing and re-combing her hair to cover as much as she could of her face, she finally conceded that there was nothing she could do.

She began her walk at two, just after Bobby got home from school to take care of Danny and Rachel. She left on that walk that she and Connie had always walked in forty or forty-five minutes at two, even though she didn't have to be at the store until 3:30, because Danny and Rachel and Bobby would drive her crazy if she had to stay in that apartment with them for one more minute, and because the other kids, the kids her age and older, in the neighborhood wouldn't be home from school yet and wouldn't be able to make fun of her white people's clothes. She left with the rolled and folded brown paper bag tucked under her arm, lest the others claim her other new clothes in her absence. She moved quickly through the neighborhood, wanting to avoid the questions of the women who were all too ready to spot whatever moved beyond their curtains or blinds. "How's your mother? I haven't seen her lately. She's not sick again, is she?" "Where you going dressed like that? Aren't you supposed to be in school?" "Has your social worker been by? Mine came yesterday. Bobby said your mom hasn't been home for a few days."

She left the neighborhood without being noticed. After she crossed the freeway, after the houses changed, she began hesitating, both in her legs and in her mind. But there was no going back. Tomorrow they would be without food, and it was still three days to the first. She moved on, already knowing at twelve, without ever having articulated it or heard it, that many things in life were done simply because they had to be done.

She arrived at Rangel's gas station, a half block from the store, at exactly 2:45, according to the big round clock that hung on the station wall. From the side of the station she could see the front doors of Giordano's Market. She stood and watched, watched white women enter and leave the store, dressed in clothes that the women on Curtis Street would never know, with real hairdos that came from beauty shops rather than from home curlers. They seemed to be smiling and nodding to everyone and everything. Would they smile at her? Would they be able to hide their shock and disgust when they saw her, not only in the store, but working in the store, a part of the store? No. At her they would laugh instead, point their fingers and laugh. And then they would become angry, and the laughs would become mean, angry laughs. She didn't belong there, and they knew it, and she knew it. She would run. Because the laughs would tear into her worse than any knife, because nothing could make her stay, not even the hunger and misery at home, not even . . .

Sally saw the gas station man staring at her through the window and instinctively began moving again, out onto the sidewalk and away from the market, because it was so early. She turned at the corner and only looked back when she was shielded by the corner house. She quickened her pace as if she had somewhere to go or some reason to be there. She turned again at the next corner, thinking that by then the man in the gas station would have forgotten her. She walked in a huge circle, widening it and shortening it by a block at a time so as not to arouse any suspicion. She was worried now, because she had no watch, no clock to tell her what time it was. The more she walked, the more worried she became that she would be late and that Ralph Giordano would fire her, and they had to eat or they would go to the shelter and . . . So she looked for some sign of the hour and found none except for her legs and feet that were telling her that she had walked a long way and that she was going to be late, and if Ralph Giordano fired her, she would have to walk out of that neighborhood again, fired. When she reached Columbus Street again, she turned and approached the gas station again, even if the man saw, until she could see that it was 3:25. Then she turned around again and began counting 1, 2, 3 . . . and walked and planned and counted so that by 296 she was standing at the front doors of Giordano's Market.

She didn't enter the store. She simply stood there, looking from side to side, but seeing nothing, hearing the cash registers and the hubbub of voices, but seeing nothing. Finally, she heard, "Sally, come on in . . ." and she saw Ralph Giordano in his brown apron moving toward her, motioning and then turning. And she followed him as fast as she could away from all the eyes that she couldn't see down a long aisle past no white people, no white women, into the back room where only Fred was, and then down some stairs to the huge basement where it seemed that only she and Ralph Giordano were. She breathed easily for the first time that day.

When Ralph Giordano had finished demonstrating and handed her the labeler, Sally asked, "Do I have to work upstairs?"

"No."

"Does anybody else work down here?"

"No . . . Is that a problem?"

"No."

"Why do you ask?"

"I just wanted to know."

Then she started. Once he was gone, she stopped and then walked down every aisle and into every corner of that basement to make sure that no one was there. She went to the stairs and saw for certain that the door was closed. Satisfied, she went back to her cartons. There were no white women. There were only the cartons and the cans between her and the ten dollars and all the food she could carry home.

She attacked the cans as if they had been the sole source of every moment of fear and anguish that she had endured over the past thirty hours, coming down hard on each can until her wrist ached, ached more and more until she stopped and cried. She thought of the food and the money and the shelter and went on, switching hands, using her right hand to lift the cans and her left to lightly label it until she had a rhythm, a method. And she moved faster and faster, telling herself that each can, and then each carton, was an obstacle, an impediment to the food and the money and the escape from the shelter.

The first time Ralph Giordano returned, she had just finished with the first stack of cartons and was beginning to worry that she might have to go upstairs. His surprise and approval were real and, as he turned for more cartons, the white women disappeared as quickly as they had appeared. Sally pounced on the second stack with greater vigor than she had on the first. Can after can after can rose and fell, vicious obstacles, ruthlessly beaten down, each one soundly defeated at its own game.

Ralph Giordano's satisfaction after the second stack propelled her onto the third and final stack. Somehow she quickened her pace, knowing that these were the last of the cans, that she was almost there, that the cans could not stop her.

As they started to leave the basement, his praises ringing in her ears, she pointed to the rolled and folded brown paper bag and asked, "Mr. Giordano, can I leave that here 'til tomorrow?"

"Sweetheart, you can leave anything you want here." Then he handed her a ten-dollar bill.

Upstairs, in the back room, as the doors to the front of the store appeared, she stopped.

"What's the matter?" he said.

"Nothing."

"Come on, you'd better get your groceries."

She wouldn't move, she just stood there staring at the doors. Finally she said, "I'm too dirty to go in there."

Ralph Giordano looked at her for a moment and then said, quietly, "I'll get them for you."

Once she stepped out the back door into the cool early evening air, she felt and then saw for the first time the large sweat stains on each side of her blouse.

⟶

The next day, she wore her best dress to school, because she would be going directly to the store from school.

In another rolled and folded brown paper bag she carried the clothes that she had worn at the store the day before. She carried the bag everywhere she went, putting it down only when she sat at her desk, and then placing it under her, up against her legs. When the others asked, "What you got in that bag, Sally?" she said, "None of your business." And later, "None of your business. That's what I got in the bag, none of your business."

At 3:25, she knocked at, and then pounded on, the back door until Fred opened the door. Before he could say anything, she said, holding up the brown paper bag, "Don't worry, I have my work clothes in here."

Fred didn't budge, saying, "You're not supposed to be coming in the back way. Employees go in the front. That's the rules. That's how Ralph wants it."

The fear struck again, as quickly and sharply as any bolt. "But he told me to come this way."

"Who told you?"

"Mr. Giordano did," she lied.

"I don't believe that. Nope. I sure don't. You're gonna have to do like the rest of us. Go on up around the front."

Fear shot out in every direction. Then she heard, "I did tell her that. She can come in the back. She's just part-time."

He knew. He knew, she thought later in the basement. He must have known from that first day, from the moment she had laid claim to Mrs. Gómez's house and put the three bags on the hot sidewalk.

At the end of the second day, Ralph Giordano could not have been more pleased, and the job that was to have lasted just two more days was extended well into a second year. Soon she could label in five two-and-one-half-hour shifts what it took any other employee two full days to label. Within two weeks, Ralph Giordano raised her wage to five dollars an hour, and two weeks later to six dollars an hour, plus whatever groceries she could carry home. Every weekday afternoon at exactly 3:20 Ralph Giordano would make it a point to be in his office so that he could hear her rap at the back door and answer it and see the thin wisp of a girl, but a beautiful girl, who always carried one of the two rolled and folded brown paper bags under her arm. "Hello, sweetheart!" he would say, and every part of him, including his bald head, would gleam, so much so that she too would smile.

Within the first week, every employee in the store had snuck a glance at the thin Mexican girl in the basement. Within the next week, everyone had found an excuse to go down to the basement to see the little brown robot who never stopped working, who never stopped stamping and lifting cans and did little more than glance at them, or rather, at their smocks or aprons. She never spoke to them, never invited or answered any question. She just kept lifting and stamping, as if there were no one else in the basement other than she and the cans. She spoke only to Ralph Giordano. And he in turn spoke to her and favored her as he did none of the others, which was not lost on them. Later, when he had two lockers installed in the store's back room because, he said, he wanted to be able to change before he went out to the golf course or to a meeting, they smirked, having already seen the second locker padlocked and knowing that she no longer carried the rolled and folded brown paper bag to and from work each day.

When Ralph Giordano sent Barbara down to Gottschalk's again for two more outfits and began sending the girl's "work clothes" to the laundry with the smocks and aprons, one of them thought it had gone too far, had gotten out of hand, and wrote an anonymous letter to Ralph Giordano's wife, Josephine. Josephine visited the store and went down, uninvited and unescorted, to the basement. She watched the girl from the top of the stairs for a full ten minutes, watched the girl whom Ralph had said was twelve or thirteen, but who looked more like ten or eleven, working alone and in silence, feverishly, as if someone or something were pushing her, as if she were in some sort of fiendish race with herself.

Josephine was already embarrassed when she went down to the girl; she was already satisfied that there was no need to go. Still she went. To introduce herself, yes. To let the girl know there was a Mrs. Giordano, no. To apologize without apologizing for even coming, perhaps. But she hadn't anticipated the girl's reaction: the girl looked up from her cans and saw her standing there and became frightened. Then, when Josephine Giordano raised her hand to reassure her, the girl became terrified. When Josephine Giordano said, "Hello, I'm . . . " the girl began backing away, looking from side to side but not at her until she had backed herself up against a wall. Then the girl put her head down, and when Josephine Giordano tried to speak to her again, the girl put both hands over her ears hard, tight, hard enough to make her head jiggle. Baffled, shaken, Josephine Giordano left, or rather went up the stairs and opened the door and closed it loudly but remained on the top stair, waiting for the girl to return. And for a moment it seemed that the girl would not return, that she would remain hunched and pressed against that back wall. But the clicking began again, slowly, hesitantly at first, then steadily, then at that non-stop pace. Josephine Giordano crept down a stair and watched, watched the wisp of a girl stamping and lifting as if she were being chased by demons, no, by all the Josephine Giordanos of the world.

When Josephine Giordano went back into the store, she said only, "My, that poor thing works awfully hard. And you know, Ralph always wanted a daughter."

Connie returned three weeks to the day from when she had left. She was sitting on a bed, curled, staring into space, when Sally came home from the store. Angie had met her outside. "Connie's home and she's either drunk or stoned." Sally couldn't tell. What she saw was that Connie was several shades darker: her skin was a deep copper brown, as if she had lived under the sun for those three weeks. Her hair was straggly and stuck together at the ends. She wore the same dress that she had worn on the day she left. Now it was splattered, threadbare, and frayed. Despite the heat, she also wore two men's jackets over the rayon dress. Her legs and arms and the right side of her face bore bruises that, at first glance, were difficult to see because of the darkness of her skin.

"Where you been, Connie?"

She was still wherever she had been: the stare and the silence were proof positive.

"Where'd you go, Connie?"

There was no answer, no response of any kind, not even a flinch or a twitch of the eye. Nothing. She was still there, wherever that had been.

"Connie, you can't do this to us again. You can't. Do you understand? You can't. We're better off without you. At least then we all know what we have to do."

Connie couldn't or didn't care. It was one and the same.

Sally squatted so that her face was level with Connie's, so that their eyes were inches apart. "Connie," she said, taking hold of Connie's knees and putting her eyes directly in the path of Connie's eyes. "Connie, you can't do this to us again." She shook Connie at the knees, bringing her eyes even closer. There still was no response, nothing, not even the suspicion that she was being seen by eyes two inches from her.

"Ahhh!" Sally finally said, rising and walking away from the hunched, stuporous woman. "Angie, Billy, get her into bed. Take those jackets off of her and get her into bed and cover her."

After dinner, Sally and Angie bathed Connie. The first tubful of water immediately turned a grimy grey-brown. So did the second. It was only with the third tubful that they scrubbed her and washed her hair. Even when they poured water over her head, Connie sat in the tub immobile, frozen somewhere under a bridge, or on a river bank, or in an alley, or under an overpass, or in a park, or under a set of bleachers.

Later, as Sally was getting ready for bed, Angie came to her and said, "She's got the shakes."

"Oh, no."

"Yeah, go look at her."

Connie was lying on the bed, curled up next to Rachel, with the covers pulled up to her ears, shivering shivers that increased in magnitude until she shook violently, until something snapped and she lay calm for a while, only to begin shivering again. This time their eyes met and this time Connie said, "I'm cold. I'm so cold." But her eyes said more, they begged: Sally help me. I need a little taste, just a little. You know where the bottle is. You always know where the bottle is. Help me, Sally, don't let me go through any more of this. Please, Sally, help me.

"Let's get her out of here. She's gonna wake the kids up, and then we're really gonna have a mess."

The two girls walked-carried the moaning woman to the other room. "It's okay, Connie, you're gonna be okay. We'll cover you in just a minute. You're gonna be okay," the younger daughter said. Sally said nothing. This had happened, everything had happened, too many times. When she did speak, it was out of necessity. "No, no, not on the couch. She'll shake herself off of it. Let's put her on the floor. I'll sleep next to her on the floor."

They laid her on the floor, and then Angie hurried back to the bedroom for covers. The copper brown woman curled up on her side, wrapping her arms around her knees tightly, so that she was almost a ball, looking up at her oldest child, pleading as only eyes can plead. The child looked down with only anger, resentment, and disgust. The child next in line returned with covers and a pillow and quickly covered her, tucking the covers under her and then placing the pillow under her head and then wiping and stroking her sweating forehead as she whispered reassurances. The oldest child simply stood with her arms folded and watched as the woman looked past the child tending to her, silently pleading with her teary eyes.

Finally, Sally said, "Okay, Connie, you win again. You don't know how hard it's been, how much school I've missed, how scared I was that those people would take us all to the shelter, how I lied for you the two times they did come . . . We had nothing to eat, but you didn't care. You win. I'll go get you your bottle."

Sally went out and down the stairs to the back of the apartments, to an air vent under the farthest unit where there were two bottles. She removed one of the bottles, hid it under her blouse, and went back upstairs. This time when she entered, the copper brown woman raised her head and said, "Have you got it? Have you got it?" Sally nodded and went to the cupboard and took a small glass and filled the glass less than a quarter full. Then she carefully hid the bottle under the sink and went out, glass in hand, to the open area where Connie lay.

"You better get to bed, Angie. You've got to go to school tomorrow. I'll have to stay with her tomorrow."

The younger girl kissed her mother goodnight, whispering as she did. Connie was not interested in kisses or whatever Angie had to say. She was interested only in the glass that Sally held in her hand, smacking, wetting her lips as she stared up at it. Then Angie was gone and Sally stood over Connie with the glass in hand, not moving, not speaking to the woman who had raised her head toward the glass and who then raised her hand toward the glass. The hand shook and trembled in the air. Still Sally didn't move. She waited, letting the outstretched appendage, which rose from the floor like a pole, quiver and shake.

Then she said, "Sit up. Sit up. We'll have this wine all over the place if you don't sit up."

Connie struggled to sit up, her body shaking. Sally watched, letting her struggle. Then she knelt, shifting the glass to her left hand, the hand farthest from Connie, and then watched again as Connie, knowing the glass was closer, within reach, struggled, panted, and gasped in a grotesque fury to sit up. Finally she sat up, and as soon as she did, she lunged for the glass which Sally simply twisted farther away.

"No! I'll give it to you when you sit up and sit still. Now sit up and sit still."

Connie knew that this time, of all times, she had to do as she was told: she had to sit up and sit still. So she tried to sit still, to somehow control her quivering body while Sally watched with the glass in hand. But the quivering wouldn't stop and she cried, "Please, Sally, please. Just a little taste. I'll make it up to you. Please, Sally."

Sally only sat silently, watching. Then Sally brought the glass closer, inch by inch. And Connie's mouth watered, and she reached. Sally shook her head no, and stopped the glass's movement, and waited until Connie was sitting upright again before she brought the glass closer and closer to the trembling woman, until Connie's lips, and then her teeth, clamped onto the glass. Then Connie clamped both hands around Sally's hand and the glass and nudged at the glass, upwards, and when the glass didn't move, she pushed upward, harder and harder until she could feel the tautness of Sally's hand against hers. Sally yanked the glass away, hissing, "Stop it! Stop it! You'll spill it!" oblivious of what she herself had just spilled. "Now sit up and behave!"

Sally waited again, wanting to wait. Finally, she was somehow satisfied and then brought the glass slowly toward Connie again. This time the panting, gasping, shaking woman let her daughter completely control the process. When the wine finally entered her mouth, she shuddered and swallowed, hard and quickly, gasped and sighed, and then laid down to rest.

It was a year and ten months before Ralph Giordano found a way to get Sally out of the basement. Even though he had concluded over and over again that, everything considered, labeling cans in his basement was probably the best thing Sally could be doing, still, the thought, the sound, the sight of that wisp of a girl lifting and stamping can after can troubled him.

It was Fred who suggested that Sally stay after hours on Thursdays and label and stack the shelves on the floor for the weekend specials. Ralph Giordano liked the idea, not only because it made business sense, but also because it got her up into the store. Sally was willing: it meant more money, and only she and Ralph would be in the store.

On the first Thursday when he drove her home, he drove past Mrs. Gómez's house without a word and stopped in front of her apartment complex. Then he said, "Sally, You don't ever have to lie about anything to me," and he kissed her forehead.

Upstairs, at the door, Angie said, "Why are you crying?"

"It's none of your business."

———

When Fred told him that Country Boy Market was using girls for bag boys, Ralph Giordano laughed. But even as he laughed, he thought of Sally. In four weeks she would be fourteen and could get a work permit.

He waited until the following Thursday, until she was stacking shelves before he said anything.

"You know, Country Boy is using girls for bag boys."

She kept stacking. It meant nothing. He repeated himself. It still meant nothing.

"I'd like you to be a bag boy for me, Sally."

She looked at him, wrinkled her brow and then shook her head no. "Why not?"

Her eyes widened. She shook her head all the more. No! No! No!

He let it pass. It was best to let it pass. He raised it again as she waited for him at the door. "Sally, someday I want you to be a checker, here in my store. And you can, in just a few years, but you have to start getting used to how things work up here. You have to work up here. You have to start working with the other employees and with the customers too. And being a bag boy is the best way to start."

She didn't answer. He went on. "Do you know how much checkers make? A lot. Let's put it this way. A checker makes as much or more in one week as your mother gets from welfare in a month."

On the way home, she blurted out, "But I like working in the basement."

"I know you do. But there's no future in it. You can't support yourself or your family by labeling cans in the basement."

Later she said, "But I don't want to be up there with all those white people."

"Sally, white people are just people too. They have their own problems too. Believe me. They're afraid of things too. Just like you."

When they reached the apartment complex, he said, "I know you don't like it here, Sally. I know you want to get out of here. And you can. Once you're a checker, you'll have enough money in two months to move you and your family out of here. I guarantee it."

The next afternoon when he answered the back door, she said, "Okay, I'll try."

It was his idea to practice, to use part of the remaining Thursday nights before she got her permit to randomly fill shopping carts full of groceries and then work the register, sliding cans and cartons and packages to her at the end of the counter where she quickly learned to stack and fill the brown paper bags with the same intensity that she had labeled her cans. It was her idea to take the smock home, to see how it would fit, to make sure it would fit, she said.

It was early October then, and the alternating summer heat and fog had given way to an Indian summer that threatened to last the winter. The days were shorter but hotter, and for Sally the sun was everywhere. On the day she told Ralph Giordano that she would try, she took to wearing a baseball cap with the bill pulled down and a long sleeved blouse and pants whenever she went outdoors to protect herself against the sun. Because it was the sun which had made her brown, which was making her brown. Sometimes, in the dead of winter, if she looked in the mirror long enough, she could tell herself that maybe she could pass for white, for Italian at least. Now she had three weeks to become as white as she could be.

After a week, her face seemed to be getting lighter, but her hands were betraying her, because even though she kept them in her pockets every moment that she was outside, the brown wasn't fading; her hands were still a deep brown. She thought of wearing gloves. But it was too hot for gloves. After the second week, her face was definitely lighter. But her hands . . .

She was shocked to see, as she stood on the toilet, that the smock she had brought home went up almost to her elbows, allowing the brown of her hands to spread up her forearms. No matter how she stood or which way she turned, the arms were brown too. So she started to scrub with the bathroom door locked, hoping it was dirt or grime or grease. She scrubbed with a wash cloth that first day, scrubbing and rinsing and drying and then scrubbing again until her arms and her hands were red and sore. Then she stopped: better red than brown.

When she went to bed, she saw that the red was giving way to the brown again. And she cried.

She scrubbed again the next night after everyone had gone to bed, in the locked bathroom, standing at the sink as she scrubbed and rinsed, and then donning the smock and mounting the toilet, as she dried and inspected herself. On that night she used a piece of rope instead of a wash cloth, a crude coarse white rope that she had seen old Mexican women use. She scrubbed and dried and inspected until her skin was red and sore again. When she went to bed this time, she noticed flecks of white on her brown arms, flecks that were even whiter in the morning.

She used the rope again the third night, but with little improvement. The next morning, Sunday, she walked to the Guadalupe River, went down into the trees and brush and dried grass of its banks, and walked along the receding October stream until she found them. Then she dried them and put them in a brown paper bag. At home she hid them. When the others had gone to bed, she took the two smooth, flat, grey river rocks into the bathroom with her and tried to remember how her old aunt (the cleanest of clean and the whitest of all her aunts) had used them. She couldn't remember, and so she started to scrub as best she could, gently at first, and then harder and harder until the blood appeared, small dot-lines of blood that frightened her. And she cried again.

The next morning, the lines looked more like scratches, which, if she kept her arms at her sides, could not be seen. That night she knew she could use neither the rocks nor the rope, nor even the wash cloth, and she also knew that come Thursday at 3:30 her arms and hands would still be brown.

———

On Thursday, Ralph Giordano was waiting for her as she entered the store.

"How are you?" he asked.

A look was her answer.

"Come on into my office for a second, I want to talk to you." He turned the light on in his small, windowless office and closed the door. "Sally, I think I understand what you're going through." No, he didn't. "The job you can do. From what I've seen, you're as good as the two boys I've got out there right now. In a week they won't be able to touch you." No matter what he said, she had to do it. "About this Mexican thing, or this white thing, or whatever you want to call it, what is it gonna take for me to convince you that we're all just people, that we're all the same, that . . ." Connie would never be like any of those white women. He talked on, and for a moment she thought of the Curtis Street people. No, they'd never be the same, and they soon gave way to the white women who were waiting for her in the front of the store.

When he stopped talking, the room fell into a helpless silence. After a pause he said, "Sally, look at me . . . Do you think I want anything but the best for you?" A look was her answer. "Come here, Sally." She went to him, and he held her, and she felt the big expanse of his belly just under her breast, and for a moment at least that belly was a shield against the women waiting.

She walked out of his office and down an aisle without seeing or hearing a thing. She went to the end of Molly's counter, the counter on which they had practiced, and opened a large bag and placed it squarely in the packing frame, and then stared at, and saw only, and heard only the cans and the cartons and bottles and packages in the cart and on the counter sliding toward her. Quickly and deftly, she built a base in the bag and packed the fragile goods above them. Then, with a twist and almost a fling, placed and fitted the bag into a waiting shopping cart. And then she began again, seeing and hearing only the cans and the bags and the carts. She followed the woman out of the store, intent only on the cart, nodding to whatever the woman said without hearing or listening. She loaded the bags into the trunk of her car with her back to the woman, keeping her back to the woman even as she pulled the cart from the car, and nodding, nodding to whatever the woman had to say as she walked away from the car back to the store.

She repeated the task again and again and again, communicating only with the cans and the bags and the carts, but intent enough, aware enough to go from counter to counter, helping other checkers whenever Molly's line slowed, and above all, frightened enough to know that she had to stay busy, had to keep moving to insulate herself from the stares and whispers and smirks that she knew were there.

At her break, Ralph said, "You're doing great, Sally! The checkers can't believe it. Molly wants to keep you as her permanent bagger. You're putting the boys to shame. Even the customers are amazed. But you can slow down, you know. You don't have to kill yourself. You can go half as fast as you're going and still beat the boys. And smile. Please smile. They'll love you if you smile."

She heard him. But his words had little meaning. Because there were still more of them out there, waiting, and there was still an hour to go.

Near the end of that hour she followed a tall, white-haired woman out to her car and quickly began transferring the bags to the car. When there were just two bags left in the cart, the woman said something to Sally, and Sally nodded. The woman continued speaking, and Sally continued nodding, and was backing away from her and the car, when the woman took Sally by the shoulder, and then stepped in front of her. "I'm not sure you're listening to me."

Sally looked from side to side and then up at her. What she saw was a smile, a warm smile: there was no mistaking that. Sally's eyes fluttered and then they looked again. The smile was still there.

"How old are you?"

"Fourteen."

"Well, I'm impressed. I watched you while I was in line and I must say that I have never seen anyone your age work that efficiently or that hard."

Sally was dumbfounded. There was no confusing or denying the smile.

"Here, I want you to have this. You deserve it."

Sally took the bill and, when she saw that it was five dollars, she was stunned.

Within the week, Sally was smiling. Within two weeks, it was systematic: once she had filled the cart, she would turn to the customer and smile, and once she had unloaded the bags into their cars, she would turn and smile again. And they too would smile. They liked her. There was no denying that. Hardly a Saturday passed that she didn't receive ten dollars in tips. Word traveled fast. She was a fourteen-year-old, Mexican, eastside, junior-high student, who worked to help support her ten brothers and sisters and her arthritic mother. Some women sought her out, lining up at the checkout stand where she was bagging, first to watch the speed and earnestness with which she filled those bags, and then to see her smile.

Ralph Giordano was beside himself. "The customers love you. They have nothing but compliments for you. I wish I had ten more like you. As soon as you turn sixteen, you're a checker." He raised her wage and extended her hours, and more often than not, noted, after she had left, no matter how cool or hot it had been, the sweat stains on her smock, always large and under her arms.

━━━━━▶

Twenty months after Sally Martínez became a bagger, she and Ralph Giordano began practicing after store hours, she as the checker and he as the bagger, for that day when she would become a checker. She quickly learned the mechanics of the registers, checking hundreds of filled shopping carts. Then she canvassed the shelves and learned the specials pricing system. Sometimes she stayed for as long as three hours after the store had closed. Now she was driven, not only by fear but also by the desire to excel, to be the best, to be the fastest and most accurate checker in the store.

On her sixteenth birthday, Sally Martínez began her career as a checker at Giordano's Market. Her speed and efficiency came as no surprise to the others, but they resented it. "Somebody ought to talk to that girl. Now Ralph's gonna expect all of us to go that fast. There's no way I'm gonna kill myself just to keep up with that little twit. I'll find me another job first." She brought to the check stand the same intensity, concentration, and effort that she had brought to bagging and to the cans in the basement before that.

Now she also brought a vocal, open charm that had already been suggested by her systematic smile at the other end of the counter. She had watched the other checkers, listened to them as they dealt with and spoke to the customers, knowing that some day she would be a checker, and knowing long before that, that she could do better. She greeted many by name. "Hello, Mrs. Falcone." "Good morning, Mrs. Venturi." There was nothing she didn't notice. "Oh, you've had your nails done. I like them." Or, "That color . . . peach, is it? It really brings out your complexion. I've never seen you wear that blouse before." There was nothing she didn't remember. "Is your mother home from the hospital yet, Mrs. Galucci?" Or, "Is your husband back to work now?" There was nothing she forgot. "Happy birthday, Mrs. Corsi." She accomplished it all with that easy, warm, appropriate smile, as she took cans and cartons and bags from the shopping carts, punched them into the register with her right hand, and slid them down the counter with her left hand at a speed that often required two baggers.

But once she left the check stand, the smile was gone. She ate alone in Columbus Park a block away. She ate there every day except for the coldest and wettest of days, and on those days she ate in the basement, alone. The others resented that too, saying that the girl who now worked full time thought she was better than them because she had Ralph wrapped around her little finger, and God only knew what was going on between them, because if you really stopped and thought about it, she was just a little, uppity Mexican from the east side.

Sally felt the resentment, but it didn't and couldn't matter. She needed that hour alone each day, first to recover from those first four hours, and then to ready herself for the next four hours. After leaving the check stand, she would go directly to the women's rest room each day, every day. There in a stall, she would take off her blouse, and then remove the large gauze pads that she wore taped under each arm to absorb the sweat. Then she would wipe herself dry and wring her sweat from the pads, often in small streams, watching as some measure or gauge of what those first four hours had been like. Then she would cut the morning pads into small rectangles, with scissors that she carried in her purse for that purpose, and flush them down the toilet.

From the women's room she would leave the store through the back door for the block-and-a-half walk to her seat in the park, walking, when no one was near, with her arms bent at the elbows, held up to her shoulders, forming two wedges that seemed joined by the brown lunch bag that she carried in either hand just under her chin, walking in that manner so that the outside air would better reach and dry and soothe the skin that the pads had covered, so that the rashes and resulting powders and ointments wouldn't return. Upon reaching her bench, she would sit where she always sat, squarely in the center of the bench, and then she would extend her arms on each side along the top of the bench and then throw back her head and close her eyes. Her arms would twitch; sometimes the back of her hands twitched, and on particularly busy days her legs twitched. She had no control of the twitching, no control over the little lumps that would pulsate at will up and down her arms. The jumping lumps frightened her at first, but soon she understood that by simply sitting, relaxing, they would pass.

Fifteen or twenty minutes into her lunch hour, she would eat, not because she was hungry, nor even because she wanted to eat, but rather because she knew that she *had* to eat to get through the remaining shift. The sandwich, the cookies, the apple or orange were tasteless, indistinguishable, as if she had a mouthful of oats that she was moistening and breaking down in order to swallow. It didn't matter what she packed in those little brown bags; it was always the same. But she chewed on, reminding herself that she hadn't, because she couldn't have, eaten breakfast. Often she would follow the food, grinding and growling, down into her resistant and violated stomach. And then the belching would begin, loud belches that she was always afraid would surface at the checkout stand. So she would begin coaxing the belches, forcing them up and out immediately after she had eaten, and continuing until she was just steps from the store.

Then she would walk. Because the walking relaxed her. But she would walk only in a small circle around her bench, to prevent anyone from claiming it. In a few minutes she would return to that bench and begin to ready herself for the remaining four hours, which she did by first thinking of the store, feeling the store and what it would be like that afternoon or evening, and then telling herself that she had to be strong, that she was a better, faster checker than any of the others, that she had proven that over and over again, that she was as smart, and smarter, than any of the women who passed through her check stand, because she knew them and they didn't know her, because she could cajole and flatter and charm them without them knowing that she was cajoling and flattering and charming them, and mostly because she had been from, and come from, and went back to, each night, a place that they could never have come from, that they could never have crawled out of. And when she had repeated her litany several times, when she had convinced herself and knew not only what she had to do but what she could do, she rose from her bench and began her walk, or perhaps her march, back to the store, making certain that she had allotted enough time to take the second set of gauze pads from her purse in the restroom and tape them just under her armpits on the sides of her thin, taut, wiry body before she began the second shift.

Ralph Giordano could not have been happier. Within six months he moved Sally to the first check stand. To the disgruntled, displaced Barbara, he said, "Don't take it personally. She's just the fastest checker in the store. And the customers naturally go to that first stand, and that causes backups in the aisles on busy days. You know that, Barbara. I have to put my fastest checker at that check stand."

On Friday evenings and all day Saturday, two baggers were assigned to Sally, something that Ralph Giordano had never done before, but which quickly proved warranted. On the busiest of days, he would make it a practice to stand in one of the aisles for a few moments and watch Sally work, work not only the register but mainly the customers, smiling and pleasing them and making them smile in return. Customer compliments for Sally were endless. And he soon dismissed the sweat stains on her smock as the product of someone who sweated easily.

Chapter II

Sally Martínez had been a checker for almost a year and a half when Joey Rocco began working at Giordano's Market. She had heard the others talking about him, but knew only that he was sixteen when she asked Molly, "Who is this Joey guy?"

"Do you know who Giuseppe Rocco is?"

"No."

"Giuseppe Rocco is the richest man in this town. And Joey Rocco is his oldest son."

"What's he doing working here, if he's so rich?"

"Don't ask me."

"Where's he working?"

"In the basement, doing your old job."

Later that day she asked Ralph, who answered, "He's Giuseppe Rocco's oldest son. He's a nice kid. Not much of a worker. But then he's never had to work. Probably never will."

"Why did you hire him?"

"Sweetheart, he's Giuseppe Rocco's son. You don't say no when Giuseppe Rocco's son asks you for a job. Do you know how much business Giuseppe Rocco brings into this store? You know all those orders we fill for the labor camps? And my son's a caterer. Do you know how many women in this town hire him just because Giuseppe Rocco's wife uses him? Do you know—"

"Did he ask you for the job?"

"Who's he?"

"The son."

"Yeah. Strangest thing. I used to know the kid when he was a little boy. Giuseppe Rocco used to bring him and his brother into the store every Wednesday afternoon for ice cream for years. Didn't recognize him when Barbara said there was some kid asking to see Mr. Giordano. He's a shy kid, and with those glasses he wears and that goofy baseball cap, he doesn't look like he could open a shopping bag, let alone fill one. So right away I told him that we didn't have no openings. He looked so beaten when I said that, that I felt sorry for him and told him

155

to leave his name and number. I just happened to glance at the name, Joseph Rocco, as he was walking out and then I saw the phone number. Shoot, I call that number twice a week at least to check Mrs. Rocco's orders. And so I said, 'Hey, wait a minute, are you . . .'"

"Molly said you have him in the basement labeling."

"Yeah, where else was I gonna put him. He doesn't know the first thing about anything and he moves even slower than that. But I gotta give the kid credit. He's trying. He's much better than he was a week ago, although he'll never be you. And you know, I don't think his family knows he's working. He just comes in every day after school, like you did, and just goes down to the basement and starts labeling."

The next afternoon, she went down to the basement on her break, armed with an excuse, but an excuse that she did not use because the boy did not look at her once, not even when she passed within a foot of him. He stayed stooped over his cans, slowly, methodically stamping them and then carefully reclosing the carton and just as carefully opening another. She watched him from the stairs and felt the resentment she had had from the beginning grow. There was nothing special about him. In fact, the gangling, awkward boy with long, shapeless, white arms, who wore a faded black baseball cap pulled down to his thick, horn-rimmed glasses, was less than special. Were it not for his rich father, he would not have been there.

Sally had all but forgotten him when she saw him again some two months later. It was a cold, wet, December day, too wet and too cold to take her lunch to the park. She heard the labeler when she opened the basement door, and anger and resentment flashed. She needed this hour alone. She thought of leaving, but there was no place to go. She went to the opposite end of the basement, as far from him as possible. Rearranging some cartons, she sat, tilted her head back, and closed her eyes. There was no twitching that day. It had been a slow afternoon shift and it would probably be a slow evening shift. Still she had to calm herself, rid herself of the frenzied state of readiness that she put herself in every morning before coming to work, to stop, or at least slow down, her racing, protesting stomach so that she could chew and digest her tasteless food. And then she had to begin to ready herself again for the inherent threat and challenge of the evening shift. Because she would never belong. She knew that. And thus the grim determination and need, not only to perform, but to excel and dominate as well.

He irritated her with his clumsy, slow labeling. The clack of his labeler broke into her closed-eyed breathing; it was in her mouth as she chewed her bland food; it competed with her growling stomach for attention; it shattered her concentration as she paced back and forth in front of the cartons. She was about to scream when it occurred to her that not once had he stopped stamping; then, that he had been down there for months like a human mole with his cans and labeler, constantly stamping; never once, that she could remember, having surfaced, gone upstairs. How strange, especially for this boy. And she stopped, as she left the basement, near the top of the stairs, and watched him again, now out of a different curiosity; watched the stooped figure with the huge feet and shapeless arms, now covered by a flannel shirt; watched the awkward figure who wore a black baseball cap jammed down onto his head, shielding his weak eyes from the dim basement light, stamping each can as carefully and diligently as anyone could.

That night, as Ralph Giordano drove her home, she asked, "Does he ever take a break?"

"Who?"

"That Joey kid."

"What do you mean?"

"I've never seen him upstairs, and today I ate my lunch in the basement and he didn't stop. I mean he's not fast, but he didn't stop, not once, and he didn't know I was down there."

"He's a good kid, and he's shy, and he's earning his money now. I mean I'm not losing anything on him. He doesn't want his family to know that he's working here, not at least until he's a bagger. Don't ask me why, that's just what he told me. So I guess he doesn't come upstairs because he doesn't want anyone to see him and go tell his family. Not until he's a bagger."

"Is he gonna be a bagger?"

"Oh yeah, I think in a month or two I'll bring him upstairs. In his own way he's a real good worker."

<hr>

Three weeks later, Ralph Giordano brought Joey Rocco to Sally Martínez's check stand. "You two know each other, right?" She looked at the boy and nodded. The boy simply nodded.

"Anyway, it's a slow afternoon, and I couldn't think of a better time to break Joey in as a bagger. And I couldn't think of a better checker to do it than you, Sally. I'm sure you can show him the ropes. Remember what I told you, Joey, use the cans and cartons and the bigger, harder stuff for your foundation, and build from there."

Then he left, and each of the two looked awkwardly in the other's direction. But only for a moment, because Barbara and Molly came to Sally's stand and chirped, almost in unison, "My God, look at this! Joey's going to be a bagger!" "Boy, you didn't stay in the basement very long! Sally was there for two years." "You can bag for me any time you want, Joey!"

"Has Sally explained the different bag sizes to you yet, and when you double bag? Here, let me show you. Actually, there's a little knack to opening a bag. Here, let me . . ." Barbara had not only Joey's attention, but Sally's as well. She wanted them out of her check stand, all of them. But Barbara went on, and Molly inserted her tips as well.

And when the first customer came through, they stood and watched and marvelled as he slowly, clumsily, filled a first and then a second bag. And Barbara added in a high-pitched voice, "Angela, do you know who this is? Of course, you do . . . It's Giuseppe Rocco's oldest boy, Joey."

"Yes, yes, of course. I should have recognized him with that cap. I guess I didn't picture him working here. Are you working here now, Joey?"

The boy nodded.

"Isn't that wonderful!" Barbara said.

And they all smiled, except for Sally. She fumed through three more customers, as they applauded his every awkward move and introduced him to all as Giuseppe Rocco's oldest son. They stayed until Ralph Giordano noticed them and said, "Barbara, Molly," and looked over at their check stands.

There were enough customers in the store by then so that there was a steady flow through Sally's check stand and there were no awkward pauses, no need to say anything to the rich boy whom she glanced at from time to time as she slid a can or a bottle in his direction. He looked and moved like a nerd, examining each item and each space in the bag as if there were a difficult decision to make as to each. If this was what he was like now, what would he be like when business picked up in half an hour?

She waited. Then, as lines began forming, she picked up her pace. He fell behind. She went faster. "What's the matter?" she said, stopping half way through a shopping cart. He dropped a can on his finger as he tried to hurry. "Owww." She went to the end of the counter and said, "Move," and then filled a bag in a tenth of the time it was taking him. "Put this in the cart," she ordered. "It's not a big deal," she added, as she started back to the register, "Just put the groceries in the bag. This ain't homework. There's nothing to think about."

He stood hunched, beet red. She went faster, as fast as she could check, until the groceries were at a standstill, halfway down the counter as he struggled, red-faced. As soon as he filled and lifted a bag, she shoved all of the backed-up groceries toward him, saying, "Come on. Let's go! There's people waiting. They've been working all day. They're tired. They want to go home. They don't want to stand in line all night waiting for their groceries."

Then she returned to her register, to her fastest speed, sliding item after item at him until they were jammed just a few inches from her. And then, just as she stopped, he dropped a large bottle of juice on the floor and for a moment stood watchful and waiting. When he bent over to pick up the broken glass, he cut himself, a deep bloody cut on his finger. Ralph was there by then and she gritted through her teeth, "Get him out of here! Get him out of here! I can check and bag faster than he can bag! Get him out of here!"

He bagged mainly with Molly and Jennie over the next several weeks, but Sally was still irritated by the coddling that he received from everyone, beginning with Ralph and Fred down through all the checkers and many of the customers. His slightest act brought compliments. On slower afternoons, she turned her back to him. She never acknowledged him, never said "Hi," or even nodded. He got enough attention. She wasn't paid to give him attention, and if it ever came to that, she would quit.

Then one hectic Saturday afternoon, one of Sally's baggers went home sick, and the boy came to her stand and said, "Ralph said for me to help you."

"Ralph said that?" She stopped and looked around the store, her hands on her hips, for Ralph. The boy reddened. Not finding Ralph, she said, "All right, you're the second bagger. Anna's the first. Move! Let her get in here," she said, motioning to a girl half his size and at least two years younger. "Go help another checker until Anna takes this cart out." Then, as he turned, "No, you'd better stay here and watch. Anna'll show you how it's done."

The boy stepped back and stooped, in a way that she had not seen him stoop since that first day with her. He needed to stoop; it didn't hurt him to stoop. Then deftly, smoothly, she began feeding Anna item after item and the girl half his size just as deftly and smoothly filled and loaded bag after bag. But Sally was careful to control her tempo so that the process would be deft and smooth. Then Anna left with the filled shopping cart and the boy brought an empty cart to the stand. And Sally picked up the tempo, but just a little at first, just enough to gauge him. The boy was better, much better. She upped the tempo again. He was better, but still clumsy. She checked at her fastest speed. The groceries began backing up. He tore a bag and then had trouble opening another. She kept up the pace. Half the counter was crowded with groceries as he finished filling the third bag. She went even faster, wanting to cover the counter by the time Anna returned. He put the third bag in the cart and then struggled with the creases of the next bag as she said, "Come on, you gotta move, the store's packed today." And then the counter was filled, and she stopped and stared at him, not wanting to move or help him until Anna returned. And then Anna was there and she said, "Get out of the way! Let Anna do it. Move! We can't keep this customer waiting here all day."

But the customer watching said, "Oh, that's all right, Sally. I'm not in that much of a hurry. Everybody has to learn."

Now it was Sally who reddened, and she left the check stand and found Ralph and said, "Get him out of my check stand! Get him out of there!"

Summer came and the boy began working full time, but no longer as a bagger, rather as Fred's helper in produce and stacking shelves. Sally thought, it took me two years to get out of the basement and two years of bagging before I was a checker, before I was full time and he . . . But she thought of it only when she saw him and she saw him less and less. When she did see him, it was usually in the front part of the store with customers who more often than not made a big fuss over him with their Joey this and their Joey that, or Giuseppe's boy here and Giuseppe's boy there. And she saw too, when the boy had been bagging, that some of the customers had begun to bring their daughters shopping. Whoever heard of teenage girls going grocery shopping with their mothers on Saturdays? They deserted her check stand and lined up at whatever check stand the nerdy, ugly boy was bagging, so that their daughters could smile at him and say a few silly words to the rich man's son.

Then, just two weeks before he went back to school, Sally saw Joey in the park and was outraged. She saw him as she walked in that little circle around her bench before she sat down to ready herself, saw him by happenstance, just happened to notice the black baseball cap pulled down to his ears, as no one else wore a baseball cap, and stopped dead in her tracks and stared to be sure, stared at the figure a half a block away sitting on another park bench with his back to her, eating his lunch. Was he following her? Did he know that she came here every day for lunch, that she needed to come here every day for lunch? Was he spying on her? Had he turned his back on her so that she wouldn't think that he was spying on her? It wasn't by accident that he was sitting there pretending to eat his lunch.

She fumed. The bastard! He had everything. Everywhere he went, everything he did, people kissed his ass. Now he wanted the park too. She started toward him. But as she neared him, she saw that he had spread out all of his lunch and his two drinks on the far side of the bench and it occurred to her that he might have come just to eat his lunch, too. She stopped, confused, but angry that he was in her park, yet no longer certain that he had come because of her. She stood and stared for a while longer. Not once did he turn, or stop eating his lunch, or give any indication that he was aware of her. Finally, she started back to her bench, back-pedaling at first, to see if he turned, to make sure that he wasn't spying, and then sat down, angry still, on her bench. Sitting, she couldn't see him.

After that, Sally noticed that he was there almost every day until school started, every day, it turned out, that their lunch coincided. He was there on his bench with that awful baseball cap jammed down onto his head and his lunch spread neatly across the right side of his bench, with his back to her, not once turning or giving the slightest hint that he was spying on her or even knew that she was there whenever she spied on him. She went to Ralph, but stopped because it would have sounded so ridiculous: I don't want you giving him the same lunch hour I get because he goes to Columbus Park too and eats his lunch there too, even though I can't see him eating when I'm eating unless I sneak up on him. She let it go, left Ralph looking up at her asking, "Did you want to see me about something, sweetheart?" In just a few days he would be back in school and there would be no problem.

And there was none, once he returned to school and his part-time hours. At least not until late October, long after the relentless summer fog had blown itself dead and September's heat and haze had extended themselves into October, relieved only by the night and the shrinking days, so that the old building was hot and stuffy and Columbus Park was needed for yet another reason. It was then, on a Saturday, just before her lunch break, that she saw him leave the store, bag in hand, and start in the direction of the park. And she began twitching, no, shaking. She shook through the last two customers, nodding yes, yes, yes, to all their silly chit-chat, wanting only to go to the park and put an end to his crude intrusion once and for all.

"Why do you come here?"

"What?" he said, looking up at her. He had not seen her coming. He had been sitting, hunched, stooped, on the bench with the bill of his cap touching the thick of his glasses, as if he were examining the sandwich that he held in his hand.

"I said why do you come here?" It was not a question; it was an accusation and its tone was cold and confronting.

"Why do I come here?" he repeated, looking at her clearly angry face and then turning from it.

"Why do you come here!"

His look shifted from one side of her, back down to the remains of the sandwich. "To eat my lunch."

"To eat your lunch!" she shouted.

He nodded, without looking up, and said, "Isn't that what you're gonna do?"

She wanted to hit him, but stormed off instead, reaching and passing her bench, but stopping and returning and sitting and looking over at him whom she couldn't see, hating him. That evening she asked Ralph for a later lunch hour on Saturdays and Sundays. And for several weekends she didn't see him at Columbus Park.

———◄———

"I love you."

She was sitting on her bench with her arms outstretched and her head tilted back and her eyes closed, and before she opened her eyes, he said it again. "I love you."

He was standing before her with his cap and his lunch bag in hand, neither flushed nor stooped, looking directly at her when she opened her eyes. He said it again, "I love you."

"What!"

"I love you."

"You *what?*" She was certain he hadn't said what he had said.

"I love you."

"You love me!"

"Yes."

"Are you crazy?"

"No. I know a lot about you, Sally, and I love you."

She looked at him, stunned and puzzled, wanting to be outraged, but only stunned and puzzled. And he looked at her with large open eyes behind those thick glasses.

"Get out of here! Get out of here before I call the police!"

He didn't move or even blink. Instead he said in the same even voice, with the same direct look, "I just wanted to tell you. I had to tell you. In a way it doesn't matter how you feel about me. Because I love you." And with that, he turned and walked away, putting the faded black cap on his head and then pulling it down as tightly as it would fit.

She sat on the bench for the rest of her lunch hour, agitated and angry, not eating, not walking, not getting herself ready, thinking instead, consumed by the word, by the concept, love, and cursing him. Love. What did he know about love? Love. The bastard, how dare he . . . But love still. The word crept, spread through her with all its warmth. Some day there would be love . . . for her. But it was not something she let herself think about, not now. There was no place for it, no time or chance for it, not now. Some day there had to be love. Some day there would be love. But not now. She was about to move herself and her family across the freeway, out of the Eastside, and there was no time for love. Working and keeping track of the kids and Connie was all there was time for. Love. She had long ago decided against the love of the barrio, the transitory passions that had left too many of the others pregnant, alone, and on welfare. And Connie, no matter what her condition, was always preaching at her: "Those white boys you're gonna meet in that store are gonna be after just one thing. Better not be bringing me home one of those halfbreed babies." Connie. As if she could take care of herself, let alone any babies. And here was one of those white boys, a very, very rich white boy. What did this twit know about love? She'd teach him about love, mash his face in his love, hang his love on his swollen dick. All of his daddy's money would never buy her.

Love. For just pennies she had heard men say it, use it over and over again in the dark of their bedroom, as they grunted and gasped over Connie, buried somewhere, drunk or loaded, under them. Love. She had held her breath and shut her eyes in that darkness so they would not know that she was awake and listening. Love. Did men love? Or was it just women that loved? She thought of the boy as she walked back to the store. The idiot. The fool. Was he crazy or just horny?

Then, during a lull, Sally noticed the dark-haired woman who came to the store every Saturday for a case of wine that Ralph specially ordered for her. She was expensively dressed, as was her sixteen-year-old daughter,who had lately begun coming with her. They waited at the front of the store. They were the other checkers' private joke. There was no need for the girl to have come, except to talk to, and walk out with, Joey Rocco, who always brought out the wine and carried it out to their car. Sally looked at the girl. She was pretty. She wore little or no makeup. But then, with the special creams and conditioners that she had probably been using for years, she needed no makeup. Her hair was probably done weekly at a shop that Sally would never see the inside of, and her dress probably came from San Francisco. Sally moved to the end of her counter to better watch this Saturday's exchange.

Then Joey came from the back of the store with the case of wine on his shoulder, and the mother smiled first, a practiced, perfect smile. And then the girl smiled too, but only when Joey looked at her, a sweet unadorned smile: she liked him. And then Joey turned, turned only his head and looked across three check stands to Sally and gave her a look that was slightly more than a glance, because that was all that was needed for the look to say, I love you. Sally turned away because, rather than anger, she felt a blush, a blush to be instinctively hidden from Barbara and Molly, who were watching too.

When Joey and the woman and her daughter left the store, Sally listened to them as she had never listened to them.

"Isn't that a bit much. My God, do you know how much time those two must have spent getting themselves ready just to come over here for that wine."

"Christ, if I wanted my daughter to land somebody that bad, I'd just have him spend the night."

"Oh, come on, Barbara."

"Why not! If she played her cards right, she'd have all the attention she'd ever want."

"Oh, come on, Barbara, they don't do that in those hoity-toity circles."

"I've got news for you, honey: everybody does it. How do you think your daughter's ever gonna get a man?"

"But they're so obvious. You'd think Joey would know."

"Oh, he knows. Christ, with the money his old man has, can you imagine all the mothers and daughters that have been after him? He's probably been running from them for ten years now. He knows."

"And the joke is that he's not only a good kid, but he's a good-looking kid too. If he'd take that God-awful cap off or just wear it like everybody else wears them, and if he took those horrid glasses off and got a pair of contacts, he'd be a very nice-looking boy."

I love you, she heard him say, as she wiped off her counter.

He looked, glanced across at her again, as he went out the front doors to go home two hours later. It was the same look. I love you.

Then Ralph was at the back door, turning off the lights. She wanted to ask him as soon as he got into the car. But he would suspect something. So she restrained herself, managed to wait until they were six blocks down Santa Clara Street.

"Do you trust Joey?"

"What!" Ralph answered.

"I mean, does he lie?"

"What the hell are you talking about, Sally?"

"I mean, does he tell the truth?"

"Of course, he tells the truth. But what the hell does that have to do with you?"

"Nothing really, except that Barbara and Molly make such a big thing about everything he says and does, that I just thought I'd ask you."

"No, he doesn't lie. He's a good kid."

⟵————➤

"Can I sit down?"

She looked up and nodded. It had been two weeks.

"I didn't work all last week or last weekend. I was sick."

"I know."

"Do you always eat lunch here?"

"Yeah, except when it rains or gets too cold."

They sat side by side, neither able to look at the other, not then. It seemed that there was nothing more to say. He wanted to leave, slip away without her seeing any more of his awkwardness than she had already seen.

Now that he had seen her for what she was—a plain, unadorned Mexican from the east side with no fancy clothes or manners, and a high school dropout to boot—she thought that there could be nothing, because she could never be what he wanted her to be. And if it were just sex that he wanted, sex from a Mexican, from an easy mark, she knew she would cry. He made no attempt to touch her or even to move closer. And she thought of his face and words of two weeks before, and she knew that there hadn't been the slightest hint of sex or deceit. She saw that now, as then, he had taken off his cap and was fingering it nervously.

"Do you like working in the store?" she finally said.

"Yeah."

"What do you like about it?" She led him as she would have a customer, but carefully, because she was a full year older, and women spoke easier than men and were smarter than them, and she didn't want to scare him away. But she hadn't expected his answer.

"I like it because it means that I don't have to take any money from my Dad. I buy my own clothes, my own books, I pay room and board. Not that my Dad wants it, because he doesn't. He wouldn't take it when

I tried to give it to him. So I give it to Maria Luca instead. She's our housekeeper. She's lived with us since before I was born. I give her my room and board because she's the one who buys the groceries. And my Dad knows I do that every week. I know he likes me doing that, even though he'll never say so. I make my own spending money, and I'm saving up to buy my own car. I think it's important to support yourself. Don't you, Sally?"

It was the first time he had said her name. And when she turned and looked at him, their look was brief and awkward still, but their fear was gone.

———————

"Can I sit down?"

This time she had seen him coming, in fact, had been watching for him, and when she saw the black cap bob up in the walkway, she had looked down at her sandwich so that he wouldn't know that she had been watching for him, so that he wouldn't see the excitement he was causing her. This time, she smiled when she nodded.

"I only have half an hour for lunch. The dairy cooler went out yesterday and nobody noticed it. Most of the milk and cream and cottage cheese went bad. So I'm cleaning all that out because the milk company's coming this afternoon. And Fred has been uptight all morning. He's really being a jerk. He's . . ."

She was surprised and pleased by the ease with which he spoke. So different from yesterday. She had never heard him say more than a few words to anyone about anything. "Do you like Fred?"

He shook his head, "No, he talks behind people's backs. Everybody. Ralph, me, you. Everybody. But in a way I feel sorry for him too . . . because he's so mean and unhappy."

Then she asked what she had asked herself a hundred times since yesterday. She asked it exactly as she had practiced it, calling him by his name for the first time.

"How long are you going to work here, Joey?"

"Well, I graduate this summer and I want to go to State in September. My Dad says that I can go to any college I want to, any college that I can get into, but I want to put myself through college and State doesn't cost that much, and I'm already paying room and board. And Ralph's pretty good to me. He lets me work the hours I want, so they don't interfere with school. He's been giving me raises right along, and I'm in the union now, and I'm pretty sure I can get myself through State working here. So I guess I'll be here another four or five years, part-time of course . . . . Why? Why do you ask, Sally?"

"I was just curious."

"And you, how long are you going to work here?"

"Probably forever," she said before she could stop herself.

<hr>

Now she returned his looks in the store. As quick and meaningful as his, and guarded too, because those looks were to be shared with no one.

<hr>

"There's five of us altogether. First there's my dad. Everybody knows who he is. When I was a kid I used to like telling people, grown-ups, that my dad was Giuseppe Rocco . . . just to see what their reaction would be."

"What's he like?"

"He's quiet. He doesn't say much. But he doesn't miss much either. He always knows what's going on around him. He doesn't have many friends. I don't either. He's real close to Johnny and me. He doesn't like town much. I don't think he'd live in town if it wasn't for Johnny and me being here."

"Don't you have another brother?"

"Yeah, Matthew. He and my dad aren't very close, and Johnny and I aren't very close to him either. He's younger and kind of a mama's boy. Papa, that's what Johnny and me call him, spends most of his time looking after his ranches and properties and businesses. Every day he leaves real early in the morning and doesn't come home 'til dinner. I've heard all the cracks about him spending more time with the Mexicans than he does with us, but that's not true."

She bristled at the word, but he didn't notice.

"Then there's Johnny. Everybody's heard about Johnny. He's in the paper all the time. He's even been on television. He's the best high school pitcher in San Jose right now and a lot of people say that he's the best San Jose's ever had. Last year, every time he pitched, big league scouts and college coaches were at the games. And he was just a junior. A lot of them have already been to our house, and Papa says he's gonna put a limit to it this year."

"And what about your mom?"

"She's kind of a society lady. Belongs to the symphony here and in San Francisco. She goes to San Francisco a lot. She likes it up there."

———

"I've got three brothers and three sisters. My Mom and myself make eight. There's really not much to say about them."

"I told you about my family."

"My brother Billy's almost eighteen. He's a year younger than me. Angie's next and she turned seventeen just last week. Bobby's sixteen and Elena's fourteen. Rachel's eleven and Danny's nine."

"And what about your mom?"

"She's thirty-three."

"Thirty-three or forty-three?"

"Thirty-three."

"Wow! That's young . . . What's her name?"

"Connie."

"Does she look like you?"

"Not really."

"And your dad?"

"I don't know him."

———

"Johnny's got everything. He's big, he's handsome, he's strong. He's got a great personality. Girls go crazy for him. He's smart, maybe not about books, but he knows people, like Papa. And he's the best baseball pitcher San Jose's ever had. He'll go to the majors easy. He'll never have to rely on Papa."

"Do you like him?"

"Do I like him? Sure I like him. He's my brother."

"Just because he's your brother doesn't mean that you have to like him."

———

"I know a lot about you, Sally."

"What do you know?"

"I know that you support your family . . . that your mother's sick and can't work, and that you support everybody. I know that you just moved your family from the east side. I know that you're practically the mother of your family."

"Who told you this?"

"Nobody told me anything, I just heard."

"From who?"

"The people at the store."

"Which ones?"

"All of them."

"They talk about me?"

"Sure, they do."

"What do they say?"

"What I've told you."

"What else?"

"Lots of things."

"Like what?"

"They talk about your mother."

"What do they say?"

"That she has a drinking problem."

"That's all?"

"That if she's sick, it's because of her drinking."

"That's all?"

"Pretty much."

"Do they talk about the garbage bins too?"

"Yeah."

She reddened. "Do they talk about me and my mother and the garbage bins behind the store?"

"Yeah."

"Oh." She felt herself burning.

After a while he said, "Some of them say that you think you're better than them, but I don't believe that."

"Why do they talk about me? I don't talk about them."

"I don't know."

⟵⟶

"I love you, Sally."

It had been three weeks since he had first said it, and she had wondered and then worried.

He reached for, and she gave him, her hand, relieved. She had touched him during those weeks, touched him lightly, gently on the arm, on the back of his hands, on his shoulder, touched him because she had wanted to be touched. And she had concluded first that he hadn't understood the signals and then that he didn't want to touch her.

"Did you hear me, Sally? I said I love you." He was looking at her there on the park bench and the words sent a shiver through her.

"How can you love me, Joey, you don't even know me."

"I know you and I love you."

"But I'm a Mexican."

"So?"

"I'm poor and uneducated and dark."

"So?"

"Would you introduce me to your father?"

"Yes."

"Would you introduce me to your brother?"

"Yes."

"And your mother?"

"Yes."

"And would you tell them that you loved me?"

"Yes."

"And would you tell Ralph too?"

"Yes."

And she leaned toward him and he kissed her.

"This is where I taught Papa to read."

It was their first day inside the banks of the Guadalupe River.

"You taught your father to read?"

"Yep. Right over there. Come on, I'll show you."

"It's a pretty place."

"We used to come here after school and sit right here and go through my books."

"But he could read Italian, couldn't he?"

"No, I don't think so. He was an orphan, and he was working when he was real young. He didn't have much school."

"You love your Dad, don't you, Joey?"

"Yeah. Probably more than anyone or anything in the world."

"Why?"

"I don't know. I guess he's always seemed so strong. Even when I was a little kid, I could see how much people respected him or were afraid of him. Just walking down the street with him was something special. People paid attention to us, they moved aside, they always wanted to talk to him, they always wanted to be on his good side. He was special, and I could feel that . . . It doesn't even matter that he loves Johnny more than me."

"I don't know if I love Connie or not. I don't even know if I like her."

They had been meeting at the river for more than a week then.

"I know she's my mother, and I know you're supposed to love your mother, but I don't know if I do."

They were lying on an old blanket that he wrapped in plastic and hid in a thicket of volunteer bamboo before they left each day. They were looking up at the sky through the branches of a giant tree that began on the far bank and rose and rose and then spread, covering both banks of the river and more.

"I think she's worn me out. I've been waiting and waiting for her to help me out with the kids, but instead it's the kids that are helping me out with her. They can't let her out of their sight because she'll sneak down to the bar, and then we have a heck of a time getting her back home, if we can find her. The doctor says she's going to kill herself if she keeps drinking. He's told her so many times that I think she does want to kill herself. I think we're going to have to move again. The bar is too close. And Billy's having trouble in school. Too many of his old friends in school. If we move closer to the store, it'll put him in a different high school."

The kisses were becoming too frequent. She knew where they would lead and she wanted more than that.

"Joey, let's eat. We've got to go back to the store. We've got full shifts to work yet and we both have to eat. Look at what I brought you. I know how much you like chili verde and . . ."

He would catch his breath and turn from her to hide, if not the anger, then frustration and embarrassment too for his hunger, although not for chili verde. In a few moments it would pass. His love and respect for her would make it pass.

———————

"No, Joey, please. I want to talk to you. I haven't seen you all week and I want to talk to you."

"You saw me in the store," he would say, sitting up and looking away. "You saw me every day this week in the store."

"But not like this, not here. Not alone and together."

"Well, tell Ralph to give you back your old shift. He's your friend, isn't he? He's like a father to you, isn't he?"

———————

"Joey, let's talk for a while first. I want to talk to you. I want to know what you're thinking. I want to know you."

And he would sigh and lift himself from her and turn and lay on his back and look up at and through the giant tree and say, "You already know me."

"Not like I want to know you."

"And not like I want to know you."

"Oh, Joey."

———————

"What are you thinking?"

"I'm thinking that I love you, Sally."

"Oh, that's nice," she'd say, squeezing his fingers in hers.

"What are you thinking?"

"That I love you . . . Joey, why do you think we're so attracted to each other?"

"I don't know."

———————

"Why do you wear that cap and those glasses?"

"I like my cap, and I need my glasses."

"But, Joey, look. I brought a mirror to show you. Look how much better you look without them. You're handsome. And nobody sees you without them except me. I want people to see how handsome you really are. Don't get me wrong, I don't want anyone else to have you. I just want them to see you."

"I like my cap."

"Yeah, but you don't have to wear it the way you do, all pushed down. All anybody sees is this nerdy-looking guy with an old, beat up cap and thick, thick glasses. You can get contacts, you know . . . And then the way you hunch over . . . It makes you look worse. You don't do that with me. But you do it with everybody else . . . Why do you try to make yourself ugly, Joey?"

He listened to the water pushing against and past the rocks on its endless way to the bay. "Listen to the water, Sally," he said.

"I listen to it all the time, Joey, and I love it. But you're not answering my question."

He listened. It was a soothing sound. Then he said, "I guess it's because I want people to like me for me. All my life people have made a fuss over me because of Papa. I know why Mrs. Candiotti brings her daughter down to the store every week. I know why she always walks on the outside and puts Julie between us. I can't tell you all the things they've invited me to. I'm not stupid. They think that some day I'll be rich. Well, if it's Papa's money they want, Sally, then at least let me be ugly."

———————

It was the day after Thanksgiving and once they spread out the blanket, it began to rain.

"Papa always says that the weather always changes right after Thanksgiving."

"But where are we going to meet, Joey?"

"It won't be long. He says it always breaks around Lincoln's birthday."

"But that's in February, and he doesn't know everything."

"I didn't say he did."

"But where are we going to meet, Joey? It'll be too wet and cold out here."

A gust of wind increased the rain and freed yellow leaves above them.

"I don't want to meet in the basement."

"We can't hide all the time, Sally."

"We're not hiding. I like it here."

"They've got to know sometime. I'm not ashamed of you."

"I didn't say you were. I just couldn't take all their looks and whisperings. Not now."

"You act like we're doing something wrong. I don't care what they say."

"But I do. I just couldn't take all their gossip and the way they'd spread it out to all the customers. I'd feel them talking about us all the time. I'm not ready for that yet, Joey."

"How about if we meet at the Koffee Kup."

"I can't afford to buy my lunch in a restaurant."

"So I'll buy it for you. You always bring me stuff."

"They'll see us there, Joey."

"Nobody from the store goes there."

"I don't just mean them. People will see us there. Everybody knows you. It'll get back to the store. It'll get back to your family. They'll laugh at us. They'll laugh at me. Your family will get mad."

"Why?"

"Because I don't belong with you."

"I think you do."

For the next two and a half months they met twice a week at St. Paul's Church. Except for an occasional old woman or man, there was never anyone in the church during their lunch hour. At first they sat in the back of the church in its darkest corner and spoke in whispers.

"Do you still love me, Joey, even though we have to meet here?"

"I'd rather meet here than not meet at all."

"How come you never go to church?"

"I guess I've never seen any reason to go. Papa never goes, and my Mom goes all the time. She and Maria Luca and Matthew. But I don't see that it's made them any better than Papa. In fact, they're not as good a person as Papa. None of them."

"But do you still love me?"

"Yes." And he kissed her.

"I'll get better, Joey. Believe me. In a few months I won't care what people think."

"Papa's good to the poor. In the winter when people aren't working, he sends trucks full of food and clothes to the labor camps. Ask

Ralph, he'll tell you. I've seen him with Mexican workers. He doesn't talk down to them; he doesn't laugh at them or make fun of them; and he doesn't take advantage of them. And they know it and like him and respect him. My mother comes to church every Sunday, and she looks down on the Mexicans. Sometimes Papa brings Mexicans from the camps to do some work around our place. She doesn't like it. She's afraid of them. I think she thinks they're going to rape and rob her and dirty up our place. I don't know what good all that church stuff does for her except make her feel important. If there's a heaven, Papa ought to go, and he never comes here."

"Will you ever love me as much as you love your father, Joey?"

"Sally, that's different."

———

Just before Christmas, they discovered the side chapel. For the next several weeks they spent the last ten minutes of each meeting standing in its corner, locked in embraces away from the eyes of anyone in the main body of the church. Two weeks later as he met her, Joey said, "Let's just go to the side chapel, Sally."

"No, Joey, if we're there the whole time someone will see us."

"Who's gonna see us? Who comes in here except one or two old women who can't even see anyway?"

"Joey, I want to talk to you."

"We talk all the time."

"Joey, we're only together for forty-five minutes two times a week."

"That's not my fault."

"I didn't say it was. But I want to talk to you. We have to get to know each other."

"We already know each other."

"But I want to spend time with you."

"What's wrong with spending it in the chapel."

"We won't talk in the chapel."

"Well, let's go out tonight after work. Guys take their girls out on Saturday nights. We can do all the talking you want to then."

"I can't. Not yet anyway, Joey. I have to get my family ready. I have to tell them about you. They won't understand. I have to get myself ready. People won't understand. Just give me a few more weeks, Joey."

They were wrapped in an embrace in the chapel, pressed tighter and tighter against each other, breathing heavily, with Joey's hands caressing her back and her waist and her buttocks, when Sally opened her eyes and saw him and gasped and jerked out of Joey's arms.

"What's the matter?" he said, irritated, collecting his breath. Then he saw her face and her eyes and he turned and saw him too.

He was a bent, stooped, shrunken old man whose strands of thinned, white hair stood straight up from his olive scalp. The years had also blurred his race: he could have been an Italian or a Mexican. He stood there just inside the chapel entry, mesmerized by them, even as they stared back at him, his mouth grinning or at least half smiling and his eyes twinkling even now that they had separated. He said nothing and they said nothing until Joey hissed, "Shoo! Go on! Get out of here!" as he would have to a stray dog or cat. Only then did the grin break and the twinkle snap, and then he was a startled old man who promptly hobbled off.

For the following week, Sally wouldn't return to the side chapel.

"Why not?"

"Because he might come."

"There's nobody here except us, Sally."

"There was nobody here when we went to the chapel the last time either."

"There's been nobody here the last three times."

"I just don't want him to see us again."

"He's not going to see us again. And even if he did, are we doing anything wrong, anything that we should be ashamed of?"

"Did you see his face?"

"Sure I saw his face. He's nothing but a dirty old man."

"We're in the house of God."

"Sally, we love each other. Are we doing anything wrong? Are we doing anything God's never seen before?"

◆━━━◆

Reluctantly she agreed to return to the side chapel. But it wasn't the same, at least not for several weeks, at least not until they left St. Paul's for good.

"What was that?" she said, pushing away from him.

"I don't know. What was that?"

"Don't tell me you didn't hear that."

"Sally, I've heard a lot of things. This is an old church. It creaks. The wind blows. People do come in, but they hardly ever come to this side chapel. That old guy's the only one that's ever come."

"There's somebody in here now."

He sighed and walked into the body of the church, into a pew directly across from the side chapel, and then stopped and looked in every direction and returned. "I told you, Sally, there's nobody here."

"Yes, there is. I heard him. Anyway, we've got to get back to the store."

"We've got five minutes yet."

"Not me. I've got to get back early."

"Oh, God."

⸺⸺⸺

They left St. Paul's church a week after Lincoln's birthday, but not before she reminded him, "I thought your father said the weather always changes by Lincoln's birthday."

"So he's off a few days."

"It sure has changed. It's pouring out there. I don't think it's rained this hard all winter."

⸺⸺⸺

It was still raining on the day they left. Sally had finally relaxed, and Joey's caresses were longer and stronger.

They had been clamped together for several minutes when Sally saw him and screamed and jumped back. Then she gasped, stepped back again, whimpered, and covered her eyes, saying, "Oh no! Oh no!" Joey looked, but saw nothing. He went to the chapel entry and looked, but saw no one and nothing in the entire church. He looked back at Sally, who was crying now, her head down and her eyes covered.

"What is it, Sally, tell me. What is it?"

But she only shook her head and cried.

And then he heard something between a gasp and a moan just a few feet from him. He turned again and still saw nothing, until he heard the sound again and looked under a pew and saw the old man of some weeks ago lying under the pew, stuck, pinned, it seemed at first, his eyes bulging and his mouth agape, but with his penis in his hand. Then it was Joey who screamed, "Get out of there! Get the fuck out of there!

Get the fuck out of there!" But the old man didn't move. He lay motionless, gasping, or at least trying to suck in air. Joey jumped into the row and bent and pulled, grunting, "Get the fuck out of here! Get the fuck out of here!" The old man was stuck, inert. Then Joey kicked him. "Get out of here, you pig! You pig! You pig!" He kicked him again. And Sally screamed, "Stop, Joey, stop! Let's go! Let's get out of here!" Then she ran out of the chapel, into the aisle, out the first set of doors, into the vestibule, and out into the street.

———————

It rained for three weeks. "Can you believe this weather. Never seen anything like it," customer after customer said. But for Sally it was a blessing. She wasn't ready for the river, for the banks of the Guadalupe. Not yet. Because the nights had become a torment, leaving her more exhausted than the days. Nights were filled with images of shriveled, toothless old men with standing strips of white hair crawling into the bed of a terrified child, amid the breathing of brothers and sisters and thuds from her mother's bed. Often the old man was the old man in the church. Sometimes he was Joey.

———————

In the basement she said, "Joey, please, they're going to see us. They're going to put two and two together. They're going to know."

"So let them know. Who cares? It's about time they know."

"I care, Joey. I'm not ready. I couldn't take all their whispers and looks. Not now."

"Well, let me drive you home at least."

"Then Ralph will know."

"Tell him you're gonna walk home."

"In the rain!"

"Oh, Jesus."

"Joey, somebody's going to come down here and see us together."

"I don't care who sees us together. I love you. Don't you understand that?"

"Joey, if you don't leave, I'll leave. I'll go out in that rain. I swear. You've got your car at least."

"Sally, it's been two weeks since we've been together. I need to talk to you. I need to hold you. I need to kiss you."

"Joey, I promise, as soon as it stops raining, I'll go to the river with you. The first day it stops, I'll meet you there."

"Let me pick you up after Ralph drops you off. You don't work tomorrow. Give me your address. I'll be there at 9:30."

"Joey, I can't. I haven't told my family about you yet. They'll worry. They'll call Ralph."

"Are you ashamed of me?"

"No, I'm ashamed of *me*."

———

It was a glorious spring day. The sun was warm and the bank was dry and everywhere there was new life. He met her at the bamboo, showed her the clearing he had made there and the new blanket he had spread out. She still said, "We have to be quiet, Joey, we have to be careful. We can't see anyone coming."

But the bamboo was anything but quiet. It rustled and crackled and shook with each of Joey's movements, as he kissed her and held her and pressed himself closer and closer against her until that wasn't enough and he slid on top of her. She now welcomed his weight and his hands. Their mouths knew each other in a new way. His hands struggled with her clothing and she not only let him, but helped him. He touched her and her mouth told him to go on, now, hurry. But when he lifted himself, frantically struggling with his pants buttons, she bolted up and covered herself with her blouse.

"No, Joey, I can't! I can't! Stop! I can't!"

Joey, with two buttons undone and feverishly working on the third, said only, "You can't?"

"I can't."

"You can't."

"Not until we're married."

And he with his fingers still on his third button, groping as hard at the button as he was struggling to understand her, said, "Well, then I'll marry you."

That was how their talk of marriage began.

———

"It's that I want it to be for love," she would say over and over again.

"But I love you, Sally."

"Do you, Joey?"

"You know I do."

"Oh, Joey, I've heard those words so many times, and they've always meant nothing."

"Where have you heard those words before?"

"Not to me, Joey, but to other women. Believe me, I have. And they've meant nothing."

"I don't care what you've heard. I know what I mean. I'll marry you."

"Will you, Joey?"

"Yes."

"Why?"

"Because I love you."

"Why?"

"I don't know why. I just know that I do."

———————

How can he love me? If he were to see the five of us sleeping on these three beds in this one room. If he could smell us, smell me, now. If he could hear Connie snoring. If he saw how I sweat and bleed. If I didn't wear any deodorant, how could he love me?

That was how it began each day, or rather, continued. Because it was in her too. She would wake to it, to the debate, or better, the lecture that she was enduring, aware in those first wakeful moments of the entire text, and then, within a few seconds, only of a few lines, the last lines, the context: how can he love me?

If he saw me, if he saw who I am and how I live, he who has everything, how could he possibly love me? If he knew me, if he really knew me, how . . . You've seen his fine home. You've snuck by it every chance you've gotten. But that's as close as you'll get, and you know it. Because he'll never take you in there to meet his family. Because they'll have nothing to do with you. You know that. Oh, maybe he might sneak you up to his bedroom when nobody else is around, but that's as close as you'll get, and you know that too. Unless, of course, Ralph has you deliver groceries there. And then you would go to the back door, just like everybody else in the store does, and especially you. More than likely, you'd scare the old woman, that Maria, because she'd see right away that you're a Mexican . . . Oh God, forget him, you don't need this. You can't think, and you can't sleep, and you can't eat. Forget him. There'll be someone else out there for you. A nice Mexican boy, when the time is right, whose family will accept you and you'll be happy.

Then, having settled it once and for all, she would be at peace with herself there in the bedroom or bathroom or on her way to work or to Rachel's school. She would be relieved, until he crept back into her mind again, or she let him creep back into her mind again with all his insidious hope: Joey kneeling in the bamboo, fingering his button, but saying as sincerely as it could be said, "Sally, I love you and I'll marry you." And she would sigh and rise on those words and let their warmth and happiness carry her on to wherever she was going or whatever she was doing in a bliss that was meant to be, until the doubt and the fear and the monologue began again.

Sex. That's what it has to be. Maybe he's never had a Mexican before. Maybe he wants to live the low life. Are you trying to say that he'll love you for any longer than it will take him to come? Wake up, girl. He wants your pussy. Isn't that what they call it? Pussy. Men and their pussy. Do you really think he wants anything more than pussy? What else can you possibly give him besides pussy?

It was easier on the days when she didn't see him, on the days when he or she didn't work. Then there wouldn't be the fall, the plunge, the bleak, black depression and despair. On those days, there wouldn't be the high, there wouldn't be the look, the first look that she waited for on each of those days, the look that came to her from wherever he was standing in the store, the look that she wanted and got, the look that said, Sally, I love you. That look sent her soaring and made everything wonderful, that made her happy when all that she wanted was to be happy. And that first look would be sustained, reinforced, fed, by any number of looks from him for the rest of the day, most of which, if not all, would say, Sally, I love you. And she would float through whatever she was doing, happier than she had ever been, happier than she had ever known anyone to be. So happy that there were times when he held her in the bamboo and said, "Sally, I love you," that she would burst into tears. And when he'd ask, she'd answer, "Nothing, Joey, nothing. I'm just so happy." And then the plunge would come, sometimes even before she left the store, when she didn't see him or he didn't look, or the look was too brief or casual, or Molly fussed over him, or a customer or her daughter flirted with him, or if she dwelt on the fact that she wouldn't see him tomorrow.

And if not in the store, then certainly by the time she got home, by the time she walked through the door of the small two-bedroom house with the cramped disarray and smells and sounds of eight bodies, eight Mexican bodies, to the cheap worn and stained furniture and tables and chairs and utensils that accommodated their daily needs, to the darkened thirty-three-year-old woman who sat in a daze most of every day in the same chair in the same place in the same room, waiting for someone or something or nothing—all of which screamed out to her that it could never, would never, be. And then she too moved about in a hurtful daze. She too sat and ate the tasteless food that Angie had prepared, and she too stared into the empty awful future as the others spoke, until the hurt again convinced her that it was better, easier now than later, to forget him, let him go, let him be, so that she too could be.

Over time, she thought of him and there was first the hint, and then the suggestion, and then the belief, that he had not lied, because the looks had been true and the words and touches, too. She saw him again, and the look said what it said, crushing the hopelessness, the despair, and she was soaring once again, not fearing or thinking, but rather savoring, enjoying the moment, happy.

"I love you too," she would answer. Their breathing would quicken and deepen as he held her or caressed her and pressed himself to her. When the breathing got too heavy, when he felt that he was about to explode, he would release her and roll over on his back and look up at the giant tree that had once again given birth. She would reach for his hand and say, "I'm sorry, Joey. Believe me, I want you too. Believe me, I love you."

"Well then, marry me."

Four weeks after they returned to the river, she said, "When?"

"Now."

"In two months you'll be out of high school. We can decide then," she said.

"Why then?"

"Because you'll be nineteen then and out of high school. You'll be a man then. And we can go to Reno and get married, and then no one can say that I took advantage of you or that we didn't know what we were doing."

<hr>

She had decided before then, some two weeks earlier, on Connie's thirty-fourth birthday. She had come home from the store and had found Joey there in the house with presents for all and a cake and wine for Connie, sitting next to Connie, listening to her as she babbled on about when she was a young girl and how everybody said that Sally looked just like her and was probably as pretty as she had been with the same figure that made most boys turn. When Sally looked at him in disbelief, he smiled.

He ate with them and led the younger kids in singing "Happy Birthday." And Connie cried and kissed him and said to Sally in her best English, "Where did you ever find such a sweet young man, Sally?"

Only Billy and Bobby didn't like him, but Billy no longer lived there, and Bobby was just parroting his older brother's words.

Billy followed her into the bedroom and said, "What're you doing with that faggoty peckerwood?"

"You better get used to him, if you're gonna keep coming around here to freeload," she answered.

She started planning that very night. They would go to Reno the day after he graduated. They would rent the little house behind them. Angie would be eighteen by then. They would have to talk about money. She would have to budget as she had never budgeted before. She would . . .

<hr>

"You *what?*"

"Joey and I are going to get married."

"Joey who?" said Ralph Giordano, hoping beyond hope that it was not the Joey that they both knew.

"Joey Rocco."

Ralph sat back in his chair and rubbed his bald head and looked around his tiny office as if there would be some answer there. Then he looked back at her and saw a nervous half-smile and said, still hopefully, "You gotta be kidding."

She shook her head no, and the smile fled, and her mouth quivered, and he turned from her again, lest she start crying.

Oh, my God, he thought, and then, Oh, my God, again. He looked past her in disbelief. The air in the small room grew heavy, and he understood, knew, that she had come seeking his approval, when there could never be any approval for anything so outrageous. She was waiting, and he knew it, waiting for that which he could never give. He still loved her, and his heart ached for her. Finally, he said, "When?"

"Tomorrow, after Joey graduates."

"Tomorrow?" Ralph Giordano said, rubbing his bald head again. "Isn't that a little soon?" Like any parent, he hoped that time would change what she didn't know, couldn't know.

"No, we decided months ago."

"But I don't think I've ever seen the two of you even talk to each other the whole time you've worked here."

"Oh, we've talked. We've done a lot more than talk."

He blushed: was she pregnant? That mattered little, because along with that thought was the thought of Giuseppe Rocco. He had seen him angry before and he could see him angry now somewhere in his store, anywhere in his store, shouting: My son! My son! I let him come to work in your lousy little store and this happens! I can break you, you know! I can . . . And Mrs. Rocco. She would be worse. With all her airs, she would be worse. She truly would be vindictive. She would never forgive him, would always blame him. Her son married to a Mexican, a Mexican from the rankest of welfare families, from a mother who was a whore and a thief and a junkie and now a sickly drunk. And he, Ralph Giordano, had arranged it and permitted it, had made a laughingstock of her Rocco family. And with all the business she brought into the store and into his son's catering business . . .

He looked at the pretty, dark-skinned girl, who at nineteen looked like a fourteen-year-old, vulnerable and needy. Doesn't she understand that she doesn't belong with those people, of all families, of all Italian families, of all white families, not that family?

It was Sally who broke the silence. "We haven't told anybody. Nobody knows, not even Connie. But I wanted to tell you, Ralph, I wanted to tell you. Outside of Joey, you're the only one I can count on, you're the only one I have."

This stopped him. He remembered the girl covered with slime as he lifted her out of the garbage bin, the girl who had lied to him about where she lived, the girl who had stamped cans as if she were haunted, taunted even, the checker who had moved her family out of the armpit of the slum, not once but twice, to the small but tidy house just blocks from the store. And he said, "Do you love him?"

"Yes."

"Do you think he loves you?"

"I know he loves me."

"Are you sure?"

"Yes."

"This is not something you think you have to do?"

"No."

"This is something you want to do?"

"I want to do it, Ralph. Believe me, more than anything else in my life, I want to do it."

"Then you should do it."

And he hugged her.

―――――――

Sally and Joey rented the small house directly behind the house where Sally's family lived. Together they painted the house and shopped for used furniture. They would work full time at the store through the summer, and he would reduce his hours in the fall when he began San Jose State. She would handle the money. They neither expected nor wanted a penny from his parents. If they budgeted, and she would, they could make ends meet.

―――――――

They started out early for Reno on a bright June morning following his graduation. Sally had planned the trip carefully. It was 528 miles round trip to Reno. If they drove at fifty-five miles per hour, the trip would take no more than ten hours. That would give them enough time to find the chapel that had been recommended to her as the best bargain in town, to have the ceremony performed, and still be back in San Jose at a decent hour. The fifty-five mile-per-hour speed was important for another reason. It gave the best gas mileage, and she had budgeted for three tanks of gas. She had taken fifty dollars more than she thought the gas and ceremony would cost, just in case, but they would use it only for an emergency, because she knew that they needed that fifty dollars to live on until the next pay day. She prepared sandwiches and drinks for their lunch and dinner, and she shifted them in the car, keeping them out of the sun, so that they would be as fresh as possible. She reminded Joey of his speed, explaining that gas was more expensive outside the big towns, and if he wasn't careful, they would have to gas up along the highway.

They arrived in Reno on schedule, passed through its daytime glitter, and stopped on a street full of chapels. They went into one and saw the smiles fade as Sally asked for directions to The Chapel of the Woods. "I can tell you where it is, ma'am. But it's not in a very good part of town, and I don't think you'll be very happy there. In fact, I don't know if they're still performing marriages over there . . . Honey, do you know if the Woods is still marrying people? Seems to me like I heard they lost their license." They went on anyway. The fifty dollars had to last them another six days. "Don't worry, Joey, it'll be nice."

It wasn't nice. It was a dilapidated, dirty old house in the black part of town, run by a shriveled, old, white man named Woods, who wore a stained and soiled maroon tie and croaked, "Want to get married, do you?"

"How much is it?" asked Sally.

"Fifteen dollars," he said, but weakly, which made her think that they could get it for ten. She let it pass, not wanting to bargain over their wedding ceremony, and nodded yes.

The old man disappeared behind a worn curtain, and then they heard voices and stirrings, and they smelled rancid grease. The old man returned with a sly smile on his face, leading by the hand an equally shriveled old woman in a rayon dress, who in turn was leading a mongoloid teenager by the hand. Each of them took a place: the old woman placed the mongoloid next to Joey and then stood next to Sally, who wanted to stop it then, wanted to run from there, but didn't, couldn't, because they needed the fifty dollars for another six days. The old man took out a wrinkled black book and recited from it old, familiar phrases while the mongoloid laughed and shook his head no.

"It doesn't matter, Joey," Sally said in the car. "All that matters is that we're married." She kissed him to reassure him. "All that matters is that we have this." She waved the soiled paper that the old man had signed. "Now no one can separate us. Now we can be happy."

She burst into tears. "I'm sorry, Joey, I'm sorry. But I wanted to budget. We need to budget."

Chapter III

It was just past eight when Fred leaned into Ralph Giordano's office and said quietly, "Giuseppe Rocco's here. He wants to talk to you."

"Giuseppe Rocco," he mumbled, feigning surprise. As he walked out to the front of the store, he was thankful that it was so early, that nobody was there. He had expected much worse. And when he saw Giuseppe Rocco standing at Sally's check stand, he stopped at the end of the far aisle and said, gesturing, "Giuseppe Rocco. Come on back to my office. I've got somebody on the phone. We can talk better there." He avoided looking directly at the man in the faded brown leather jacket, not meeting his eyes. He looked only in his direction, and turned as soon as Giuseppe Rocco nodded, and then half waiting, half starting, moved toward the back.

When Giuseppe Rocco caught up with him near the end of the aisle, he stopped again and shook Giuseppe Rocco's hand, but quickly, still not meeting his eyes. He mumbled, "I've got to finish this call," as he led Giuseppe into his office. Ralph wondered how much of the shouting the others would hear with the door closed. After entering his office, he stationed himself at the door, then closed it as soon as Giuseppe Rocco entered. He spoke first, seizing the moment.

"I know why you're here. And I want to tell you, believe it or not, that I didn't know a goddamn thing about it until a few hours ago. Not a goddamn thing. You probably don't believe me, but I didn't know a goddamn thing."

Giuseppe Rocco said only, "Can I sit down?"

"Sure." Ralph was taken off his guard by the other's quiet, his calm, but he nevertheless seized the moment again and added, "And I want to tell you, Giuseppe Rocco, that that is one damn fine girl! I don't care if she's Mexican or not, she's one damn fine girl!" And then, regretting it even as he said it, but saying it because he had vowed so many times to say it, "I think Joey's lucky to have her."

Giuseppe Rocco looked up at him from under the brim of his grey khaki hat. His eyes were quiet. He said calmly, "Take it easy, Ralph, I only came here to meet my daughter-in-law and speak to my son."

Then the two men sat in silence, one embarrassed and one at peace with himself.

"She's a damn fine girl, Giuseppe."

"Yes, I think I saw some of that last night."

"This is an exceptional girl. I don't think there's anything she can't do if she puts her mind to it . . . And she's very pretty . . . Don't be too hard on them, Giuseppe, they're both good kids."

"What time do they come in today?"

"They both start at one."

At exactly 1:15, Giuseppe Rocco stepped just inside the front doors of Giordano's Market and stood there unnoticed amidst the comings and goings of others. He looked at the checkout stands and saw her. There could be no question as to which of the three checkers she was. She was more than pretty, she was beautiful. He watched her nimble hands and her quick eyes and her magnificent smile through two customers, nodding to himself. Then she was free, and he went to her and, standing at the far end of the counter, said, "My name is Giuseppe Rocco. And you must be Sally Rocco, my new daughter-in-law."

Sally turned, startled and wide-eyed, as the words scrambled about in her mind for some meaning, even after there was no denying who he was, not because of his face or his body, but rather because of the old leather jacket and the grey khaki hat that Joey had so often described. And more, she had seen him before, she had known him before. She knew that too, even as she watched and waited for the anger that she had long expected. Instead, she saw him open his arms and smile and say, "Welcome . . ."

Sally went to him, and he hugged her and kissed her and said, "Welcome to my family! I'm so happy to have you! We've needed a good, beautiful girl like you for such a long time!"

Then Giuseppe Rocco turned to everyone in that part of the store, most of whom were already watching, and said, "Hey, all of you! I want you to meet my new daughter, Sally Rocco! Sally Rocco! Isn't she beautiful!"

And there were cheers and clapping, and when those subsided, he said, just under a shout, "Where's Joey? Somebody get Joey! We need to celebrate! Get Joey!"

When Joey appeared, he said, "Come here, my son! You did good! You did real good! I'm so proud of you. I'm so proud and happy for both of you! Let's have a party!"

And a party was had—a huge party in the parking lot of Giordano's Market. The store was closed. "I'll pay you three times what you've been taking in on Mondays, Ralph, so don't worry!" Food and drink were taken from the store at first, until caterers arrived with tables and chairs and Italian and Mexican food. A mariachi band appeared within the hour. Everyone was invited. Customers and would-be customers and passersby all joined in. The crowd swelled to well over two hundred. The first dance was danced by Sally and Joey inside a huge circle formed by the crowd. The second dance belonged to Giuseppe Rocco and his new daughter. She was certain by then, there was no doubting it. Still, she cried through the second dance, just as she had through the first. And when Giuseppe Rocco asked her why she was crying, she said, "Because I'm so happy. And because this is where it all started."

"Where?"

"Over there by the garbage bins."

❧ Book Three ❧

Chapter I

Later on the evening of the wedding party, Matthew Rocco found his mother in the study. "Peter just called. He says that Giuseppe's throwing a big party for Joey and his wife down at the parking lot of Giordano's Market. He says that there's music and food and drink and that everyone's invited. He says it's getting loud and rowdy."

Rita Verducci looked up from her book, thought for a moment, and then said, "Peasants."

That night, Giuseppe Rocco entered the old Victorian house for the last time. He had planned to take the few remaining things he had in his room the night before. Instead, he had witnessed, was fascinated by, the scene between Sally and Rita Verducci and Joey, all of it, including the arrival of the police, the escorting of Joey to and from his upstairs room by a uniformed officer, Rita's blocking of the girl's path not only with her body but with her insults: "Whore! Slut! Mexican gold digger! I want her out of here now! Do you hear me, now!" And finally, "You'll never set foot in this house again!"

Giuseppe Rocco entered for the last time, knowing it would be the last time. He entered through the servant's entrance as he had for many years now, careful not to wake the sleeping two, the same two he had been careful not to wake even when Johnny and Joey had been there. Once he was in the open space of the kitchen, he understood how drunk he was. Each step was an adventure: his stationary foot bent, leaned, tilted, and wobbled, making it impossible to gauge where his moving foot would land. He tittered and held back a laugh. He grabbed onto a counter as he started to fall; he hung on tightly until the kitchen stopped swirling. All he needed was for Matthew to be standing over him with a gun drawn. The little bastard would shoot and then claim that he thought he was a burglar.

He started up the rear stairs, holding onto the railing with both hands, feeling for each stair with the clods of his feet, frightened lest he stumble in the dark and topple back and down to a large crash. When had he become so servile in his own house? He remembered how he had scrambled and struggled to buy the house from owners who did not want to sell to someone as crude as he. He relived that struggle there in the darkness as keenly as he felt for the next stair. When had he lost the house? When had it become theirs? When had he become so servile? He wanted to cry out in the darkness as much in defiance as in anguish. He didn't, and he knew he wouldn't. He knew he would meekly, anxiously feel his way up those stairs until he reached what, after tonight, would no longer be his room, and then what, after tonight, would no longer be his bed.

In the hall, in his drunkenness, as he leaned against the wall and took one careful step after another, he conceded, as if there were anything left to concede: the house was theirs. There was nothing there for him. He was a stranger in a strange land. Johnny's departure had precipitated his departure. But he had not expected Joey's departure, not so soon. And he had not expected the total void, the barrenness that Joey would leave behind, that he felt now.

When he reached his room, as he felt for the door knob, he took back his concession. He was tired of concessions: life now was nothing but a series of concessions. So he sank to the hallway floor and there, sitting, shook his head no, no to life and no to death and no to Matthew and his gun and no to Rita and her house. It was his house. He had already made too many concessions. Johnny was gone and death was coming.

What did he have left: five, ten, fifteen years, if that? And then all would be gone. All of his sweat and struggle and sacrifice would be gone. It was not the money that mattered. It was the awe, the respect, the reverence even, that everyone had for him wherever he went. He loved the busts of A.P. Giannini in all the Bank of Americas; they made A.P. a great man. Johnny could make him a great man, carry him past the grave too. Because everything he was, everything he had, had been passed on to Johnny. He had seen it in what he now hated most, the baseball. He had seen the fire and the drive and the ruthlessness and fearlessness that had made him what he was, he had seen all of that in Johnny, most clearly in his silly baseball. But now that silly baseball had taken his Johnny, maybe forever, maybe never to return.

That left him with Joey, good, kind, sweet Joey. The money world would eat him alive. Better that he should give everything to charity now, rather than let those vultures pluck it at will from Joey. And Joey had married. She was a strong girl. How strong remained to be seen. But any child of theirs would still carry Joey's blood, and Joey's was not his blood, or at least not that part of his blood that Johnny carried.

In the morning, he waited until he heard Rita's car. Then he looked from behind the curtain and saw that it was the two of them. Only then did he gather what few things had any meaning for him, and in a single trip downstairs, left.

He drove south and then west through Morgan Hill along the back roads that straddled the base of the coastal range. At sixty-three, he was beginning the final phase of his life just as he had begun the first phase: alone. An occasional oak gave way to redwoods interspersed by madrones and maples. He turned right off the two-lane road onto a narrower road that pointed directly into the mountains. After a little more than a mile, the mountain receded briefly and a large clearing, an indentation, appeared, one in which a vineyard had been planted on one side and an orchard on the other. In the center was a small, cream-colored house with a red tile roof. The road ended at the driveway that led to the house. As Giuseppe Rocco unlocked the gate, he turned and looked across the valley floor toward where Angelina's house stood. He had thought of living there. But now, more than ever, it was important to keep it as it had been.

———————

"Is Joey home?"

"No, he's not, Mr. Rocco. He went to have the car checked. Something about the carburetor. He should be back soon."

She was standing behind the screen door. The light was such that he could see her, see her eyes clearly. They were clean, brown eyes, beautiful eyes, and they looked at him as few people did, open and direct, without deference or intimidation, neither hostile nor servile, but rather, calm and serene. Giuseppe Rocco did what he seldom did anymore: he looked away. And then started to leave. "Just tell him that his father . . ."

"Oh, don't go, Mr. Rocco. Really, he should be back any minute. Please come in, Mr. Rocco. He really does want to see you. He tried to call you to invite you over, but he didn't know how to contact you. Nobody has your new number, not even your lawyer."

"Please don't call me Mr. Rocco. Call me Joseph, Giuseppe, Idiot, anything, but not Mr. Rocco."

She nodded and smiled, thinking that he was not at all what she had expected, not what she remembered. But then, she remembered so little.

"Won't you come in," she said, unlatching the screen door. "Joey will be here any minute."

He nodded and entered and stepped past her, noting as he did her long, smooth arm, lithe and lovely in its youthfulness.

"Please make yourself comfortable, Mr. uh . . ."

"Just call me Papa. All my kids do."

"I don't have a father."

"You do now."

They laughed uneasily.

"Can I get you something to drink?"

"No, it's too early for wine."

"I meant a Coke or water. We don't have any wine."

"And you said Joey wanted to invite me over. Are you sure of that?"

Again they laughed uneasily.

It was not his intention to make her uneasy. "I'll take a glass of water, thank you." When she rose and left, he looked, but just for a moment, catching himself, reminding himself that this was his son's wife and this was his son's home. And he looked about the small front room instead. It was spotless and neatly arranged.

In the kitchen she thought, It's him.

He drank from the glass and said, "You know, I've heard nothing but good things about you." He repeated some of the many good things that Ralph Giordano had told him about her. As he looked at her from time to time, he was struck by the fact that her look remained the same: calm, open, unintimidated, and direct.

When he finished, she was ready, saying without hesitation, "I know you don't remember, but we've met before."

"We have?"

She nodded.

And his eyes moved over the vast expanse of the past, and he shook his head and said, "I don't remember."

"It was a long time ago. At my aunt's house."

"Your aunt's? Who's your aunt?"

"Yolanda. Yolanda Parra."

The words staggered him. His face fell. "Yolanda." His eyes froze, deserted him, returned to the warmth and softness of that wonderful woman.

"I was a little girl and she lived in Salinas then, at the edge of town. Twice when you were visiting her, my sisters and I were staying with her because my mother was sick . . . I guess you could say. I saw you come with the food and the presents, and, the second time, you gave me a doll. All the kids there liked you, and so did I. And my aunt loved you."

He looked up. There was no malice in her eyes, no glee as he staggered. He looked away and once again said softly, again to himself, "Yolanda."

They sat silent, he studying the specks of bubbles at the bottom of his glass, and she studying him, knowing now that he too had loved her.

Then he said, without looking up, "Where is she now?"

"The last I heard was that she was somewhere in Tennessee."

"Tennessee?" She might just as well have been in the jungle.

"Yes. She married an American man . . . a white man who treated her good. And when most of the kids were out of the house, they moved to Tennessee. That's where he's from." Then she added, thinking that she shouldn't add it, but adding it anyway, "I saw her daughter Ofelia, on the street not too long ago, and she said that her mom was really happy over there."

"That's good," he mumbled, "That's good," even though it wasn't good, even though it hurt, even though he longed for Yolanda then as much as he ever had. "That's good," he said for the last time and then sighed and returned to the minute bubbles that filled the bottom of the glass when all that filled him was Yolanda.

Perhaps to make amends, Sally said, "She really loved you. You could see it whenever you came. She lit up. She was a different person. She was . . ." Sally stopped. He was hurting.

It was a quiet back house in a quiet residential district. And it grew quieter by the second, until he said, "Does Joey know?"

"No, I thought it was you after I first saw you at the store, more after we danced. But I wasn't sure until you came this afternoon, when you were standing at the door. So there was really nothing to tell him."

"Will you tell him now?"

"There's nothing to tell him. That was between you and my aunt."

Again they sat in an awkward silence until he said, beginning his exit, "Maybe Joey got stuck somewhere." Just then, a boy crashed into the screen door with a loud bang and then bounded into the room.

"Sally, Bobby took my marbles and he won't give them back! He says they're his, and they're *not* his! They're the ones you bought me the other day, remember! He says I took them out of his drawer. But I didn't. You bought them for me. Remember!"

Sally flushed. "What did I tell you about running in here anytime you want to?"

"Joey's not here. This ain't Joey. And his car's not here either."

She flushed even more.

"Where's Angie?"

"She went to the store. That's what she said anyway. But I saw her boyfriend waiting for her at the corner. And Connie's passed out."

It was getting worse. She took the boy by the arm. "Excuse me, Mr. Rocco . . . I mean, Giuseppe, but Danny and I are going to have to talk. I'll be right back."

From the kitchen he could hear the boy protest, "But that's not Joey."

"Shhhh!"

"But it ain't. That's an old man."

"Shhhh!"

"All you said was that when we saw Joey's car out there, we couldn't come in, and that's a truck."

Then there was a smack and the boy started to cry, and he heard the kitchen door open and close and then the kitchen was quiet.

Sally returned within the minute. Now it was she who was flustered. "That's my little brother. My mother and brothers and sisters live in that white house right behind us, right over there."

"Yes, I know."

"How do you know?"

"Ralph told me." She was strong. Flustered, he could see the strength. And she was beautiful.

"Well, I better get going. It looks like Joey's stuck with the mechanic," he said, rising, putting on his hat, which he now realized for the first time that he had removed.

"He should be here any minute now. Are you sure you don't want to stay just a few minutes more?" Sally said in that even, calm voice again and with that open, direct look from those pretty, brown eyes.

"No, I better . . ."

And then they heard the car in the driveway, and she said, "That's Joey."

Giuseppe Rocco sat down again. When Joey entered, he hugged him as he seldom did and kissed him several times too, saying, "I'm so happy for you, Joey. I'm so proud of you. You did good, Joey. You married a real good girl. I'll help you kids any way you want."

Giuseppe Rocco stayed for dinner, but only after he had gone to Giordano's Market and purchased a truckload of food, which included a case of his favorite wine. It was enough food for at least a month. He bought presents too for Sally's brothers and sisters.

"I want to help you kids. Just name it and it's yours," he said as they began eating.

"I know that, Papa."

"You don't have to go to college, Joey. You can start running the scavenger business tomorrow morning and make more money than ninety percent of the people that are gonna graduate from that college."

"But I don't want to go into the scavenging business, Papa."

"I'm not saying you have to stay in the scavengers. But it's easy and it's good money and a good start right now, and you can make a good living for your family right away. Sally won't have to work. You kids can have babies. I wouldn't mind some grandkids. And you can start learning the properties and some of the other businesses and the investments too. And eventually you can pick the ones you want to run, or run the whole thing. I don't care. I'm getting older. And Johnny with his baseball . . ."

"But I don't want to do that, Papa. I want to go to college, I want to have a profession."

"A profession? What kind of profession? What do you wanna be? A doctor or a lawyer or—"

"I'm not sure yet, but I think I want to be a lawyer."

"A lawyer. Well, that's good, son. Carlo Rossi's older than me. He's not going to last forever. I'm gonna need a good lawyer to handle all my things."

"But that's not the kind of lawyer I want to be, Papa."

"What you wanna be, one of those big corporation lawyers? You know with that mall I got connections all over. San Francisco, Chicago, New York, you name it. I could get you into one of those big corporations easy."

"I don't want to do that, Papa."

"Well, what kind of lawyer do you want to be?"

"I want to be a lawyer that makes the world a better place."

"*What?*"

"I want to make the world a better place for everybody to live in, not just the rich, but the poor too."

"The United Nations can't do that, how the hell are you gonna do that?"

"I don't know yet. But I want to try."

Then there was silence. Giuseppe Rocco stirred about in his plate, and Joey Rocco wished that his father could understand.

Finally, as much to break the silence as anything else, Giuseppe Rocco said, "Well, being a lawyer is a long way off and we don't have to worry about that now . . . Let me at least pay for your college, let me put you through college."

"I want to do it myself, Papa. The tuition at State's not very much, and I already paid it for this semester."

"Well, do you want to move over near the college? I've got some houses over there. It'll make it easier for you. You'll be closer and you won't have to pay rent. You don't have to live here."

"But we want to live here, Papa. We picked this house and we like it."

"I'm not saying there's anything wrong with this house. I guess I just don't understand. Why do you want to do it all by yourself, son?"

"You did everything yourself, Papa. Why can't I?"

"But I'm sending Johnny money every month and he's on a full scholarship. Why can't I help you?"

"Papa, Johnny and me are different people. You know that."

From that night on, Giuseppe Rocco went to dinner every Tuesday at Joey and Sally's for almost two years, arriving in early afternoon and staying until eight or nine, bringing food and presents for all.

Through that first summer, Giuseppe would usually help Joey with whatever chores or repairs he had around the house. When those were finished, he would usually pour himself and Joey a glass of wine and then the two would sit and talk. Inevitably, Giuseppe would steer the conversations to his properties, his businesses, and holdings. "I know you're not interested, Joey, but Johnny's gone and with his baseball he won't be around for the next ten, fifteen, or twenty years. Who knows, he may never come back. I'm sixty-three and I'm not gonna live forever. I need somebody in the family to know about these things, to be ready to handle these things in case something happens to me. So listen for a minute. Try to understand that it's for your sake, that it's for your family's sake . . ."

Giuseppe had an ally in Sally. If Joey's lack of interest became too obvious, she would break in. "Joey, listen to your father. It's important."

Giuseppe Rocco was a keen listener. From the beginning, he drew the two out at the dinner table. As often as not, Joey would dwell on the plight of the poor: there had to be some way of alleviating their suffering, of eliminating the inequity in their lives. Sally, on the other hand, was much more specific. She had hated being poor, and whatever it took, she would never be poor again. Joey went to extremes, vowing at one point to give up every penny he owned if it would change the condition of the poor.

This caused the otherwise smug Giuseppe some concern, and he promptly turned to Sally and asked, "Would you do that, Sally?"

Sally answered without hesitation, "No, not me."

On that first Tuesday as Giuseppe Rocco had risen from the table, had gotten ready to leave, he had reached into his pocket, taken out a roll of bills and held them out to Joey. Joey had stiffened, moved back, and moved his hands back.

"Come on, Joey, take it. It's really not a lot of money. And I didn't get you kids a wedding present."

Joey didn't change his stance. As Sally looked on in disbelief, he said, "No Papa, we don't need anything right now. We're doing fine. You already gave us a big party. We really liked that. And today you brought us enough food for the rest of the year. We don't need that right now. Believe me, if we ever do, you'll be the first to know."

"Joey . . ." Giuseppe had said, taking another step toward his son and extending his arm a little more, "Every young couple can always use some extra cash."

But Joey had stood firm, shaking his head. "No, Papa, you know I love you and I really appreciate what you're trying to do, but I don't want to start taking money."

Then it was Giuseppe Rocco who shook his head and slowly put the wad of bills back into his pocket, but not before he noted Sally's disappointment.

The following Tuesday as he brought in the first two bags of groceries, and as Joey went out to the truck to help him with the rest, Giuseppe Rocco turned to Sally and said, "Here, young lady. I know you kids can always use this."

Sally looked down at the two hundred-dollar bills in his hand.

"If nothing else, save it. You'd be surprised how fast you can save up for a down payment on a house. I know you don't always want to live here. Joey's not always of this world, and he doesn't have to know."

She took the money without hesitation and without a word, and thought, Joey doesn't have to know.

For the next several weeks as he brought the first bags in, he said to her quietly, "There's something for you kids under the first bag." And there was. Later he said, "There will always be something for you under the first bag." And there was, every week, a crisp one hundred dollar bill. They never spoke of it again. And Joey didn't have to know.

They seldom spoke to each other when they were alone, when Joey wasn't there. And when Joey's classes began in September, except for Danny's and Rachel's occasional visits, they were alone every Tuesday afternoon from two to five. Then they would pass each other like two awkward dancers, with unnecessary nods and exaggerated gestures. And they would speak to each other, break their awkward silences, with short direct phrases that said only what had to be said and nothing more. Almost never would their eyes meet, and when they did, it would be only for a moment, only long enough to skitter. Until Joey came home, like clockwork, between five and ten minutes after five; then they could speak to each other and look at each other and pass each other with almost a calm indifference.

Sally thought of her awkwardness. Much of it was the man himself. Giuseppe Rocco was still a local legend. Hated, envied, distrusted by many, he was nevertheless respected by most, and he still intimidated all. As soon as anyone learned that she had married Giuseppe Rocco's son, there was an unmistakeable change in the way they viewed her: deference abounded. The customers said it best. "*You* married Giuseppe Rocco's son! Oh my God, Giuseppe Rocco's son!" "I don't believe it!" "And you're still working here!" "My God, girl, how did you do it!" "Giuseppe Rocco's son! Here, let me ring up my own groceries! You can buy and sell everyone in this store! If not now, some day for sure!"

This was the same Giuseppe Rocco who, for the first hour or more of every Tuesday afternoon, worked their portion of the yard, weeding, turning the soil, trimming bushes, or mowing the lawn, and then did other chores and made repairs that Joey was too busy to do. Afterward, he would sit down in the shade of their tiny porch and pour himself his first glass of wine, pour it into a kitchen glass that was as plain and sturdy as the big jug from which it came. Sometimes Rachel or Danny or both would be there, and he would give them the small gifts that he had brought. He watched as their eyes shone, probably never realizing, she thought, that his eyes shone too. And sometimes he would assemble the toys or fix toys from previous Tuesdays and play with them and talk to them, enjoying the glow of their faces.

Sally watched him from behind curtains and from the corners of windows and from the darkness of the house, watched him out of amazement and respect. This powerful man, who was known to none, played with the son and daughter of a damaged, penniless, Mexican drunk, for no apparent reason other than that he enjoyed it. But even as she watched, she knew that he was watching too, if not with his eyes, then with his mind, because she knew that he was aware of her, of what she did or was doing in the house or on the phone or with her brother and sister, that she was under scrutiny. Somehow she expected that of Giuseppe Rocco, and rather than annoy her, it challenged her, challenged her to continue to gain and keep the respect of the man she so respected.

Often she thought of his beginnings, of what it had to have been like at fourteen or seventeen, alone and poor, a stranger in a strange land, and she compared herself to him. Had she been a man, would she have been able to accomplish the same things, acquire the same riches? She would have liked the opportunity. And more than once it occurred to her that some day she might yet have the opportunity to work with those riches, to multiply those riches. And then she would see.

There were times on Tuesday afternoons, too, when she felt him looking at her as a woman, when she felt his eyes on her body. Then she would stiffen and walk without movement, and take in her breasts, and take care not to stoop or bend, take care not to let him feast his old, lecherous eyes on her body. She had heard the stories of the labor camps and his Mexican whores. And sometimes at the dinner table when he had had too much wine, he called her Angelina.

Once Joey was home, the awkwardness would pass, and she would feel herself relax. She was then able to approach Giuseppe Rocco with food or drink, completely at ease, and look and smile at him as she had not looked or smiled at him all afternoon. As she prepared the meal, she would listen to the father and the son talk, listen to and note the old man's curiosity and questions about college and what Joey was learning there. And it soon became clear that she thought more like the old man than did Joey. And invariably at the dinner table, Giuseppe Rocco's eyes would meet hers for a moment or two, just long enough to acknowledge that they knew each other, had and would always know each other, before they looked away.

For Giuseppe Rocco, the awkwardness was based on the fact that she was a beautiful woman whom he admired and respected, but a woman who was his son's wife, a woman whom he was seeing in his son's home. You violated neither. This was now, and might always be, his only family. Johnny was gone and might always be gone. He admired her greatly, and his restraint was the awkwardness.

He admired her strength and energy. She never stopped. If she wasn't cleaning the house, she was washing and ironing clothes, or preparing meals, not only for that evening, but for the rest of the week when she would be working. And it occurred to him over and over again that she did precisely what he always expected a wife to do, but what his own wife had never done. Beyond that, she was still raising another family, determined that the first would not interfere with or damage the second. It didn't take long for Giuseppe Rocco to recognize that at exactly 4:45 on Tuesdays, Rachel and Danny would disappear through the back fence . . . And she was beautiful.

He watched her with Rachel and Danny, watched the young woman who would someday extend his line. And he liked what he saw. She was clearly their mother, or more mother than their mother. Her directness and firmness were tempered by love and warmth. Rachel and Danny were good kids. So it troubled him when Joey and she said that they did not want children of their own for as many as ten years. It surprised him that it troubled him. He had not thought of Joey or any of his offspring as capable of carrying on and multiplying what he had begun. But now with Sally . . .

It was after they had spoken of children that Giuseppe Rocco sought out and found the apartment complex that had been Sally's home for much of her early life.

"What you want?" the haggard Mexican woman said as she tucked and tied her robe.

"I want to rent an apartment."

"What?"

"You heard me."

"Why you want to rent an apartment here. You don't belong here, mister."

He answered with a large wad of bills and by asking, "How much is it?" Flipping through the bills so that she could see the large denominations, he added. "There's some here for you too if it's a good one."

He rented the apartment for two months, but stayed only two days and two nights, watching from the bare and empty rooms that reeked with the smells and stains of hard, confined living, the daily lives of his new neighbors. He watched the constant comings and goings of young men, boys even, some of them sober, some not, at all hours, to the abodes of women little more than girls who had already stretched and distorted their small-boned bodies with baby after baby and more to come. He listened to the loud and raucous music that he didn't like or understand and that more than anything seemed to guarantee that there would never be a solitary moment for its listeners. Through the thin sheetrock, he heard their belching and their farting and their fighting, he heard their sex and their snoring. In the morning, he saw the children emerge, but only the children, as if in a wasteland or a war zone, as the young mothers slept with their lovers. He watched those children, from the youngest, who were loaded down with their bulging and drenched disposable diapers, to the ten-year-olds, who were already practicing for their lives to come. He understood by the second morning that he was watching the beginning of another day in a hopeless, endless cycle. When he left the apartment after the second day, he had gotten all he had come for and more.

If anything, the stay at the apartment made the following Tuesday afternoons more awkward than before, made Joey's arrival more momentous, something he anticipated and waited for from the moment he set foot on the lot, even measuring when and how much wine he would drink before he came. Once Joey arrived, he could look at her, look and talk to her openly and freely as he would have to any beautiful and sensuous woman, without fear of violating his son or his home. And he did look at her, and he did talk to her, more and more to the exclusion of Joey. Theirs was a common language, one that needed little explanation or refinement. Whatever they spoke of at the dinner table, from the need for a new water heater to a new group of approaching developers, to the plight of the poor, they understood and accepted each other's position almost immediately, almost always. When he looked at her as they sat across the table from one another and their eyes met and locked for a moment before she looked away, the meeting and looking away was not the meeting and looking away of an old man and a young woman, of a father-in-law and a daughter-in-law, but of a man and a woman.

He too was aware that when he had had too much wine, he called her Angelina. He was aware too of Joey's and her embarrassment when he did so. What he didn't understand was why he called her Angelina and not Yolanda.

Chapter II

Two weeks before the end of the winter league, Johnny hurt his arm. He had pitched a full nine innings for the first time against a team of young professionals and had been overpowering, giving up just two scratch hits. After the game, he was surrounded by scouts from several major league teams. As he shrugged and grinned and came out of his state of planned intensity, he thought, You guys ain't seen nothing yet.

But the next morning as he turned in bed, he felt a sharp twinge in his upper arm. He felt it again in the shower and twice more as he sat in class, enough so that he decided to throw in practice. There was no pain with the first soft tosses, none with the medium speed throws, but with his first hard pitch, a knife-like pain shot up to his shoulder and he groaned and winced and grabbed his right arm. He did not pitch another game that winter and, two weeks later when he tried to throw again, the pain was still there.

Johnny Rocco spent his Christmas vacation at his father's new home.

"What's the matter, Johnny?"

"Nothing, Papa."

"No, no. I know you good enough to know something's wrong."

"I hurt my arm, Papa."

"You hurt your arm? What arm?"

"My right arm, my pitching arm."

"I thought you said the winter season was over."

"It is, but I hurt my arm just before it ended, about six weeks ago."

"How did you hurt it?"

"Pitching."

"Have you been to a doctor?"

"Oh sure, but the doctor says there's nothing I can do about it except not throw for a while, let the arm rest. He thinks I strained a tendon."

"A what?"

"A tendon . . . It's up here. It's over on this part of the arm."

"So you don't pitch. So you rest for a while. The real season doesn't start for another month, right? You'll be okay by then."

"I'm not so sure, Papa. I tried throwing a few weeks ago, and it still hurt. It hurt worse."

"So Johnny, what's the worst thing that can happen? So you don't pitch for a while. You'll be okay."

"Papa, you don't understand. Baseball's my life. I live for it. I'd die for it. It gives me a rush like nothing else can."

"Johnny, you're eighteen years old. You got your whole life in front of you. You're smart, you're tough, you're good-looking. People *like* you. With what I have here in this valley, you can do anything you want. Anything. And it's all yours."

"Papa, I just wanna play baseball."

———————

Training for the regular season began in the third week of January. Johnny threw lightly that week and began throwing harder the following week. The phone rang every night. "The arm feels good, Papa. I think it's almost a hundred percent." Two nights later. "I cut loose today, Papa. I let it all hang out. Threw as hard as I could for fifteen minutes. The arm feels great."

The news was bittersweet. Giuseppe was happy with whatever made Johnny happy, and he knew he had to let him live his life, but there had been a suggestion that Johnny's baseball days might be over, and there was so much for him there in the valley. So much more.

"I pitched three perfect innings against Flagstaff. I struck out four and didn't give up a hit. In fact, they only hit one ball out of the infield. Coach said I'm everything he expected and more. The scouts are here in bunches. I can't turn around without one of them wanting to talk to me." It could be twenty years before he came back to the valley.

"I went five innings against Arizona U. They got a bloop single off of me. First hit I've given up all spring. Coach is talking about letting me start against the Oakland A's. Can you imagine that, Papa?"

Giuseppe Rocco imagined more. If he signed with one of the major league teams, the odds were that he would end up on the East Coast or in the Midwest.

"I'm definitely going to start against the A's, Papa. Coach said he might let me go five innings against them. Can you come down, Papa?

It's only an hour on the plane. I want you to come down, Papa. They're the world champions and you've always brought me good luck."

Sure he could go down. If it meant that much to his Johnny, he would be there.

The park was bigger, more brightly painted, and the playing field far more manicured than any Johnny had ever played on. The boys were no longer boys, or at least their bodies were those of men: fine, highly toned physical specimens. But for Giuseppe Rocco it was much the same: twelve years of watching Johnny play this game. In many ways it was still the same. The coaches, as always, went out of their way to be nice to him. Johnny's teammates were all very respectful, as they had been when they were younger. The scouts said all the same things they had said at home: Johnny was a can't-miss talent, a pitcher who came along once every thirty years. And Johnny's ritual was the same.

It began in the locker room. He stopped his father just inside the doorway and said, "I'll see you after the game, Papa." And that was all. Then he undressed and dressed, staring into the void of his almost empty locker. Each garment that he removed brought him that much closer. Slowly, deliberately, he put on his uniform; each piece of that uniform seemed to carry its own significance. Then he sat on the bench and removed his cleats from the locker, into which he was still staring. He banged the cleats several times on the concrete floor to shed the caked dirt. Once he tied his shoes, he remained seated, still looking at the rectangle of cramped darkness before him. His cap sat beside him, sweat-stained and hand-shaped. He sat in silence for at least five minutes and, as he did, the room seemed to grow more silent and solemn. Others were dressed too, but they seemed to be waiting for Johnny. Then Johnny took a deep loud sigh, picked up and fitted his cap, stood up and took his glove from his locker, closed the locker door and then walked to the clatter of his steel cleats on the concrete toward the door, walked past several of his teammates, not seeing them, not speaking to them, his mouth fixed and his eyes intent on the field which was two doors beyond. As he reached the inner door, someone yelled, "Come on, you guys, let's show these hot dogs what we're all about!" And the room erupted into shouts and cheers.

✄ Giuseppe Rocco ✄

In the corner, Giuseppe Rocco shook his head and smiled. They were still boys. But it was a big game for them, and as he smiled, he felt a warm shudder.

From his seat behind home plate, Giuseppe Rocco watched Johnny stretch, jog, and then stand alone next to the batting cage, swinging the two bats that he held together up and over his head. There was that same grimness to his eyes and mouth that he had known for so many years; if anything, it was more pronounced. Then Johnny took his turn in the batting cage, swinging ferociously, driving each pitch as if it were a matter of life and death. Giuseppe loved his son's fire. Not many people in life would devote themselves to anything the way Johnny did to his baseball. If only that fire could somehow be applied to running Giuseppe's empire.

When Johnny left the batting cage and went into the dugout, Giuseppe stayed and watched the team in the grey and green uniforms. They were the world champions. To Giuseppe they looked ordinary enough. They were big men, but few as finely honed as Johnny. They were on average ten or fifteen years older than Johnny, and they strode and swaggered about casually, laughing and talking easily, perhaps too easily, but none had Johnny's fire. Their faces were lined and sun-burned and a few had paunches. In ten or fifteen years, Johnny would look and act like them. Johnny could have chosen to do almost any-thing with his life, but he had chosen this. And from the looks of many of the men, the hangers-on who surrounded these champions, it could be a life-long pursuit.

Once Johnny reached the bullpen, a crowd of men, most of them scouts, gathered. Boys of all ages and sizes joined them. On the bullpen mound, Johnny Rocco was already locked in another place and time, already fighting the battle, waging the war that he loved to wage and win. "He's got a helluva motion." "Gets his whole damn body into the pitch." "His legs are real strong. Look at the way he uses his back leg to push off." "Shit. His concentration alone will eat them up alive." One of the scouts said for the fifth or tenth time, "He can't miss, Mr. Rocco, he's gonna be a great one." And as the ball whistled past them and popped into the catcher's mitt, Giuseppe Rocco wondered how any man alive could hit it in the split second it took to reach the catcher. Maybe he would be great. Let him be great. Let anyone be great at whatever he chose. He wasn't dead yet; his businesses weren't dead yet; God willing, he could live another twenty years. By then, Johnny would be back, and if worse came to worse, Sally could hold Joey up until Johnny was ready.

As Johnny left the dugout to begin the game, the public address system announced, "Today's starting pitcher for the Arizona State Sun Devils is Johnneeee RRRoccooooo!" The Arizona fans rose in unison, cheering, stomping and shouting. It was the largest crowd that Johnny had pitched before. As Giuseppe Rocco heard his son's name repeated and embraced by all those people, he thought again, let him be great.

Johnny struck out the first world champion on three pitches, and the crowd went wild. The next batter fouled the first pitch back, and there was a groan from the fans, as if they hadn't expected any of the world champions to make contact with any of Johnny's pitches. The next pitch was a blazing fastball, called strike two, and the fans were screaming again. Then Johnny stood on the infield grass, rubbing up the baseball. He sighed and then slowly but firmly walked back up onto the mound, and with his mouth set and his eyes narrowed, he stared down at the batter who looked back at him undaunted. He started his windup, kicked his leg high, and then there was a pop, an ugly pop, a pop that had nothing to do with the ball, a pop that Giuseppe Rocco would never forget. His eyes found Johnny on the ground clutching his arm, writhing in pain.

Giuseppe Rocco remained in Arizona for two weeks. During the days before the surgery, Johnny saw no one, spoke to no one, except for his father. He would just sit in his father's hotel suite, staring out at the vast expanse of the desert.

"Johnny, you're only eighteen. You have your whole life in front of you." By then Giuseppe Rocco didn't expect an answer. "You can do anything you want with your life. I have so much to give you. So much opportunity." It was as if someone had died. "You're still alive, Johnny. You've got fifty or sixty years ahead of you." He thought he knew what baseball meant to his son; now he decided that he didn't know.

After the surgery, the doctor said that there was a better than fifty percent chance that Johnny would pitch again. He advised Johnny not to throw for a full year. Thereafter, he would probably be able to throw without any pain or discomfort. How well he would pitch again was hard to say.

It was a long year. Johnny attached himself to the team; had he not, it would have been an even longer and harder year. He was at their practices, meetings, and games. He traveled with them and even went to northern California with the nucleus of the team for most of the summer to watch them play in a semi-professional league. During those few weeks when there was no baseball, he returned to Giuseppe Rocco's home at the base of the coastal range. But he saw no one and went nowhere. Instead, he sat in front of the television set for most of the day, and by early afternooon, was sipping on a beer.

He gained weight; none of it was muscle. A dead glaze had set in around his eyes and he showed no interest in anything. Each time Johnny returned to Arizona, Giuseppe felt a greater relief. By the Christmas break, Giuseppe had given up all attempts at coaxing or criticism: Johnny's hostility was biting. By then, all that Giuseppe hoped for, at times even prayed for, was the day that Johnny would begin pitching again.

Johnny began throwing during the first week of January.

"But it's not a year yet," Giuseppe said as he listened to the excited voice on the other end of the line.

"It's just a few days shy of eleven months, Papa."

"But the doctor said a year, Johnny, not eleven months."

"It's not like I threw hard, Papa, or for very long. I threw yesterday, not hard and not long, and it didn't bother me this morning. Nothing. I feel great. And I threw again this afternoon, and then I iced the arm and it feels great! I think I'm gonna be all right, Papa, I think I'm gonna be all right!"

That was how the nightly calls began.

———————

"I threw for fifteen minutes straight, Papa! Fifteen minutes! And I don't feel a thing! Of course I'm not throwing at a hundred percent yet, but that'll come, that'll come. What do you think, Papa?"

"What does the coach think?"

"He thinks it's great!"

"What does the doctor think?"

"I haven't told him yet."

"It's not a year yet."

"Papa, you got to listen to your body."

"No, *you* got to listen to your *head,* for a change. But I love you, you son of a gun. And it's good to hear you alive again."

<hr>

"Papa, I threw three innings of a simulated game! You know, where there's a batter and an ump and the batter doesn't swing and the ump calls balls and strikes. Well, I threw three innings of that, Papa, and it felt good."

"Did you throw a hundred percent?"

"No."

"Why not?"

"It's not a year yet, Papa."

<hr>

"I didn't throw today, Papa."

"How come?"

"Coach wanted me to take the day off, give the arm a rest."

"So maybe you studied a little, huh?"

"I didn't say that. Coach still had me dress out, and they worked my butt off."

"It won't hurt you."

"Hell, you ought to try it. First they had me do burpies, all kinds of exercises, stretching, wind sprints, twenty laps around the field and that's a big field. Then more exercises and running. They ran my ass off. They worked my butt off."

"It won't hurt you."

"They think I lost strength in my legs and that I put on a little too much weight."

"Both."

"What?"

"I said both. Every time you were here all you did was sit in front of the T.V. and drink and eat."

"Jesus, Papa, with friends like you who needs enemies."

"You know your Papa loves you."

<hr>

"He says they're gonna start me in two weeks. Let me go three or four innings. See how I feel."

"At least it'll be more than a year then."

"Thirteen months to the day, Papa."

"What does the doctor think?"

"He says it's all up to me. That only I know how my arm feels. He says what he always says, listen to your body."

"I want you to come, Papa."

"I already told you I was coming."

"But I want you to bring Joey."

"Joey? Why the hell you want Joey there for?"

"I don't know, Papa. It's kind of like old times, superstition maybe. You guys were always there at the big games for me. You and Joey were always good luck for me."

"But this is no big game."

"It is for me, Papa, it is for me. Bring him, Papa, please. It's a big game for me. One of my biggest."

"Johnny, you want me and Joey there, me and Joey will be there."

<hr>

But Joey didn't understand. "He wants me to go all the way to Arizona for a game?"

"It's important, Joey."

"And you don't even know who they're playing."

"He says it's important, Joey, so I have to believe him."

"He didn't ask me to go last year when they played Oakland."

"I don't know anything about that, Joey. All I know is that he wants you to come and he says it's important."

"But Papa, I got classes on Friday and I work a full shift at the store."

"Sally says you only have one class on Friday, and I already talked to Ralph and he said it's okay."

Joey resented them: they would have never done the same for him.

Sally insisted, "Go, Joey. If your father thinks it's important, I think you should go."

<hr>

The flight was delayed. When they arrived at the park, the team was in the club house. There was only a handful of fans in the park. A guard stopped them as they started to enter the dugout.

"I'm Johnny Rocco's father and this is his brother, Joey."

"I'm sorry, sir, but no one is allowed in the club house except players and coaches."

"I've been in there before. I'm Johnny Rocco's father."

"Johnny who? I'm sorry, sir, but . . ."

A man in a uniform poked his head out of the dugout and said, "It's
all right, Sammy, let them come in."

Giuseppe Rocco nodded to the man distractedly. No one on a baseball field had ever said that they didn't know Johnny Rocco.

In the club house, the players were gathering their gloves and caps
and starting to go back onto the field. But Johnny wasn't there.
Giuseppe went to the coach.

"Where's Johnny? I thought he was supposed to pitch today."

The man who had showered him with attention just the year before,
the man who had traveled to California two years earlier to watch
Johnny pitch and meet his family, didn't recognize him until he repeated, "Johnny Rocco, my son, Johnny Rocco."

"Oh, yeah, Mr. Rocco, Johnny. Johnny's in the training room."
That was all.

Johnny lay on his stomach on a padded table that filled most of a
closet-like room. A short, thick man dressed in white was rubbing
Johnny's shoulders and arm.

"Aren't you pitching today, Johnny?" Giuseppe asked.

"You came!" Johnny said, sitting up and then hugging them. "It got
so late that I didn't think you were coming."

"We only got seven minutes, Johnny," the man in white said.
"Come on, you'd better lie down."

"Aren't you pitching today?" Giuseppe asked again.

"Yeah, in seven minutes," the thick man in white said.

"What's all this about?" Giuseppe said, waving at the table.

"Coach thought it would be good for my arm. Keep it loose." And
then, with his chin buried in the top of his fist, he turned to Joey and
said, "So what's married life like, big man?" And he laughed loudly,
too loudly, at Joey's answers. When Joey finished, he was ready with,
"How many units you taking this semester?" Then, "So what's your
major gonna be?" He listened and laughed until the thick man in white
said, "It's time to go, Johnny."

Giuseppe Rocco didn't like any of it.

As they left the training room, Johnny said, "I want you guys to sit right next to the dugout." And then again, at the inner door, he said, "I'll show you where I want you guys to sit when we get out there. There should be room. Nobody was out there earlier. There's not gonna be too many people out here today." And then Johnny turned back to Joey and began asking him about Giordano's Market.

Giuseppe did not like it.

After pointing out the seats, Johnny began his walk to the bullpen. Except for Giuseppe and Joey, no one walked with him. When they reached the bullpen, there was no one there, no scouts, no fans, no kids, not even a catcher. Johnny stood on the mound for several minutes talking to Joey again about his classes until a catcher trotted down to them. Even as he warmed up, Johnny talked to Joey, occasionally smiling between throws.

More than not liking it, Giuseppe didn't understand it.

The first batter hit Johnny's first two pitches over the fence but foul. Johnny then walked him. The next batter hit a long drive off the top of the center field fence for a triple. The center fielder made a miraculous catch of the next batter's hit, but the following batter hit a homerun. From the dugout Giuseppe could hear the coach's raspy voice: "Throw the ball, Rocco, throw the ball!" Johnny did throw the ball, but the next batter hit it to the outfield fence as well. The coach's voice was louder, "Throw the fucking ball, Rocco, throw it!" And when Johnny finally looked over toward the dugout, it was not to coach that he looked, but rather to Giuseppe. On his face there was something close to a smile, a bewildered nervous smile.

Johnny walked the next two batters and only a diving catch by the third baseman ended the inning. The score was three to zero and Giuseppe Rocco watched his son walk off the mound as he had never seen him walk off before: meekly, timidly, embarrassed, his head hung in shame.

"Are you afraid to throw that fucking thing?" Giuseppe heard, even before Johnny was in the dugout. "Throw it, goddamn it! This isn't batting practice! I don't give a shit if your arm falls off! Don't toss it! Throw the fucking thing! Show me some guts!"

Giuseppe looked around at the few people seated near them, humiliated. He said something to Joey, not knowing what he said and not knowing what Joey answered. Then he said something about the

Arizona desert, something about the sky too and how he wouldn't want to live there, as his flesh burned and his heart ached for his son. And for himself too.

The first batter of Johnny's second inning was the ninth batter in the lineup, the weakest hitter in the lineup. He promptly drove the ball well over the drawn-in outfielder's head to the base of the fence and scored. The coach called time and walked angrily out to the mound, his hands stuffed into his back pockets. He barked at Johnny for what seemed an eternity as Johnny's head and shoulders slumped more and more. "That son of a bitch," Giuseppe mumbled, "that dirty son of a bitch." Then the coach walked back to the dugout and shouted again, "Now throw the fucking thing! Throw it!"

Johnny looked over at his father, looked at him as he had not looked at him since he was a little more than an infant, helpless and frightened. Giuseppe Rocco ached all the more for his son. Then Johnny walked back up on the mound, only, it seemed, because there was no where else to go. And he went into an exaggerated windup, kicking high, and threw a blur that the batter missed, that slammed into the catcher's glove with a whack that was heard throughout the park. "Now you're throwing the ball, Rocco!" the evil voice boomed. "Do it again!" Johnny did it again and the batter swung and missed again, and for the first time there were cheers in the stands. "One more, Rocco!" the coach shouted. And again Johnny went into an exaggerated windup, then came the high kick, and then the pop, the same ugly pop in the same ugly park on the same ugly mound. This time Giuseppe was the first to reach Johnny as he writhed in the dirt, clutching his arm, crying.

Johnny cried quietly, as Giuseppe and the trainer and one of the coaches helped him to the clubhouse. Once inside the clubhouse, Johnny burst into a loud wail, "It's over, Papa, it's over! I'll never pitch again!" And Giuseppe held him and cried too, cried as Joey had never seen him cry. At that moment, Joey Rocco knew better than ever what he had known all his life: that there would never be a replacement for Johnny in his father's heart.

At the end of the week, the doctor told Johnny what he had told Giuseppe in those first hours, that he would never pitch again. Giuseppe remained in Arizona for a second week, trying to convince Johnny to return to California. Johnny said, "There's nothing there for me, Papa. At least here I have school and friends."

Four days later, Giuseppe Rocco received a letter which read, "Papa, I'm leaving to find myself. I don't know where I'm going or where I'll end up, but I have to find myself. I love you. Johnny."

Over the next six months, Giuseppe Rocco spent thousands trying to find his son. But Johnny hadn't left a trace. The only suggestion of a clue was a pair of shoes that were found on the Golden Gate Bridge on the day Giuseppe received the letter. They were identical in size and appearance to those that Johnny had been wearing on the last day that Giuseppe Rocco had seen him.

Chapter III

It was two weeks after he had received the investigator's report that Giuseppe Rocco sought out Sally. It was early in the afternoon on a Tuesday when he arrived. He could not stay for dinner, but had come to talk to her anyway. He asked that she send Rachel and Danny home. He seemed grim. Whatever it was, it had to do with Johnny and it wasn't good.

He was sitting on one of the two white, plastic chairs when she came out. She sat next to him. "What is it, Papa, what's the matter?"

He stood up and moved his chair around on the tiny porch so that it was directly in front of hers. Then he sat again and scooted his chair under him until his knees were but inches from hers. Then he looked at her with a calm, clear look but said nothing.

"What is it, Papa, what's the matter? It's Johnny, isn't it? Tell me, Papa."

He shook his head slightly and then said, "I want you to have my child."

Her eyes blinked, and her head jerked, and she brought her hand just over her breast as if to help her breathe.

"I want you to have my child," he repeated. "If you do, I'll make you the richest woman in this valley . . . Don't say anything now. Think about it. You would only have to be with me a few times. I want a child by you, Sally. I want to see it before I die. I'll pay anything for that, anything. Even Joey knowing. Of course, I hope you won't tell him. It would break his heart. But if it comes to that, I'm ready for that too."

And with that, he left.

She sat for a long time, stunned. She had heard the words and had even understood them, but they had left her in shock, immobile, numb.

She left the porch only when her mind had settled enough to allow in another thought, or at least a piece of a thought. If nothing else, her instinct at least told her that if she remained on the porch, Connie or the kids might see her, and she did not want to deal with Connie or the kids. Not then. In the cool shade of the house, she cried. She cried for Joey. She cried for Johnny. She cried for Giuseppe, and she cried for herself.

She was cooking when Joey came home. She had told herself even before she began cooking that she did not know what she would say, what she would do when he got home. She had timed her cooking so that she was standing squarely in front of the stove when he entered, stirring and tending to two pans and a pot. She didn't have to turn when he said, "Hi, Babe, I'm home." She only had to tilt and twist her cheek toward him when he approached for his greeting kiss. She did not once have to look at him before he began talking. She could answer without looking at him, until she was ready, until she was comfortable, when it would be less likely that he would be looking directly at her.

"Is Papa coming for dinner?"

"No."

"Did he stop by or call?"

"He came by early this afternoon."

"What'd he say?"

"That he couldn't make it."

"Why?"

"Oh, I think it had to do with Johnny."

"What about Johnny?"

"I don't know. He didn't say."

"Well how do you know it's about Johnny?"

"He was upset and the only thing that upsets him these days is Johnny."

That was all she said, all she said of what Giuseppe Rocco had said.

It meant nothing, she told herself that night and all the next day. She had chosen not to tell Joey, not to hurt Joey. It did not mean, suggest, hint in any way that she was acquiescing or even thinking of acquiescing to Giuseppe Rocco's insane, outrageous proposal. For the next two days she worked her register, her customers by rote, by memory. Her mind wasn't there. She was in the realm of what couldn't be and what could be—mostly what couldn't be. The idea, the thought was still outrageous, preposterous. How could that old man, and a dirty old man at that, think that he could buy her at any price? How could that old man be so cruel to his son, a son who loved him as she would never love a parent, or perhaps, anyone? But it was the act itself, or the acts, however many it would take, that repulsed her most, even though she never got past the image of him on top of her, bringing his head, his mouth down to hers for that first kiss. She shuddered at the register as she felt him, felt the first pressure of his weight and the first touch of his lips.

There were other moments too during those two days, moments when she gave her fortieth or fiftieth forced smile of the day, forced it and felt it more than ever on those two days and then bent over a shopping cart and lifted a ten-pound bag of sugar for the thousandth or two thousandth or three thousandth time, knowing that she might still be lifting ten pound bags of sugar out of shopping carts and smiling forced smiles ten years from that moment, given Joey's reluctance to accept anything from his father. And she thought too of the satisfaction it would give Barbara and Molly and even some of the customers to watch her, Sally Rocco, ten years from then, a long-time member of the Rocco family, still bending over shopping carts. At those moments she heard, I'll make you the richest woman in this valley.

There was little to say at night.

"What's wrong, Sally?"

"Nothing."

"Something's bothering you."

"Nothing. I'm just tired."

"It wasn't that bad at the store today."

"I know. But you've got to remember, I've been working at that store going on ten years now, Joey, and that's almost half of my life. I get tired of it, you know."

"I know."

"Do you really?"

Saturday was a grueling day. The store was packed. There was a constant line at her register. On busy days she had estimated that she lifted at least a ton, two thousand pounds, of groceries. On Saturday it felt like two tons. Her back ached and her feet and legs were sore. When Joey asked her that night what was wrong, she quietly began crying and said only, "I'm exhausted, Joey, I'm exhausted."

Sunday was a slow day, but early that morning customers began commenting on a party that Rita Verducci had hosted the previous Sunday, a party that had been extensively covered and photographed in the morning paper. "That must have been quite a party." Sally simply nodded, hating them, knowing that they had to know of her relationship with Rita Verducci.

"What was the party like, Sally?" She answered, "I didn't go," and later added, "I wasn't invited," burning after each admission.

On Monday, Barbara had her chance, taunting in a loud voice across three checkstands, "Hey, Sally, tell us about that big bash your mother-in-law had last weekend. It must have been a blast. Anybody that was anybody was there." And Sally said for the last time, "I didn't go. I wasn't invited." That afternoon, she decided that at most it would take only three or four times.

That night, Sally waited until Joey had asked for the fourth time before she answered, or rather, before she said more than "nothing." He had asked when she started cooking, "What's the matter, Sally?" and again when she served the meal. The longer she waited, the more "nothings" she repeated, the more seriously he would take her, the more concerned he would become. They were just finishing dinner when she answered. He had been readied by then.

"I want to quit working, Joey."

"*What?*"

"I want to quit working."

"What do you mean you want to quit working?"

"Just what I said. I'm tired of working. I'm tired of working at that store. I hate it there. I don't think I can take another day there."

"What're we gonna do if you quit working?"

"You figure that out. You're the man around here, aren't you?"

"What are you mad at me for?"

"I'm not mad at you, Joey, I'm just tired of working. I want to stop."

"How are we gonna pay the rent, the bills, not just here but at Connie's house too? I would if I could, but you know I'm only working part time. I've got to finish my education."

"I don't know and I don't care. All I know is I hate that place. I hate those catty women there, and I've had it."

"What happened today, Sally? Tell me, what happened?"

"Nothing happened today that doesn't happen every day."

"If Barbara and Molly are getting to be too much, just tell me and I'll go to Ralph."

"Don't you understand, Joey? I'm tired of being there! I do not want to be there anymore!" He had stopped eating, the fork fixed in his hand. There was no need to say any more. No need to look at him.

She waited.

"Sally, I know you make twice what I do. But I think I pay half of everything around here. But with Connie, if you stop working, we just can't make it."

This time she didn't wait. "Are you crazy, Joey, you're the son of the richest man in town and we work like dogs!"

"I don't mind working hard."

"And I don't either. But your father's offered you jobs, offered you things that would mean that we wouldn't have to live like this."

"What's wrong with the way we live?"

"Nothing's wrong with the way we live, except that we could be living a lot better and not be killing ourselves."

"Are you saying that I should quit school and go to work for my father?"

"No, I'm saying that you should go to work for yourself. At least half of that's going to be yours some day. It might as well be yours now. Nobody else seems to want it, or is gonna get it."

He didn't answer and she didn't look at him. She didn't need to. She could feel him burning. She had never broached the subject before, and now she had gone too far.

Now it was he who waited for her, and when she didn't look or speak, he said, "I thought you married me for me, Sally."

Now it was she who was frozen.

Then he said, "Let me tell you what you've heard me say at least fifty times already. I don't want any of my father's money. If he were to die tomorrow, no, tonight, I'd give every last penny he left me to charity. All of it! Believe me. I just want to be me, and my father's money is never gonna let me be me."

———————

Although Giuseppe Rocco thought about his proposal constantly during the following week, he acted on it only once. That was on a Friday night when he went to Giordano's Market just before it closed, at 8:45, knowing that Sally would be home by then and that Joey would be at the rear of the store working alone on Saturday's produce. He pushed through the swinging doors to the huge back area as if the store were his. He cleared his throat and deliberately bumped against a row of cartons so that Joey would hear him, so that Joey would look up from his produce and see him, look at him from a distance, so that he in turn could watch Joey's face, his reaction before he got any closer, and know what it was that he had to say or do.

Joey looked up with a head of lettuce in one hand and a produce knife in the other, and he said, "Hi, Papa," as innocently and warmly as he always said it. "What brings you here?" This meant that he didn't know, that she hadn't told him.

For a moment Giuseppe Rocco wished that he had known, regretted that his son didn't know, so that it could have ended there, so that all of the deceit, all of the anguish, all of the lies and the suspense could have ended there. But that was only for a moment, because he nodded and continued toward his son and his innocence.

"What's the matter, Papa, what's wrong?" He really didn't know; she really hadn't told him.

For the past three days, Giuseppe had mulled over the three possibilities. She would tell Joey. That was the worst of the three. She would not tell Joey, spare Joey, but refuse him. He could and would have to live with that. Or, and he tried not to dwell on the third possiblity too much because it sent him spiraling in so many different directions, she would accept. Now as he walked toward his son, he knew there were only two possibilities, and he had decided before coming that her silence would favor him.

As he neared Joey, he reached for the pretext about Johnny that he had concocted for coming. But he didn't need it, because Joey raised it for him.

Joey asked, "It's about Johnny, isn't it?"

Giuseppe stopped just across the crates of lettuce from Joey and looked neither up nor down, but rather at Joey's chin from under the brim of his khaki hat and nodded slowly, haltingly.

"What is it, Papa, what's the matter with Johnny?"

"They found some shoes like his," he answered, hating himself, fearing he might be tempting God.

"What do you mean shoes like his?"

"You know, those fancy tennis shoes he liked to wear."

"Papa, everybody likes to wear those kind of shoes!"

He had to have come for a reason, so he finished. "But these were on the Golden Gate Bridge."

Joey smiled and shook his head and said, "Papa, that doesn't mean anything. Do you know how many people wear shoes like those?

Thousands. Millions maybe." And with the head of lettuce in one hand and the produce knife in the other, he stepped around the stacks of crates and hugged his father. "Oh, Papa, I know how much you love Johnny. He's gonna be okay. He's just trying to find himself."

Giuseppe stiffened until he realized that he had stiffened. And then he embraced Joey, tentatively at first, but then hard, pressing his fingers into Joey's back, feeling Joey's chest and his stomach and his thighs against him, as he would have a woman's. And he kissed him and said, "I love you too, Joey."

───────

It was the following Tuesday. She knew he would come. In fact, she sat waiting in the cool of the house to escape the early afternoon heat of October. She sat at the kitchen table rather than on the couch in the living room of the tiny three-room house, because that was where they would talk, where they could best talk, where she could best see him. She listened for and heard the truck enter the front driveway. Then she rose and tiptoed, though there was no one else in the house, to the window above the kitchen sink, and from behind the blind, watched as he parked the truck, and then as he sat motionless for several moments before he opened the truck door. Then she saw what she must have seen many times before but had never noticed: she saw the slowness and stiffness with which he got out of the truck, watched his first leg slowly descend, feeling for, anticipating the ground, and then saw his pant leg slip over his boot and sock, exposing a patch of pale, yellowish flesh around his calf. She shuddered. And she shuddered again when she saw his first, stooped steps and then his deliberate effort to straighten himself. She closed her eyes and clenched her teeth and with one shake of her head chased those images from her mind.

───────

He, in turn, had been awake since 3:30, had lain in his bed looking up at darkness, until just before 5:30 when he left the house in the darkness, having chosen a ranch that he had recently purchased just south of Carmel as his destination. They were still harvesting there, and at that distance it would be dawn or near dawn when he arrived, and no one would give his presence a second thought. When he drove up, the workers were warming themselves around the pre-dawn fires that they had built against the chill of the fall morning. He mingled with them, talking about the crop and asking what they would do and where they would go for the winter. As they answered, he noted that this was the third generation of workers that he had known since coming to San Jose and that he still liked interacting with them, however bad his Spanish might be.

From there, he crossed over into Salinas and later went south to Chualar and Soledad, where he also had ranches, biding his time until he could return to San Jose and the small rear house on 20th Street, using as a pretext wherever he went that he was looking for Ramiro, whom he had heard was working again since his surgery in June. At exactly noon, he left the Righetti ranch in Soledad and started for San Jose, shielding himself as best he could from the barrage of would-she-or-wouldn't-she that mounted. He stopped only for a bouquet of flowers. It was that bouquet that caused him to sit for a few moments in his parked truck as he tried to decide whether to take it with him or leave it, whether to give it to her or not. He left it.

Giuseppe Rocco rapped lightly on the screen door. From the darkness within she said, "Come in, Giuseppe, the door's unlocked." It was the first time she had called him by that name in a long, long time. She had almost gone directly from Mr. Rocco to Papa. And now this. She had said it matter of factly, without any adornment. He opened the screen door gently, delicately even, and then saw her sitting at the kitchen table without a smile or hint of a smile, making no effort whatever to meet or greet him, and he was glad that he had left the flowers in the truck. She wore a long-sleeved dress that buttoned at the neck and fell almost to her ankles. She watched without a word or expression as he approached, and he knew what her answer would be; he also knew that it was he alone who had humiliated himself.

When he reached the kitchen table, she gestured to the chair across from her and said, again matter of factly, "Sit down, Giuseppe, we've got a lot to talk about."

No one talked to him like that, not in that tone of voice. Now or ever. Least of all a Mexican girl who was forty years his . . . he sat down, nevertheless. Because the answer was not *no*, the answer was *we've got a lot to talk about.* He took off his hat, without knowing or thinking that he had taken it off, maybe because he was breathing heavily as he was waiting to hear about all the things that they had to talk about.

225

She returned to her chair once he had gotten down from the truck and then watched through the screen door as he walked slowly, an old man's walk, not stepping, not lifting, rather shifting, shuffling down the narrow walkway to the porch. And she thought what she had been thinking for days now, what she had condensed from days of thinking. That he was no different than any of them, no different than the multitudes that had visited Connie, no different than the boys in the foster homes and shelters. Except that he had put a new twist to it. He wanted a child, he said, and was willing to pay for that child, he said. Well, in a few moments they would see how willing to pay he was.

She told him to come in just as she had told Connie's to come in. Because now he was no different than they and she no different than Connie. Except that she wouldn't give it up quite as easily as Connie. Not quite. That was what she was thinking as he opened the screen door and shuffled in. At that moment he looked as lustful as all of them, and as weak as them too. And she told him to sit down because they had to talk. Not as Connie would have done, because Connie wouldn't have done that. In that sense she wasn't Connie either.

He took off his hat and she was surprised at the years the hat saved him. She had never seen, or at least never noticed, the severely receding hairline, the deeply wrinkled brow, and the yellowish hue of his balding skin until moments before, when his pant leg had slipped over his boot.

"You said you wanted me to have your child, Giuseppe, and you took me by surprise. You said that you would make me the richest woman in the valley, Giuseppe, and I heard that part too, but I was so shocked by the first part that I didn't pay much attention to the second part for days.

"I want to be blunt, Giuseppe. Frank. Because about these things there is no other way to be. To have a child, Giuseppe, we have to fuck. So when do we fuck, where do we fuck, how many times do we fuck? And let's say that after two hundred fucks I'm not pregnant, what then, Giuseppe? Are all those fucks free?"

He had heard that word a million times. He had heard women use it, to be sure. But never in his life had it been more offensive. He lowered his eyes so that she wouldn't see. Because each time she used it, it was if she had a knife attached to it, a knife that not only pierced, but once inside, twisted and hacked too.

They were silent, and when the silence thickened, he began to let his fingers rise and fall gently on the brim of his hat, watching them rather than her. He couldn't raise his eyes to her. Not then. She, in turn, had no trouble watching him, studying him, determined that he would answer, that the question wouldn't fade unanswered. When he didn't answer, when at least two minutes had passed and he had not yet answered, she asked again.

"What about the free fucks, Guiseppe? What if I don't get pregnant? What if I don't get pregnant? What if I don't get pregnant after a year and you decide that you want to try for another year, or a year after that? What of all those free fucks, Giuseppe?"

And he, without raising his head, without stopping his fingers, answered quietly, "I did not come for free fucks, as you call them, Sally. I do not want free fucks. Not from you or anyone. I came because I want to have a child by you because I respect you. I respect everything you've done and everything you are. There is no woman that I respect more. If you try to have a child with me, whether it's once or a hundred times, you will be paid, and paid well. I will keep my word."

He stopped there, but only for a moment, just long enough to stop his fingers and raise his head, so that his eyes met hers softly, openly. He said, "Money means so little to me now. Life is much more important. I have little of the last and much of the first. You have just the opposite. Like you, I was very poor. And like you, I accomplished much. And now I want someone to take up where I am leaving off, someone who will have my blood in his veins, who will go far beyond where I have gone, someone who will be as strong or stronger than I was, as strong as you are. I want him to have this beginning.

"You say you wanted to speak frankly, well, so do I. So let me be frank. I always thought that Johnny would be that someone. But Johnny is gone now. He might come back and he might not. He might be dead. I don't know. When I last saw him, his spirit was broken. They might have taken the best part of him. I don't know.

"Matthew is his mother's son. He hates me and I hate him. It has always been that way. I mention him only because I think you should know how I feel about him. I never consider him. On the day my divorce was final, I disinherited him.

"And that leaves Joey. Joey is a nice boy. You know that. He's a good boy. Sometimes I wonder where that goodness came from. He didn't get it from me, and he didn't get it from his mother. He wants to make the world a better place. Can you imagine that? Making the world a better place. He doesn't even know what those words mean. How do you make the world a better place? Where do you begin? Where does *he* begin? They would eat him alive when he started his mission. No, I guess I always wanted more than Joey. I wanted someone who was tough and full of fire. Like I was . . . like you are. Who knows, maybe that someone will turn out to be you in the end. But before that, I would like that someone to have my blood in his veins. No, Sally, I did not come here for free fucks, as you call them. I came here to buy a child, a child who can carry on where I left off, a child who can go far beyond where I left off."

She was sitting upright and firm when he began, and she was still sitting upright and firm when he finished. Nothing about her had moved or changed, except for her eyes: they had blinked more than they should have. They had blinked to some of his words and to his eyes, eyes that were neither combative nor hostile, yet strong in their softness and convincing in their directness. Still, she had prepared herself for anything, prepared herself over the past few days for any and all ploys, not the least of which was endearing words. She had heard them by the thousands from Connie's visitors, and in the foster homes too, heard them by the thousands in each visitor's moment of need, heard them twist and disappear once each had gotten what he had come for. So she said, exactly as she had practiced it, "What do I get besides promises before I go to bed with you, Giuseppe?"

"Two ranches, and I will change my will to include you with Johnny and Joey—in equal shares."

"A will can be changed at any time, can't it? Look at Matthew."

"Yes, but the deeds to the ranches will be yours before we begin, and each month there will be another piece of property until you are pregnant or want to stop. And once you are pregnant, there will be what they call a trust set up for you and the child. You will never have to think or worry about money again, Sally."

⟵——————▷

They met on the following Tuesday at a fast food restaurant on the outskirts of Gilroy. His pick-up was there when she drove into the lot, and she saw his silhouette through the plate glass even before she got out of her car, saw the outline of his hat and a cup held up to his mouth, and she shuddered. But she wanted this, or at least all that it would bring, and there was no turning back now.

"Can I get you a cup of coffee?" he said when he saw her standing next to him.

"No, thank you," she said, shaking her head as well, wanting to get away from the eyes of the customers and the help, who had to be wondering, suspecting what she was doing with such an old man.

"Sit down," he said softly, gesturing with one hand to the chair on the other side of the table. It was neither a demand nor an order, but a request.

"Relax," he said once she was seated.

She tried to smile but couldn't. She wanted to get on with it, get away from the suspicious, snickering eyes that she knew would look away once she looked back at them. But she couldn't. Then she realized that that, too, was part of the bargain.

"I want you to see these, read these before we go on," he said, taking two small stacks of papers from under a newspaper that he had at his side.

She looked at them and then looked back at him, puzzled. They looked like the contracts or credit applications that she and Joey had signed when they had bought furniture and appliances.

"These are the deeds that I promised you. This one here is a small ranch near Saratoga. It still has fruit trees on it. It's worth a lot of money, not for the trees but for the land. Everything around it has been developed. If you sold it today, it would be worth $300,000. If you wait five years, it'll be worth at least three times that much. This one over here is twenty-five acres on the other side of Morgan Hill. The valley's growing that way. It's worth $250,000. Give it ten years and it will be worth . . ."

She didn't hear any more. Her eyes watered and she shook her head, no longer aware of the customers or the help.

"What's the matter?"

"Why are you giving me so much?"

"Because I want your child."

"But this is so much."

"If you have my child, he will have it too. It will be his as well. I know you will never deprive him."

"And if I don't, if I don't have your child, if I can't have your child, what then?"

229

"It's yours."

"But why?"

"Because we agreed."

"But it's so much. Nobody is worth that much."

"It means that much to me and more. I want you to have my child. It's something I want. And there's not much I want anymore. It's important that I try to have that child with you . . . Shall we go?"

Just outside the door he said, "There's no need to take two cars. We can go in my truck. I have to come back this way anyway."

In the truck, she fingered the deeds, rubbing those sheets of paper that gave her more than she would earn in twenty years, in a lifetime perhaps. They were well out of Gilroy before she realized that she didn't know where they were or where they were going.

"Aren't we going to your house?"

"No, not the one you're thinking of."

"Where are we going?"

"To my other house."

"Your other house? I didn't know you had another house."

"Nobody does."

"Why do you have two houses?"

"I've always had two houses. For forty years now, I've had this other house. I've never left it. Even when I was in San Jose, when I was with Johnny and Joey, I would come out at least twice a week, at least to take care of the dogs. Most every week I would spend at least a night out here. Now, until it gets cold, until the end of next month, I spend almost half my nights here."

"There's nothing out here," she said, looking in every direction at the tall, dead grasses that had turned to a faded gold, now in the flatlands and soon in the hills.

"There's more than you think."

"There's no houses."

"There's a few."

"There's nothing."

"There are trees."

"I don't see any."

"You will."

The road left its flatness for dips and then a long, mild grade. Only the tips of the dry grasses moved, and they were dead. She fingered the deeds.

"Are you sure you have a house out here?"

"I'm sure."

The truck left the paved road and climbed onto a dirt road that quickly became a long, dusty corridor into the hills.

"From here until we get to the house, and even past the house, I own everything that you can see. I've bought it piece by piece over the years so that nobody could change it."

Most of what she could see was dust, a white-brown dust that spumed up heavily on all sides of the truck. She coughed and rolled up her window.

"You should have worn pants."

"Pants?" She looked at him, but he only smiled.

They drove on, down that endless corridor of dust until they came to a pass between two mounds. He stopped the truck and pointed. "There it is." Before them, halfway up a rise that ended at the base of the first row of dry hills a mile away, sat a small house surrounded by clumps of rust-colored masses, all of which seemed enclosed by a fence. There was no other house or sign of life anywhere for as far as she could see, and there was no reason for the house to be there.

"You stay there?"

"Yes."

"Alone?"

"Yes."

"For forty years?"

"No, I haven't lived there every day for forty years. But it's been a home to me for forty years. It's been a special place."

"Does anyone else live there?"

"No."

"Has anyone else lived there?"

"Before me there was Angelina Mendoza."

She turned and looked at him again.

"Yes," he said.

She fingered the deeds as the truck descended, running through the dust and challenging the ruts. Behind them was nothing except spiraling clouds of dust. Before them was the house, growing smaller and more dilapidated as they neared. The closer they got, the more worn and shabby and isolated it became. So this is where I will conceive my first child, she thought. And she looked down at the deeds.

Then she saw a pack of dogs leaping and clawing at the gate, heard their barking and cries over the bumping and rattling of the truck. They were huge, black dogs that looked as if they would break through the gate at any moment. But they turned to pups, yelping and leaping and whining, when Giuseppe approached and opened the gate. They surrounded him, struggling among themselves to get next to him, to lick him and nudge him, begging for his hand. For a few moments he petted and patted them and then with one wave of his hand moved them away from the big gate, which he then swung open.

He got back into the truck, drove it past the gate, stopped and got out again and closed it and locked it while the dogs yelped and licked and whined. Sally studied the house, repulsed by the shabbiness of its weather-stained planks. She accepted it again as part of the bargain until he drove around, and then past, it to, and through, a back gate to the protest of the dogs. He proceeded along the hillside over a path or road that she could not see.

"Where are we going?"

"I want to show you the trees and the water."

"What trees?"

"You'll see."

He zig-zagged through the tall dead grasses, occasionally hitting rocks and mounds that he was trying to avoid, following an indiscernable line or path, leaving the house behind. Then, just as they were about to lose sight of the house, as they were about to drop into a gulley, he stopped the truck and said again, "You should have worn pants."

"Why?"

"Because we're going on a hike."

"To where?"

"To the trees and the water."

"But there's a tree."

And there was: a huge, magnificent, sprawling oak that burst through the faded-gold grasses and ran to the sky, first with its grey-white trunk, then with its branches and then with its green, as isolated and unexplained as the house itself.

"There's a lot more of those where we're going." He looked at her dress again and said, "I think you'll be okay. Just stay close behind me."

He got out of the truck and from behind the seat took a worn, filled knapsack and another khaki hat. He strapped on the knapsack and handed her the hat. "You better put this on. It's gonna get hot real soon." He started away from the truck and then stopped and turned and looked back at her. This was part of the bargain too. So she got out of the truck, taking the deeds and the hat with her and stepped down into, and then jumped up from, the grasses that had gotten under her dress and had run up her legs.

"There's a path over here. It won't be so bad."

Behind him she saw and felt that the waist high, chest high grasses had been cut in a long thin straight line that dropped down into the gully and then up again.

"Who made this?"

"It's a deer trail. They've been using it for years. They come down from the hills and use it to get to the water. Other animals use it. I use it too."

"I don't see any water."

"You will. Try to follow in my footsteps. I'm wider than you, and my body will brush back the grass. It won't scratch your legs as much if you do that." Then, looking down at the deeds in her hand, he added, "Are you sure you want to take those with you?"

"Yes."

"You better put on the hat," he said again.

She looked at the hat. It was an awful-looking thing. "I don't want to wear this hat," she said and returned it to the truck.

He nodded ever so slightly, waited until she returned, and then started down the gully. He moved briskly and effortlessly. It wasn't until they started up out of the gully that she remembered his labored shuffle as he moved toward her door just a few weeks before, because he was leaving her behind, moving away from her up the hillside. Already the morning sun was hot on her head. She had to say, "Slow down, Giuseppe."

He stopped and waited and started again, raising his old legs in short, steady, unbroken strides that she couldn't match or repeat.

"Wait, Giuseppe," she said, less than halfway up the hill. The sun was hotter with each step and her bare, heavy legs were being eaten alive by the grasses.

Again he stopped and waited, then he started again with a slower pace, but it was still a steady pace. She seemed to wander aimlessly and fall behind him, searching for her breath and her balance as the sun mercilessly bore down on her. At the top of the hill, he stopped and gave her water and his hat.

"It's just over the next ridge," he said.

She looked over at the next ridge. She would never make it.

They started down again and she thought only of the next ascent, certain that her legs would collapse under her, or that she would double over in pain from the ache in her breathing. His pace was even slower, but steady still. He would stop every few yards, not looking at her, not humiliating her, but rather looking about at the dry grass and the hillsides and the unblemished blue sky that stretched from every ridge or edge or horizon up over them. There was no sign of fatigue, not a drop of sweat on him, and everywhere he turned, everything he saw seemed to give him pleasure. She, in turn, stared repeatedly down at her best dress, which was now matted to her body with sweat. Again and again, she kept saying to herself that it was ruined.

They stopped, and she sat on the trail three times during the last ascent. Sweat poured from her. She had never hiked anywhere, let alone in those hell-hole hills. Each time they stopped, he looked at the twisted, rumpled, sweat-stained deeds in her hands and asked, "Are you sure you don't want me to put those in the pack?" Each time she simply shook her head, not speaking, not looking at him, clutching onto the deeds tightly.

When they reached the final ridge, he gestured down and before him with an open hand, beaming as she trudged those final steps. "There it is."

What she saw was a long row of green at the base of the next gully about a half a mile away. "Oh, Giuseppe, I can't. I can't make it there. I really can't." She tasted the make-up that was running down her face and saw the sweat-laden strands of hair that were further staining her dress.

"Let's just do it here. Right here on the grass. I can't get any more pregnant down there than I can right here. Please, Giuseppe, I don't think I can take another step. Let's just do it here."

If he heard her, he didn't show it, because he continued looking down at the base of the gully, beaming as one would to a loved one. "Rest. Let's rest. Have some water. But drink it slowly. Wash your mouth out first. Here, have a piece of bread and some cheese. In a few

minutes you'll feel much better. And it's all dowhhill from here. You'll
love it there."

She looked down at the green line and then at the wet, wrenched,
dirty deeds in her hands. It was part of the bargain.

They went on, down that last half mile of dried grasses to the trees,
with him turning every few moments, smiling, saying, "We're almost
there," or, "You're gonna like it."

And she did like it, because there was shade. There were trees everywhere and it was cool. And the tall, raspy grasses stopped where the trees
began, and the ground beneath her was of packed dirt and rock, and she
wasn't being scratched, and she could drop her arms and hold her deeds
at her side because there was nowhere to lose them, not there.

Smiling, Giuseppe kept motioning to her, "Come on. Come on. It's
just a little ways more."

She knew that it would have to end soon, that the trees did not go
on forever, and that when they came to the end of the trees, they would
have to do it, regardless of how they did it, or what she looked like, they
would have to do it, and then she could go back to San Jose.

Suddenly, she heard water running. Then she saw it, and saw him
too, grinning, as if he owned it, no, as if he had made it. And maybe he
did or had, because with his money, he seemed to own everything everywhere, and he could probably make anything or have it made. It was no
more than three feet across and at most no more than six inches deep,
but it was swift and clean and all the rocks under it gleamed. She
touched it, and it was cold. She scooped it, and it was pure.

He took off his boots and rolled up his pants and stepped into the
middle of it. "This is what the deer do, especially when their hoofs or
legs have been hurt. I've seen them limp into this water and then carefully put the sore hoof down. And when you stand in it like this, you
understand why they do it. Try it. Take off your shoes. You'll like it. See
what it does for your feet."

She shook her head. Ridiculous old man. He'd brought her all this
way just to do it here. Sooner or later he'd get to the point. They always
did.

When he got out of the creek, he went to the pack and took out a
blanket which he carefully spread next to the creek. Then he removed
bread and cheese and salami and wine and two cups and two plates and

said, "Here, have some. You'll see how good everything tastes here, especially after a hike."

She sat with him and ate, and it was good.

"Have some wine," he said, pouring some into her cup. "I know you don't drink, and I understand why. But wine is nothing but fermented grapes. It's good for you. It tastes good, and it makes you feel good."

She took the wine as well, thinking that that too was part of the bargain and that it was the prelude to what had to be.

She woke to the gurgling of the water and was startled and confused until she saw the trees and looked around and saw him sitting with his back to her on a large rock in the creek with his feet dangling in the water, looking up at the trees. She saw that her dress was above her thighs. She felt her underpants for any wetness and, finding none, examined her thighs and legs for any sign of what might have been. Finding none, she looked at her watch and saw that it was just past three and that she must have slept well over two hours. She went to the creek and sat on the rock next to him, letting the dress slide well up her thighs, because if they hurried, there was still time enough. He looked at her and smiled and then looked back up at the top of the trees.

"What are you doing, Giuseppe?"

"I'm looking at the trees."

"Why?"

"I'm watching them move."

"I don't see them moving."

"Oh, they're moving."

"So."

"They're beautiful when they move. I think they're more beautiful when they don't move very much, when just parts of them move, when just some of the leaves on some of the branches move."

She slid further on the rock, letting her toes touch the water, letting her dress slide too, exposing the fullness of her thighs. And when he didn't look, she began splashing the water with her toes, kicking her naked legs and thighs back and forth. Now he did look, but only for a moment, because his eyes went upstream.

"You know, the wonder of this place is that the creek just comes out of the hill about a quarter of a mile from here, goes for about another half a mile from here and then disappears back into the hill. No one knows where the water comes from and no one knows where it goes . . . at least I don't. But it runs all year long. This is our driest time, and look at it, look at all the water. I've thought of getting some heavy equipment out here to dig into both sides of the hill to see where it comes from and where it goes. But I know that I'd never find out, and what a mess I'd make besides. And maybe I'd kill all this. With all that digging and blasting, the water might end up going a different way. And it's the water that's made all of this. There's no other place in these hills like this. Without the water these trees wouldn't be here."

"Why did you let me sleep so long?"

"I don't know. I guess I wasn't keeping track of the time. I went for a little hike, like I always do when I come here, to where the water begins. I can sit there a long time, just looking at it and listening to it, watching it start its run and wondering about it. Then I came back and saw that you were still sleeping, and I walked down to where the water disappears. I can sit there for a long time too without knowing how long I've been there . . . What time is it?"

"It's 3:20."

"3:20! Oh, my God, we got to get going or we'll never get you back to San Jose in time." With that, he slid off the rock into the creek and then went back to the blanket, leaving her and the dress that had slid up to the V of her legs behind. She sat on the rock as he packed, thinking. Is he crazy? Is this some sort of game? He hasn't touched me once. Has he changed his mind? Is he going to want his deeds back?

Those were still her thoughts as she followed him along the deer path over the hills to the truck. As they approached the house, she thought he might stop there, might try there. But he didn't, and once they were on their bumpy, dusty way again, going back to Gilroy, she said, "We can't have a child this way, Giuseppe."

"I know. "

"But we didn't even try."

"We will when we're both ready."

————➤

At the dinner table Joey asked, "Did Papa come today?"

"No," she said looking directly at Joey. Because he hadn't.

"I guess that Johnny thing still has him all shook up."

She nodded.

————➤

237

As she washed the dishes she said, "Joey, I'm thinking of asking Ralph for the rest of the week off. That's if you don't mind."

"I don't mind. But why?"

"Connie said that she heard that my aunt Yolanda is back around Salinas again, just visiting. I'd like to go down to Salinas and see if I can find her and visit with her. You know how I've always liked her."

"I don't have any problem with that."

"It could mean that I'll be late some of those days, or even stay over for a night, depending on where she is. Of course, I'd phone you and let you know."

"I don't have any problem with that."

———

Later, as he was working on his assignments, she said, "I'm tired, Joey. I think I'm going to go to bed now."

"Okay," he said without looking up from his book.

She went over and kissed him on the cheek. "Goodnight, Joey."

"Goodnight, Sweetie."

She paused and said, "I just want you to know that I love you very much, Joey, and I always will."

"I know, but what's that got to do with saying goodnight?"

"Not much, I guess."

———

He was waiting in his truck in the parking lot, just as she had asked, when she arrived at one o'clock. She wore jeans and tennis shoes and had a large, brimmed hat in her hand. They smiled at each other as she climbed into the truck, but said nothing. On the way out of Gilroy, she told him that she had taken the week off and that she had told Joey that she would be looking for Yolanda. "That ought to give us enough time," she concluded. She hoped so.

At the gate, she disregarded the dogs and studied the house, trying to imagine what Angelina Mendoza was like. Today she knew he wouldn't stop at the house, wouldn't take her in, and today she thought she knew why. She wondered how she resembled Angelina Mendoza.

At the deer path, she put on the hat even before she got out of the truck. It was the hottest time of the day, and all around here the grasses crackled. She was sore for the first few hundred yards, but with her movement and the heat, the soreness soon diminished and she was able to keep up with him, although not without effort. He, in turn, moved quickly and quietly and effortlessly with the pack on his back over the first and then the second hill, at most slowing his pace some for her.

They reached the trees and the creek with only a few stops. He took out and spread and anchored the blanket in the same place that he had before and then hoisted the pack onto his back again and said, "Let's go."

"Where are we going?"

"To where the water ends."

"But why?" It was already past two.

"Because I want you to see it."

She had not brought the deeds, but she thought of them, saw them. This too. It wasn't much of a price to pay.

They walked along the creek. "See how most of the trees are on our side of the creek. See how the trees on the other side are only two and three deep, but on this side they're eight to ten deep."

Where the trees were meant nothing to her. But she listened because she might have to answer.

"So the creek has shifted. There's no way that all the trees over here could have gotten water from where the creek is now. If you look close, you'll see that these trees over here are bigger, older; not that they're big trees, they're all scrub oak."

She didn't know an oak from a pine and didn't want to know.

"So the creek had to be way over here at one time, many . . ." The way they were walking and stopping, it would be dark before they reached the end of the creek. "Look at how healthy they are. They need no tending, no care . . ." They had been walking for more than a half hour, and the creek seemed nowhere in sight. She didn't want this to go on for months. She wanted to get pregnant now, this week, today.

"And it started from a single seed, a seed that the wind or a bird brought by chance. And the water that comes from nowhere brought it to life. Look at it! Isn't it wonderful?"

She looked for what seemed the hundredth time, a hundred times more than she needed to look. Still, it was a small price to pay.

At the end of the tree line, the water seeped, sank into the base of the hill, and disappeared. He began comparing it to life itself, to the end of life, to death. Now she stopped listening. Old people were always talking about death, needing to talk about death. Young people didn't. Death was far, far away. What was important now was the hour. It was nearing four and he had not once touched her, had not once looked at her, not the way a man looks at a woman. In an hour or so they would have to start back. Another day wasted. What was he doing? She couldn't keep on telling Joey that she was looking for Yolanda forever.

Finally, they started back, Giuseppe explaining that these trees were evergreens. The only tree she had ever cared about was the Christmas tree she bought each year off the Giordano's Market parking lot.

Just a few hundred feet into the trees, he stopped. "Come on. I want you to see this." He went to the low branch of a tree and climbed up onto it and kept climbing until he was more than halfway up the tree. "Come on up," he said, sitting on a branch.

She shook her head. "I can't."

"Oh, come on."

This too was part of the price. Slowly she pulled herself up to the branch just below him.

"When you're up here in the trees, it's like you become part of them. You can feel them and hear them and really see them. Look at the top branch. There has to be wind up there that we can't hear or feel. See how the color of the leaves changes, how the light changes. And look . . ."

Was he crazy? Was this some kind of a game? He knew why they were there.

When he paused, she said, "Giuseppe, you know there are only a few days each month that a woman can get pregnant. If we wait much more, we might lose those days."

"Oh, don't worry about that," he said from above, flicking one hand downward without so much as lowering his eyes, let alone his head, to look at her.

Gradually, he stopped talking, but then he simply sat there, as he had yesterday on the rock, looking up at the trees. She was determined to wait him out. At two minutes to five, she got up from her branch, knowing that this was another wasted day, and said, "I'm getting down, Giuseppe."

He came to the blanket some twenty minutes later, saying, "We better get going. This time of year the sun sinks real fast out here, and it can get cold once it goes down." That was all he said.

"Giuseppe, you know there are only a few days a month when . . ."

"We should get to know each other," he said curtly.

"But we do know each other."

"Do we?"

He was quiet when they met the next morning. He said nothing except to answer, as briefly as he could, the few questions she asked as they drove. Once they were inside the gates, he looked up at the house for a long time and then, rather than driving around it, drove to it, stopped the truck and said, "I want you to see it."

It surprised her, but relieved her. Maybe he wanted to begin. She followed him up onto the old porch that swayed with their weight and then moved with his efforts to unlock the two padlocks that fastened the front door.

"Did you stay here last night?"

"Yes."

He opened the door and let her into a stuffy darkness. In a few moments the darkness passed, and she saw four small bare rooms, each of the same dimension, each with a single, window and each with the same unpainted, rough, broad planks for floors and walls. One was a kitchen with a stove and sink. One was a bedroom with a small, iron bed. Another had old, stained boxes and nothing more, and the room through which they entered had two plain, wooden chairs and a tiny table between them. He was watching her, saying nothing, following her as she went to the door of each room, entering none except the first, because she felt nothing except repulsion. She stood in the doorways and said, weakly at first, "It's nice." She was not able to say anything else.

Tension gushed from her when he said, "Let's go." She could not have lain on that iron bed with its thick, coarse, worn blanket. She could not have conceived his or anyone's child on that small, iron bed in those dark, cramped rooms.

Outside he said, "You know, you're the first woman that's been in there since she died."

She let it pass. It was best to let those words pass. All along the deer path, as she followed him, as she looked repeatedly at his bowed but supple moving figure, she couldn't help but think and wonder about that small, dark, bare house and about him and Angelina Mendoza.

He went directly to the place where the water began, where it sprung out of the ground at the base of the hill. There he laid out and anchored the blanket, set down the pack, took off his shoes, rolled up his pants and walked into and stood in the flowing water just a few feet from its origin. He looked up at the sun, letting it warm him as the water cooled him. He stood there for some time, fascinated as he always was by the water and its source. When he turned, he saw her. She was lying on the blanket naked, and she was beautiful, as beautiful as any woman he had ever seen.

She smiled, because seeing him, seeing his face, she knew it had begun. He went to her and took her, as loudly and hungrily as anyone had. And when it was over, when the last grunt of strength was strained from him, he rolled over on his back, exhausted. Then he became conscious of his pants at his knees; he raised his back, pulled up his pants, zipped and buttoned them and laid down again and looked up at the speckled sky with her.

After a while, he stretched out his arm, reaching for her, and she raised her head and let his arm slide under her shoulder. He brought her to him saying, "I know what this is, but there's no reason I shouldn't enjoy the moment." She curled up next to him and said, "You can take off your clothes, Giuseppe."

"I'd rather not."

They lay for some time under the trees, she pressed to him, talking occasionally, quietly, randomly of small things as old friends would have, she naked and he fully clothed.

Three weeks later, Sally sent him an unsigned note. "I missed my period. No one knows."

It was Joey who told Giuseppe that she was pregnant. It was the second week of December. He saw Joey's car come up the long driveway. He saw him jump out of the car and run up the walkway. He saw the excitement on Joey's face and he knew.

"Papa! Papa! Sally's pregnant!" He hugged his father, and Giuseppe Rocco hugged him too.

Giuseppe's eyes watered, and he tried to control them so that Joey wouldn't see, but couldn't. "I'm happy for all of us," he said.

"I knew you'd be happy, Papa! I knew it! I tried calling you, but you won't answer the phone. We want you to come and spend Christmas with us, Papa. We want you to celebrate with us. We haven't seen you in months."

"It's your brother, you know. I still have them looking. I still have them searching. They tell me they maybe found something. But I'll come for Christmas, if that's what both of you want."

―――――

A week later, his investigators, and then the police, told him that a skull that had washed up at Pescadero was Johnny's. Dental charts confirmed it. There was no doubt.

―――――

Giuseppe Rocco had a simple private ceremony for Johnny at the Holy Cross Cemetery. Only he and Joey and Sally and the priest were there. Johnny's skull was sealed in a casket and lowered into a grave next to the plot that he had already purchased for himself.

After the brief ceremony, Giuseppe Rocco hugged Joey and said, "I love you, Joey. In my own way I've always loved you and always will. Forgive me for any hurt I've brought you."

When he hugged Sally, he said, softly, "It's all in your hands now, Sally. I couldn't ask for anything more. Not now."

―――――

It was more than three months before he saw either of them again. Then he went to the store, knowing that Sally was no longer working.

"Has Sally had those tests to see if it's a boy?"

"She doesn't want to, Papa."

"They can tell ahead of time now if it's gonna be a boy."

"I know, but Sally doesn't want to know."

Thereafter he went to the store weekly.

"She's fine, Papa, and the baby's doing good too. No problems. No complications. Hey, we'd like to see you. We miss the Tuesday dinners. Sally's starting to think that you don't like her."

"Sally knows I like her. It's not that. I need time right now. When the baby's born I'm sure it'll all be different."

―――――

The baby was born on July 26, nine months to the day from when he had turned and seen her, as beautiful a woman as any he had ever seen. It was a boy. Carlo Rossi had the sheriff's office locate Giuseppe and send him on his way to the hospital.

Joey was waiting for him in the maternity ward.

"He's big, Papa, and strong. And he looks like our side of the family."

"Good," Giuseppe said, breathing heavily with excitement. "Where is he?"

"If we go to Sally's room, they'll bring him out."

When he saw Sally, he stopped.

"Hello, Giuseppe," she said from the bed, and then closed her eyes and turned her head as if exhausted.

"How are you, Sally?"

She nodded with closed eyes, and Giuseppe was relieved that their eyes wouldn't meet, not then, not with Joey there.

"Good," he said.

Then a nurse came with the baby, and Giuseppe took him before she could reach Joey. He was beet red, with slits for eyes and a mouth. Giuseppe stared at the sleeping infant, absorbing every line and blemish, thinking, this might be the one. And then the infant writhed, and Giuseppe felt his tiny arms struggle mightily against the blanket, watched the tiny head turn in struggles, even redder now, and then saw the lipless mouth open and heard a long, loud cry fill the room, punctuated only by the need to breathe.

"He's strong," Giuseppe Rocco said. "He's strong." And tears ran down the right side of Giuseppe's face.

He thought of the baby constantly, more so when people began saying that he looked more like him than anyone else, and not at all like his father. When Joey insisted that they name the baby Johnny for his brother, Giuseppe said, "Joey, you've made me very happy."

For Sally it was a different matter. "He's here almost every day, Joey."

"I don't understand the problem, Sally."

"Why should you? You're not here."

"What does he do that bothers you so much?"

"He's in my way. He's always in my way."

"How?"

"He never leaves the baby alone. He's always with the baby. I'm the mother, not him. Instead of sitting in the park with all the other old men where he belongs, he sits in the baby's room, next to the crib, and stares at him."

"I still don't see why that bothers you. He's in the baby's room and the baby's sleeping. Why does that bother you?"

"This is *my* house, Joey. Our house. I don't want an outsider here all the time. Yes, I know he's your father. But he's not part of this family, and I don't want him to be part of this family."

"I can't tell him not to come over, Sally. I've never said anything to your family and they're here every day."

"It's not the same, Joey. It's not the same."

And it wasn't. In fact, it was getting worse. Each day the baby looked more and more like Giuseppe. At six months, there was no denying it. At nine months, she knew it was a curse. Each time she looked at the baby, she was reminded of Giuseppe and of her betrayal. Because of his constant, reckless energy, Joey compared the baby to his namesake, but Sally knew better. It was just a matter of time, she thought, until they were found out.

By the time the baby was walking, Giuseppe was there every day, watching his every move, his every breath, talking to him constantly. Those were the only words spoken in the house, because by then Sally had stopped speaking to the old man. She would tense up as soon as she heard the truck in the driveway. And Giuseppe, thinking that she thought he had come for her, was determined to show her that that was not the case.

"He's got to go, Joey. I can't have him here practically every day. I can't take it any longer."

"But what can I tell him?"

"I don't know and I don't care. But he's got to go. Either he leaves or I leave. I can't turn around and see the two of them all the time. It's bad enough seeing one."

"What are you talking about?"

She paused, catching herself. "I'm talking about this being our family, our home. And I'm tired of seeing him here all the time. I just want to be with you and the baby, Joey."

The next day Joey said, "What if I tell him that he can only be here when I'm here? That'll let him see the baby and I'll keep him away from you."

"That means that he'll be here every night for dinner."

"No, it won't. I won't let that happen."

<hr>

Two days later Joey said, "I talked to him. He's hurt. But he said he'll come over only when I'm here."

He was hurt. He wouldn't look at her, not even greet her. But she preferred it that way. At least at first. But soon, that too became oppressive, because he came and stayed for dinner, just as she had predicted, every night, sitting next to Johnny in his high chair at the table, constantly talking to him, feeding him, coaxing him, almost as if she and Joey weren't there, were intruders in their own home.

<hr>

"I can't take it anymore, Joey. It's got to stop."

"But he's my father. How do I tell him that he can't come over to his son's house and see his grandson?"

"I don't care what you tell him, but it's got to stop."

"He's an old man now, Sally. He really doesn't have much else. I mean, he doesn't want much else. Johnny was his life. And little Johnny's his life too. He didn't expect Johnny to die so young."

"Nobody did. But that's not my fault."

"I didn't say it was."

"If you don't talk to him, I will."

<hr>

And they did talk, two days later, when Joey was detained at the store and Giuseppe arrived at his usual hour. "I don't want you here anymore, Giuseppe." She wasted neither time nor words.

Nor did he. "You're going to keep me from seeing my son?"

"Which one? Oh, excuse me. You've always only had one son, haven't you, Giuseppe?"

"That's none of your business."

"It is my business. Because he's my son too, and you're destroying my life with both your sons. I can't have you here and have any kind of relationship with Joey or Johnny. Don't you understand that, Giuseppe?"

"You're not going to keep me from seeing my son."

"If you don't stop coming, I'll get a court order against you."

"Don't threaten me. Let's go to court. I'll tell everybody I'm his father and I'll fight for custody too."

"Nobody will believe you. They'll think you're a crazy old man."

"Oh, they'll believe me. Just look at him. They'll know. And where did you tell Ralph and Joey you were that week? With Yolanda? Ha! And what about the deeds? Did I just happen to give you two pieces of property that week for nothing? No, Sally, they'll believe me. And I'll take a blood test, too. Will you make Joey take one, Sally? Do you really think I can't prove that's my son?"

———

Two days later she drove out to the old, colorless house, knowing she'd find him there. At the gate, over the barking, yelping dogs, she said to him, "Here are your deeds. I don't want anything of yours. Please take me off your will, if I'm on it. I'm going back to work. You can have the baby every Tuesday, all day Tuesday, for as long as you like. Joey's home on Tuesday mornings, and you can drop the baby off at my mother's house at night . . . I just can't see you in our house with them anymore, Giuseppe. And I don't want you telling the world that you're Johnny's father . . . I can't do that to Joey. We've already done enough to him."

———

For months he came precisely at 8:45 every Tuesday morning. He no longer entered the house and he had little to say to Joey.

"Is Johnny ready?"

"Yes, Papa."

He would smile as soon as he saw the toddler. "Hello, big boy!" he would say to the bounding, smiling child. He would squat and open his arms to hug and kiss and laugh with the teetering child. Then they would leave, as quickly as he had come, with the old man laughing and smiling at the non-stop reports and observations that rose from the end of his hand in undecipherable words and sounds as they walked to the pick-up.

"Where do you take him, Papa?"

"Everywhere."

"What do you do with him all day?"

"Everything."

That was enough of an explanation until the child began returning with scratches on his legs and burrs in his clothing and his shoes as often as not soaked.

"Papa, Sally asked me to talk to you. She doesn't like the scratches on Johnny's legs. She's worried . . ."

"You tell Sally for me that she can go straight to hell! I love my boy, my grandson, every bit as much as she does!"

He said nothing to Sally, choosing instead to follow Giuseppe and the boy the following week, at a safe distance, down the highway to Gilroy, and then, trailing even further behind, on an isolated country road that headed into the barren brown hills to the east. He parked on the road and watched the truck raise large clouds of dust as it drove to and through the first set of hills. Once the clouds settled and the truck disappeared, he too traversed that bumpy, dusty, dirt road and stopped at the pass from which he could see the truck approaching a solitary house halfway up the next set of hills. The truck stopped and then continued past the house and up into the hills behind it and disappeared.

When he told Sally, she said only, "I don't think you should be following your father around. He loves Johnny. He'll take good care of him."

"You don't think he's losing it? What's he doing up in those hills? And with our son, no less."

"He has property in those hills. He's always talked about those hills."

"Not to me he hasn't."

"He has to me."

She imagined them on the deer trail, with Johnny on his back, turning in every direction. And then she imagined them at the beginning of the water, and at the end too.

After the first rains, Ralph Giordano said to Joey, "You know, a couple of Tuesdays ago, I saw your dad coming down the street with your son. Remember how he used to bring you and your brother to the store when your brother was about your son's age and was just barely walking? Like your kid is now. It sure took me back a ways. I thought he was gonna bring your boy into the store, so I went and told Sally. Well, she got all upset and left her checkstand and went to the back of the store. I went back there to see what the problem was, but she wouldn't talk to me. Then I came back out thinking they'd be in the store, but they weren't. I looked out the front doors and saw your dad down at the next corner lifting your boy into one of those baby backpacks. Yesterday I saw him do the same thing again. I didn't tell Sally, and I only mention it because . . ."

There was no need to follow him. The next Tuesday Joey not only knew where Giuseppe would be, but what time he would be there. So Joey parked a block away on Broadway at exactly five minutes to three and waited. Nine minutes later the pick-up truck drove past him. It stopped at the next intersection, crossed it and parked. He watched his father get out of the truck, then go around to the other side of the truck and take Johnny from its cab. Then the two started up Columbia Street, just as Giuseppe had walked up that same street some twenty years before with Johnny and him.

As soon as they were out of his view, Joey drove to Columbia Street and from there watched as the two walked towards Giordano's Market. It was pretty much as Joey remembered. The thick, stocky man, now more bowed, holding the tiny boy at the end of his long arm, walking slowly, patiently, as the child looked in every direction, walking distractedly without any pattern or rhythm, except to bolt as often as he could from Giuseppe. Giuseppe would chase him and catch him with a few steps, and hug him and chide him good-naturedly, and hug him some more, and then begin again. What Joey did not, could not see was the look on Giuseppe's face, a look that wasn't there twenty years before. It was not quite a smile, but rather a calm, peaceful look, a look of contentment. It was a look for no one, except perhaps for himself and the boy, a look directed down that funnel of streets and beyond the hills to the east. He saw no one and nothing with that look except life itself; he saw all of its hardships and joys. His time was limited, but he had survived better than most, perhaps better than all. And he had been given a second chance. He felt the vibrancy and warmth of that chance in his hand.

They walked past Giordano's without stopping or pausing or even looking in. A cold, dark wind blew in from the north; rain couldn't be far behind. Giuseppe stopped at the corner and took off the Gerry-Pac he was wearing, strapped Johnny into it, raised it onto his back again, and then crossed the street at a brisk pace, away from the store, away from Joey, and disappeared.

Joey had no idea where his father was going. He drove to the end of the block. From there he watched as Giuseppe moved quickly down one block and then down another. Giuseppe was in a residential neighborhood now, and Joey knew of no friends or acquaintances that he had there. Only then did he realize how little he knew of his father's private life. When Giuseppe was halfway down the third block, Joey turned the car and slowly followed. Giuseppe was still moving at a brisk pace. Two raindrops fell on the windshield. Johnny's head bobbed in the Gerry-Pac. The northern sky was rapidly spreading its blackness; still Giuseppe kept moving further and further away from his truck.

At the end of the third block, Giuseppe veered to his right out of view. Joey sped up. Soon he saw that Giuseppe had crossed over into a park, had passed the picnic area, and was now heading across the park's grass toward play structures at the far end. He was about to turn the car around when he saw Giuseppe leave what was also the outfield grass of the park's baseball diamond and, instead of heading toward the play structures, turn onto the dirt infield. Then he walked directly to the pitcher's mound. Reaching it, Giuseppe took off the Gerry-Pac, set Johnny squarely on the mound, tossed the pack to one side, took a baseball from his jacket pocket, moved a few feet from the toddler and then began rolling the ball to the boy, who repeatedly chased the slowly moving ball around the mound, falling at times, but stopping the ball or at least reaching it, picking it up and somehow managing to propel it back in Giuseppe's direction. And then the boy would teeter excitedly about the mound, laughing, eagerly awaiting its return.

What Joey could not see was the fixed smile on Giuseppe Rocco's face. What he could not hear were Giuseppe Rocco's words after each roll of the ball, after each of the boy's movements. "Atta boy, Johnny . . . Atta boy, Johnny."